Twenty-Eight First Kisses

Endorsements

"For everyone who couldn't help rooting for the likable-but-rebellious Cyndray in *Presence of Cyn,* she's back … but this time, her best friend, the seemingly-perfect Janaclese, is struggling with the impending divorce of her parents and falling for her first love. Why do everything right when even the adults disappoint and fail you? Author Sandra Barnes weaves together the points-of-view of both girls as they deal with a reality all teens face: is waiting till marriage for sex just old-fashioned nonsense or something worth saving? Especially when life gets complicated and everything around them is not always what it seems. An important read for today's teens!"

—**Neta Jackson**, Award-winning author of the *Yada Yada Prayer Group* series

"At last, a YA author willing to take on the delicate subject of abstinence and purity with a book that pops with teenage authenticity. This is not a lecture in the form of a novel. It's a funny, gritty, deep story that breathes the message from its soul. All that AND the genuine African-American voice we've been waiting for. Read this. Read it now."

—**Nancy Rue**, Award-winning author of *the Real Life* series

Twenty-Eight First Kisses

Sandra D. Barnes

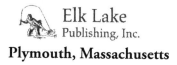
Elk Lake
Publishing, Inc.
Plymouth, Massachusetts

Dedication

I commit this book to the ONE who has blessed me with the gift of storytelling. Thank you, Heavenly Father, for your incomprehensible love that daily covers and sustains me. To everyone who yearns to love and be loved, I pray you also experience God's greatest offering.

"Do not to excite your love until it is ready.
Don't stir a fire in your heart too soon,
until it is ready to be satisfied."

Song of Solomon 2:7; 3:5; & 8:4
(The Voice)

Acknowledgments

I am thankful for my critique partners, affectionately called my c-peeps— Kiersti Plog, Marilyn Turk, and Sarah Tipton—who graciously offered advice and read my rewrites without complaining. To Neta Jackson, who continues to inspire and encourage me. To the awesome young adults who contributed to this work in many aspects from feedback on the manuscript to modeling for the cover. Karis Barnett, Jordan Lopez, Christain and Sascha Barnes, I'm especially grateful for your support. LaShaw Photography, thanks for your patience and professionalism in working with the giggly teens. To my agent, Jim Hart of Hartline Agency, for trusting me to "git er done." To the entire Elk Lake Publishing family for your prayers, guidance, and support.

To my husband, Gentry, who constantly reminded me to "just write" until I had a finished product. Thanks for the long walks, the brainstorming, and simply holding my hands when I wasn't typing. Love you forever and a day!

Chapter 1

JANACLESE

The average person has 28 first kisses before marriage. The words in the article almost jumped from the page and pressed into my chest.

I bit my lower lip. That sounded like a lot. And at sixteen, I'd never even had a boyfriend.

My stomach churned. What was so hard about being in love, anyway? Whoever fell in love with me, I'd love them right back. And vice-versa. Not like Mom who couldn't seem to love past her anger. Or Dad, who refused to stick around even for my sake. Did they even care how I felt about their separation?

Footsteps padded in the hallway. I tucked the *TotalDiva* magazine into my bag and scooped up the art supplies I'd placed on a nearby desk. I wanted to experience true love that lasted through thick and thin. Not the pain, and not pretending that everything was hunky dory when it wasn't. With all the brokenness in my home, I had to focus on one day building my own perfect family. The kind that loves unconditionally.

Based on the article, I was late in getting started.

Thuds clomped louder outside the doorway, then stopped. I shook my head, trying to regain focus on why I'd come into the art room in the first place.

I stood on my tippy toes trying to place art supplies back on the top shelf. My diamond necklace swayed as the wooden stool teetered beneath me. I held my breath, waited for it to balance and then inched higher. I blew out a frustrated breath. When they asked me to volunteer at Vacation Bible School, I had no idea they'd place me in life-threatening situations. The pointe technique and lengthening maneuvers I'd learned in dance class were of no use in practical matters like this.

"Looks like you need some help." A male voice filled the silence.

Careful not to lose my balance, I glanced sideways but couldn't see anyone. "I got it."

Man, this was worse than the kitchen cupboard above the refrigerator at home. Why build extra space if you couldn't reach the shelves to store stuff anyway?

"Okay, Shawty. You sure you don't need help?"

Shawty? I swiveled to face the speaker. "No, I told you ... um, um ..."

My heart skipped as my eyes traveled up his long legs and settled on his strong jawline. Who was this guy?

"Name's Hassan." A toothy grin met my gaze. "My class needs an easel. Thought I'd offer a hand. You sure you're all right?"

I floundered for words, but nothing came out.

Suddenly, I stumbled from the stool and practically dived onto the floor like I was sliding into home base.

In a split second, he rushed to my side. "Are you okay?"

Heat burned my ears. Why hadn't I seen him before the last day of VBS? Light brown eyes—so clear, they looked like gemstones—seemed to suck me in, making me lightheaded. Was I smelling tempura paint or had I spun around too quickly?

"I'm fine." *And so are you.*

"You'd have better luck if someone held you up. Here, let me show you."

I glanced at the top shelf where the other tubes of paint had been shoved toward the wall. If I could get enough balance, I could place these tubes back where they belonged. We could be just like ballet class where the male dancer lifts the female above his head.

"You think you could lift me?" I barely recognized my own breathy voice.

"Sure, on the count of three, I'll boost you up." Hassan spread broad fingers around my waist.

Butterflies fluttered in my stomach. *Why was I feeling so giddy?*

"Not like that, like this." I turned away from him and faced the shelf, standing en pointe. "In my dance class, we do a pas de deux lift. If you provide support long enough for me to make a jump to reach the top shelf, it will work. Think you can do that?"

Hassan gauged the distance with his eyes, then gave a slight nod.

"Okay." I gestured for him to move nearer. "Now stand behind me and place your left hand on the small of my back for stability. Put your right hand here."

"Shouldn't be that complicated," he grumbled while wrapping his right hand below my ribcage as instructed. "Just jump."

Ignoring his annoyance, I leaped into the air.

"Janaclese Mitchell!"

At the sound of my name, I jolted from Hassan's safety net and landed on top of him. My attempt to place the paint tubes on the shelf was an epic fail.

Mrs. Dunning stood with her back perfectly straight, head held high and eyes fixed in a low, steady gaze. "Are you two in here alone?"

Hassan flinched as I sprang from my awkward position and backed away from him.

"Are," she repeated in her stern voice, "you two in here alone?"

No, you're in here too. I kept my mouth shut and looked away at the collage of paintings plastered on the walls. Musical notes flowed from a seashell nestled beside a midnight blue ocean. I couldn't help wishing I could drift away with them.

Hassan gestured toward the paint tubes. "We were—"

"Young man, get to where you're supposed to be. And young lady, follow me."

I hustled out of the room, suddenly feeling weak. What did Mrs. Dunning think she saw Hassan and me doing? I reached her make-shift cubicle seconds behind her, barely able to stand.

"Yes?" I forced an innocent smile and my usual upbeat expression.

"I'm disappointed to find you, of all people, breaking the rules." She placed one hand on her hip and used the other hand to point her index finger. "And with a boy at that."

"We were just putting away art supplies." I held up the tubes I didn't have time to place back on the shelf.

The seam between her eyes pronounced dissatisfaction. "Indeed, I did see."

"Mrs. Dunning, I know what it probably looked like in there, but I promise you Hassan was helping me put the art supplies away."

She arched one brow, pinning me with a stare. She didn't believe me, the girl who never even had a boyfriend. I looked at the floor.

"We weren't doing anything wrong," I muttered.

"Don't argue with me, Janaclese. Since you refuse to talk to me, perhaps your *mother* could convince you to give an honest explanation."

I cringed. If I'd thought about doing anything with a guy, my mom's instincts would've already alarmed her. She would've crashed through the walls just to prevent a simple hug.

Mrs. Dunning held out her hand for the paint tubes. "I expect you to be a role model. You can start by helping with the children outside and by *staying outside with them*. Am I clear?"

Sometimes I think the adult mind is more X-rated than a teen's. I blinked back tears and nodded. I hated crying when reprimanded by an adult.

I passed Mrs. Dunning the tubes, then left her cubicle and headed outside, tucking away the feeling of being misunderstood. Whatever. My parents' separation had already taught me that arguing was pointless. I fingered the diamond infinity necklace Dad had given me, its meaning shattered like Dad's promise of always and forever.

I plunged through the doors, no longer in the mood to play games with the children. The whiff of freshly mowed grass stung my eyes. Even the canopy of oak trees didn't provide relief from Maryland's summer heat. A papier-mâché star-shaped piñata was suspended from a limb. Streamers in an array of metallic colors—gold, red, purple, orange, yellow, green, and blue—cascaded from each point of the star.

Cyndray's face brightened when she saw me. "Janaclese, you're just in time."

She held up a large stick. "Ready?"

I was ready alright. Ready to leave this church and never come back. But I bounced up front and stood next to her. She passed me the stick and my heart pounded, still trying to recover from the art room disaster.

"These points on the star symbolize the seven deadly sins." She cleared her throat and waited. The kindergartners looked totally confused, but when no one asked her to explain, she continued. "Um…that includes uncontrolled anger or wanting other people's stuff and not appreciating what God has given you."

Appreciate what? I swallowed, wishing I were young enough to just blindly buy into that. How was I supposed to appreciate my parents divorcing?

I glanced toward the church building. Was Hassan a member of our church? He should've been easy to spot. He had to be at least six feet.

Cyndray pointed to the splashes of paint and then wrapped a streamer around her palm. "All of these colors represent temptation. That's when you want to do something that you know is wrong."

I smiled, playing my role, but my mind strayed. If I hadn't opted to be an assistant teacher, would I have met Hassan in the teens' class?

"Yeah, like biting or kicking," one child yelled out.

"How about pushing in line?" another one asked.

"Good examples," Cyndray said. She glanced at me like she expected me to say something.

I blinked. I needed to focus. *Was it really wrong for me to daydream about a guy I'd just met?*

The children, sitting in a circle on the grass, competed for compliments.

"And stealing is bad, too."

"One time Miguel hid my toy, and I couldn't find it."

"Whoa. Hang on." Cyndray held up one hand. "You're all right. Now how do you suppose we should handle temptation?"

I swatted a gnat, ready for this class to be over. Maybe I'd see Hassan after class. My heart dropped. I couldn't, not after Mrs.

Dunning made me feel like my underwear was showing. How could I ever look him in the face again?

"Now watch." Cyndray approached me with a cotton blindfold. "Janaclese, would you please turn around and stand still?" I turned my back to her as she tightened a handkerchief over my eyes. "Sometimes we can't see what God is up to, but we must always trust him to help us in our fight."

As much trouble as she got into, it was odd to see Cyndray teaching about temptation. It was also weird she'd mention trust while blindfolding me. I'd been fumbling around in the dark, waiting on God to let my parents get back together. I raised the stick, and Mrs. Dunning's face came to mind. I swung at the piñata, thrashing, swinging again and again.

Hissing and booing confirmed I'd missed the target each time.

"Good and bad are always fighting," Cyndray explained. "When evil is broken, then Heavenly rewards are released."

Wham. I finally struck the piñata. It had only been a year, but I'd apparently lost the battle against my parents' separation. *Whack.* Was unconditional love even possible between humans? *Smash.* One last wild swing sent me crashing to the ground with a loud thud.

"Let me try. Let me try." One after the other, the kids screamed for a turn to break open the piñata.

Cyndray knelt down and removed my blindfold. She didn't look happy. "You're swinging that stick like a crazy woman. What's wrong with you?"

I hopped up and giggled. "Just illustrating for the kids."

She eyed me a second longer, then clapped her hands and addressed the children. "Okay, sometimes we have to help each other in the fight."

My facial muscles cramped from the fake smile. Striking out had provided some emotional relief, but deep down I still cringed as I watched the kids. The truth was, with so many unanswered prayers about the divorce, my faith had waned.

The boy who'd asked to be first raced to take my place. One good swing, and WHAM. Candy, gum, and other treats flew from the broken star. I sighed. Life was so easy for some people.

Chapter 2

CYNDRAY

I was different. Maybe not the "new creature in Christ" kind of different that Janaclese always talked about, but I'd definitely changed. What else could explain why I hadn't found that loser Tommy Dawg and already clawed his eyes out?

Yesterday, I'd taught about temptation at Vacation Bible School. Even gave my testimony—*or part of it*. Today, I would give testimony in court.

I crossed my arms, then uncrossed them. Didn't know why flirting with temptation usually cost more for people like me. Even in a court of law, there was no real justice. Not for people like me.

"All rise!" The burly clerk, who looked like a heavyweight wrestler, yelled out into the courtroom.

With wobbly knees, elastic like rubber, I rose to my feet. An older woman with short brown hair wearing a long black robe entered the courtroom—the Honorable Judge Raffinan. I gazed around the room, hoping no one from school was here to witness how dumb I was to get mixed up with criminals. I wiped my palms on my jeans. Even though I was only a witness, I had to constantly remind myself that I wasn't on trial.

Hanging out with my so-called "friend" Danielle was like running blindfolded through a winding maze with sharp scissors. She'd taken my scissors, so I wouldn't accidentally cut myself, and then she stabbed me with them. *Such a traitor!*

I sucked in a breath as the judge glanced at me. When her gaze shifted elsewhere, I whispered a promise to God. *From this day forward, I will never get into trouble again.* I had a plan, too. Glue myself to good girl Janaclese Mitchell.

"You may be seated."

I slid into my seat, wishing I could fade into the bench like a chameleon.

The bang of the gavel against the wooden desk got my attention. "Court is now in session."

I twisted my WWJD bracelet as the clicking of the court reporter's stenotype filled the chamber. Partying in a hotel with Danielle and her drunk buddy, Tommy Dawg, was a mistake. Now I had to testify.

I glanced at the defendant's table. A bushy-haired lawyer, neck bowed, seemed to be reading notes. An icy chill snaked down my spine. I didn't know what happened in court the previous days. Didn't particularly care, either. Normally, I'd refuse to rat out anybody, but I had to do this. I'd kept secret the other repulsive hotel drama.

No man on earth would *ever* touch me again.

"The court calls Miss Cyndray Johnson to the stand."

I shuddered, the heavy thud of my heart weighing me down. Mom offered an encouraging squeeze of my hand, as I pried myself off the hard bench and made my way to the witness stand.

You're only a witness, you're not on trial ... only a witness.

Heat from the burning gaze of too many unfamiliar eyes crawled up my neck. I glanced two rows behind where I'd sat and noticed Mrs. Samson, my former English teacher, the only person who had ever seemed to truly understand me.

God is your vin-di-ca-tor, Mrs. Samson mouthed.

I wanted to bolt through the double doors and run like I always did, but now that I was supposed to be different, I had to behave differently. So I sat still, convincing myself that good had to come from all the bad like Mrs. Samson had promised.

"State your name."

I took a deep breath, raised my right hand and placed my left hand on the Bible that was held out to me. "Cyndray. Marie. Johnson."

You're a witness. I straightened my back and prepared myself for questioning. *Not on trial.*

The prosecuting attorney, who I'd already spoken to in private approached me. "Miss Johnson, tell us about the night of the party."

I swallowed, pushing down the fearful memory of being trapped in a hotel room. "Like I told you before ... I was hanging with my friend, and her boyfriend picked up alcohol from a guy, then we drove to a hotel, and they got drunk."

"Miss Johnson, do you recognize the man sitting there?" The attorney pointed at Mr. Grungy sitting next to the bushy-haired lawyer.

"Yes, sir, but barely." Once again, I was honest. It's amazing what a clean shirt and a tie will do.

"Where do you know him from?"

"He's the father of Matty—uh-Matt-Matt."

I only knew the nickname I'd heard the little kid called by when he attended a children's event I'd worked to get community service hours. I'd called the little boy "Booger" after he stuck a rock up his nose. The lawyer was patient, so I continued. "I met Matty last fall at a holiday event for children—uh, at the Women's Wellness Center."

"Miss Johnson, I want you to think clearly. Is there any detail you remember about the person you saw giving alcohol to your underage friends?"

"Yes, sir. I remember the guy had animal tracks tattooed on both arms. They looked like some type of paws leading up from the wrist to the elbow."

"Thank you, Miss Johnson. That will be all."

I breathe a sigh of relief. Maybe this wouldn't be so bad after all.

The tall, thin, Q-tip looking defense lawyer, whose head seemed too big for his body, approached me. He pointed to his client, Mr. Grungy, who sat on a bench in front of the witness stand. "Miss Johnson, do you recognize this man as the person you saw giving alcohol to minors?"

"No, sir." Although his client wore his Sunday best and didn't look grungy from grease stains, I recognized him. But I couldn't identify him as the same man who had given Danielle and her boyfriend the alcohol.

"And you recall, for sure, that the person you saw that night was a guy?"

"Yes, sir." I nodded.

"Describe his face. Did he have a beard? Was he bald? Eye color? What else do you remember?" The Q-tip pitched questions like a batting machine.

"It was dark." I bounced my knee. "I couldn't see the man's face."

"How can you be sure it was a male if you didn't see the person's face?" The lawyer peered at me.

I squirmed, sinking lower into the seat. "Uh, I don't know, but I'm pretty sure it was a man."

"Can you say with certainty it was a man?"

"No, sir, I guess not."

"Speak louder for the court to hear!"

Sheesh, why was the Q-tip yelling at me? "No, sir, I cannot say with certainty it was a male, but—"

"That will be all."

The cleaned-up Mr. Grungy looked relieved. He sat on the bench, grinning.

No one else cross-examined me. Good. I'd already told the court everything I knew, which apparently wasn't much. I was granted permission to leave the stand and I felt relieved my part was over and I could go home.

Judge Raffinan cleared her throat. "Council, please approach the bench."

Both of the lawyers approached the judge and whispered about something, seemingly urgent. The judge requested that Booger's grungy dad roll up his sleeves to show his arms.

My heart raced. The animal paw prints that I'd described were stamped along Mr. Grungy's arms. *I knew that man was creepy!*

The excitement suddenly faded as reality knocked me to my senses. People like me didn't get to be happy. Not that easily. As I walked back to my seat, I felt like someone was slowly licking the icing off my cake.

Mom placed her hand on my shoulder, her eyes gleaming. "It's finally over."

I nodded and gave a weak smile, not believing for one second this was the end. Although I'd changed, my world hadn't. Nicely wrapped presents didn't exist in my world. There were no happily ever afters. With my luck, Mr. Grungy would escape from jail and kill me.

Mrs. Samson had kept her promise by supporting me. She reached to hug me, and I felt frozen. "Cyndray, you did so well up there."

"Yeah, too well. Should I enroll in a witness protection program?"

Mom and Mrs. Samson laughed. Seeing Mom unworried and well again felt good, but didn't she know bad luck followed me? At least that's how she'd made me feel.

"I'm so glad that case is sealed," Mom said to Mrs. Samson.

I sure hoped so. But the only thing really sealed was my promise to God. No more trouble for me.

Chapter 3

JANACLESE

I brushed my fingers across the row of soft nylon swimsuits hanging from the metal rack. Two more weeks before Miracle's pool party, so my friends and I were scouring the mall for new swimsuits. Kehl-li had insisted we bring our fashion A-game to the party and look red-carpet ready like Sports Illustrated supermodels. Didn't make sense to me since our parents had pre-approved the guest list. Everybody coming was from school or church. Nobody new, nobody interesting.

Just as I grabbed a two-piece aqua bikini, my cell phone rang.

"Are you going to get that?"

I swiveled around to face Cyndray holding a purple one-piece, then pressed the bikini against my body. "Why? Does this one say *Janaclese?*"

She lifted an eyebrow. "I was talking about your cell."

"Oh." I reached into my shoulder bag and pulled out my phone. "Hello?"

"Are you driving?" Mom asked.

I inhaled a long breath. "No, Mom. I'm still shopping."

"I didn't expect one purchase to take all day. Who did you tell me you were with?"

Why did she always put me through this annoying process as if she didn't already know? "Cyndray, Miracle, and Kehl-li."

The playful look in Cyndray's eyes told me she was getting a kick out my conversation. But I didn't find anything humorous about my mom checking up on me, especially since I was labeled "Your Righteousness" by Cyndray.

"Hey, Mrs. M!" Cyndray grabbed the swimsuit from my hands and tried to yell into the phone. "You gotta see your daughter's hot bathing—"

I pressed the mute button and shooed Cyndray away. Mom wouldn't get her jokes. She'd cancel our party and give us a lesson on modesty instead. "Stop fooling around, will you?"

Cyndray chuckled. "Your mom's not letting you walk out of the house in that teeny weeny bikini."

"Is that Cyndray in the background yelling?" Mom's voice sounded serious through the phone. "What's hot?"

I hit unmute and glared at Cyndray as I pressed the phone to my ear. "Noth … nothing's hot, except this summer heat that's making my hair all poufy. Did you need me to run an errand before coming home?"

"No, but I need you to come straight home after dropping your friends off."

I rolled my eyes. No need to ask why. "Yeah. Okay."

"And call me when you're on your way." Another one of Mom's odd parenting rules.

"Yeah. Okay," I agreed before clicking off.

I tried grabbing the bikini from Cyndray. "I was just looking at it. Besides, my mom doesn't know what's *under* my clothes."

"Mrs. Mitchell? Humph … she's always one step ahead of everybody. Wouldn't surprise me if she had spy gear in that bathing suit." She touched the tags and fabric, pretending to search for a hidden camera. "Might be why she called as soon as you took this wretched thing off the rack."

One look at Cyndray's purple one-piece and Kehl-li turned her nose in the air. "I see you couldn't find anything worth a dollar either. We should try a designer boutique."

"Everybody's not rich like you. With my summer pay, shopping for swimwear is a luxury." Cyndray held out the bathing suit I'd selected. "This is Janaclese's. You like it?"

Kehl-li tossed her long dark straight hair, refusing to touch the clothing as if she thought something unclean might rub off on her.

She gave me a sinister look. "Are you buying that to impress your boyfriend?"

A tingling sensation swept across my cheeks, as I thought of Hassan despite myself. I shook my head. "You know I don't have a boyfriend."

Kehl-li crunched up her face. "Then what's the point?"

"Why does your every thought begin and end with boys?" Cyndray's cold eyes bore into Kehl-li. "You think you know so much, but you don't even have a boyfriend yourself."

Those two couldn't breathe the same air without arguing. Miracle's gaze swapped back and forth between Cyndray and Kehl-li, her fingers twisting the tail of her cotton shirt at warp speed. My stomach muscles twitched too. Couldn't stand fighting—not my parents and not my friends.

"Betcha I can snag a guy before you do!" Kehl-li challenged Cyndray.

Miracle released the wrinkled shirttail from her hand. "You'd lose. She's already dating the hottest guy in school."

"You have a boyfriend?" Kehl-li squinted at Cyndray.

"Trevor is not my boyfriend." A motionless Cyndray looked down at the tiled floor.

"The hottest guy at school is not your boyfriend?" Kehl-li's eyes twinkled. "That means he's up for grabs?"

I wasn't fooled by Cyndray's cool exterior. With her, a spark could ignite an explosion. I eased between Kehl-li and Cyndray. "Trevor isn't up for grabs. You talk like he's a piece of meat or something."

Cyndray skirted around me to get in Kehl-li's face. "If you think you can get Trevor, then you can have him."

"Is that a dare?" Kehl-li brushed a strand of straight black hair from her naturally tanned face.

"How do you say 'no' in Korean?" Cyndray's nostrils flared. "As you don't seem to understand English."

"Aniyo," Miracle said. "Aniyo means no in Korean."

Cyndray shot Miracle a look of irritation, then spewed off at Kehl-li. "Aniyo, I'm not challenging you. Aniyo, Trevor's *not* my boyfriend. Aniyo, I can't afford boutique prices."

Kehl-li sneered. "Temper, yes?"

"Aniyo-opposite!" Cyndray tossed my bikini across the rack. "Let's go."

"Cyndray, wait!" I grabbed the swimsuit before it hit the floor and watched my friend storm away with the one-piece in her hand. Kehl-li seemed to enjoy getting Cyndray riled up. "Was that necessary? You know how she is."

Kehl-li's smirky lips spread into a wide smile as she looked past me and pointed while addressing Miracle. "MiCha, isn't that Hassan?"

Hassan? My stomach fluttered at the familiar sounding name. Could it be …

My heart picked up pace as I rotated in the direction of Kehl-li's index finger. The pounding threatened to explode my chest. It was him—the guy from VBS. *God, don't let him see me.*

"Come on, MiCha, let's go talk to him." Kehl-li grabbed Miracle's hand, then waved as she called out his name.

Hassan glanced over, squinted and broke into a toothy grin like the first time I'd ever seen him. I busied myself with the swimwear, stealing glimpses as he talked to Miracle and Kehl-li. Part of me wanted to hide between the clothes rack, and part of me wished I had Kehl-li's boldness. But he probably thought I was weird after the way I fell on top of him. Mrs. Dunning whisking me from the room hadn't helped either. I grabbed the rack with both hands as a troubling thought circled my brain. *What if he didn't remember me?* That would be even worse.

I peeked over the rack and locked eyes with Hassan, who now stood facing me. My slippery hands tilted the bar forward, and hangers clattered to the floor.

Hassan reached out and righted the rack. "Janaclese, right?"

The piercing sound of the store's alarm diverted our attention.

"Don't touch me!" Near the store's exit, Cyndray's eyes flashed wide open like two round bagels popping out of a hot toaster, her arms flailing away from a security officer. "I wasn't stealing! Get your hands off of me!"

My heart lunged into overtime, but my legs froze. How were we going to explain this to my mom?

Chapter 4

CYNDRAY

So much for my promise to God. Trouble just seemed to stand in line waiting for me. I hadn't meant to steal the swimsuit. Also hadn't meant for my entire life to be ruined in an instant.

Kehl-li and all her talk about boyfriends had ticked me off, and I'd stalked out the store not once thinking about the swimsuit in my hand. But try telling that to a cop. Hadn't worked with the judge either.

"I don't need anger management." I banged my fist against the car door as Mom drove me to my first court-ordered therapy session.

When Mom glanced in my direction, I tucked my hands beneath my bottom. Had to control my hands or I'd smash something else.

"You have to go." Mom eyeballed me as the car glided along the curvy road. "Therapy was one of the conditions for your release."

"Release?" I'd been given a Consent Decree, something I'd never heard of until this stolen swimsuit incident. I had to pay a hundred and fifty dollars and for six months, attend court-ordered therapy. "They should've put me in jail since I can't do anything anyway."

"You're allowed to do things, Cyndray. This situation is bad enough without your extra drama."

Mom couldn't handle what she called drama—which was basically life. People got mad all the time and made mistakes. But Mom was a bit too "delicate" to have any real emotions. The only time she seemed to feel anything was when she lay in bed for days, too depressed to face the world. I'd vowed to never be like her. I rolled my eyes. Just because she was too weak to face her feelings, didn't mean I was. I certainly didn't need anybody to manage my anger.

Mom clutched the steering wheel. "Six months isn't long. The time will pass quickly and be like nothing ever happened."

"It's my entire summer and part of next school year." I wiped my sweaty palms on my jeans. "If they'd put me in jail, at least I could've pretended I'd visited relatives for the summer. Should've put me in a facility like A—"

I stared straight ahead. Talking about A.J. upset her more than anything. Another reason to hate having a brother in a psych ward that I could only visit twice a year.

"Locked away? Is that what you really want? To be considered a social threat and confined to jail or a mental institution?"

I twisted in my seat, wishing I hadn't brought this topic up. All those meds had made A.J. so moody. He'd had so many diagnoses— ADHD, Bi-Polar, Schizophrenia—nobody knew what was wrong with him. But I knew, for sure, he wasn't crazy. Didn't matter what anybody else said. "Everybody gets mad sometimes. At Redemption, the preacher said Jesus got so angry he turned tables upside down in the temple."

"I'm sure there's another side to that story." Mom's lips turned slightly upwards.

I sighed, giving up.

She pulled into the parking lot of the Youth Center and turned the car off. A humongous sculpture of a crib stood in front of the building.

I pointed at the odd artwork. "What's that for?"

Mom shrugged. "I don't know. Might be a logo for the SOS program."

"The Save Our Seed program?" I offered a half-laugh. "Yeah, right. Crib's a great place to lock-up babies, keep 'em from crawling and endangering themselves and others."

That's what the judge had ordered. For me to be a part of SOS— the town's youth rescue mission. If the community didn't save me now, I was apparently destined for bigger trouble later down the road. I leaned my head against the window. *God, am I that bad?*

"Honey, anger management therapy is only one day a week. It'll fly by." She sighed. "Be happy the judge dismissed the theft charge."

"That's because I wasn't stealing!" Heat rose from my belly. "Ke-hl-li, with her stupid talking, made me mad and I marched out of the store. I got distracted, that's all."

"Will you listen to yourself? You got mad, and now you're blaming someone else for your impulsivity. It's your temper everyone's worried about. You struck an officer."

"Whose side are you on? I didn't assault him. I just jerked away when he touched me." I hated when she didn't trust me. And I *hated* being touched—especially by males who tried to control by force.

Mom grew quiet and leaned against the headrest. After a few seconds, she looked over at me in the passenger's seat. "We're trying to help you. Nobody's trying to ruin your life."

"Then why did the judge also order me to stay away from that store? Why do I have a 9:30 p.m. curfew unless I'm with my parents or in a supervised, structured activity?"

"You can still attend Miracle's party. Mrs. Mitchell will be there to chaperone."

I rolled my eyes. This was so not about anybody's dumb pool party, even if the rest of the world was excited.

"Your father and I want what's best for you. Would you rather be placed on electronic monitoring where you'll be forced to comply?"

"No!" I opened the car door and stepped one foot onto the pavement. Steam had literally clogged my pores, but somehow, I had to keep from exploding. "You'll wait right here for me, right?"

When she nodded, I hopped out of the car and entered the building. The ankle bracelets the court strapped on teens were a bad fashion statement, but if it ever became necessary, a girl like me could work with them.

I'd sat through my first group counseling session for fifteen minutes—long enough to be introduced to everybody and long enough to know I wasn't supposed to be in anger management therapy. Sheesh! Even among this circus of three clowns posing as hardcore criminals, I was still a misfit.

What was wrong with me?

Dr. Reed, the counselor, sat in the midpoint of our semicircle. My eyes focused on his scuffed-up brown loafers. Probably a size thirteen like my dad's. The air-conditioned room made my forearms look like chicken skin. Wish I'd known to bring a sweater. I hugged myself to stay warm and wondered if Dr. Reed felt cold on his bald spot.

"You on papers, Cyndray?" The kid sitting next to me wiggled his foot as he addressed me.

I mean-eyed him on general principle. "What?"

"What they get you for?" he asked, wildly shaking his foot.

"Nothing." I rolled my eyes. Why was he even talking to me?

A wide stretch of duct tape covered random holes in the wall behind Dr. Reed. I looked past his receding hairline at the silver-gray patch work.

"So let's talk about what happens to our bodies when we become angry, and what we can do to stop the anger," Dr. Reed said.

I stopped jouncing my leg, mentally answering his question. *My insides burn just like right now and only running makes me feel better.* I didn't dare speak those words aloud, though the urge to run was about to overtake me.

"Ricardo don't play." A light-skinned dude with curly hair squeezed a stress ball and looked directly at me as he spoke. "If Ricardo says don't go there, then that's what Ricardo means."

"Who's Ricardo?" I scrunched my face.

"Ricardo is me." He stopped squeezing the ball for a split second like I'd asked an ignorant question. "I'm Ricardo, that's who he is." He pressed the ball against his palm with his fingers, resuming the squeezing. "And Ricardo ain't nobody's fool neither."

"O-*kay*, Ricardo." I lifted an eyebrow, wondering why this nut was referring to himself in third person like Elmo from Sesame Street.

"Shari, would you like to share?" Dr. Reed addressed the tattooed girl whose arms and neck looked like newsprint. Something about Shari's smile was spooky.

She drew her legs up onto her seat and hugged them close. "My heart feels like it has to pound its way out of a tiny box. I'm all sweaty, trying to ignore the voice in my head."

My heart staggered. *She heard a voice in her head too?*

"Very good, Shari. How do you calm yourself?"

When Shari giggled, her eyes lit up, and her smile stretched from ear to ear. "I break something. Last time, after I busted a couple of windows, I was all smiles again."

Chills iced my spine. A really weird jack-o-lantern. The shiny metal in Shari's pierced tongue was like a candle. How could I possibly have anything in common with her?

I pressed my palms against my temples. *These people know nothing about anger. I could let loose right now and churn up a few chairs like the Wizard of Oz tornado. Bet that would clear the room. This is so stupid.*

"Jimmy, we haven't heard from you? Any comments on anger?" Dr. Reed stared at the orange-haired boy with freckles sitting across from me.

"Fire!" A high-pitched voice said.

I jumped from my seat and looked behind me.

"Sit down, Cyndray. Jimmy's talking." Dr. Reed spoke in a calm voice.

"I thought someone said …" I hesitated. I didn't smell smoke; everyone else seemed collected. Had I imagined a voice saying 'fire'? I glanced behind me and got more chills. Nothing. No one was even there.

Sinking into my seat, I eyed Jimmy's expressionless face.

"Fire rages inside. Helps seeing it outside." The imaginary voice behind me spoke again.

"Ooh, so that's why Jimmy sets trashcans on fire." Shari beamed like she'd solved a million-dollar riddle.

I sighed, thankful somebody else had heard the voice. But Jimmy's mouth hadn't moved. I stared at his tight lips.

"Guess so. When the fire suffocates outside, it dies inside too."

My stomach clenched. How was Jimmy throwing his voice? Was he a ventriloquist pyromaniac?

The real million-dollar riddle was why anybody would assume I needed therapy to control my anger? I'd never had a rage that made me want to break windows and set fires. But six months of group therapy would send me straight to the looney bin.

I had to come up with a plan to make this my first and last group session.

Chapter 5

JANACLESE

"Ouch!" I accidentally banged my head against the side of the pool at Miracle's.

"Gotta work on those reflexes." Cyndray grinned. "Didn't you see the edge of the pool launching an attack?"

I climbed out of the water, streams rushing down my body forming a puddle at my feet. Cyndray's jokes weren't always funny.

"You'll live." She floated on her back and watched me massage my head.

As I rubbed my head, Cyndray flipped over and swam off in the opposite direction.

My hand-crushed lemonade waited beside the lounge chair I'd claimed when I arrived at Miracle's pool party. I raised the cup to my forehead hoping a knot wouldn't form.

"So we meet again."

I turned and feasted my eyes upon the most handsome face I'd seen in my entire life. "Hassan! You're here?"

A flawless complexion the color of pumpkin spice latte. My heart leaped.

"Yep." A grin exposed straight front teeth, separated by a tiny gap between the middle two.

Had he come to see Kehl-li and Miracle?

"Miracle is around here somewhere." I scanned the many faces around the pool.

He took a step forward, lowering his tone, "Kehl-li invited me. Thought I'd roll through and holler at y'all."

I stepped back. "Holler?"

Hassan squinted. "You know? Say hello."

"Oh." Heat rose to my cheeks. For a minute there, I thought he wanted to yell at us, seeing how rude we must've been at the mall.

Hassan looked around, and I tried to tear my gaze away from him.

"Nice party. Your peeps rent the place?"

"Nope. This is Miracle's house." Why couldn't I take my eyes off this guy?

"Somebody's loaded with Benjamins." Hassan walked in a circle, taking in the view.

"Yeah. Must be," I replied, wondering what he thought of the conservative, racer-back one-piece Mom made me wear. At least the color was a popping red.

Was it rude to keep looking at him? I darted my eyes away. My mom was standing near the DJ talking to some man I didn't recognize. Probably another strict parent who agreed to help Miracle's mom chaperone.

"That beat is pumping." Hassan bobbed his head up and down to the music. "You dance?"

"Not really." I doubted he meant ballet or liturgical.

Hassan and I stood next to each other, silently awkward.

I fingered my diamond necklace. *Think, think.* There must be something to talk about. What had Kehl-li said about Hassan?

"What are—"

"Is that—"

We both grinned at our attempts to speak at once.

"Sorry." Hassan and I sounded like a duet.

"You first." We pointed to each other and this time laughed out loud.

I cupped my hand over my mouth, concealing more giggles and hinting he could speak without being interrupted.

Hassan pretended to zip his lips and throw away the key.

We stood staring at each other, smiling, and daring not to be the first to speak. I finally gave in. "So sorry I interrupted you. You were saying?"

"I have no idea." Hassan shrugged his shoulders. "But, I like your dimples."

"These old things?" I waved my hand. "I got 'em on sale at Target."

My heart danced, and I noticed he was wearing a white tank tee and patriotic red, white and blue swimming trunks. We matched!

Where had this guy been hiding? "Are you from around here?"

"Nah." Hassan cleared his throat, a twinkle in his eye. "I'm from Red Hill."

"Oh, then I should probably introduce you to some of the guys. Some we know from church, but most of them are from our school, Unity High."

"I'm straight."

Oh, God, did I say something to make him think I thought otherwise?

"Um ... when I said guys, I meant people like the boys *and* girls here."

Hassan raised his eyebrows at me. "Your homies, right? I follow you."

I brushed a sweaty palm against my hip. *Why am I so nervous?*

We walked over to the pool, where two teams of guys hit a volleyball across a net.

"Hey, Trevor ... Micah." I waved the guys out of the pool. "I want you to meet someone."

A trail of water zigzagged a pathway on the concrete as Trevor and Micah swished over to Hassan and me.

"S'up?" Hassan pointed his chin upwards.

After the introductions and a few fist bumps, Trevor and Micah whisked Hassan off to the game of water volleyball. I returned to my lounge chair and closed my eyes.

Pictures of Hassan bombarded my mind—his skin, his eyes, that tantalizing smile.

"Hey. Saw you grinning in some guy's face. Is he new around here?"

I opened my eyes as Cyndray flopped next to me.

"Oh, Cyndray. It's Hassan—the one from VBS I've been trying to tell you about!" I couldn't contain my excitement. "The other day at the mall, he called me Janaclese."

"Calm down. I do *not* want to talk about the mall." She rolled her eyes. "Besides, Janaclese is your name, and I can certainly think of worse things to be called."

"The point is, he remembered *me*." I pointed to my chest. "He's here. Can you believe it?"

"So, what did y'all talk about?"

"I'm afraid I did more stuttering than talking. I kept backpedaling, correcting myself."

"You like him, don't you?"

I hesitated. "I can't stop thinking about him. His skin is perfectly flawless. Nice teeth. No acne."

Cyndray pressed her lips together and narrowed her eyes. "And that's enough to fall madly in love?"

"No. He just seems ... different. Says he's from Red Hill."

She laughed. "Trust me. He is different. Hassan is a boy from the 'hood."

"What do you mean?" I looked at Cyndray. I hated when she judged people. "He attends Redemption, I think. At least he was at church that one time."

"He's a bad boy. Why do good girls always want a roughneck?"

"Stop generalizing." I shoved Cyndray. "Where's Red Hill anyway?"

"Trust me. You're better off not knowing." Cyndray looked at her arm where I touched her. "Feels a little tender. Got any sunblock?"

"Yeah. Check my bag." I leaned back in my lounge chair.

As Cyndray reached for the sunblock, an issue of *TotalDiva* fell out of my bag.

"You subscribe to this?" She held up the magazine, dog-eared on the page with the article heading "Twenty-Eight First Kisses."

I shifted, glancing in my mom's direction. "I'm returning it to Kehl-li. She left it in my car."

Cyndray leaned forward. "Did you read it?"

"The entire magazine? Of course not."

"Stop being funny. I'm talking about this '28 First Kisses' article. The one that *prepares you for marriage*." Cyndray's index and middle fingers formed air quotations.

I gripped my glass of lemonade and took a deep swallow. "Uh-huh. I read it."

"What did it say? Hardly sounds possible since you only have *one* first kiss. Bunch of hogwash, right?"

"Maybe." I lowered my gaze. "Just interesting how people come up with crazy ideas concerning the opposite sex."

"No, what's crazy is this flirt fest disguised as a pool party. Have you spoken to Miracle and Kehl-li at all?" Cyndray jerked her head. "See that huddle of boys over there? Guess who they're surrounding?" She threw her hands up in the air. "Miracle and Kehl-li, that's who."

I laughed. "Cyndray, you're so animated today. Where's Trevor?"

"Same place as Hassan—yapping around Kehl-li's heels like a weak puppy, just to get a whiff of that stinky perfume she keeps spraying. That girl's totally responsible for destroying the ozone layer. I couldn't stand it anymore, so I left the pool."

I looked around. Everybody who wasn't playing volleyball did seem to be closely engaged with somebody of the opposite sex. What did the chaperones think about that?

I scoured the perimeter of the pool to see if the guards were on duty.

My heart plummeted.

Was that my mom still talking to the man from before? My mom practically had her head resting on the unfamiliar guy's shoulder. The man whispered something in her ear, and a flood of laughter erupted, soaring into the air.

When was she ever that happy?

"I don't think Kehl-li will mind if I take this article home to read it for myself," I heard Cyndray say.

I didn't bother to respond. I locked my gaze on Mom and the unfamiliar man. A cold shiver coursed up my spine and prickled my scalp.

"Janaclese? Girl, are you even listening to me? What are you staring at?"

Cyndray followed my line of vision. "Is that your dad? Cool. Looks like your prayers for your parents to reconnect were answered."

"That's. NOT. My. Dad," I said, rising from my seat.

My heart pounded with the same force as when my parents announced their legal separation over a year ago. Was my faith for my parents' marriage to be saved in vain?

The weight of the ball and chain attached to my legs slowed each step, but I moved forward and finally approached Mom.

I hoped my imitation of a smile worked. "What's up?" *And who's this baldheaded man?*

Mom spun around as if I'd startled her. "Oh, Janaclese. Are you having a good time?"

My stomach quivered. *Obviously, you are. Now who is he?* "I guess so. I'm just chilling with Cyndray. How's it going with chaperoning?"

"I think we're having just as much fun as you kids."

I arched an accusatory eyebrow. *I can see that.*

Suddenly Mom was distracted. "Good Lord, what is that child wearing?" She placed her hand over her heart and bolted off.

I turned around to see what all the excitement was about. I fell back on my heels. Miracle had finally taken off her cover and made her grand entrance into the pool, revealing the swimsuit she and Kehl-li had raved about.

What *was* she wearing? Her skin-toned bathing suit exposed most of her body. Three sequined eye patches, strewn together with a thin strip of lace covered her essentials.

The music stopped, and the DJ's voice transformed into a woman's voice booming into the mic, "MiCha! *ije an-eulo deul-eo wass-eo-yo.*" The harsh tone spouted Korean words without interpretation.

Miracle's face looked like the red coating from a fireball had bled through on her cheeks.

"Come inside ... NOW," the voice demanded.

A horrifying, deafening sound of screeching forced us to cover our ears.

I turned toward the music platform. Miracle's mom slammed the mic down and zoomed through the sliding glass door in her wheelchair.

I swiveled back around to look at Miracle. My mom's crumpled face was stern as she held out Miracle's wrap. Miracle grabbed the swimsuit cover and dashed into her mansion.

Chapter 6

CYNDRAY

After Miracle's swimsuit debut, which closely resembled her birthday suit, Janaclese and I were headed home.

"Epic fail." I couldn't help giggling as I placed a beach ball in the trunk of her Prius.

Janaclese looked over at me and frowned, and then slammed the trunk shut.

"What?" I asked, getting into the passenger's seat.

"That wasn't funny, Cyndray." She slid behind the steering wheel. "Did you see Miracle's face?"

I laughed harder. I wished that was *all* I'd seen. "I saw more than just her face. Why would she even do something like that?"

"Attention. Why else?" Janaclese's flat tone reminded me of a toy whose batteries had grown weak from overuse.

"With all her money, she could buy attention."

She buckled her seatbelt. "Money isn't the answer to everything."

"I'd sure like to find that out from my own personal experience." I needed a hundred fifty dollars to pay restitution to the court. *Rich girls like Miracle don't have real problems like me. Ugh, the haves and the have-nots. That kinda stuff just makes me mad.*

I shook my head and watched Janaclese biting her lower lip, emphasizing the perplexed expression registered across her face. Why was she so worried about Miracle?

"Okay. You're right. The thing with Miracle wasn't just ha-ha funny, but maybe a little odd funny to me too. Weird, you know? After tonight, I'm convinced that anybody is capable of doing anything under the right, or should I say *wrong*, influence."

Janaclese still didn't respond. She pressed the start button, and the dashboard illuminated.

"How do you suppose her mother wheeled herself outside so fast?" I asked.

"The house is equipped with elevators." She stared into space, resting both hands on the steering wheel.

"You think her mother was watching the party all along?"

"Probably. Somebody sure needed to, since the chaperones were engrossed with each other."

So that was her problem. Something about her own mom was troubling her. "Did you get a chance to talk to Hassan again?"

"A little."

"What'd he say?"

"Nothing I care to share."

Had Hassan upset her? I couldn't understand why everybody was suddenly so interested in boys anyway. I sighed. Small talk was hard enough for me, but Janaclese wasn't making our conversation any easier.

She glanced at me. "Did you talk to Trevor?"

I shrugged my shoulders. Not talking to Trevor wasn't a big deal to me. "He was in that swarm of bees buzzing around Kehl-li and Miracle."

"Don't worry about that. I've known Trevor as long as I've known Miracle. He only has eyes for you, and I don't think he's easily distracted."

"Well, you certainly are tonight." I pointed to the shrubbery. "You hit the camellia bush."

"No, I didn't. I've started my car, but it's still in park."

"Then why is the bush shaking?"

We watched leaves fall to the ground.

"Janaclese, you'd better get out and look to be sure. We don't want any more mayhem at the mansion tonight."

When Janaclese opened her door, Kehl-li stepped out from behind the bush, grinning.

Kehl-li straightened her blouse and brushed off debris. "The engine on your Prius is so quiet. Are you stalking us?"

Us? She was the only person visible. Maybe Kehl-li had multiple personalities or something.

The bush shook some more.

Just then Trevor's head bobbed up from behind the greenery. He tied the drawstring on his swim trunks.

Janaclese's mouth opened and closed. My body caved in as she stepped back into the car. "Cyndray, sit tight. I'm sure it's not what you're thinking."

Heat stirred inside my pit. "What is it that you *think* I'm thinking? I honestly don't care."

"Cyndray, things aren't always as they seem." She tried to console me.

I held up my palm to her face. "Save it." I really didn't appreciate Janaclese trying to make me feel better. Who cared if Trevor and Kehl-li hooked up?

A block of ice formed around my heart.

"Cyndray, Trevor wouldn't—"

"Janaclese, I don't believe in fairy tales." Sheesh. Hadn't I just told her that people are capable of anything? "Sometimes you've gotta remove those rose covered glasses that are blinding you and see life for what it is. Relationships are tricky, and people aren't always as nice as you think they are."

That should have been enough. Problem is when my temper flares a floodgate opens, and the water gushes out. Without a plug, I had no restraint.

"Here are the facts: Trevor has a thing for Kehl-li. Hassan's skin is not flawless. There's a scar above his right eyebrow." I couldn't control the waves of anger. "And you saw your mom enjoying someone else's company. You might as well accept the fact that your parents may never—"

"Cyndray stop. Please." Her voice trembled. "When we're hurting, we sometimes say things to hurt other people. Please don't say anything about my parents."

"Who's hurting? I'll never be emotionally battered and bruised like a sensitive wuss." I pressed my lips together, bringing my words to a complete halt. I twisted my mouth, sorry that my anger toward Kehl-li and Trevor ricocheted and hit her.

"Janaclese, I'm just saying—"

"Cyndray, you've said enough. Please don't say anything else."

Janaclese's jawbone was tight, but she was kind enough to say please. Was she capable of being as angry as I was? Why did it feel like I'd lost my best friend. And my boyfriend. How could I convince my pounding heart that it really didn't matter?

Chapter 7

JANACLESE

I placed my feet together, heel to toe.

Assemblé ... passé ... relevé ... and triple pirouette. I spun and stumbled. Both my focus and rotation were definitely off today.

Plié ... developpé ... arabesque ... "Ow!"

Another attempt to turn en pointe with a perfect landing sent me clattering to the floor, writhing in pain. Grimacing, I clutched my ankle and scooted to the barre. The music I'd chosen for the allegro steps was too light and lively for my heavy spirit.

I'd spent the last few days trying to figure out what was going on with my friends. Why hadn't Miracle returned any of my calls? Was she grounded?

Leaning against the mirror, I removed my dance slippers and examined my foot. Maybe I hadn't properly exercised. Flexing my ankle in the pointe position, I winced as I held my toes downward for a few seconds before relaxing my foot.

Why didn't Hassan ask for my number at the party? Could a guy like him possibly be interested in a girl who danced ballet?

A ... B ... I wrote the alphabet with my toes to stretch my ankles. C ...

Cyndray had judged Hassan too harshly. So maybe I'd missed the scar above his right eyebrow, but that couldn't be as bad as her scarred perception of people.

But it was hard not to consider some of the things she'd alluded to. What if Trevor had fooled around with Kehl-li? What if Mom ...

I wrestled the thought, banishing it from my head. My parents still loved each other.

Stuffing my shoes into my duffle bag, I hobbled from the basement to the main level of my house, the stairs aggravating my throbbing feet.

The clickety-clack of the keyboard alerted me that Mom was home. Good. I walked toward her office. I needed answers.

"Decided to work from home today?" I stood in the doorway of her office.

Mom sat at her desk, her head bent over a pile of papers, spectacles propped on her nose. "Trying to meet a deadline for another grant proposal. What's up?"

She was back to acting like a normal businesswoman and not some love-struck teenager.

"Nothing really." I stalled a few seconds. "Um … who was that man you were talking to at Miracle's party?"

Mom squinted at the computer and scratched her head like she was trying to figure something out. Then she glanced up and said, "Just an old friend."

She went right back to working, crunching numbers on her calculator. I eased further into the room. "Is he a parent or relative of someone I know?"

Just like Cyndray had never met my dad, maybe there were fathers, stepfathers, or uncles within our tight circle that I'd never met either.

Mom typed something on her computer, stared at the screen, then pounded the keys on the calculator again. I stood waiting for her response.

She finally looked up and sighed. "I'm sorry, Janaclese. Were you asking me a question?"

"Yeah. Who was that man with you?"

"What man?"

My muscles tensed. *Was she avoiding my question on purpose?* "The guy you were talking to at Miracle's pool party."

A light flashed through Mom's eyes. "Oh, Curtis? I was about to introduce you when Miracle unveiled herself. Have you spoken to her since her party? She seemed pretty upset when MiShelle scolded her."

What was Miracle's mom thinking shaming her in public? "No. Miracle isn't accepting my calls."

"Well, I said some things to her about modesty. She might be avoiding you because she's perturbed with me." Mom gathered a few papers. "What about Cyndray? Has she spoken to Miracle?"

"I don't know. We haven't spoken since the party either."

She swiveled around in her chair. "Everything okay with you girls?"

Mom had a sixth sense that told her when something wasn't right. Except today she didn't seem to notice that I was more concerned about Curtis—the man she was hanging all over at the party.

"I guess we're fine. Maybe just a little girl drama."

She pursed her lips.

"Nothing that can't easily be resolved," I added.

"Good." She presented a half-smile. "By the way, Mrs. Dunning called."

Shoot. My breathing slowed. Had she exaggerated what happened at Vacation Bible School? "What did she want?"

"To discuss her ideas about the summer lock-in."

"Already?" I crumpled my face. "I thought the lock-in was always the weekend before school starts."

"That hasn't changed." She hole-punched a document. "Mrs. Dunning suggested we add a few topics to our discussion. She feels strongly that purity and abstinence need to be covered."

Mom stopped what she was doing and looked at me as if to challenge any opposing response. I shifted the weight on my aching feet. What did she expect me to say?

"At first, I thought the subject about sex might be too heavy. After all, the age range for those who attend is so broad. With her being so adamant and after seeing Miracle expose herself, I think it's necessary. Do you have any thoughts?"

"Thoughts? About sex?"

Mom's eyes searched me.

My head was foggy. Did I say something wrong?

She cleared her throat. "Actually, I meant do you have any thoughts about the lock-in?"

"Um-um." I shook my head.

"Mrs. Dunning also said she didn't think you girls fully understood the importance of appearances as far as purity is concerned."

"Appearances?"

"Yeah, apparently there was a recent incident where this needed to be addressed."

Uh-oh. I braced myself for a verbal thrashing.

"Let me ask you something. If you see a customer hurrying out of a bank during normal business hours, what would you assume?"

God, help me. I know this is a set-up.

I hunched my shoulders upward. "I don't know. Maybe the customer made a legitimate banking transaction and was rushing to another business meeting."

"If you see a customer hurrying out of a bank when it's supposed to be closed, what would you assume?"

I crossed my arms. "That doesn't mean he robbed the bank! Why are people so judgmental?"

"People can be judgmental. And you're right, that doesn't mean he's a bank robber. But notice how that was the first thing that came out of your mouth."

The only thing I'd noticed was the quickening of my breathing. I needed to relax.

"Appearances are important, especially when we're leading other people to do the right thing. We have to be careful that they're not led astray by our *assumed* behavior."

Why didn't Mom just come out and say that being alone in a room with Hassan gave the impression we were doing something we weren't supposed to be doing, even if we were putting away art supplies?

"I understand." Sagging, I turned to leave the room.

"Janaclese," Mom called after me.

I turned back to face her.

"You have no reason to worry about Curtis and me."

So she did pick up that I was bothered. *Funny, she didn't seem concerned about her own appearance.*

"The man has several children. Apparently one of them was at the party."

"Ahh." An unexpected heave of relief escaped.

Ignoring my sore ankle and pained feet, I raced over and flung my arms out, hugging her from the back with a tight grip.

Mom looked up over her shoulder at me with a smile stretching almost as wide as her eyes. "Okay? What's this all about?"

"I love you, and I'm so glad you're my mother."

I hopped into Mom's lap like a big baby, not permitting my almost grown-up age and body to block me from the embrace I needed so badly.

Mom rubbed my back. "Jana. Are you sure nothing is bothering you?"

Imagining myself looking ridiculously immature, I jumped to my feet.

"Sorry, I ... I just."

"Yeah, baby I know." Mom stood up and held out her arms, beckoning me back into her safety net.

I nestled my head against her shoulder, sniffling and laughing, the emotions warring.

No words were exchanged; but somehow, I knew she understood whatever I was communicating.

"Me too," she said. "Me too."

Chapter 8

CYNDRAY

I pulled out Kehl-li's magazine, *TotalDiva,* hidden underneath my bed. After running my finger through the table of contents, I flipped to page 24. The article began:

In a recent survey sampling 1,041 college students, researchers found only five who had never experienced romantic kissing and more than 200 who estimated having kissed more than 28 partners. Kissing between partners occurs in more than 90 percent of human cultures. It is a part of an evolved courtship ritual.

Blah, blah, blah. How was this supposed to keep Trevor from Kehl-li? I skimmed for the stuff that related to my situation.

Tip Number One: Interest yourself in whatever your fellow is interested in.

Hmmph, now that's just wrong. Why couldn't the guy interest himself in whatever the girl found interesting? So, what did Trevor like anyway? We'd spent hours together playing online games but had never dated.

Tip Number Two: Make yourself available.

Now, what the heck did that mean? I continued reading.

Position yourself where he sees you.

How was that possible when school was out for summer, and I had a court-ordered curfew along with supervised, structured activities?

The author of this article was lame. No doubt it was written from a male's point of view, even if it was supposed to be girl talk.

I texted Janaclese. "Bored. Call me." I was about to hit the send button when I remembered we weren't speaking. She'd politely asked me not to say anything else to her, and we'd ridden home in silence.

Everything that had gone wrong over the last few days was Ke-hl-li's fault—from my court problems to losing Trevor and Janaclese, to being reduced to reading this stupid article written by an ignoramus. I threw the magazine across the room. It thudded against the wall.

That felt better. A little anyway.

I picked up my phone and checked for new messages. None. What now?

Reluctantly, I dialed Kaci's number and waited for her voice to answer. We were running mates on Unity's track team, but more like arch rivals.

"Hello?"

"Hey, it's Cyndray."

"Whatever it is I don't know anything about it."

Sheesh. She acted like I was the po-po.

"Quick question. You and Trevor still spar each other at the gym?"

"Yeah. So?"

"So, I'm thinking of trying it out for some exercise."

Kaci was too quiet. Maybe she'd hung up on me.

"You there?"

"You gotta fax machine?" Kaci asked.

"A fax machine?" Was this chick weird on purpose?

"Yeah. I'll ask Coach to fax over the waiver. Your parents need to sign it, and you can bring it when you come to class."

"Oh. Sure thing, Kaci."

As soon as I gave her my information and ended the call, I started shadow boxing.

"Okay, Kehl-li. IT'S ON!"

Shuffling my feet, I pretended to land a knockout punch.

If I was going down, it wouldn't be without a fight.

Hanna ... Dool ... Seth ... Neth ... Dasaul ...
The instructor, who'd introduced himself as Coach Gray, counted in Korean as the class did seventy-five jumping jacks and fifty sit-ups, followed by thirty push-ups.

Kaci had clued me in on the one-week free trial. The price was right, so I'd walked over to the gym after work with a signed waiver ready to get my workout on. But now, I didn't know which would kill me first—the extreme workout or the smell of a thousand sweaty feet soaking in sulfur.

Beads of sweat rolled from my forehead and settled on my cheeks. I was making myself visible to Trevor—positioning myself so he could *look upon* me. After this boot camp, I doubted there'd be anything left of me to see.

"How's your first class going?" Kaci patted my back as her voice rose above the chorus of grunts surrounding the gym.

If I had any breath left, Kaci slammed it right out of me. I stumbled to the wooden floor. Maybe the pat was well-meaning, but I'd swear in court she'd directly assaulted me!

"You okay, Cyndray?"

I rose to my knees, and Kaci helped me to my feet.

"Everybody find a punching bag and a partner," Coach Gray said.

"C'mon. I like this one. It's already adjusted for my height."

With gloved hands, I followed Kaci to the red and white free-standing bags.

"Left jab, right jab, hook, uppercut." The instructor demonstrated as he yelled out more commands.

"Follow the sequence, Cyndray," Kaci encouraged me.

Trevor, you better be worth it.

Kaci and I rotated on the bag, which barely moved when I struck it.

Kablam. I hit the bag hard.

Kaci hit harder.

"Kiai!" I mimicked the other students' sound and swung with all my might.

Kaci proved to be mightier.

I tried to talk between punches. "Is it ..." *Wham.* "Almost over?"

"What?" Kaci screamed above the pounding.

That girl had a nice set of strong lungs on her.

"What time is it over?" I used my last breath to blow out a question.

"Six forty-five," came the fierce bellow.

I turned to look at the clock.

Whack.

The bag clipped me. I did a double backward flip, with a clean slide clear to the other side of the room.

Kaci ran to my side. "Nice! I didn't know you were a gymnast."

I rolled my eyes. Slapping her down to the floor beside me was not a feasible option. Besides, she could breathe on me, and I'd blow like a leaf in the wind.

I clutched my chest and whispered, "Must. Get. Air."

Kaci bent down and leaned her ear toward my mouth.

I had enough energy for one word before departing this earth. "Thirsty."

"Did you bring a bottle of water?"

I shook my head.

Kaci ran and got a bottle of water from somewhere.

I slugged down sixteen ounces in sixteen seconds. Now there's a contest I could win.

Kaci motioned for me to follow her. "Come on. It's time to spar."

"What? I thought the class was over now."

"That was a warm-up routine and technique training. We've got fifteen more minutes to execute what we've learned."

Sheesh. I thought walking the two blocks to get here was a pretty good warm-up. And as far as technique training was concerned—I'd learned to watch those bags. They punch back.

Coach Gray divided the class in half. I eased beside Kaci just to be certain Amazon girl and I would be on the same team and not matched against each other.

After studying the opponents, I smiled, satisfied with the good decision I'd made. They stood tall and slender like blades of grass. But we were mean machines ready to mow them down.

I watched girl after girl get beaten by our team. Kaci's match lasted only two rounds since she'd racked up too many points over her opponent.

Finally, it was my turn to enter the ring. There was only one person left to spar on the opposing team. I'd already sized up the shy little redhead, peeking behind the giant assistant coach. This would be easy.

I stuck out my chest and stepped into the ring, revved up and ready to kick butt.

When the assistant coach jogged into the ring and stood across from me, I knew something was wrong.

"This is Cyndray's first time," Coach Gray explained. "Use control."

I searched the sidelines for my opponent. The redhead had disappeared.

"This is a non-contact match," Coach Gray announced. "You're both relatively new students."

Wait a second. The giant assistant coach was actually a student?

I studied my enemy. How was this even fair when I didn't have a slingshot or a bag of stones to bring down Goliath? If she came even close enough to hit me, I'd swing like a wild caged animal.

Goliath threw a punch. I sidestepped. Countered. Missed.

I charged forward. Goliath blocked my attack and belted me in the gut.

So much for non-contact. I wanted to crumple in a heap just to stop the clock.

New tactic—stay far, far, FAR away from Goliath.

Bobbing and weaving to avoid contact, I danced around the ring. Goliath zigzagged after me. I'd determined that my speed and fluidity was a secret weapon against her slow, bulky mass. I pranced in all directions—backward, forward, side to side. Goliath seemed dizzy from spinning in circles and nearly pummeled herself.

Ding. The timer buzzed, signaling the end of the fight.

Whew. I'd survived my first rivalry.

"Great defense, Cyndray," Kaci said and backed away like I had a new virus.

I checked my deodorant. What did she have to be all embarrassed about? I outsmarted my opponent, didn't I?

I limped to the locker area to get my gym bag. All of that hard work and no sight of Trevor!

"I saw your match." Trevor's wide smile greeted me when I turned around. "You interested in sparring?"

No. I'm trying to be interested in you, Bonehead.

"A girl's gotta exercise." I kept walking.

Trevor's footsteps matched mine. "You looked pretty good in there."

Killing myself just to impress you, so you'll like me, and I can finally feel normal.

Ignoring him, I entered the women's locker room and didn't look back.

Was it against the rules to pretend I couldn't care less? Maybe I shouldn't have just skimmed that article. I quickly gathered my belongings so I could catch Trevor before he left.

I slowed my pace as I entered the common area. I didn't want to appear too eager. Where was he? I looked down both ends of the hallway, but I didn't see Trevor anywhere.

I spun around at a tap on my shoulder.

Trevor winked at me. "Looking for me?"

"No." *Sorry, God.* "Yes."

Trevor's contagious laugh was an ice pick chipping away the frozen mound that engulfed my heart last week. I forced a smile, wondering if I should ask about seeing him with Kehl-li. Did he even know that I saw him?

"I'm proud of you." He draped his arm across my shoulder making me wince. "Not many people have the stamina to spar on their first night."

I felt like a Marine—The few. The proud.

My body ached to the tune of the "Star-Spangled Banner" playing in my head. The clash of the cymbals sent spasms throughout every muscle. But I couldn't ask Trevor to remove his arm. Normal girls who liked boys didn't do that.

"So when are you gonna let me whip up on you in 'Hanging With Friends'?"

He wanted to play online video games with me again? I couldn't allow any thoughts about Kehl-li to spoil this moment. Maybe both of our pasts should be kept secret.

I looked into Trevor's deep-set eyes. I felt another drip from the ice melting. It hurt to smile, but if it meant gaining our friendship, the pain was so worth it.

Chapter 9

JANACLESE

I skirted down the hallway through the row of closed doors at Redemption Temple. The door decorated with sparkling silver stars grabbed my attention. Its message, "*Let your light shine,*" was outlined in gold. I glanced at my watch. Sunday School would be over in another minute, and I still hadn't seen anyone who even resembled Hassan. Did he really attend church here?

Deacon Jackson jingled hand bells alerting the end of class. Doors burst open, and the vestibule flooded with chatter and people rushing to get to their favorite pew in the sanctuary or row in the balcony. I scooted among the crowd, looking for any sign of Hassan.

My heart sank. Where was he? No Miracle, no Cyndray, not even Kehl-li in sight. I bit my lip, realizing I hadn't really expected to find my friends waving at me over the crowd. How had things between us changed so quickly? My body felt loaded with bags of heavy metal, and I dragged my feet toward the sanctuary.

"Isn't she darling?" Mrs. Etheridge embraced me from my blind side. "You looking for your me-maw?"

Her senior circle closed in on me, and my cheeks were attacked by kisses, squeezes, and pinches as if I were still a toddler. I smiled, not wanting to talk. At least somebody cared.

I huddled among the scent of Bengay and mothballs mixed with spearmint gum, breathing in the familiar smells of love, admiration, and safety. I sighed, releasing about ten pounds from my load.

"Your me-maw headed out of class early to get her front row seat. You know we old people can't hustle to the sanctuary like you young folks. We already went to early morning service. Gotta go by the hospital now." Mrs. Etheridge puckered her red lips and smacked me on my face again. "Tell Betima hello, and y'all enjoy the service, hear?"

"Yes, ma'am." I waved and walked toward the sanctuary doors, pausing at the foot of the balcony as about twenty people clomped down the stairs. I sighed. That only happened when the balcony was full, which meant I'd waited too long and now had to sit in the sanctuary.

Along with smiling ushers in white uniforms and white-gloved hands passing out programs, the stained glass picture of Jesus with outstretched arms located directly above the pulpit welcomed me into the sanctuary. Ambling down the aisle, I spotted Mom in her usual church section. She looked up at me with pinched brows, then motioned for everyone to squeeze further down. She scooted over for me to sit next to her. I eased onto the pew.

"What's up?" Mom leaned over and asked.

I shook my head. She already knew about my friendship situation, but I couldn't tell her the other sorry excuse for why I wasn't in the balcony today—I got stuck on the main level looking for Hassan when praise and worship ended.

Silence permeated the congregation. I couldn't resist scanning the perimeter, hoping to catch a glimpse of Hassan. Uncle Sam's voice boomed from the pulpit. "No one likes to admit being wrong. Today, I have one question: Do you want to be right or reconciled?"

My eyes twitched. *God, please help me concentrate on your message.*

"Be aware of the Ego trying to take God's proper place in the center of relationships. Ego destroys bonds by demanding its own selfish desires."

Mom dabbed her eyes as Uncle Sam continued to preach another hard message for people in broken relationships. My mind switched to Hassan. How could I get to know him? He seemed shy, yet confident—so different from the other guys I knew. I must've been mistaken about him going to this church, though. My mind wandered, and I rehearsed what I'd say if I ever had another chance to speak to him again.

Cyndray claimed that Hassan was a bad boy from the 'hood. He hadn't seemed that way to me. More like my knight in shining armor the way he tried to help me put the paint brushes on the shelf. *Where was Red Hill? Would Cyndray be willing to ride there with me?*

"Let us close in prayer." Uncle Sam bowed his head.

What? Had I daydreamed through the entire sermon? My body readily assumed the prayer position.

"Amen," the congregation chorused, and I opened my eyes.

"Who kissed you?" Mom raised her brows.

"Huh? Kissed what?" *Lord?*

"You're so jumpy." Mom rubbed my face with her thumb. "There's red lipstick on your cheek. Hold still."

"I got it." Touching my face, I sprang from my seat, "See you at Aunt Alicia's." I raced toward the back door but was cut off when Cyndray blocked my path.

"Hey." With a blank face, she sized me up and down.

I forced a smile. "Hi."

"We cool?" Cyndray held up her hand for a high five and gave me that 'you better not leave me hanging' look.

A neon sign flashed in my brain. *Do you want to be right or reconciled?*

I broke into a wide grin and hugged her instead, releasing the bottled energy that made me heavy one minute and jittery the next. "I missed talking to you. What've you been up to? Have you spoken to Miracle? I didn't see either of you at Youth Encounter last Tuesday night."

Cyndray laughed. "Missed you, too … Bored like you wouldn't believe … No, Miracle's missing in action." She paused for a moment. "And what else did you ask me?"

"It doesn't matter. I'm just happy we've made up."

Cyndray rocked back and forth on her heels and rolled her eyes upward. "I suppose somebody should still apologize."

"You already have." I grabbed her hand and spun away from the back door. "Come with me. I have something important to show you."

"Slow down, Janaclese. Where are you taking me?"

I thought maybe I'd given Cyndray the wrong impression about faith before, and now I could redeem myself. We headed back toward the sanctuary and walked over to where Uncle Sam and Aunt Alicia were shaking hands with members as they left the front entrance of the church.

"Look at Aunt Alicia's stomach." I pointed.

Cyndray's eyes were as big and round as Aunt Alicia's belly. "Wow. Looks like Mrs. Samson swallowed an entire watermelon."

I cupped my hand over my mouth to conceal my laugh. "Girl, you are cra—" I halted, remembering how much Cyndray hated being called "crazy" because of the mental issues in her family. "Anyway, I'm showing you faith in action."

Cyndray wrinkled her nose. "Faith in action?"

"Yes. Aunt Alicia has believed for twelve years that she would one day have a baby."

"She told me she was pregnant and lost a baby boy a few summers ago."

"And that was after several miscarriages," I added.

"If she's been pregnant before, then getting pregnant again isn't a big deal." Cyndray paused, looking over at Aunt Alicia again before continuing. "How's that faith in action?"

I gazed into Cyndray's eyes, seeing sincere curiosity. She wasn't challenging me.

"This is the first time I've ever seen her stomach grow so full of the promise. She's never been this far along. You know after all she's been through, she could've given up, but she didn't."

Cyndray nodded. "Most people probably would have."

"Yeah. And seeing her stomach reminds me that God hasn't forgotten my prayers either. God answers prayers, Cyndray. That's what faith can do."

"I believe that." Cyndray stared in amazement.

"So, about my parents' separation ... faith is all I have that they'll somehow get back together. I'm never going to stop believing real love endures all things."

Cyndray looked at the floor. "Sorry. I shouldn't have said those things about your mom."

I reached out and touched her arm. "Hey, it's okay. I just wanted you to know why I have faith my parents will get back together."

She twisted her bracelet but didn't speak.

"And I really need you to not judge people so harshly."

Flexing her shoulders, Cyndray looked up, her stare meeting my gaze. "I hear you, but you've gotta understand that I'm new at this Christian stuff and sometimes ... well let's face it, sometimes I'm gonna mess up."

"We all do. No one is perfect. It'll be better if we both understand that."

"Well, since we're talking about what happened, I need you to honestly answer something for me."

My head bobbed up and down. "We're friends. Anything you ask, I'll tell you."

"Okay. You mentioned Hassan said something that you'd rather not share, but you seemed upset. What did he say?"

I looked away. Was she going to think I was stupid for still liking Hassan after what he said to me?

Cyndray's eyes widened. "Spill it, friend."

I sucked in my breath. "I think he called me fat."

"What?" She burst out like a lid blown from a pressure cooker. "That thug has some nerve thinking he's God's gift to—" She frowned and slowly rolled out another thought. "Wait a minute, Janaclese. What were Hassan's *exact* words?"

I sighed. "He said 'your swimsuit is tight.'"

"So you were in a funky mood after the party because he said *that*?"

I crossed my arms. "I know. I'm too sensitive."

"Too sensitive and too ... too sheltered." She struggled for words. "Hassan complimented you. He didn't call you fat. He meant P.H.A.T."

Hope surged through me. "Really? How do you know that?"

"Tight means well put together. It all fits perfectly." She looked at me like I should've known that.

I beamed. "So he was checking me out?"

"Yeah, and he liked what he saw." Cyndray shook her head. "Anyway, I have something to show you too. C'mon."

Practically floating, I followed Cyndray downstairs to the fellowship hall, where people were grabbing snacks for the car ride home from church. Redemption started doing that for the kids about a year ago since the services lasted so long. Seemed like the adults appreciated it more than the kids.

"Over there." Cyndray signaled for me to look in the direction of the kitchen.

My heart fluttered. Was that my dreamboat at church?

"Hassan was in the new members' class with me and my mom." She threw her hands up. "He apparently joined Redemption earlier this summer. And he asked about you before class."

"He did?"

"That's why I searched for you right after church. I wanted to know if he'd said anything to offend you at Miracle's party."

Instead of twirling and leaping like I wanted to, I locked arms with Cyndray and rested my head on her shoulder.

"Whadda you doin'?"

"Trying to keep my balance." My feet jerked, wanting to dance, but I was too dizzy with excitement.

Cyndray brushed me away. "That's just creepy."

She stood in front of me. "Keep facing me. Hassan just spotted us, and he's coming this way."

I leaned against a table for support, fearing I might faint.

"Yo, Janaclese." Hassan perfectly pronounced the three syllables in my name, and I loved hearing him say it.

"Yeah?" I turned my back to Cyndray to face Hassan. Could he hear the horses galloping across my chest?

His eyes danced. "Your name matches your beautiful smile."

"Thank you." I blushed. What were the lines I rehearsed?

"Saw you at VBS, but didn't know this was your church too. I'm a new member. When did you join?"

"It's been quite a while." Like my entire life. My uncle was the pastor. But he'd discover that soon enough.

"Yo, Shawty, uh … I was wondering if I could hold your digits." His hands gyrated as he spoke. "I asked your friend, but she wanted to speak with you first."

I spun around and stared at Cyndray. "He wanted my digits?"

"Don't look at me. I'm not an operator, sheesh." Cyndray sucked her teeth. "If he wanted your *telephone number*, he should've dialed 411 for the information."

"Oh!" I looked at Hassan. "My cell number is three oh one, nine three four, twenty-eight fourteen."

Hassan grinned. "I'll call you tonight."

He stored my number into his cell and walked away. Too wobbly to stand, I fell against the table.

"Breathe, girlfriend." Cyndray fanned me with her hand. "Janaclese and Robin from the 'hood. What a pair." She laughed. "Seriously, unless you want me tagging along on every date as your translator, you'd better google urbanslang.com."

I couldn't stop smiling. "Are you still judging him?"

She mimicked Hassan's gestures. "Yo, Shawty, I'm just saying…"

Chapter 10

JANACLESE

The smell of roasted chicken floated from the oven in Aunt Alicia's kitchen. I could barely focus on helping her and Mom prepare the side dishes.

Six days, twenty hours and eighteen minutes had passed since my first telephone conversation with Hassan last Sunday after church. Since then, we'd called or texted each other at least twice a day. So, why wasn't he in church today? And why hadn't I heard from him?

Maybe something was wrong.

I fiddled with my phone, checking the volume and searching for any missed text messages.

"Are you expecting a call?" Mom asked, removing a dish from the oven.

I leaned against the counter in Uncle Sam and Aunt Alicia's kitchen, my stomach rumbling at the smell of Sunday dinner. I checked the volume and searched for missed text messages again. Nothing.

"Will you stop checking your cell phone?" Mom scowled, frustration marking her face because I wasn't focused on helping her and Aunt Alicia in the kitchen.

I picked up the bowl of blueberries—Aunt Alicia's favorite. She had so many delicious blueberry dessert recipes she could publish a cookbook. Unfortunately, I had to fix a blueberry walnut salad. Now that she was pregnant, we all suffered a loss from sweets.

"Janaclese, I'm almost finished with the love song I've been working on. There's an unedited CD in my studio. Interested in giving me some feedback?" Taking the bowl from me, Aunt Alicia winked and placed the blueberries next to the sink.

"Sure." I grabbed the opportunity she offered to check my messages without Mom hovering over me, took a fistful of blueberries, then headed to her studio.

Leaving the door opened, I dialed Hassan's number. After the third ring, I heard breathing on the other end.

"Hassan?"

"You reached me."

Relief filled me. I picked up the love song CD from the desk.

"It's Janaclese." We both hesitated. "You sound different today."

"Definitely me, Shawty. S'up?" he responded.

My insides fluttered. Hassan automatically nicknamed me Shawty. Pretty cool to already have a pet name.

"I didn't see you at church this morning, so I thought I'd call you."

"You keeping tabs on me or something?"

"No, just checking to make sure you're all right."

Swallowing blueberries, I traced the cover of the CD with my finger. Why did this call seem so awkward and strange?

"You're pretty *and* sweet, huh?" Hassan chuckled.

"So ... what've you been doing all day?" I asked.

"Chilling."

"Really?" That was an odd reason to miss church.

Hassan was quiet on the other end. I fingered a button on my blouse.

"Are you sure you're okay?"

"Just a little exhausted, I guess."

"I thought you said you were chilling all day." I squinted. Maybe "chilling" meant something else in Red Hill.

"I'm at my aunt's house. The one that lives near Pastor Sam. Had to unclog a drain."

My heart skipped. We were only a few blocks from each other. "Is that why you didn't go to Redemption today? I missed seeing you."

"Yo, Shawty, I know you're a church girl and all, but that's not the only place we can see each other. *Is it?*"

Laughter floated up from the kitchen, so I closed the door. "No. Of course not."

"Then, when can I see you … other than at church, I mean?"

My voice lowered to a whisper. "Are you asking me out on a date?"

"Whatever you wanna call it. I just wanna kick it, you know?"

I could be at his aunt's house in less than five minutes.

"Hassan, I'll call you right back."

I tucked my phone into my pocket and slowly walked down the steps. Excitement and fear set off a string of firecrackers in my stomach. Could I sneak to my car? Surely no one would miss me if I paid Hassan a surprise visit—I'd only be gone maybe fifteen minutes tops.

Mom and Aunt Alicia's silhouettes reflected in the china cabinet. Aunt Alicia shredded lettuce while Mom chopped nuts. While listening to their conversation, I stood on the last step and planned my escape.

"Curtis and I are having lunch tomorrow," Mom said.

Curtis? I frowned, pausing my attempt to slip out of the house unnoticed. Why did that name sound vaguely familiar?

"I thought you had lunch with him last week." Aunt Alicia stopped shredding and stared at Mom. "You two have been talking an awful lot, and you wouldn't want him to get the wrong idea."

Wasn't Curtis the man I'd asked Mom about? A noose wrapped around my insides.

"Don't look at me like that." Mom arched her brows. "He knows I'm still officially married."

"If I were you, I'd still be careful. He's widowed, and only God knows what you and Franklin have going on with your marriage." Aunt Alicia paused, and then spoke over her shoulder. "It would be another matter if he wasn't your old boyfriend."

The noose squeezed tighter. Had I heard right? Was Mom secretly rekindling an old flame?

"We're just catching up. It's so strange that he still knows how to make me laugh. He practically had me in stitches at Miracle's pool party, until that child publicly disclosed her personal secrets."

Grasping the banister, I sank down onto the stairs. Mom told me Curtis was an old *friend*. There was no mention of an old *boyfriend*.

"I don't know what's getting into teens today. We didn't act like that," I heard Mom say.

"Actually, I don't think we were that different when we were teenagers. Wisdom comes with age."

"There were always fast girls, but I don't remember anyone in our generation being in a big hurry to have sex. We waited for marriage."

"Not all of us," Aunt Alicia muttered.

"What's that supposed to mean?"

"I'm just saying ... all of us didn't wait for marriage."

My hand gripped the banister.

"Well, speak for yourself. I won't pretend it was easy, but I remained pure until my wedding day."

Aunt Alicia rubbed her stomach but didn't say anything.

Mom leaned across the counter and whispered like a schoolgirl sharing a secret with her BFF. "Alicia, I don't believe it. So you were experienced when you married my brother?"

"Come on, Betima. Don't act like we don't have a past. Or like you really expect me to kiss and tell?"

A throbbing pain stabbed my stomach, folding my body inward. The noose around my insides worked its way up my neck, and I gasped for air, accidentally banging my head against the wall.

Had Aunt Alicia ... no! Not my God-loving aunt. My example of faith in action. My confidante for all those things I couldn't talk to my mom or my friends about...

A long groan escaped from me, triggering an urgent response from Mom and Aunt Alicia. They rushed to my aid. A dish crashed to the floor as my flawless image of Aunt Alicia also shattered into pieces.

"Jana!" Mom knelt beside me. "Is it your stomach?"

I nodded. The intense pain felt like a jackhammer crushing through my intestines. I rolled onto my side, praying for the spasms to stop.

"Israel," Aunt Alicia called out to Uncle Sam while passing Mom a wet towel. "Didn't you take her to the doctor? ... Israel, come quick," she yelled again before Mom could answer her.

"No need to wake Sam." Mom massaged my stomach. "She's gonna be okay. Just breathe, baby."

"Betima, this has been going on for weeks, and Jana's doubled over in agony. Shouldn't we head to the emergency room?"

"It'll pass in a few minutes." Mom wiped the sweat from my forehead and coached me through the pain. "Inhale ... now, exhale."

Did Aunt Alicia have premarital sex? Was Mom cheating on Dad with her old boyfriend?

"I feel nauseous," I spluttered, my stomach heaving.

Aunt Alicia grabbed a small trash bin. "Surely, you'll take her to see the doctor first thing in the morning."

Blueberries surged from my insides, splattering everywhere except the bin.

"Yes. I'll call Dr. Abby first thing tomorrow," Mom said, eyeing the dots of blue sprinkled on her clothes.

Chapter 11

CYNDRAY

As soon as Mom parked near the big crib, next to the SOS building, I blurted my usual mantra. "I don't need anger management." Must've sounded like a broken record, but it was true.

"Cyndray, we've already been through this. The judge said—"

"I know, I know." I grabbed my white windbreaker from the backseat and opened the car door. "Are you going to wait for me?"

"I have to run an errand, but I'll be back before the session ends. I promise."

I snatched my water bottle from the console, slammed the door, and stomped into the building. Going to therapy automatically made me angry.

Mom didn't understand, and she didn't care. Nobody did. I'd given my life to God three months ago. Wasn't He supposed to keep me out of trouble?

Empty chairs already formed the shape of a horseshoe when I entered the room with duct-taped walls. Dr. Reed twiddled with the thermostat until the fan roared to life and spewed a blast of cold air. He noticed me standing in the doorway. "Come on in, Cyndray. The others should be here shortly."

The others ... the jack-o-lantern vandal, third person Elmo, and the pyromaniac ventriloquist. I scowled, wondering how they described me.

Something in the room felt strangely odd—like Shari's jack-o-lantern smile the last time. Maybe it was the room itself, maybe it was Dr. Reed ... or maybe it was just me who was strange.

I didn't get it. Seemed Janaclese was falling in love, and all I could do was fall into trouble. Girls like me had one emotion—anger. That couldn't be all that normal. Still, no one was gonna make me crazy with the gross therapy stuff.

"Dr. Reed, my mom has to run an errand, so I won't be attending today's meeting."

"Oh." He seemed startled, then pleasantly surprised as a crooked smile formed on his face. "That was very responsible of you to drop in and tell me. Usually, the teens just don't show up. I'll note it in my records."

That's because I'm not criminal-minded like them. I erased the thought.

"Yeah, thanks." I walked out of the room, then turned back. Maybe I could prove I was different in a good way, a productive citizen who didn't need therapy. "You know, Dr. Reed, I won a state track competition at my school."

"That's nice." He presented the fake 'good job' smile that adults give pitiful little kids. "Maybe you should share your accomplishment with the group sometime."

That ain't gonna happen. I squinted, zooming in on his half-shaven face. "I don't do too well with 'Show and Tell.'"

He raised his eyebrows. "It takes some people a while to appreciate group work."

I swallowed. "How do people do that, anyway? You know … sit and tell strangers personal stuff?" I drummed my fingers against my water bottle. Dr. Reed wasn't Mrs. Samson. I'd gotten lucky with her one-on-one mentoring. Luck didn't last forever. "My friends don't even know everything about me."

He pointed aimlessly around the room. "In here, there's no judgment. Common struggles are better understood by those who've experienced them. Not necessarily by friends."

I don't have anything in common with the Motley Crew! I wanted to scream the words, get them outta my head, even if they sounded mean. My ears burned, and I wanted to tell him he was so wrong about the judging thing. Just like I'd judged them, they were probably judging me.

I twisted my foot. Dr. Reed was probably judging to see if I could control my anger. That's why I couldn't speak my mind. And that's why the head voices were getting stronger.

He stared at me. "Are you okay?"

"Yeah, I've gotta go. After Mom's errands, I've got a Youth Encounter meeting."

"Youth Encounter?"

"At my church."

He twisted his lips. "Okay. See you next time."

Like everybody else, Dr. Reed didn't seem to care either. My good works didn't matter. Or maybe it was hard to believe I was a gold medalist athlete and a church girl.

Maybe it really *didn't* matter, because nothing mattered much when people saw you as worthless.

Chapter 12

CYNDRAY

Hassan hunkered down in the seat next to me in Youth Encounter class and stared at the door.

"Don't worry," I whispered. "She'll be here."

"Who're you talking about?" Hassan murmured back.

"Boy, you know good and well you're sitting next to me and watching that door for Janaclese." *Ha, I flat-out busted his cover.*

He shrugged, trying to reclaim his cool.

"She never misses Youth Encounter. Besides, she's giving me a ride home tonight."

"You sure? Said she'd call me back two days ago, but she didn't."

"Quit stressing. She likes you, okay?" I glanced at him. Didn't know what Janaclese saw when she looked at *that* face. "I just can't figure why."

He grinned. "I ain't sweating it."

"Can you keep it down in the back? We're about to begin." The friendly girl flashed pink gums larger than her teeth.

No, she didn't just call us out in front of the whole class.

"Sorry," Hassan apologized, holding up his index finger.

Back in my BC days—*before* I accepted *Christ*—I'd have held up a finger too, but it wouldn't have been that one.

I concealed my rolling eyes. I was so not in the mood for this, but I promised Janaclese I'd show up if she could take me home. I needed to learn as much as I could so I wouldn't revert to the old Cyn. Seemed to be a thin line some days. And I especially needed Youth Encounter to save me from therapy. It was a supervised, structured activity like the judge wanted.

The girl batted her fake lashes. "Hi. I'm Brianna Nicole, and this is Jon. Minister Jeffries asked us to lead some of the Encounter classes this summer. We're both excited to share our coming-of-age experiences as Christians in today's culture."

"Exactly," Jon added.

Soft giggles burst out from behind me. "He's sooo cute," a girl mumbled.

Jon and Brianna looked like supermodels. If this was a promotional tactic to get young people interested in God and Heaven, it just might work.

They continued, "We'll be here to assist this age group until we return to State College in the fall. Whatever is on your mind is what we'll discuss on Tuesday nights for the rest of the summer. That includes partying, good movies, peer pressure and bullying, drugs and sex, friendships, and of course, parents who just don't understand."

Seriously, lots of teens would be lined up for miles to get into Heaven if they thought it was full of images like Jon and Brianna. The Pearly Gates would need a "No Vacancies" sign.

I doodled a cartoonish version of Brianna standing under a cloud, her extended lashes keeping her clothes dry from the pouring rain.

"No umbrella needed," I said to Hassan.

"Nah, she's wearing bat wings." Hassan made the cartoon fly above the clouds.

I felt my brow lift. Bad boy was actually pretty good at art.

"Feather dusters." I pretended to sneeze and clean furniture with my lashes.

"How about flippers?" Hassan pantomimed snorkeling.

We acted like simple-minded idiots.

"Which would you choose?" Brianna pointed at Hassan.

We both sat up straighter. I flipped over our drawing as Brianna held up a slice of chocolate cake displayed on a crystal platter in one hand. Her other hand held broiled mango in aluminum foil.

I rolled my eyes again. This time, uncovered. Was this church or some awful cooking class?

"Chocolate cake, I guess." Hassan hunched his shoulders.

"Why would you choose the cake?" Jon looked serious.

"Uh ..." Hassan raised his brows and inflected his voice like that was a dumb question. "I like chocolate cake?"

"But you haven't even tasted this cake, how do you know you'll like it?"

"I know what chocolate cake tastes like."

"Hmmm ... have you ever tried broiled mango?"

"No, and I won't tonight either," Hassan teased, making the entire group laugh.

"But why not?" Jon challenged.

"Man, I wouldn't eat nothing served like that. I'd have to be starving *and* blind."

More laughter rang out along with high-fives and fist bumps.

"There we go. Your decision was made based on what looked appealing to you, even if it's a less healthy choice. You chose the cake because it was familiar. Reminds me of our bad habits we can't seem to let go of."

That got our attention. The group settled down, but something stirred in me.

"Okay, this young man also says he'd have to be starving *and* blind to try the broiled mango, which is packed with nutrients. Sounds like a state of desperation to me, what do you think?"

I pressed my lips together, waiting ...

"Psalm 34:8 says *Taste and see that the LORD is good; blessed is the man who takes refuge in him.* Why do we ignore what is power-packed with goodness until our moment of despair?"

No one answered. My mind raced back in time.

Brianna interrupted the silence. "Reflection is good. But it's even better to talk among like-minded friends. Look around the room. Isn't it great to know they're others just like you who are here to learn more about Jesus?"

I scanned the room. Janaclese still hadn't arrived. I recognized several faces, but other than Miracle and Kehl-li, who sat on the opposite side of the room, I didn't know anyone else that I'd call "friend."

"I don't want you to move from your seats. But you'll notice you're already sorta arranged in groups of four for your discussion. No need to be shy. We're all here for the same purpose."

I looked over at Hassan, then turned to the two girls behind us who'd giggled about Jon being cute. Sheesh, why was it always a set-up?

"What are we supposed to be doing?" Grumbling came from every direction.

"Simmer down." Jon spoke above the noise level. "This isn't a root canal or a torture test. You're simply sharing your testimony about God's goodness once you decided to taste and see."

Hassan and I turned our chairs to face the girls behind us, and we all stared at each other for a moment.

When no one spoke, Hassan rubbed his head like he was about to enter a fiery furnace. "I guess it is on me to start."

I twisted my WWJD bracelet and silently prayed. *Help me to be brave and unashamed.*

Hassan shifted in his seat. "Yo, I'm Hassan ... and uh, a while back I was really angry. You know, I ... uh ... lost my moms and had to step up to help my pops raise my two little sisters."

Lost his mom? Was he talking about death?

Hassan gestured with his hands. "I was like, what's up with that God? How you gon' just up and take my moms? I know she's up in Heaven and all, but man, we needed her down here."

I swallowed hard. *Wow. That was deep.*

His eyes blurred. "I spent every second I could with Moms before she died. Just wanted to be near her, and she taught me how to cook, clean, sew buttons, comb my sisters' hair. Just name it. Lotta pressure on a brotha' being called a mama's boy ... but I took it like a man."

I sucked in a big breath, then slowly squeezed it out. Sheesh, he had gall.

"I gotta knack for fixing things too. And now, with Pops working *two* jobs, I can see why Moms took time to teach me. My little sisters really need me, and I help Pops with odds and ends."

I gulped for air, following Hassan's pause. One of the girls brushed away a tear while the other girl lightly touched his arm.

Hassan hit his knuckles against his chest. "I gotta give God credit for how He sustained my family. See, my sisters look up to me. But it ain't me doing all this. I hafta make sure they know it's bigger than me. Gotta show them God. Like Moms showed me."

My heart skipped. How many times had Janaclese warned me about judging him?

The next girl introduced herself as Tiffany. After her—if we were going clockwise—I'd have to share how God rescued me. What would they think if I mentioned the hotel, attempted rape, the gun … going to court and needing therapy for my so-called anger issues?

"Cyndray, it's your turn." Hassan nudged me.

I sat on my shaky hands, took a deep breath and opened my mouth to begin.

"I apologize, but we're out of time, folks. If you didn't get a chance to share, we can pick this up next week. I see a hand over there. You have a question, young lady?"

Relief spilled from me as I glimpsed Kehl-li tossing her hair. "Yes. How can someone prove to a non-believer God is real?"

She and Miracle glanced at each other. What were they up to now? A church girl like Miracle could answer that question. And when did they start looking so much alike? I hadn't noticed before.

"Good question. If you have a moment, I'll speak with you after we close in prayer," Jon responded.

"Oh, and don't forget about the lock-in. Information is right outside the door," Brianna Nicole added.

As soon as prayer was over, Kehl-li sprayed perfume and bounced over to Jon, Miracle right next to her. Strangely, Miracle introduced herself as MiCha.

I didn't have time to be bothered with those two clowns. Janaclese was a no-show, and I still needed a ride home. I checked my phone. One text message: *My mom will give you a ride—JM.* Maybe Mrs. Mitchell would explain what happened to Janaclese. I hoped everything was alright.

Miracle and Kehl-li brushed past me with the coldness of the Arctic winds. Not speaking tonight, huh?

"Stop, thief!" I yelled louder than intended.

Everybody froze and stared at me.

I pointed to Kehl-li. "I'm talking to the person who swindled Miracle's identity."

Some people rolled their eyes and muttered like I'd interrupted them from something major. But the cool ones snickered at my joke. Still, the class emptied leaving the three of us behind.

Kehl-li's sparkling lips tightened. "Poor Cyndray. Don't you have any friends you can annoy?"

Just then, Mrs. Mitchell popped her head in the door. "Hi, girls. How was class tonight?"

"Awesome, Mrs. Mitchell." Kehl-li's smile swallowed her eyes. "Hello, First Lady. I didn't see you standing there."

Mrs. Samson's stomach entered the room first, then the rest of her followed. She lifted her chin. "What's that smell?"

Kehl-li whipped out her perfume and sprayed again. "Must be this. You like it?"

Masking her nose and mouth, Mrs. Samson scurried from the room, sending Mrs. Mitchell on her heels racing after her. She called over her shoulder, "Cyndray, I'm supposed to take you home. Stay put. Just need a minute to check on Alicia."

Kehl-li was evil. Period.

I snatched her perfume bottle and whirled it into the trash. "Two points."

She transformed into a flesh-eating T-Rex. "You better give that back to me NOW."

"It's garbage, now. See, all gone. Perfume go bye-bye." I waved my hand and used a toddler's mommy voice.

Kehl-li stepped closer to me. "Get. My. Perfume."

"What? You might huff and puff like the big bad wolf, but if you mess with me, I'm gonna blow *you* down. I *ain't scurred*."

She pointed without blinking. "Ihae!"

Really? What was that? Korean or a command in huff-n-puff language? Was she that serious?

I walked over to the trash bin, bending to get her perfume when my notepad fell out of my pocket.

Kehl-li scrambled to get the pad and dangled it in my face. "Is this the little love letter you and Hassan were passing back and forth?"

"Okay, Kehl-li. Let me have that." I held out my hand.

"Not before I read it."

Kehl-li turned to walk away. I grabbed her arm, but she jerked and elbowed me in the nose. Blood spewed.

"Look what you made me do," she snarled without the least concern but tossed my notebook to me.

I held my head back trying to keep from dripping. Miracle politely passed me some paper towels.

Mrs. Mitchell glided back into the room. "Let's go, Cyndray. Alicia's fine now."

I didn't move.

"Cyndray?" She looked at me, lines forming on her forehead. "What happened here?"

What did she want to hear? A gang of heathens broke into the church, possessed our bodies, and she needed to perform an exorcism?

"Fight." Miracle stood all stoic and pointed at Kehl-li and me. Did that girl even have a pulse?

Mrs. Mitchell squinted. "In the church?"

No one spoke.

"Fighting? In the church?"

Why was she stuck on where the fight happened? That made no difference when you mixed decent humans like me with beasts of the jungle like Kehl-li.

Mrs. Mitchell addressed Miracle and Kehl-li. "You girls drive straight home. I'll speak to MiShelle about this later." Then she reached into her purse and pulled out a sewing kit.

I frowned. Was it that bad? Did I need stitches?

She pulled out a small plastic package, whose label I recognized from my mom's stash of feminine care products, and kept mumbling about how unbelievable it was that we'd fight in the House of the Lord.

I shifted my weight. *Lady, it was just a scuffle—no guns and knives. Give it a break, Sheesh.* Now I understood why Janaclese walked the straight and narrow. Who wanted to hear all of this preaching?

I offered the most spiritual explanation I could think of. "The Word says come lay your burdens out." And Kehl-li was definitely a burden.

"Down, honey. Come lay your burdens down," Mrs. Mitchell corrected me. "Take your problems to the altar and leave them there."

She unwrapped the wad of cotton and cut off the string.

"Shouldn't that still be interpreted literally?" I asked.

"No fighting!" Her voice was stern. "That verse encourages you to let God handle what you cannot."

I opened my mouth, then closed it. The red fluid continued to flow from my nostril.

"Be quiet and hold your head forward, Cyndray. Here, plug this up your nose to soak the blood."

My heart sank. Wasn't that a ... was she sticking a ... sheesh.

Chapter 13

JANACLESE

I arrived only minutes before Cyndray clocked off work at the Hen Pen and waited for her in the mall parking lot at our usual entrance. After overhearing Aunt Alicia and Mom share their secrets, I waited for my stomach to stop aching, and then I'd thrown my clothes in a duffle bag ready to leave this entire fantasy island I'd been trapped on with the hypocrites.

Cyndray sailed through the double doors, spotted my Prius and whisked over laughing uncontrollably.

"Watch this." She found a video on her phone and passed it to me. *ADRENALINE JUNKIE OVERDOSES* showed some guy crashing to the ground after flipping through the air on a skateboard. A girl's shaky voice screamed, "Is Judah moving?"

"Is that Kehl-li?" I asked.

Cyndray nodded, choking with laughter.

I twisted my face. "Who's Judah?"

"Don't know." She tried to catch her breath. "The crackhead boyfriend?"

Her referral to his head smashing on concrete wasn't funny to me. "Delete it, Cyndray. It's a cruel joke."

She stood outside my car for a few minutes. After drying her eyes, she looked at me with a straight face. "So what's this *huge* favor you need from me?"

I blurted without hesitation. "You gotta take me to see him."

"Him? Meaning you want me to take you to see Hassan?"

"Please. I need to know how to get to Red Hill."

"You've got a GPS. You don't need me to hunt down your man."

"But I don't have an address."

Cyndray stared at me like I had two heads. "Well, do you at least have a shoe?"

"Huh?" I gazed back at her.

"If we're going house hopping in the 'hood looking for CinderFella, it might help to have his tennis shoe or something." She jumped in the front seat, then a somber look crossed her face. "I gotta be home by 9:15. Promise or no deal."

"You have a summer curfew?" I smiled but saw her seriousness. "No problem. I love how you can never pass up an adventure."

"The doc must've fixed your stomach up real nice since you're so pressed to go to a war zone," she muttered. "What'd he say anyway?"

I shrugged. "*She* said to get plenty of rest. Thinks it's abdominal migraines. My mom suffers from migraine headaches, so Dr. Abby said I might be predisposed to the condition."

"So what's the cause? What triggers it?"

"Don't know ... maybe stress."

"Stress? Ha! Stress doesn't live on your street." Cyndray rolled her eyes and fiddled with the knob on the car's stereo system, switching from FM radio to the CD player. The music blasted, knocking over an air freshener on the dashboard.

"got me feeling things I didn't know I could ... and I'm doing things I never knew I should." The lyrics blared from the music track.

"Girl, I'm feeling this rhythm. When'd you start grooving to jazz?" Cyndray bobbed her head to the beat.

"That's Aunt Alicia's new CD. She wanted feedback."

"Mrs. Samson's singing club music now?" Cyndray yelled above the music.

"No, it's a gospel track," I screamed back, then turned the volume down.

"Gospel? I don't think so." She pushed the reverse arrow. "I'm rewinding it—no way she's singing about Jesus like that. That's somebody in some serious love."

The track replayed from the beginning, and we listened.

"Never felt love like this before. I'm drawing closer just to know you more."

Cyndray was right. The song sounded like someone crazy in love, and every time I tried to listen to it, I ended up thinking about Hassan. Would he be surprised to see me this evening? I let my mind wander with thoughts of Hassan taking center stage while everything else dimmed into the background.

"And then your mom stuck a tampon up my nose."

"What?!" I jerked my head around to look at Cyndray. I hadn't heard a word of her conversation until now.

"Yeah. Rather embarrassing, but it worked. Your mom's pretty cool, you know? I mean she's serious and what not, but nurturing."

Cyndray liked my mom? She raved about riding home from Youth Encounter with her.

"She's strong like superwoman. Totally the opposite of my mom. Janaclese, you're so lucky."

"Blessed, not lucky." Don't know why I corrected her. Habit, I guess.

"WhatEver ... you know what I mean." Cyndray rolled her eyes and continued talking.

If she'd overheard what I had on last Sunday, she'd probably have a different opinion of Mom and Aunt Alicia. I didn't want to talk about them, especially not how good they were.

"And I've decided that I just can't stand that Kehl-li. She's a vicious snob. She deliberately sprayed her stinky perfume in Mrs. Samson's face. Sheesh. Poor Mrs. Samson needed a gas mask to keep from gagging."

I stared straight ahead at the road. If my mom had a boyfriend, then why couldn't I have one? And if she was keeping him a secret, then well, I could do the same with Hassan. But then Mom would be as angry with me as I am with her right now.

"Janaclese, are you listening to me?"

"Yeah. I'm thinking about something Uncle Sam said in his sermon last Sunday."

"What?"

"If somebody irks you that much, maybe it's a God-orchestrated relationship for your spiritual growth."

"God-orchestrated? You mean God wants me to be friends with *Kehl-li*?"

"Uh … at least be friendly toward her. Maybe it's an opportunity to practice patience and learn to control your temper."

Cyndray paused and tilted her head to one side. She squirmed in the passenger seat and leaned back on the headrest quietly thinking. After several moments of reflection, she finally spoke. "That can't be possible. God would *not* want me to be friends with Lucifer."

"Cyndray, where are we?" I looked around, too unsettled to pull over and ask for directions. A strip mall on my left had a pawn shop, tattoo parlor, and an exotic video store. To my right was a giant liquor store with a drive-through window. A tiny church, positioned right next to this establishment, displayed the message, "*Soul Food Served Here.*"

"Welcome to Red Hill." Cyndray smirked. "You sure you wanna continue this little quest of yours?"

I bit my bottom lip. "Shouldn't there be a welcome sign or a name on a water tower or something?"

"Janaclese, this isn't Sunshineville, it's Red Hill. It's the resident dwelling of the Jerry Springer cast. Ever wonder where those people come from?"

"Okay. I get your point. But how am I supposed to find Hassan?"

"We'll stop and ask further down the road. Keep driving until we get out of this section of town."

I drove another mile or so down the unevenly paved road, barely visible lines dividing the lanes. The driver behind me honked his horn and swerved past me, giving me a hard stare.

I looked over at Cyndray. "Did you see that impatient driver?"

"You're lucky … *um, blessed* … he didn't shoot you. Driving all slow like Miss Daisy." She pointed to a convenience store next to a neighborhood. "Pull into that gas station over there." She grabbed her messenger bag as I stopped the car. "In this small community, everybody probably knows everybody. What's Hassan's last name?"

"Rayfield. Hassan Rayfield."

"I'll be right back. Lock the door and keep the car running."

"I'm coming with you," I said, switching the car off and unbuckling my seatbelt.

"No, you're not. You're a dead ringer for trouble, Pollyanna—too innocent looking and naïve."

Cyndray opened the car door, twisting her body to place both feet on the parking lot. Suddenly she paused. "If I'm not out in five minutes, call the police."

I gulped, covering my mouth with my hand and watching her escape into the store. My eyes, a pendulum, oscillated from the door of the store to the clock on my cell. Did she literally mean what she said?

One minute passed, and I switched the engine on for a second, rolling down the windows to avoid baking to a crisp. At five forty-five p.m., the sun's heat still simmered like midday. Stagnant, musky air hovered without much flow, but the opened window eased the stuffiness of being closed in.

The steady tick, tick of a water sprinkler and giggling children pulled my gaze to the tall wire fence separating the convenience store from a row of cookie cutter white stone houses—all identical in size and style. On the opposite side of the fence, a little boy in light blue Bob the Builder swimming trunks and a tiny girl in a bright pink Dora the Explorer bathing suit took turns running, jumping, and sliding through the water, while an even younger child wearing colors of a summer fruit basket—orange and lemon-lime—waded in an inflatable pool. At least somebody was wet on purpose. I dabbed the sweat trickling from my forehead. Three minutes had passed. *Come on, Cyndray. What's taking you so long?*

I sighed, breathing in a whiff of mouth-watering barbecue chicken floating in the air. Anything grilled would ease my hunger right about now. I glanced at the clock—close to six p.m., dinner time for most people who worked day jobs. *Close to six p.m.?* What time had Cyndray entered the store?

Eyeing the door, I pushed the power button to start the ignition just as my cell phone dinged a text from Cyndray. "HE—" is all the message said. *He what?* My heart thumped. Was this about Hassan? I studied the letters. Was she trying to write "help?"

I jumped out the car and moved toward the store just as Cyndray bolted through the door, her face tight and cramped with distress.

"Run. Get in and drive!" she screamed. "Hurry!"

Snapping around, hopping back into the car, I snatched the car in reverse and sped out of the parking lot. "What's happening? What's going on?" I demanded, my heart pounding and my vocals screaming a million decibels.

"Gotcha!" Cyndray collapsed into a fit of laughter.

My foggy mind didn't register her words. "What happened back there?"

Cyndray's shoulders shook like tremors from an earthquake. "Did you leave your car running to rescue me from inside? What were you about to do—quote Scriptures?"

"That wasn't funny." My hands trembled as I gripped the steering wheel.

"If you could see yourself, you'd find it hilarious." She slapped one hand on the dashboard and held her stomach with the other.

I tensed, each cackle plucking another nerve. "For your information," I said pulling the car over to the side of the road, "the Word of God is a weapon of defense."

"I was just kidding." Her giggling slowed. "Did I scare you that bad?"

I leaned my head against the steering wheel.

"Janaclese, are you mad? 'Cause if you're mad, it might help prevent those awful stomach aches if you just say so."

"I'm not mad, but how would you feel if your heart was suddenly ripped from your chest? I like your sense of humor, but you shouldn't joke around about stuff like that."

I could feel Cyndray staring at me.

"Will you chill out? It's not that serious," she said.

Lifting my head, I met her gaze. "It's serious because that was a stereotype. And that's wrong."

"Stereotyping?" Steam registered in her eyes. "Really, Your Righteousness?"

"That stunt you pulled was because of the neighborhood we're in. You're determined to make me think Hassan is a bad boy from the 'hood."

"Is that what you think? Look around. How much convincing do you need from me about where Hassan is from? You can see what Red Hill is like for yourself."

She had to know that being dirt poor didn't mean you were a bad person. Hadn't she learned anything during her time at Unity? I swallowed the words on my tongue. "I'm sorry. Let's not fight."

"No, let's do. I enjoy challenging those who think they know so much about my intentions."

I fought the welling tears. "It's just that I've been a little emotional for the past few days." I pictured the overnight duffle bag I'd hidden on the top shelf of my closet. I needed to get away. And I wanted to see Hassan. "Can we just forget all of this?"

Cyndray took a deep breath then reported her findings. "An older gentleman said 'there ain't but one set of Rayfields' over here." She mimicked the male voice, then became serious. "Take a left at the light. Go about three blocks, and make the first right onto Oliver's Shop Road. You'll see an off-white house on the right."

"That sounds easy." I pulled back onto the road. Relieved she wasn't mad, relieved we could continue our journey.

"He didn't know the number, but there's a blue birdbath in the front yard. Says we can't miss it."

We headed in the direction of the house. Pretty soon, we'd found the blue birdbath. And after entering a neighborhood filled with run-down houses and front yards filled with clay and rocks, this house stood in amazing contrast. The crème vinyl siding house with blue shutters plastered on freshly mowed green grass offered cheerful hope in a community with a bleak backdrop.

We strutted up the walkway where a young girl jumped rope. She took one look at us and froze, her feet seeming to dangle in mid-air from our surprise visit.

"Hi. Does Hassan live here?" I asked, smiling big and friendly so she wouldn't be afraid.

Bouncing beads click-clacked in her hair as she ran to the door and retrieved an older girl, also with long braids framing her heart-shaped face.

The older girl, who looked no more than eleven or twelve years old, scooted the younger one inside and stood behind a screened door. "Get back, Nneka." She shooed the younger girl who peeped from behind her.

"Yeah?" She looked at us.

"We're looking for Hassan Rayfield. Does he live here?" I asked.

"He might. Depends on who's asking and why."

"Oh. I'm Janaclese, and this is my friend, Cyndray."

"Janaclese?" She wrinkled her nose. "What y'all want with Hassan?"

"We're friends stopping by to say hello."

"Friends?" she huffed. "Yeah, right." She kept her eyes on us and yelled out, "Talent! Taaaleeent!"

Hassan appeared with a wrench in his hands. One look at us and his face exploded into that toothy grin I loved. "Come in."

The older girl stood blocking the door with her hands on her hips. "Boy, you know what Daddy said about having girls in the house. And you promised to take Nneka to get a slushy when you're done fixing her bike."

Hassan passed the wrench to the older girl. "Just chill, Khadijah. I got this."

Taking the wrench, she and the younger girl left the door.

"Why don't you come out here?" I said, extending my hands.

"Talent? You shoot three-pointers?" Cyndray smirked.

Was she stereotyping on purpose since I called her out? I shuffled my feet hoping Hassan wouldn't notice.

Hassan's grin widened like he caught what Cyndray was implying. "That among other things." He stepped onto the porch. "Sorry about my sister's rudeness. We're all a little overprotective of each other."

"No problem." I punched his shoulder when I should've punched Cyndray's for her sarcasm. "Somebody probably needs to keep you straight. How old are they?"

"Ow." He smiled rubbing his shoulder. "Khadijah's twelve in middle school and Nneka's five almost six, she'll be starting first grade in the fall. Y'all came to beat me up or hang for a bit?"

I looked over at Cyndray. She shrugged and looked away.

"Sure, we can hang … for a bit. Can you show us around your neighborhood?"

Hassan pulled keys from his pocket. Jingling them, he walked over to the dented Ram truck with peeling brown paint parked in the driveway. "Maybe old faithful will act good today."

"We can kick it." Cyndray twisted her hips and headed for the back seat of my Prius. "But we're *not* rolling around in *that* ghetto mobile."

Chapter 14

JANACLESE

I sat on the park bench next to Hassan, slurping on a blue raspberry Slurpee and taking in every inch of him—gentle eyes, deep-set and inquisitive; full lips that smiled even when he seemed lost in thought; soft black hair curling at the nape of his neck.

Hassan stared back at me. Up close, a smooth band of hair barely peeked through his skin's surface and lightly lined his upper lip. Had he started shaving yet?

"You look like Nneka," he said.

What'd he mean by that? I bent my neck down then looked up at him, without lifting my head. "Your cute five-year-old sister?"

"Yeah. You seem so innocent and carefree, but with attractive blue lips."

My insides melted, despite the solid mass my stomach carried. If he only knew the stuff going on in me.

"I'm glad I joined Redemption. So how come I didn't see you at the beginning of summer?"

"I was on a cultural tour of Costa Rica with my school. Then my mom set up a three-day mission for some of us with the Tico children."

Hassan leaned forward. "What was that like?"

"The tour was cool. Definitely an eye opener."

"No, I mean what was it like doing missionary work in a foreign country?"

I bounced up. "Oh, Hassan. I absolutely loved it. It's an incredible feeling to give yourself to so many needy people."

"Hmm ..." Hassan chuckled and leaned back on the bench.

"What about this one?" Cyndray called from across the lawn, holding up a white wildflower and inspecting it. She always asked about scientific names of plants for some odd reason.

"*Lonicera*," I said, taking a whiff of the fruity fragrance of honeysuckle drifting in the air.

"You know about plants?" Hassan reached for my hand as he stood up.

"Some." I pretended not to see his gesture. "My mom's hobby is gardening. I'm around her a lot." *Actually, too much lately.*

We eased over to Cyndray, where the honeysuckle crept along a hedge. "Like this." Plucking the flower from the bush, I pulled the stem away and tasted the sweet nectar. "Mmm, try it."

"I'll pass, but you're sooo cute." Hassan reached for my hand again.

"With blue lips? Boy, you're sinking fast." Cyndray smirked.

I emptied the flower from my hand, then scooted next to Cyndray, leaving her between Hassan and me.

"There's a garden maze at the back of the park. Y'all wanna try it? My sisters think it's pretty fun." Hassan nodded toward a wooden bridge that led to a castle-like entrance.

Cyndray checked her watch. "Might take too long. We've gotta get home soon." She raised her eyebrows. "*Before dark.*"

Hassan's lips curled upward. "Oh, so you heard about the after-dark gangsters around here."

I pressed my lips together and walked away. At least they could joke about that stuff together.

"Hey, Shawty. Where you headed?" Hassan called after me.

"To the car. I need to get Cyndray home."

Hassan took double steps to catch up with me. "Oh, before I forget, your signal light is flashing too fast. The bulb's about to blow. You buy a new one, and I'll replace it for you."

"Thanks." I smiled and hopped into the driver's seat as he held the door open for me. "You really enjoy fixing things, don't you?"

As Hassan walked around to his side of the car, Cyndray yanked her door open and piled into the backseat. "He needs to enjoy fixing his own raggedy truck," she muttered.

Why was she trying to mess this up for me? I glanced at her in the rearview mirror and mouthed, "Be nice."

Hassan nodded. "You're right."

Was he talking to Cyndray or me? I pressed the power button to start the engine. "So if you're good at fixing things, what're you gonna be when you grow up? An engineer or builder? And for goodness sake, don't say architect like my dad."

"None of the above. No more schooling for me. Twelfth grade is enough."

Cyndray cleared her throat. Another "told you so" poked the back of my neck.

My hands hugged the steering wheel as Hassan gazed at me. "So your mom's a gardener and your pops designs buildings. Anything well-known?"

"Not really. A few downtown buildings, and the house our family lives in. Um, sorta." I swallowed. *God, don't let my parent's separation come up.*

"Sorta?" Hassan's eyes narrowed. "He kinda, half-way designed buildings and your house?"

I glimpsed in the rearview mirror hoping Cyndray would switch the subject. Miracle and I knew the cue to do that for each other. My belly flopped. Hadn't really spent time with Miracle since the pool party. Without her, some days I felt handicapped.

"Um … my family sorta doesn't live in the same house." I clutched the wheel.

"Divorced?"

"Separated. Temporarily." I bit my lip.

"Mrs. Mitchell is not a gardener." Annoyance rang in Cyndray's voice. "She works *in a garden* at the Women's Wellness Center she owns. After practicing law and putting hoodlums off the street for years, she became an advocate for women by offering free services for those in need."

"Did my mom give you her resume last Tuesday night?" I flushed. When did she get so buddy-buddy with my mom?

"Tuesday night was awesome. Right, Cyndray?" Hassan held his gaze at her for a few seconds like they shared a bond. I tightened my lips. *What was that all about?*

As we drove along, night fell soft and easy. The sky, a velvety dark, sparkled with glittery sprinkles. I turned onto Hassan's street.

"Drive past my house. I wanna show you something."

I continued down the road.

"Turn here and park the car there." Hassan pointed to a vacant lot.

Cyndray hissed in the backseat. "I knew you were a little off, Hassan. But why're you acting like a new fool? We're going home."

"Cyndray, you know I'm not about to do anything stupid." Hassan's voice was even. "You *know* me."

She did?

Cyndray stepped out of the car, and I followed.

"You talked about your far away mission trip and your mom's Center for women in need. I just wanted you to see the need right here in our town."

"Hassan, it's dark. We can't see anything." Cyndray bobbled her neck.

"Just look. Take a moment and really see." Hassan challenged us.

I concentrated in the darkness. And then I saw—shotgun houses from the 1800s.

As a cultural tribute, my dad had architectural pictures of these narrow-framed houses on the wall of his office. Lights flickered in windows that held no curtains or blinds to shield their privacy. Children walked around in torn bottoms, with no shirts or shoes.

Cyndray walked in a circle. "So what if some people like candlelight? Maybe it's romantic to them."

"Are you too blind to see that they have no electricity? Doors are open to catch a summer breeze because it's hot and stuffy inside. Some have no money for battery-operated flashlights, so they've removed the curtains to prevent a fire hazard. You see that man over there?"

"Yes, I see someone stooping." Cyndray stopped in her tracks. "No, two people bending." A head bobbed up. "Are there more?"

"Lots of families in this section of town have no homes. It's summer, so they'll be fine until the season changes."

Without warning, a spontaneous outburst of tears exploded from me. I looked up at Hassan, unable to speak, yet his eyes held many questions. Was he judging me for being so unaware? We'd worked so hard abroad, when there was so much to do here at home, literally across town from my nice suburban world.

Hassan searched Cyndray for the answer I couldn't explain. "Did I do something wrong?"

"Uh … about Janaclese." Cyndray touched my shoulder. "She's really sensitive, Hassan. She can't handle this. You shouldn't have brought her here."

Cyndray was right. But hearing her say I couldn't handle what I'd seen made me feel weak and helpless. I ran to my car, trying to distance myself from the responsibility of knowing.

When Hassan reached me, I'd buried my face against the roof of my Prius. He placed his hands on my shaking shoulders, forcing me to look at him.

"Hey, you." He shook his head. "It's not your fault, Shawty."

"But I—" Sobs interrupted my attempt at a coherent sentence.

"Shh …" Hassan placed his index finger to my lips and moved his body closer to mine. "Their living condition has nothing to do with you. Do you understand that?"

Looking me in the eyes, he brushed away the moistness from my cheeks. His tender touch sparked a different emotion, and my spine tingled. He leaned in closer, face-to-face, cheek to cheek. A fluttering sensation filled every part of my body—lashes meshed against his, stomach laced with butterflies, my heart skipping rapid beats.

I closed my eyes and puckered my lips. Waiting …

"That's way too much PDA." Cyndray's voice stole the moment.

I opened my eyes as she shoved Hassan aside. She didn't like any public display of affection.

"I feel really bad about seeing all of this," Cyndray said. "But we've lost track of time. We've got to head home now."

Before I backed out of Cyndray's driveway, I turned on my cell phone. The chime alerted me that I had messages. Cyndray had done the right thing. She'd called her parents twice—once to let them know that she was still hanging out with me and a second time to say she was on her way home.

I hadn't bothered to call my mom.

Mom had tried to contact me a million times, leaving both voice messages and texts. The phone rang again as I was about to place it in the console—Mom's one millionth and one attempt to reach me.

I still didn't answer.

By now, either her anger had turned into worry, or her worry had dissolved into anger. I didn't want either emotion to destroy the warmth from Hassan. I pulled into my driveway and sat and stared at the lit windows of our family room. What would I face inside?

The motion sensitive porch light blinked on as I made my way up the steps. I turned the key in the front door and walked into the foyer. The vroom of the vacuum cleaner confirmed my suspicions of her emotional state. She was beyond upset—too dark to play in the dirt outside, so she'd cleaned every speck of dirt inside.

Could I sneak to my room without her noticing? One step into the hallway and the motor stopped.

Mom glared at me. "The rules of this house haven't changed." Her greeting was stern.

"I left my phone in the car."

"And?" She stood with one hand on the vacuum handle.

"And … and." I bit my lower lip. I had no words. No satisfying excuse for my behavior.

"Janaclese, what's going on with you?" She cradled her forehead in her hand and massaged her temples.

I stood still, silent. *I'm sixteen, going on seventeen. I'm almost a legal-aged woman, but you treat me like an infant.*

"Janaclese, I'm not doing this with you. I refuse."

I'd always obeyed my parents. I'd never lied to them or given them any trouble.

"If you can*NOT* abide by the rules in this house—"

I didn't wait for her to finish. I hustled to my room.

Mom followed me and stood in my doorway blocking the exit.

"Janaclese, please don't walk away from me."

Another rule my parents had broken, yet they wanted to enforce the law with me. They'd vowed 'until death do us part' but it hadn't stopped them from walking away—from me, each other, or our family.

"I'm speaking. Please look at me."

I looked up, barely able to see through my tear-streaked eyes.

"Janaclese. Please just talk to me. What's wrong?"

I grabbed the duffle bag I'd packed three days ago and slung it over my shoulder.

Mom's eyebrows crinkled. "What are you doing?"

"I'm leaving."

"Leaving? To go where?"

"Dad's." A low whisper escaped.

Without another word, she stepped aside.

Somehow I knew Mom wouldn't stop me. Maybe on some level, I wanted to make her mad. Force her to fight with me—*for* me, *for our family.* Do anything to justify these strangely mixed emotions burning inside.

But it was as if she didn't care.

Chapter 15

JANACLESE

The fuzzy room came into focus as I recognized where I was. My unexpected arrival last night at Dad's cottage called for a bit of flexibility in sleeping arrangements.

The ratty den sofa where I rested my exhausted head had seen better days. "Vintage furniture shouldn't be slept on" is what Dad said, giving me a sheet to cover the couch and a throw to cover myself.

The sofa creaked underneath my weight as I shifted away from a loose spring. Squeezing my eyes shut, I worked to block out everything from the previous night, except thoughts of Hassan. Had he been about to kiss me before Cyndray shoved him away?

"Pull the hose this way, son." Outside, Dad barked out instructions to Kharee. I squinted from the sunlight glinting through the half opened blinds. What time was it anyway?

The digital numbers glowed 7:45 a.m. on the DVR sitting on the TV console—much earlier than I wanted to start my day. I placed my finger between the slits in the blinds and peeked through.

Kharee tugged until the hose loosened, then turned on the faucet. Gushing water whirled as it beat against my Prius. How nice to see father and son washing cars together like the good ole days when we were a real family.

My phone dinged with a message. Hassan! I tumbled from the bed to check it. Sure enough, a good morning text from Hassan. *Up for a bike ride this morning?*

My fingers worked overtime to text back. *Sure. What time?*

Leaning back on the sofa, I waited for his response. Nothing. Was I too anxious? Too forward in saying yes?

My cell sat motionless on my lap, and I stared, wishing it to life. Where'd Hassan go?

Startled by the ring, my jerking leg knocked the cell from my lap and onto the floor. I hopped like a jack-rabbit to answer it.

"Hello. Hello?"

"Good morning. That's certainly a much brighter greeting than I expected."

Mom. I should've known Hassan would text, not call.

"Did you sleep well last night?"

Knowing her, she was referring to my conscience, but I wasn't going there. "Dad needs a new sofa and at least one decent pillow in the house." I massaged my neck.

"Where's your dad? I've been calling his cell for an hour."

"Outside with Kharee. They're doing chores together." Like we all used to do.

"Tell Franklin I'm on my way over with the papers we discussed. I should be there shortly."

My heart thumped. I choked the words from my throat. "What papers?"

"Just give him the message, Janaclese. I'll see you in a bit." She paused. "And sweetheart ... I love you, and we still need to talk about last night."

"Yes, ma'am." We ended the call.

Mom didn't have to tell me they were divorce papers. Moaning echoed in my hollow heart, but no tears escaped. I ambled into the shower and turned the knob.

"Yikes!" A cold blast of water slapped me fully awake. I fumbled with the knob and waited until warm water sprayed from the shower head. The water drummed against my skin, sloshing away the outer ickiness, but somehow failing to clean the yucky feelings inside. How could Mom and Dad be so selfish?

On the bathroom counter, my phone dinged. I scurried to dry off and check the message.

How soon can you get here?

I stared at the text. Should I make Hassan wait and wonder for a few minutes? Pushing down the nagging excitement, I lined my Oral B toothbrush with Colgate. I held the brush to my mouth and then placed it down on the counter.

Leaving in fifteen minutes. My fingers danced as I typed a response.

I rushed through my morning hygiene ritual, suddenly remembering I'd only packed two outfits in my duffle bag. Should I dress cute in a miniskirt or athletic in jeans? I mixed and matched the outfits, wearing myself out with indecision. Off again, on again ... cute had to work.

Charging onto the porch, I spun around and doubled back into Dad's cottage to grab my duffle bag. Felt like something was missing without it. I swung open the front door and raced back outside.

"Hey, watch out." Dad plunged onto the porch and scooped me into his arms.

I shrieked. "Dad? Whadda you doin'?"

"Saving your life."

Caught in the whirlwind of Dad spinning to the ground, I buried my head in his chest, ducking from possible flying objects, as he cushioned me while jumping onto the grassy front yard.

He set me on my feet and pushed against the white porch column. "Be careful, pumpkin. See? It's loose." He rubbed the back of his head, suddenly looking tired. "Gotta fix it before somebody gets hurt."

Mom's number one complaint—Dad designed great blueprints for building stuff for other people, but he never fixed anything around our own house.

His gaze moved from the porch to the nearby crooked window shutter. "Your mom calls this cottage a shack, but just wait till it's all fixed up."

"Okay." I shrugged, I didn't have time for this. "You finished with my car?"

"Hold on a minute." Dad placed a hand on my shoulder. "What happened to good morning? Thanks for detailing my car and saving my life?"

I curled my lips upward. "Sorry, Dad. Good morning and thanks for everything."

"Heard you and your mother had a rough time last night. You okay?"

"I'm good." I lowered my head. Unlike Mom, Dad never pried.

Tires crunched onto the gravel pavement, and I lifted my head as the phone call thundered back. Mom! I totally forgot. "Mom-saidshe'sbringingsomepapersover." The words spilled from me in one string.

Dad's brows met for a split second, then his face relaxed into a smile. He winked, grabbing the water hose. "Wanna see your mom freak out when I tease her?"

Mom stepped out of her minivan, using the door as a shield. "Franklin, I'm warning you. Put the hose down."

"Or what?" Dad clutched the hose, aimed and ready.

I certainly didn't have time for this. "Going bike riding with a friend," I yelled over my shoulder and hustled to my car. Tearing out of the driveway, gravel sprayed into the air. After zipping across town, moments later found me knocking at Hassan's front door.

"How are you, Khadijah? Is your brother home?" I smiled until my cheeks burned.

The brown-skinned girl with braided extensions glared at me through the screened door. "Janaclese?"

My heart leaped when she remembered my name. "Yes."

She sized me up. "You can't come in, but Talent'll be out in a minute."

"No problem." I sat down on the steps.

"You going bike riding?"

I turned and looked up at her. "Uh-huh."

"In a miniskirt?" Her eyebrows arched.

Had I dressed inappropriately, trying to be cute? I fingered a pleat. What was taking Hassan so long?

"Taaaleent!" Khadijah screamed for Hassan.

"I'm right here. Stop yelling." Hassan shoved his sister from the doorway and shuffled onto the porch. Dressed in royal blue padded biker's shorts and a muscle tank top, he plopped down next to me. "Where's your girl, Cyndray?"

"We're not glued at the hips." Why'd he ask about her?

"She acts like your body guard."

I narrowed my eyes. She wasn't *that* protective.

"Glad you could make it." His smile ignited a spark in me. "Wanted to get an early start before the sun shoots blazes. Where's your bike?"

"She ain't got no bike. And she ain't dressed to go biking in that miniskirt." Khadijah stood at the door with her hands on her hips.

I looked down at my sandals, pink toenails peeked up at me. "She's right. I don't know what I was thinking."

"You're straight. Khadijah's got a three-speed you can borrow, right, baby sis?"

"I don't care if she's your little girlfriend, she crashes my bike, then I'm gonna … I'm gonna …" She paused searching for tough words. "Well she betta not crash, you hear?"

"It's all good. I got it." Hassan eyed my shoes.

"Oh. I've got ballerina flats in my duffle bag. Is that okay?"

"Yep." He tossed me a helmet and a pair of fingerless gloves. "You'll need these."

Hassan zoomed past me and raced ahead on his ten-speed bike. "Catch me if you can."

Already breathless, I turned the dial on Khadijah's bike and pumped my legs until they were limp spaghetti noodles. Why hadn't I suggested an alternative date, something cozy and relaxing?

"On the left." The steady whirring of tires approached from behind. I eased toward the curb, and a line of bikers passed me.

The paved pathway, lined with mile markers, fountains, and portable potties, also had benches along the route, engraved with dedication messages. A female jogger skittered from side to side as she filled her water bottle at a fountain. Not completely stopping for one second, she fiddled with the iPod attached to her hip, checked her timer and sprinted off.

When and how would I ever get to know Hassan? We hadn't spoken much in the truck because his Dad called for an update on his weekend chores, including everything he had to do for his sisters. After this bike ride, who'd have energy left for talking?

My pedaling slowed at the five-mile marker where Hassan sat just a few feet away on an engraved metal bench, located diagonally from a lake filled with lily pads. I slid off my bike and walked toward the bench. My legs, wobbly like Jell-O, felt like they were still pedaling.

"I've been expecting you." Hassan grinned and held up his watch.

"Ha. Ha. You're funny." I wanted to poke him. "Why'd you leave me so far back there?"

"I didn't leave you. I'm sitting here waiting for you, right?" He placed his forearm across his brow, wiping away the sweat. "Besides, I took you as the kind of girl who likes a challenge. Ready for five more miles?"

"Are you kidding me?" I let down the kick stand, staggered to the bench and plunked down. "Let's enjoy the view for a few minutes."

Hassan passed me a bottle of water, and I chugged it down, forgetting to be cute. "You come here a lot?"

"Once a week. Go fishing in that lake sometimes too." He pointed to the lake, where a man, a woman, and two small kids were throwing breadcrumbs to some ducks. "Used to be an old railroad track, but the city turned it into a walking and biking trail. Nice outing for families."

Across from the lake, another younger couple sat on the grass, holding hands as they chatted. The guy leaned forward as the female talked, then rested her head on his shoulder. I smiled, warmed by their affection.

"What're you smiling at?"

I lifted my water bottle. "That couple over there. They're in love."

"Really? What makes you think that?"

"He's so attentive. They're holding hands ... talking ... laughing."

Hassan chuckled. "We're laughing, talking ..." He laced his fingers through mine, squeezing gently. "*And* we're holding hands. Are we in love?"

I blushed. The spark from earlier grew into a small flame.

Hassan curved his neck to look into my eyes. "So, Janaclese. Talk to me. I'm listening."

How could my heart beat faster than it did from the bike ride? "It's awfully hot out here."

"Not as hot as it was the day we met."

"Ah, yeah. That seems so long ago." My sweaty hand squeezed his. "So what made you come into the room to help me?"

"Told you, I was looking for an easel, but then you looked like you could use a hand." Hassan threw his head back to sip his water. "I think you're an angel."

"Stop." I snuggled against him, and the fluttering started again.

If he knew the thoughts and emotions going through me, he'd retract that last statement. I jerked my body away and twisted my hands together. "I'm certainly no angel."

"Says who?" Hassan's eyes peered without judgment.

A flood of emotions tackled my heart and my body trembled. *God, he's so wonderful. Is it wrong to want to kiss him? Either way, give me a sign.*

Chains, jingling, caught my attention. An older gentleman jerked his collie's leash when the dog lunged after a poodle. The collie barked a complaint until the poodle was out of sight.

Hassan draped his arm across the bench. "Hey, did your mom's Center donate this seat?"

I read the inscription. *In Honor of Women's Wellness.* "Probably. She's always contributing to some cause, especially if it concerns women and health."

"Cool. My moms used to do all that stuff. She started an annual clothing drive so poor women in our community could have business suits for interviews and professional jobs."

"Sounds like our mothers have something in common. I should warn you, though. My mom has spies *everywhere.*"

"She's overprotective?"

"Controlling, you might say. What about yours?"

Hassan squinted. "Cyndray didn't tell you?"

"Tell me what?"

"About my mom?"

"How would she know anything about your mother?" Heat crawled up my neck. Why'd he keep bringing up Cyndray?

"Moms died three years ago."

I blinked, not really knowing what to say. "I'm so sorry. I … I didn't know."

"Not that I'm a hot topic, but I'm surprised your girl didn't mention it to you."

"She wouldn't." I swallowed hard. "She knows it's your story to tell."

I looked away. With everything my mom and I were going through, I'd never survive without her. I just wanted things back to normal.

"I wish my parents were back together," I said.

"I wish *my* parents were back together," Hassan said.

Leaning against the bench's metal back, I squeezed my eyes shut. How could I be so selfish? Say something so stupid and insensitive?

Hassan cupped my hands in his. "What's the point in wishing our lives away?"

I opened my eyes to find him deliberately staring into my face. His lips were moving, but the depth of his gaze captured me and silence is all I heard.

He angled forward, closer. "And I know a secret."

This is it. *Is this it?* My heart pounded. Fire stirred in me. I needed a hand fan.

"This moment is special. You've got to seize it. A gift called the present."

I nodded, tilting my head upwards. *I'm ready to seize it without interruption this time.*

He popped up, pulling me toward him. "So let's go. The sun's gonna be crazy hot in another hour."

My heart sank. Huh? What happened to the special moment? I looked at my ballerina flats, new scuff marks glistened in the sun. Was he teasing me? No, he wasn't the type. But maybe I wasn't his type. Maybe he wanted a street-wise girl like Cyndray. Somebody he didn't have to explain things to. Maybe … I pushed down disappointment.

"I don't wanna be the guy who makes you sad whenever we're together."

"I'm not sad."

"Well, I'm about to guarantee that if you'll trust me." He hung his arm across my shoulder, pulling me to his side. "Once we pass the lake, there's a hill over to the left that we'll climb."

"Your idea of happy is pedaling up a hill? I'm so choosing our next date." If this was even considered a date.

"We'll walk our bikes up, then cruise down. You'll feel nothing but pure joy."

We huffed up the hill, barely able to breathe—never mind talk.

"How do you feel?"

Sweat trickled down my forehead. "Hot."

As in on fire from the sun, as in hormones dancing every time you're next to me, as in mad when you pull away. I shook my head. It was getting harder to control my thoughts.

"Shawty, I promise it'll be great. And I always keep my word."

"I don't know. It looks pretty steep." I bit my bottom lip.

"From this perspective, yeah. But once you tackle the fear, you'll fall in love."

"I'd like that."

Hassan grinned.

"The whole tackling fear thing," I stammered, "is what I meant."

He shook his head, his smile never fading.

"Ready, set, go!" Hassan shot down like a speeding bullet. I hesitated.

"Help me, Lord." A few seconds later, I was along for the ride. "Dear God … Dear God … Wheeeeee!"

Sunlight bounced between the trees. Though I propelled downward, the wind lifted me higher and higher. Something inside me burst wide-open, loosening chains, releasing freedom. I spread my legs wide, away from the pedals, soaring in the cool breeze. Peace wrapped around me, hugging me, soothing my heart and mind, drifting me to a place of no worries.

I coasted until the bike slowed to a stop.

At the bottom of the hill, Hassan stood away from his bike, arms wide-open.

I hopped off Khadijah's three-speed and raced into his embrace.

"How do you feel now?"

"Exhilarated." I jumped up and down. "We've gotta do that again."

He grinned. "But I thought you wanted to choose our next date."

My heart thumped. Was he asking me out again? "What about a quiet picnic?" A moment to sit still?

"You like quiet? You seem rather chatty to me."

I elbowed him. "Just a slower pace, that's all."

"Sure. And if you want quiet, I know a secluded place near a good fishing hole. It's my very own uninhabited island and the best part of all …" He winked. "No spies."

"Don't be so sure about that. Betima Mitchell sees all."

"You bring the food. I'll bring the good time. Deal?"

"You bet."

He pulled me into a quick hearty squeeze, then let go. "So, did you fall in love?"

I narrowed my eyes. "Riding downhill?"

"Uh … yeah." He grinned and kissed my nose, rekindling the flame.

"I'm getting there."

Chapter 16

CYNDRAY

I stood before the Honorable Judge Chan for my status hearing. Tightness stretched across my chest, thickening the phlegm in my throat, as my court-appointed attorney provided details on how I was progressing since I last appeared in court.

Judge Chan held up a document in her slender hand. "I see that Miss Johnson has paid in full her restitution charges."

"Yes, Your Honor. I have a copy of her receipt," my attorney said.

She flipped a few papers, then looked up again. "Why was the respondent spotted at the mall? Was Miss Johnson not ordered to stay away from the complaining witness?" She clasped her fingers together and placed them on her desk. "Do I need to implement electronic monitoring?"

Heat crawled from my belly and reached my face. My lawyer had better straighten this mess out. I tugged the tail of his fancy coat jacket. He stooped so I could whisper in his ear. "The Hen Pen is in the mall. How else was I supposed to pay my charges if I couldn't go to work?" My whisper became a bark. "I ain't seen no complaining witness, and I'm not wearing no jewelry on my leg!"

He gave me a "let me handle this" nod. I hope he was worth more than I was paying, which was nothing since the court made him represent me for free.

"Your Honor, Miss Johnson works at the Hen Pen, which is located in the mall. Her parents report she has used her own money to pay restitution. Also, Your Honor, I do not think she needs electronic monitoring. The respondent, Miss Johnson, has usually obeyed curfew when her probation officer has randomly checked."

They've been checking on me? My heart staggered. Sheesh. Good thing I'd only hung out late with Janaclese and her pseudo-boyfriend one time.

Judge Chan unlocked her long fingers. She scanned another document, then looked up again. "How's Miss Johnson doing in the SOS program?"

My counsel and I both swallowed. I'd refused to do anger management classes.

"Your Honor, group sessions do not appear effective for Miss Johnson."

The room grew silent, as Judge Chan scribbled on her notepad. She glanced up. "Go on, counsel. Why is it not effective and do you recommend an alternative plan of treatment?"

My heart dropped. *Treatment?* I wasn't sick.

"Ah, yes, Your Honor." My counsel dropped his notepad and bent to pick it up. He fumbled with a stack of papers, trying to reorganize them.

Why did dude seem more nervous than me?

"Your Honor, Dr. Reed reports that Miss Johnson has only attended one session. She wasn't forthcoming, and he feels one-on-one would be a safer environment for her to express why she's so angry."

Dr. Reed said what?

"Your Honor, Miss Johnson attends Youth Encounter at Redemption Temple. Her parents feel this program is working."

"I'm familiar with Youth Encounter, and it's an excellent program, but not sufficient for Cyndray's needs. I ordered anger management, not a Bible study. We have many more community-based programs, but if Miss Johnson feels a faith-based anger management program would better serve her, then I am willing to consider the option."

"Miss Johnson." When Judge Chan addressed me, I gave her eye contact. "SOS has a successful track record." She hesitated like she expected me to disagree. "But, of course, therapy does not work if you do not participate. Am I clear?"

Not really, but I nodded anyway.

"Court can be a scary place, and I'd like for you to get on with the business of being a happy, well-rounded, *law-abiding* teenager. I'm not sure why you are struggling, so the court is ordering a psychological evaluation. I want to see you back here in two weeks."

My knees buckled. Was this what A.J. felt? Maybe I should've tried harder at SOS.

Sheesh. How did I go from being angry to crazy?

Chapter 17

JANACLESE

As I stood outside the Youth Encounter class waiting for Bible study to begin, I scrolled through my cell phone checking for messages from Hassan. Nothing.

"Hey, you." Cyndray's voice sounded winded.

I popped my head up, flashed a smile, then noticed my overly anxious Mom zooming down the hall alongside Cyndray. My smile faded. "What's going on?"

Mom embraced me. "Are you okay, baby?"

"Of course, why wouldn't I be?" I narrowed my eyes. "Why're y'all acting so weird?"

"'Cause you gotta bad habit of not returning calls, that's why," Cyndray piped in, cutting through the tension that was slowly mounting.

Mom's face registered the same question.

"I'm saving my battery, so I only cut the phone on at certain times," I said.

"Isn't that the purpose of a charger?" Cyndray laughed, though nothing seemed humorous to me. She turned to my mom. "It's not just you, Mrs. Mitchell. Janaclese does that to me all the time and gives me the same excuse."

Mom pursed her lips. "Well, if you're not going to use it to communicate, then why do you need it?"

"Actually, Mom, when you gave it to me, you said to use it for emergency purposes only. I guess I haven't had any real emergencies." Sometimes she was so annoying.

"I also said that about your credit card, but you're using *that* liberally."

I lowered my head. "Just so you know, I'm giving Cyndray a ride home tonight."

"Thanks for informing me of your itinerary," she snapped, then softened. "You girls be careful."

Cyndray waited for Mom to walk away before tugging my shirt-tail. "Details. What was that about?"

I tried to glide into Room 201, and she pulled me back.

"Not another step until you tell me what's going on."

I sighed. "My mom's a little over the top."

She scrunched her face. "What's new? You just figuring that out?"

"No." I shifted my weight. "But I'm just getting tired."

"Tired as in fatigued? Or Rosa Parks tired as in you can't take no more?" Cyndray skipped on her toes and shadow boxed. "See, if you're Rosa Parks tired, then you're willing to fight harder and go to jail for your freedom." She slapped me on my back. "Get off the back of the bus, girl. These be the United States of America."

Noticing Miracle and Kehl-li approaching the classroom, I elbowed Cyndray in the side. "I'll tell you later."

"So where's your boyfriend tonight?" Every sentence out of Kehl-li's mouth seemed to contain the word "boyfriend."

I smiled. "He's running a little late, but—"

"Not you." She tossed her hair and pointed a red rhinestone pen at Cyndray. "I'm talking to Cyndray."

"If you mean Trevor, for the umpteenth time, he's *not* my boyfriend, and he doesn't attend Redemption." Cyndray's fingers twitched like she wanted to squeeze something on Kehl-li. *Probably anything.*

"Well, I figured you and Trevor broke up seeing how chummy you were last Tuesday night with—oh, there he is." Kehl-li pointed at Hassan, then strode off with her evil grin.

Hassan waved in our direction and tilted his head in an upward nod to say hello. I returned a weak smile, then walked into the classroom without saying another word to anybody. *What was Kehl-li talking about?*

Cyndray scooted into a chair next to me. My mind flitted to how she and Hassan were always joking around. *Did they secretly like each other?*

Hassan entered the class and walked over to us. "Yo, what's up?"

"Please excuse me." I sprang up and bolted toward the hallway.

"Me, too." Cyndray raced behind me, leaving Hassan standing with his mouth open. She caught the bathroom door, just as it was about to slam in her face. She watched as I rushed to the faucet and splashed water over my eyes.

After a few minutes, I gazed at her. "What's Kehl-li talking about?"

"Search me. I'm clueless," she responded, throwing her hands up.

"Be honest. Do you like Hassan?" I leaned my back against the sink and crossed my arms.

She seemed to be struggling for an answer. She dug her hands into the back pockets of her jeans and sighed, "Yeah, I sorta—"

My heart dropped. "I knew it." I moved away from the sink and turned my back to her. "That's why I couldn't understand your jokes. They're all coded when you two are together."

"Are you serious? You think I ... me and Hassan? Girl, you really don't know me do you?"

"Apparently not. I trusted you."

"And now you don't trust me because of that silly comment Kehl-li made?" She sucked her teeth. "Humph, maybe I should've never trusted you either."

I turned and looked at her, my blinking eyes warning of the bucket of water that was about to spill from them.

Cyndray twisted her WWJD bracelet and waited a few seconds before speaking. "Look. I don't know what that girl's problem is. Or why she doesn't want me to be friends with you or Miracle."

Confused, I shrugged and shook my head.

"I like Hassan, but not like that." She rolled her eyes. "Trust me, Hassan ain't all of that. If there's anybody I'd want to be my boyfriend—and I'm not saying I'm ready to date—it's Trevor."

My face relaxed. "Then why's it so hard for you to admit your crush?"

She hunched her shoulders. "Let's just say I understand what betrayal feels like. Remember when we caught Trevor behind the bushes with Kehl-li?"

I nodded. "Did you ever ask him about it?"

"Nope. I'm not sure I wanted to know the answer. But I was positive I still wanted to be his friend, so I didn't let Kehl-li take that away."

"You think that's what she's doing? Trying to destroy our friendship?"

"When was the last time you hung out with Miracle?"

I squinted. "You think Kehl-li is misleading and dishonest on purpose?"

Cyndray's face rolled into a knot. "Dishonest? Surely, you mean a lying snake. The one thing I learned from Pastor Sam is 'the devil is a liar.' Kehl-li is the devil. Therefore, Kehl-li is a liar."

I leaned against the sink again, my head swirling with questions. "Kehl-li seems mean sometimes, but I don't think we should resort to name calling."

"Sometimes I just wanna get her back. Are you sure there's no loophole in the Bible that gives me a right to slap her?"

A small smile crept on my face.

"You know like … what if I pretended I was stomping on the devil?" She raised her foot and stomped it down with a thud. "Just beat that girl down real good."

"Nope. Nothing gives you the right to treat your enemies bad. You could try using kind words. That's what I do."

"Well, you're not me, and I'm not you."

I twisted my hands. "I know that."

"Then I suggest you do you and let me do me."

Not knowing what else to say or do, I splashed more water on my face.

Cyndray stubbornly planted herself against a neighboring sink, looking as lost as I felt.

We waited in awkward silence for what seemed like an eternity. Guess neither of us wanted to go back to class and face the stares.

"Sorry." Finally, I decided to apologize. "Cyndray, you're a really good friend, and I do trust you."

"I don't know. You weren't saying that a few minutes ago."

"Give me a break, alright? Sometimes I mess up too."

By now, she seemed calmer, so she held her hand up for a high-five. Instead, I tackled her in a bear hug.

Eyeing me, she shook her head. "Is all that really necessary?"

"Definitely," I said as we headed back to class.

We were just in time to see everyone leaving. Brianna Nicole stood at the door. "Don't forget the lock-in." She jammed a flyer in our hands.

"Oh, Janaclese." Kehl-li's voice filtered through the crowd before she reached us. "I'm sorry. I mistakenly thought Cyndray and Hassan had hooked up, but Miracle set me straight."

Miracle's face looked like she'd been sucking on sour patches. Cyndray touched her shoulder. "Girlfriend, it's time you make that call."

She nodded, probably thinking Cyndray meant for her to call me, but with her face all sunken, I knew Cyndray meant the crisis hotline.

Kehl-li pressed her peachy scented lips together and stared at me. "So Hassan's your man, huh?"

I just looked at Kehl-li.

Kehl-li's critical eyes bore into me. "Have y'all been on any dates?"

A thrill rippled through me. "As a matter of fact, we have."

"Really? Where'd you go?"

"The park, bicycling ... we're supposed to go on a picnic this week."

"Hassan sounds cheap." Kehl-li stretched her long neck and looked down her nose. "Those are all free dates. My Judah is so romantic. He spends money on me." She jingled a tennis bracelet on her arm.

As I was struggling to remember Judah, the video image that Cyndray had laughed about came to mind. *Oh, the adrenaline junkie with the crackhead.*

I smiled. "Hassan and I have been having loads of fun together."

Kehl-li leaned in. "Have you kissed him?"

My insides twitched. A big gulp swallowed my words.

"If you haven't kissed, then he's not really a boyfriend. Just a friend who happens to be a boy."

"Are those real diamonds?" Cyndray pointed to Kehl-li's tennis bracelet.

"Of course," she snipped.

"Wow, they're so beautiful. Did Judah buy that tennis bracelet? He must really love you."

"Of course." She smiled, tossed her hair and walked away.

I swallowed hard again. "Cyndray ... about that loophole in the Bible. I'll start researching tonight."

Cyndray chuckled. "Little Rosa ready for battle, huh? No need. I think your 'killing with kindness' suggestion actually just worked."

We walked to the foyer. Suddenly I stopped and gasped. "It's him."

"Who?" Cyndray scrunched her face, following the direction of my eyes. "Isn't he the baldheaded dude from Miracle's party that had your mom cracking up?"

"Yeah. What's he doing here?"

"Um, I think Redemption's a church, not a members-only club."

I crumbled the flyer and threw it into the trash bin as we walked outside.

"Did you even read what the lock-in's about?"

"My mom's coordinating it. I know what it's about. No sex 'til marriage."

"Sounds like a good idea to me. You going?"

"No." I turned a challenging glare toward her.

She backed away, her hands held out. "Hey, I'm not your enemy. Us be real good friends, okay?"

I didn't laugh at her joke or correct her broken English.

Acting surprised, she looked up at the sky as if it was falling. Then, she turned in a circle and stopped abruptly.

"Whadda you doing?" I asked.

"Redemption having an after party? Your boyfriend's raggedy lemon's still here. Probably won't start."

"Just because the brown paint's peeling doesn't mean it's raggedy. And stop calling his truck a lemon."

"That's right. An unreliable rust bucket is a 'Mater.'" She laughed. "Did you see *Cars*, the movie?"

I still didn't laugh. We settled into my Prius.

"Aren't you going to check on him?"

As soon as I turned on my phone, I texted Hassan. Within seconds, he dinged back, *I'm good.* Pressing the power button, I started the car engine and rolled out of the parking lot.

"Okay, let's talk," Cyndray said. "You're worried about your mom and Mr. Clean? Things aren't always what they seem. You said so yourself."

"And you said I should remove my rose-colored glasses."

"Are we back to the night of Miracle's party? When did you start listening to me?"

"When I found out that people you trust really do lie."

"Janaclese, make it plain English. I'm not good at the cat and mouse chase, secret squirrel stuff."

"I think my parents are divorcing because Mom might be having an affair with her ex-boyfriend."

"Whoa. Your imagination is running buck wild. How far back did you have to reach to get that? Betima Mitchell is a woman of highest—"

"Will you stop putting my mom on a pedestal? I heard her. And I heard some stuff Aunt Alicia said too. Your precious Mrs. Samson may not be as pious as you think."

"So that's why you're not going to the lock-in? You're mad, and you're rebelling? Sheesh."

"Who wants to listen to hypocrites? Anyway, I moved out last Friday night."

"What? You're kidding, right? You must've bumped your head because all your good sense is oozing out."

I glanced over at her and frowned.

"So you just left?" she asked wide-eyed.

"I stayed out too late without calling. Made Mom angry. That's why she was all weird tonight."

"Okay, forgive me for acting retarded. I just don't understand. Did you quit your summer job at the Wellness Center too?"

"Of course not."

"So you still work for your mom, and you'll still have to see her every day if you wanna get paid?"

I looked over at her. "I hadn't thought about all of that."

She shrugged. "Maybe that's why she let you leave. She knew you couldn't go far."

"At least now I can date Hassan." I imagined Hassan and me together. "Saturday was awesome."

Cyndray shifted in her seat. "Did you kiss him?"

"No, but I wanted to." I stared straight ahead, focusing on the road.

Silence settled between us, but Aunt Alicia's smooth jazzy voice hummed on the love CD.

"You ever think about it?" I asked.

"Huh?" She cocked her head and rubbed her palms against her jeans. "Whadda you mean by *it?*

"You know... *it?*"

"As in sex?"

"Yeah. Do you think about it sometimes?" I flicked the washer fluid button, and the wipers cleaned bug juice from the windshield.

"Uh ... like in doing *it?*"

I gripped the steering wheel. She seemed suddenly uncomfortable, like she wanted to say something, but couldn't.

"Be careful," she finally said.

Blinding headlights barreled toward our lane. I slammed on brakes, thrusting both of us forward. My seatbelt tightened. Cyndray threw her palms out just in time to keep her head from banging into the dashboard.

"Thanks." I flashed an appreciative glance. A long, deep inhale helped to even my short breath. Cyndray had just helped me avoid a head-on collision.

"Thank God for protection," she said. "I didn't see the car either."

She didn't? Deep in thought, I swerved into her driveway.

Cyndray opened the passenger door. One foot outside, she hesitated. "About sex, sure, I think about it. But doing it? That'd definitely be a no. I don't like being touched."

"Really?" I smiled, unable to control the sarcasm in my voice. "I'd never guess that. Not from your affectionate hi-fives."

"Thanks for the ride, Janaclese." She paused like she wanted to say something more, but changed her mind. "Goodnight."

I drove away, leaving her standing in her driveway watching me. *If she hadn't seen the car, wonder what she meant by 'be careful'?*

Chapter 18

CYNDRAY

The talk I'd had with Janaclese made me wonder even more if I was a little off when it came to being intimate. I had two options concerning sex: talk to an expert or learn from experience. I just needed to feel normal.

My attention jumped from one form of media to the next in search of answers—the Internet, the Bible, and even the old time sappy romance movies. But googling 'Frequently Asked Bible Questions' came up short, and fumbling through the Bible, I found nothing.

Why couldn't I find answers when I needed them?

My idea for a crash course wasn't working, and the best expert I knew was my old mentor, so I dialed her number.

"Hello. This is Alicia Samson." The muffled greeting sounded like an underwater current.

"How are you, Mrs. Samson? It's Cyndray."

"Cyndray! How nice to hear from you. How's your summer?"

A fish blowing bubbles popped into my head. Was she swimming?

"Good," I said, not bothering to tell her about my court problems.

"So glad to hear it. You'll have to fill me in on how you're keeping busy."

I paused. I hadn't called to talk about my summer.

"You sound hesitant. Is everything okay?" Mrs. Samson asked.

And you sound like you're snorkeling. "Uh … yeah. I had a question about the Bible. And I was wondering if you could help me?"

"I can certainly try. What's up?"

"What's the big deal about sex?"

"Urk ..."

A loud gagging sound preceded abrupt silence. One click and the line went dead. I stared at the phone. Had she drowned? Sheesh. It was just an innocent question.

I clicked the remote and turned the volume up on the TV, hoping to block thoughts of my conversation with Janaclese, her desire to kiss Hassan, her questions about going all the way.

My parents' library of classic movies usually relaxed me, but not today. Today Scarlett and Rhett's flirting in *Gone with the Wind* got on my nerves. Did she want the man or not?

My cell phone rang. I turned the TV down. "Hello?"

"Cyndray, I'm so sorry. I'm dealing with a little morning sickness."

"Oh. I thought my question threw you."

"It did surprise me a little, but perhaps I'm not 100% clear on what you're asking."

Here we go again. How'd I forget Mrs. Samson only answered what was asked?

"Sex seems to be a big deal. Why?" I waited for her carefully crafted response.

"Am I right to assume your parents have spoken to you about the birds and the bees?"

Seriously? This had to be an avoidance tactic. "My question is not about creation or conception. I get how babies are born."

"Oh. Um ... well, what exactly is your question?"

Was she kidding me? Sheesh. "Why shouldn't a man and woman, in love, have sex before marriage? I can't find the reasons in the Bible."

She repeated the question, then cleared her throat. "Actually, uh ... it's like this. See, God ..." She cleared her throat again. "Do you need an answer today? Like at this moment?"

When I held my breath, excitement rose in her voice.

"Did you know sex is the theme of this year's lock-in?" she asked.

"Yeah. I knew that."

"Every question imaginable will be addressed at the lock-in."

I fingered the remote, switching the movie off. Only Danielle had known about my secret love of classic movies. Didn't want anybody thinking I was soft.

"I kinda need to know right now. Is it a big deal or not?" I asked.

"Of course it's a big deal. God cares about our body *and* spirit."

"Like protecting ourselves from catching a disease?" I frowned. "I'm talking about safe sex. Like if you protect your body, why's it wrong?" And if the answer was "'cause God says so,' I'd crawl through the phone.

"Sex is intended to be enjoyed only in the context of a marriage covenant."

I sighed. "Yeah, I know that. I'm asking *why*? Why can't unmarried people enjoy sex without being called sinners?"

"There's a whole list of consequences besides diseases. Unwanted pregnancies, unhealthy emotional ties—"

"Yeah, yeah ... but I—"

"Are you going to let me finish?"

My bed creaked as I fidgeted. "Sorry. Go on."

"Sex is an intimate act that allows a person's spirit to connect with another."

I sat still. Something about having a spiritual connection sounded serious.

"As I was saying, sex is intended for marriage because when two people join, they become one."

I shook the visual from my brain. "You mean physically one, right?"

She cleared her throat. "No, Cyndray, not entirely. Sex doesn't just involve biology and emotions, there's a spiritual aspect as well." She paused before continuing. "Your anxiety makes me wonder why we haven't had this conversation before. Your question doesn't sound like simple curiosity. Is there something you need to tell me?"

"No."

Awkward silence invaded the line.

"Cyndray, I've been meaning to ask you. Did you ever talk to anyone about what happened to you that night in the hotel? Someone like a counselor?"

Did she think I needed help too? Like maybe I was mixed up or crazy? Heat crawled up my neck. "I already told you I was fine with all that stuff that happened."

"Yes. I know what you said. But you also seem to have unanswered questions regarding sex. Sometimes when we bottle our emotions, they escape unexpectedly. Our bodies aren't equipped to carry anger."

"Who's angry?" I tensed, hoping she hadn't noticed my sharpness. "I'm good with what happened. I don't plan to let anybody put their filthy paws on me. Not now. Not ever."

"That's a bit extreme, don't you think?"

"So I'm supposed to be okay with being touched?"

"You know that's not what I meant. Waiting is the right decision. But one day you'll probably desire a husband, so you'll want any anger or sexual issues resolved."

Why was she making this about me? "Like I said, I'm good. I'm not asking for myself."

She sighed. "In response to your question, I don't understand everything God asks me to do. But I believe He knows what's best for me. He can see down the road what I cannot see. You may think purity is unimportant, or too difficult, or doesn't make sense. But obeying God's Word to not have sex outside of marriage, despite our feelings, shows our trust in Him and our faithfulness to Him."

I leaned back on the headboard. Was she saying she didn't know why either?

"Do you understand what I'm saying?" she asked.

"I guess so." Disappointment settled in my stomach. I wanted to give Janaclese a Biblical perspective, a Scripture, something that warned her not to give in to Hassan. Any advice other than God says 'my way or the highway.'

"Are you sure you're okay?"

I pushed her question to the background. "Isn't that just like saying, 'do it because I said so'?"

"God's not a bully. You have freedom to choose. However, I do believe obedience leads to God's favor and His blessings, while disobedience brings disappointment."

I didn't expect a lecture. Just a simple answer to a simple question. But since the door opened, Mrs. Samson ran straight through it.

"Do you trust anybody?"

"Yeah. I trust people."

"Don't answer flippantly." She paused. "Is there one person you can rely on without a doubt? Somebody you know has your best interest at heart?"

"Uh ..." I thought for a second. Used to be Danielle, until she got me trapped in a hotel room with that gun-toting octopus Tommy Dawg. "My mom? You?"

Sudden movement echoed in the background of our call. "We've got to hang up. Right now, Cyndray. Hang up the phone." Urgency rang in her voice.

"Sure." I clicked off. What was that all about?

Deep thoughts settled in my head. Why was this sex thing so complicated? Kissing seemed innocent enough to me, but how far was too far?

The ringtone jolted my heartbeat to gallop. I grabbed my phone. "Hello?" My eyebrows furrowed.

"See how easy it is to obey without questioning when you believe someone truly cares about you? God's care and protection are even greater."

My face relaxed. "O-kay." Her plea for me to hang up was a test of blind obedience? Sheesh. "You got me."

She laughed. "It's natural to be attracted to the opposite sex. As you mature, you'll also likely experience certain feelings toward boys that further arouses your curiosity."

"Yep." Seemed like everybody, except me, was further aroused.

"And don't believe Satan's lies. Everybody your age is *not* doing it. Some kids are lying just to fit in with what they think is popular."

How'd she know what I was thinking? I pressed my ear against the phone.

"The Bible teaches fornication is wrong. You want my advice? Don't awaken sexual desires until the time is right. That time is right *only* in marriage."

"I hear you."

"You ready to write down a few Scriptures?"

"Hold on a minute." Looking up at my ceiling, I mouthed, *Thank you, Lord*. I grabbed a pad and pen from my dresser. "Ready."

"1 Corinthians 6:18 and 1 Thessalonians 4:3 are good places to start."

"Thanks." Maybe this could convince Janaclese to hold up a minute. Not move so fast and keep her virginity.

"May I ask you a question?"

"Sure, Mrs. Samson, shoot."

"You said this was one of those 'asking for a friend' type questions. Do I know this friend of yours?"

I chuckled, glad I was no longer her focus. "Much better and way longer than me."

My big mouth clamped shut a few seconds too late. I kicked myself.

Awkward silence now ruled the line.

"So ... is it Janaclese or Miracle?"

Chapter 19

CYNDRAY

I sat in the salon playing 'Hanging with Friends' with Trevor and his crew while three African stylists hovered over Janaclese's head. As the braiders added extensions to her hair, their interactive foreign dialect rose to a dramatic crescendo. It was hard enough to spell words but almost impossible to concentrate with so much energy bouncing around.

Apparently, Janaclese didn't know about my sex talk with Mrs. Samson. If she had known, she would've confronted me. Asked why I ratted her out, then probably would've ignored me the rest of the summer like she did Miracle.

Tapping my fingers against the keys on my phone, I added letters to the challenge word. A ding from somebody's hair dryer forced me to look up as some lady lifted the hood and peeped out. I glanced at Janaclese. "We're still going to the mall, right?"

Today was payday, and my first full check since paying restitution was about to slash a hole in my messenger bag, begging to be cashed and spent. The only good thing about my summer job was the money. I'd also upgraded my cell phone. And having every app imaginable came in handy on a day like today, where I'd sat hours waiting for Janaclese's stylists to finish her hair. Good thing the salon had free wifi.

When Janaclese didn't respond, I looked up again. She held her palm to her forehead, her face scrunched as the braiders pulled and twisted weave onto her already long hair. Don't know why she was torturing herself. Don't know why I agreed to hang out with her either, especially over here in Red Hill—Hassan's dumpy neighborhood. Like she couldn't find decent braiders where we lived.

Pictures of famous actresses and models, with the latest trends in hair and fashion, were slapped onto the light gray walls. Or were the walls actually a dingy white? Who could tell from the smoke haze of clients' natural hair being heated and straightened?

Some three- or four-year-old kid named Western raced back and forth yelling loud enough to drown out the droning sound of blow-dryers whirring in the background.

"Janaclese." I stretched my legs out. "You think you'll be done in time to catch the mall?"

"Maybe." She shrugged.

Trevor's face popped onto my phone, a request for FaceTime. Virtual dating—another perk of my handy upgraded phone. This gadget gave me a chance to be with Trevor, without *being* with him. That way, I avoided temptation at the same time. Not that I'd be tempted to kiss him, but he'd probably think I was weird if I wasn't in the least bit interested.

I glanced around the salon. Everybody looked preoccupied, but as soon as I opened my mouth, they'd be all up in my business. I pushed decline, though I wanted to chat face-to-face with my man, even if it was online.

"Beep. Beep." Western sped past me, sucking on sunflower seeds and spitting them onto the floor. One landed next to my foot.

"Grrr," I growled and clawed at him.

Janaclese shot me a disapproving glance. "Cyndray, what're you doing?"

"Did you see that kid?"

"Yes, I saw him. What're you doing?"

"That child's acting like he's been raised by a pack of wolves, spitting in my direction. I'm about to show him who's boss up in this camp."

"Calm down and be patient. My hair's almost done."

I stood up. "I need to stretch. I'm going for a walk."

Greasy smells like French fries and onion rings teased my stomach as soon as my feet pounded onto the concrete outside. Didn't even realize my hunger till my taste buds salivated. Music—likely a contest for the loudest stereo—blared from one passing car to the next.

Looking up and down the sidewalk, I headed in the direction of the gigantic sign flashing Korner Liquor Store. Easy choice for a casual walk since the opposite direction looked like the city dump.

I giggled. Were the owners of Korner Liquor drunk when they ordered the sign spelled with a K instead of a C? The store advertised an ATM, check cashing, and settlement loans on its window. Sounded like a bank hidden inside, which reminded me I needed to cash my check before going to the mall with Janaclese.

Jarred by a honking horn, my knees buckled then launched me into a trot. The car rattled past, stealing my composure. I stopped to catch my breath when my eyes locked on the red mustang across the street in front of a pawn shop.

That couldn't be Kehl-li's car, could it? Probably not. That snob wouldn't be caught dead in Red Hill. Not with its reputation for shoot 'em up gangs. The reason Janaclese was secretly getting her hair braided at Hassan's little sister's salon was probably because she was hoping to catch a glimpse of Hassan and impress him. Acting all desperate. No telling what her parents would do if they found out she visited a war zone.

A leggy, dark-haired girl, head downward, walked to the car. I couldn't see her face. Seconds later, another dark-haired girl exited the pawn shop, swinging her hips like angry waves in an ocean. She tossed her hair back and slid on sunglasses. Seeing mannerisms so much like Kehl-li's, I wanted to dash across the street and tackle her like a linebacker.

Before I could cross the street, the red mustang sped away, and I headed back to the salon, wondering why these "rich" girls were so obsessed with poverty-stricken Red Hill.

When I pushed open the salon doors, a bell chimed alerting my entrance. Janaclese and a different stylist, sporting a Mohawk, were waiting by the door.

"Love it!" I pointed to the stylist's hair. Yet, I wondered how Native Americans felt about outsiders adopting as a fashion trend what was probably a sacred ritual to them.

"Humph," the stylist grunted. "I'm sure you like your friend's hair too."

I smiled at Janaclese. She had to know me well enough to expect a joke about her fake hair. "Her hair looks unbe-weave-ably beautiful!"

Janaclese's eyes welled up, Mt. St. Helens threatening to erupt.

"What's wrong? I was kidding … just playing, girlie."

The stylist smacked her lips. "Well, I ain't playing. She betta get me my money."

Burn! The stress lines on my friend's face, her trembling lips, announced trouble in paradise.

I stared at Heap Big Talk. "What's going on?"

The Mohawk bounced up and down like a hammer when she bobbled her head to speak. "This girl owes me one hundred and seventy-five dollars for her micro-braids. Plus a tip. Claims she didn't see the sign in the window. We don't take no credit cards."

What kind of decent business establishment didn't accept American Express? Janaclese had a gold card at that. Why was Heap Big Talk treating her like a common criminal? Wasn't like she snatched some weave and made for the door.

"Cyndray, what're we gonna do?" Janaclese asked.

"We? We didn't get our hair braided."

Janaclese's eyes widened like two full moons, then lowered. "What am I gonna do?"

"Try bartering like we studied in our Econ class." I stretched my eyes to match hers. "Can you braid hair? Sweep a nasty floor sprinkled with sunflower seeds?" I swirled around and nodded toward Western. "What about babysit hoodlum junior?" Nah, I'd much rather beg God to drop the money from the sky.

Janaclese shook her head, ignoring my suggestions. "I can't call my parents because they don't know I'm over here. I don't know what I'm gonna do."

I stood next to her, thinking, fingering my WWJD bracelet. And then it hit me.

"Ugh!" I stomped my foot. "I'll be right back."

I turned toward the door, and Janaclese followed close on my heels. "Cyndray, where're you going?"

Heap Big Talk tapped Janaclese's shoulder. "Question is ... where're you going?"

Janaclese twirled around to face her. "Uh ... nowhere. I promise I'm not leaving until I pay for my services."

"You got that right." The spiky blades of the Mohawk shook.

My fingernails dug into my skin from clenching my fists so tight. "Sheesh. Why don't you give my friend a break? Nobody's trying to steal from you. If we can't work this out and get your money, then I'll personally unbraid her hair and give you the strands back."

The stylist rolled her eyes at me, then walked away so Janaclese and I could talk in private.

"Cyndray, please don't aggravate the situation by annoying her."

"What's she gonna do? Act like Edward Scissorhands and snip your hair? She doesn't want your hair. She wants her money."

"You think she'll call the police?"

"Over some weave? Get real. This is not a big deal. Trust me."

As I turned to leave, Janaclese tugged my arm. "Where're you going?"

"To cash my check."

"Your bank's over here?"

"No, Korner Liquor Store. They'll cash my check."

"You can't go into a liquor store. My mom says as Christians we have to be careful about evil appearances."

I rolled my eyes. Was she seriously lecturing me about evil appearances? Had it occurred to her it *appeared* she was trying to steal her micro-braids? I couldn't remember all the rules, but clearly stealing was ranked high on the 'do not' list.

"Listen, I respect your mother, but let me handle this my way," I said.

"But what if—?"

"I think Jesus will be okay with it."

She squinted her eyes.

"Jesus was cool. He did all kinds of stuff with wine. He wasn't against alcohol." I waved my hands in the air. "Sheesh, will it make you feel better if I attach a sign to my back saying 'non-alcoholic Christian?' That way nobody'll get the wrong idea."

She sighed. "Promise me you'll be careful. And you'll call me if anything happens."

"Uh … Yeah … Okay." I pushed open the door, wondering what she'd do if something really were to happen.

Squeezing my messenger bag into my side like it was sealed to my hip with hot glue, I hustled down the sidewalk, jerking my head around. Why'd Janaclese have to pick a salon in Red Hill of all places? Next time, I'd get the details before agreeing to tag along.

The liquor store buzzed when I entered. Check and state ID in hand, I walked over to the check cashing counter.

"May I help you?" A gray-bearded munchkin peeped over the counter.

I wrote my signature on the back of my check, then passed him everything he needed for my transaction. He opened the register and then counted out my cash.

What in the world? Could the little man count? "Excuse me, Sir." I showed him my stub. "You gave me less than the amount on the check."

He pointed to a small sign above his head. "Ten percent service fee."

"Really?" I frowned. "You charge to convert one form of money into another form of money?"

My hard-earned paycheck disappeared right before my eyes. After paying the stylist, I'd only have $1.30 left. Made me wanna change my mind.

I looked around the store at the customers milling around. *Lord, can't you blow everybody's mind by making money fall from the sky like manna?* What was I going to do with $1.30?

"Would you like to donate a dollar to the Children's Miracle Network?" The midget pointed to the colorful paper balloons on the wall with names on them.

Oh, so now he wanted to act like Robin Hood. Stealing ten percent of my money, then giving to the poor like it was an honest deed of service. But what was the point of clinging to one measly dollar? I wrote my name on the balloon and stuck it on the wall of fame. Just thirty cents left out of my big paycheck. *Lord, I'm just saying ... You could've converted a whole slew of people in one swoop with the money from the sky thing.*

Shaking my head, I stashed the rest of my money in my bag, then raced back to the salon to complete my rescue mission.

One look at me and relief flashed across Janaclese's face.

I passed her the cash. "There's not enough for a tip."

Her deep dimples exploded. "Thank you. I have the rest. I wanted to treat you to lunch for hanging out with me." She blinked innocent eyes. "Do you mind if I use that money as a tip?"

When God created Janaclese, He broke the mold. She had to be the final sweet and considerate person sent from Heaven to earth. If that stylist had lit into me the way she'd burned her, the last thing on my mind would be a tip. I'd pay her all right—*pay* her no attention and *tip* right out the door.

"I guess so." I shrugged my shoulders, ignoring my stomach's angry growl disagreeing with my words.

When the matter was settled, we clamored into her Prius, leaving the stale air and humidity rising from the busy city street. The smell of coconut, emanating from the air freshener dangling from her rearview mirror, welcomed us. Her car soon felt like an air-conditioned haven.

"Thanks for bailing me out, Cyndray. I promise to pay you back." She switched from the radio to the CD player.

"That was easy. I've been in worse situations," I said.

"I can't imagine anything worse than being accused of false intentions."

"How about being guilty of false intentions? Which you weren't, so don't start tripping." I sat still, silent and waiting.

"Sometimes the right decision doesn't seem as obvious to me."

"Really?" I turned to look at her. "I wouldn't have thought that about you. I've always felt like such a mess-up because you seem so together. It's like you never struggled with making poor choices."

"I struggle, but what you did back there was a good thing—the right thing."

Warmth padded my insides. I never wanted to be a Christian because I couldn't remember all the rules. But someone once told me I didn't have to memorize the dos and don'ts in my mind. When I gave my life to God, He wrote the rules for right and wrong on my heart. Seems they were right.

Chapter 20

JANACLESE

I sloshed my hands in the warm soapy water, then swirled the dishcloth around the floral dinner plate. Mrs. Patterson's fat cat, LeMew, purred at my feet. I moved aside. He couldn't possibly be hungry again.

"How long you planning on washing that plate?" Mrs. Patterson's amused voice said from behind.

The slippery dish landed in the water, splashing lemony-fragrant suds on my face.

I dabbed my face with a towel, then fished around the sink for the dish. "I didn't notice you'd come back into the kitchen."

"You're lost in your own little world." Her slightly plump, caramel face looked soft and concerned. "Something heavy on your mind?"

"No. Just thinking about stuff in general."

With hands aged by wrinkles, Mrs. Patterson slid a chair from the kitchen table, its legs screeching against the hardwood floor. When she sat, LeMew pounced into her wide lap and curled into a ball.

She motioned for me to sit. "Leave the dishes. Come chat for a bit."

"No, ma'am. I'm almost done." I placed the dish on the drying rack. "Don't want my mom thinking I'm shirking my responsibilities and burdening you with my problems."

"What kind of problems can a pretty girl like you possibly have?" She winked her eye. "I dig your new hairdo. You ain't pining over some boy, are you?"

I twisted my wet fingers around a braid. "No, ma'am. Not sure my parents would even allow me to have a boyfriend."

"Is that, right? Hmm ..." LeMew purred as she stroked the fur behind his ear. "I was about your age when I ran off and married my first husband."

My leg twitched. Had she been like the woman Jesus met at the well who had five husbands? *Please spare me the backstory.* I didn't want to know about anybody else's wild BC days. Aunt Alicia's and Mom's were difficult enough to handle.

"I don't borrow trouble," she said.

I cocked my head. What in the world was she talking about? I scrubbed a fork until my reflection shined.

"The old gray mare may not be what it used to be, but trust me, honey, it used to be."

I narrowed my eyes. "I'm sorry. I don't understand."

"I'm old, but I could always tell when something was eating at somebody. And I'm perfectly capable of loading a dishwasher."

I smiled, hoping she'd change the subject. "I know you're not helpless. I don't mind washing your dishes. It might sound crazy, but it relaxes me."

"Nothing boggles Mrs. Patterson, except maybe why a smart girl like you wouldn't seize the opportunity to rest her mind." She hesitated. "Better or bitter?"

Not certain why she acted like she was offering me a cup of tea—sweetened or unsweetened—I turned and gave her a questioning look.

Mrs. Patterson stroked LeMew's head. "You can talk about what's eating you and feel better, or you can harbor ill feelings and grow bitter. The choice is yours."

Drying my hands with a towel, I turned around and leaned against the sink. "I can't figure out what's wrong. I've got this gnawing feeling in the pit of my stomach like something bad is about to happen."

"Hmm ..." She nodded for me to continue.

"And I've been praying. But the one thing I really needed God to fix, He didn't. He couldn't give me this one thing? I don't understand why He allowed me to hope, then shattered my hope into a thousand broken pieces. I guess He had to make His point clear so I'd give up. You know what I mean?"

"Not yet. But keep going."

I walked over to one of her hanging plants. "You see this flower pot?"

She nodded.

"If I knocked it against the wall, a piece or two might break off, but we could probably fix it. Glue it back together or something. But if I forcefully slammed it, I could do real damage. It could break into so many pieces you wouldn't be able to find them all in order to fix it." I stared at her. "Now do you understand?"

"How about lamps?"

"Ma'am?"

"I used to have an old lamp. My grandmother's it was. Well, I don't suppose lamps can be included in your example, can they?"

My shoulders slumped. "It was just an analogy. I guess it covers anything that's broken and irreplaceable."

"Oh good, then you're wrong." Her eyes danced. "I'm not excited that you're wrong. Just glad to demonstrate there are exceptions to shattered things being unfixable. See that green porcelain lamp on the end table in my living room? Go get it for me."

I returned with a multi-colored lamp. It was the only lamp in the place she'd indicated. "Why'd you say green?"

"'Cause this here is the color it used to be all over." She pointed to a teal color. "The first time I broke it was when my first husband and I moved to St. Louis chasing his dream of being a trumpet player. Didn't pack it good, I reckon. But we found a man to patch it up."

I studied the lamp, looking for signs of previous damage.

"Then I had four rough boys wrestling in my house. Told those boys a thousand times some playing was for outdoors only. Somebody jerked the cord, lamp came tumbling down. I tell you, there was more blame going on in that room than in the Garden of Eden."

I laughed, running my fingers over the smooth porcelain, still looking for signs of brokenness.

"Grounded all of 'em for a month. Tucked this poor lamp in the closet. When it got missing, I figured my husband finally got tired of looking at it and threw it away."

"What happened? How'd you get it back?"

"My boys. Supposed the hubby helped them a little. For Mother's Day, this broken lamp came back looking brand new. Had all these different colors on it." She outlined the lamp with her index finger. "They couldn't match this original green. Such an odd color, you know? Then the boys got to arguing over what my favorite color was rather than just ask me. As you can see, they each decided a different color. If I didn't know the history, I couldn't tell it'd ever been broken. The new parts make it better—more colorful and interesting if you ask me. That's what restoration is about. Reminds me of relationships."

She eyed me, and I turned away.

"How's your gut?"

"Huh?"

"That ole feeling you had in your stomach … better or worse?"

"Was better until about two seconds ago."

"You fretting what's going on with your parents, aren't you?"

"Not really. A little, I guess." I took a long deep inhale, then exhaled. "Maybe, a lot."

"Your parents will be fine."

"Everybody keeps saying that, but—"

"What? Don't you believe it?"

A twinge of guilt forced my eyes to lower. "I used to. Now I can't see how it's remotely possible."

"And you're still praying?"

"Yes, that's all I know how to do."

"If you're praying and not believing, what's the point?" A knot formed between her eyes. "That feeling in your pit? Evil foreboding it's called—having heaviness about what hasn't happened." Her stomach bounced up and down when she chuckled. LeMew stretched his limbs.

"Sounds like insanity, doesn't it? Child, you can't predict the future. And if you could, why paint it so dark?"

The wall clock chimed, and I turned to check the time.

"Do you need anything else today?" I asked, comparing the time to my cell.

"Other than seeing a smile from my favorite helper?"

"I can do better than that." I wrapped my arms around her shoulders and planted a kiss on her cheek. "Thanks, Mrs. Patterson."

She patted my hand. "No problem. You gonna see your momma today?"

I withdrew my embrace. Did she know I'd moved out?

"If LeMew'll let me get up from here, I've got a thank you card in that drawer for her." She pointed to a drawer next to the sink.

"Oh. I'll get it for you." I opened the drawer, relieved she hadn't asked about my moving out. Maybe Me-maw hadn't mentioned it. "I'm actually headed to the Center now. Gotta get my paycheck. Shoulda picked it up last Friday."

"God laughs at our plans sometimes. I'd planned a trip to the post office to mail that card for your momma, but I think my cat needed a little cuddle therapy today. And it's a good thing you showed up to hand-deliver the card."

LeMew, eyes still closed, rested peacefully in Mrs. Patterson's lap. I rubbed his fur. "Cuddle therapy. Looks like he's got the right idea."

With the envelope addressed to Mom in my hand, I turned to leave.

"Janaclese?"

I swiveled around. "Yes, ma'am?"

"Don't borrow trouble. I believe your parents are like lamps. They carry the Light."

Mrs. Patterson's words echoed through my head as I drove to the Center. However, the gnawing in my stomach grew stronger as I got closer. Last Friday I'd avoided Mom, but today our meeting seemed inevitable.

I had enough of my own trouble to deal with, without ever borrowing more. And yes, I wanted to feel better, not bitter. But if trouble was brewing like how I felt, how was that even possible?

Chapter 21

JANACLESE

I walked into the tangerine-colored lobby of the Women's Wellness Center, immediately recognizing the familiar smell of Egyptian musk candles burning. Shirley, Mom's receptionist, held the phone to her ear, scheduling an appointment. She glanced at me and smiled, then pointed to my employee mailbox behind her desk.

Walking past the counter, I scooted around her and grabbed my mail.

"Needed money, eh?" Shirley's grin swallowed her eyes as she placed the receiver on the hook. She peeked through the tiny slits. "Love da hair. Exotic. You be a Jamaican girl like me now."

I smiled and opened the envelope containing my paycheck, inspecting the stub. "Did Mom ever tell you we have relatives in the Caribbean?"

"Your father's people, eh? Ya. She tell me. She tell me lots. Not all so good lately."

I looked up at her fading smile, her eyes now visible and penetrating.

"This note's for you. Miz Betima said give it to you if you come in today."

I took the note written on Mom's personal stationery: *From the desk of Betima Mitchell.* Two words were scribbled on the paper: *See me*, followed by Mom's signature.

"Where is she?" I asked.

"Out back. Playing in dirt." Her face begged to say more, but she hesitated.

Closing my eyes, I drew in a long breath, then retraced my steps to the front entrance. I pushed open the outside door, pausing only when Shirley spoke again.

"Miz Betima ... she trying to be a good mother. Why don't you let her?"

My insides tightened. Everyone seemed to be taking Mom's side like she was innocent. Not even Mom knew the truth about why I'd moved out.

"Mom will be happy to know you've joined her fan club," I said.

"I hope she already knows how much I admire her. But I'm rooting for both of you. You be so much alike."

I snapped my head around and walked out the door, muttering under my breath, "She's a light-carrying lamp, Shirley. I'm more of a dull flower pot."

The soft ground was silent as I walked to where Mom stooped in her garden, her head bent over a small plot. She moved with incredible rhythm, scooping out seeds from a container and placing them into holes she'd already dug. I stood for several minutes, slowing my breath so I wouldn't disturb her, but also trying to slow the bomb threatening to explode inside of me.

"Wanna help?" Mom reached into her bib and tossed me an extra pair of gloves.

"Nah ... I'm good." Had she sensed I was there the entire time? "Shirley tell you I was walking out back to see you?"

"Nope." Mom used the trowel to dig new holes then slid the hand rake to flatten the pile of dirt.

"Then how'd you know I was standing here?"

"Your shadow, the pace of your breath, your smell ..."

"Gosh, you sure you're not an undercover detective?"

"If you're ever trying to sneak up on me, don't do it when your body casts a shadow in my garden, and please don't wear those scuffed-up ballerina flats you can't seem to outgrow."

Crossing my arms to hold in annoyance, I wiggled my toes in my favorite shoes and looked at the top of Mom's head as she leaned over. A patch of gray hair crowded the part in the center of her head. I'd never noticed any evidence of her aging until now.

Another long deep inhale. I had to stop the bitter. Get better.

"Why'd you want to see me?"

She patted the dirt, not bothering to look up. "Nice braids. Felt like making another change?"

"Just thought I'd give my hair a break," I said.

"So many recent changes." Mom inched over to another section in her garden. "I want to know what's going on with you."

"Why does anything have to be going on with me because I moved in with Dad?"

"I don't care if you live with your father. That's not what this conversation is about."

My heart skipped. I figured she didn't care about my leaving. But hearing her admit it was another story. Sweat trickled down my spine, but I needed answers.

"Why'd you leave Dad?"

"Your dad was the one who moved out. Technically, I'd say he left me."

"Why'd you *let* Dad leave?"

"Janaclese, your dad's a grown man."

The pace of her digging accelerated, her focus unmoved.

"Then why'd you let me leave?"

She tensed, then wiped her forehead with her arm before picking up the rake. "If I'd tried to stop you, would you have stayed?"

"I don't know. Maybe, maybe not. But at least I'd know you cared."

Mom stopped raking and looked at me. "Is that what you think? That I don't care about you?"

"Sometimes, I don't know what to think. Sometimes it seems like you spend so much time helping everybody else in the world, you ignore those closest to you."

Mom blinked, opened her mouth to speak, then hesitated. "Has it ever occurred to you that I'm doing the best I can?"

I kicked at the dirt in the garden but remained silent. A cloud of dust formed around my ankles.

She lifted one knee from the ground. "You mind taking a walk with me?"

I hunched my shoulders and followed her into her greenhouse. Mom slid off her gloves, placing them next to the sink. As she washed her hands, her cell phone dinged, downloading a message.

She looked down and smiled. After reading the message, she belted out a gut-wrenching laugh.

"What's so funny?"

"What flower grows right under your nose?"

I shrugged.

"Tulips. Two lips, get it?" She threw her head back and howled.

"Rather corny if you ask me."

That joke was so not funny. Not even LOL and certainly not ROFL. Bet it was from baldheaded dude. I blinked back tears. *God, I promised not to cry. Help me hold it together.*

Smiling and shaking her head, she hung her apron on a nail, then turned to look at me. Straight lines replaced the parenthesis around her smile. "Are you crying?"

"What's that pine scent in the air?" I asked.

"Rosemary." She pointed to a potted plant on the table next to me, wrinkles punctuated her forehead. "You've never had allergies to rosemary." Her eyes narrowed, searching me. "Better ventilation outside, let's walk."

If she didn't think I had allergies, maybe she'd assume sweat caused my facial moisture. We walked down an old familiar path I hadn't visited once the entire summer. But this had been an unusual summer.

Maybe I'd changed, but so had she. I fought thoughts of her enjoying Mr. Clean's company, him making her giddy, all teenagery over some silly joke.

I spotted a patch of sunflowers with their long necks and big round faces raised toward the sun. Butterflies danced around their golden yellow petals and chocolate brown centers. "When did you plant those?"

"Pretty nice, huh? The kids created a sunflower fort during camp. I can hardly believe how fast and tall they're growing."

"Is that what you wanted me to see?"

"No." She nodded into a field of dandelions. "That big oak over there is where I sit and think sometimes."

When we reached the tree, Mom lowered herself against the tree trunk. I stood, propping my arm on a branch and staring at the sunflowers.

Finally, Mom broke the silence between us. "I didn't want you to move out, but I saw it coming."

"Then why didn't you stop me?"

"You see that tree underneath this big oak?"

I spotted a skinny tree with much smaller branches that looked like a Charlie Brown Christmas tree.

"The roots of this tree are so deep, it takes most of the soil's nutrients. And look at the wide branches. Can you see how they soak in the sun's rays, yet block them from the smaller tree?"

I gazed at the two trees. What did this have to do with us?

"Though I love the big oak tree, it's hard for another tree to survive next to it." She rubbed the oak tree. "Sometimes it's like that with people in relationships. I understand you needed to breathe your own air. I never meant to smother you."

She thought I left because I wanted my own space? Any clue I didn't want to see her with another man?

"What about Dad?"

Mom turned to face me. "What about him?"

I bit my bottom lip. "You still love him?"

"Of course. He's your father."

"Not like that. Do you still want to be married to Dad?"

"I *am* still married to him."

I ignored her irritation. "But do you want to be?"

"Sometimes, yes." She hesitated. "Look, Janaclese, I don't know what you're expecting me to say." Her eyes set in a daze. She tucked a lock of hair behind her ear, leaving her hand next to her face, her cheek resting against it. A pale ring circled her finger where her wedding ring had been.

"Where's your wedding ring?" I followed Mom's gaze to the field of dandelions. What was so captivating about weeds? "Did you stop wearing your ring because of Mr. Clean?"

"Yes." She nodded slowly, her stare unbroken.

My heart hammered from her casual response, anger swelling in my throat.

Mom stood up to leave. "I've gotta transport the rosemary into the ground, water those sunflowers—"

"I hate that you're hiding things from me."

"Hiding things? Now that's a great topic."

I swallowed, uncertain of her strong reaction.

Mom squinted. "When are you planning to divulge your secret dates? What's your fellow's name?"

"I don't have a fellow. Nobody sends me ROFL text messages."

"Rah … What?"

Mom's face crumpled in a knot, mirroring my stomach. If she was gonna text, she needed to catch up on the lingo.

"You roll on the floor laughing every time you talk to him. Just like a few minutes ago. No secret fellow does that for me."

"Maybe if you kept your cell phone charged and turned on, you'd get jokes of the day. Occasionally your dad sends me garden jokes. Though I wish it were true, you know we don't laugh every time we're together."

I didn't believe for one minute Dad sent her that text, not with divorce papers waiting to be signed. I'd removed my rose-tinted glasses. Now she needed to stop the pretense.

"I overheard you talking to Aunt Alicia in the kitchen about seeing your ex-boyfriend."

Cramps marched across my stomach. I wasn't sure if their intensity was being driven by our conversation or the memory of hers with Aunt Alicia. I wrapped my arm around my middle.

"That's exactly what Alicia figured. Said our conversation upset you and caused the migraine that day." Mom stepped closer, extending her hands. "Are you okay, baby?"

I backed away.

"You said that man was an old friend, not *boy*friend," I said, hugging myself tighter, not wanting to loosen the grip and feel the pain.

"Curtis and I dated long before I ever met your Dad. As I said, we're old friends." She opened her arms wider as if I'd dare let her hold me. "You're gonna make yourself sick worrying."

"I never imagined it like this ... you and Dad apart, an old boyfriend in the picture ... and why would Aunt Alicia preach abstinence when she didn't wait herself?"

"I can't change what's already happened. And neither can Alicia. She can clarify her own actions." Mom gestured for me to follow her back toward the Center, keeping her eyes on me the entire time. Probably afraid I'd collapse in the field if she didn't get me inside.

"I know you're confused and hurting, but I can't say what'll happen with your dad and me. I believe we'll always be friends and no matter what, we'll always be here for you."

I dragged alongside her. Was their split like mine and Miracle's—drifting apart for no solid reason? Could any relationship survive that kind of separation?

She stopped walking. "There's something else I want to discuss with you. Your dad and I have some business to take care of. We're going away for a couple of days, and I don't want you alone in Franklin's shack."

"I won't be alone. Kharee's there."

"Most of the time he's not. I wish that boy would get serious about his future," she added, talking more to herself than to me. She picked up her pace again. "Staying with Kharee is not an option, and Khara's college dorm room is out, so that leaves spending a few nights at Miracle's or Alicia's?"

Sleeping over Miracle's would probably be good, but Kehl-li was still in town. And I'd have to suffer harassment about Hassan. On the other hand, I could barely look Aunt Alicia in her face without seeing a hypocrite.

"Can I think about it?" I mumbled, glancing in her direction.

"Sure. But I hope you don't mind my suggesting you stay with Sam and Alicia. Might give you a chance to talk to your aunt about your feelings."

When we reached the front of the building, Mom patted the pockets of her overalls, reached in and pulled out a set of jingling keys. "Your dad's suits are in my truck. Mind taking them to him?"

"Huh?" Was she moving the rest of his stuff out of the house?

"Close your mouth and fix your face. No need to be astonished. I picked up his dry cleaning today."

My eyes widened. Did I hear right?

"And now you're amazed?" She smiled. "Your dad and I aren't enemies. Besides, we still share the same dry cleaners." She winked at me. "Tell Franklin I'll call him later."

I scratched my head and walked away. Were all relationships that complicated?

Whirling around, I yelled out to her. "Hey, Mom?"

"Yes?"

"Let's say I was interested in a fellow ..."

She froze.

I opened the trunk. "Hypothetically speaking, that is. What would you say?"

"Hypothetically speaking?" Her eyebrows met. "Well, when you get a real fellow you're interested in dating, we'll talk about it then."

Shaking my head, I watched her walk toward the Center. Didn't seem she could handle the truth about me, any more than I could stand hearing about her.

Still, my heart flickered. Mom and Dad being nice and thoughtful toward each other? Friends? I smiled. Maybe there was hope.

I ambled in the direction of the parking lot, then turned and watched Mom glide through the Center's doors, strong and tall.

Maybe talking could turn the bitter into better. Maybe everything was gonna be fine.

Jingling my keys, I headed to her car to pick up Dad's suits.

Maybe ... just maybe.

Chapter 22

CYNDRAY

"What might this be?"

After four and a half hours of being interviewed, composing puzzles, and doing basically what felt like school work, I squinted and stared at the fuzzy image on the card that the psychologist, Dr. Connel, held in my face.

None of the pictures on the flashcards looked like anything to me. Still didn't get why Judge Chan had ordered me to have a psychological evaluation just because I refused therapy. That didn't make me crazy. What idiot sat in a circle telling strangers their business?

"I don't see anything." I looked away.

"There's no right or wrong answer, Cyndray." She passed the card to me. "Just say whatever comes to your mind."

Did she want me to make something up? I took the card from her and tilted it to the side. If I said the first thought that came to my mind, she'd really think my head was screwed up. But maybe then I could go home. "Looks like a dead beaver split in half."

She scribbled notes on her paper. "What makes it look dead?"

"It's split in half." *Was she pretending to be dumb?* "I don't think any mammal could live after being cut in half."

I watched her short, nubby fingers hug her pencil as she scrawled more markings onto her pad. Our little guessing game continued.

Dr. Connel held up the last card in her batch. "What might this be?"

I sighed and tried not to roll my eyes. "I don't know. Food fight, maybe?"

"Food fight?" Her stare went through me. "What makes you think of a food fight?"

I bit my lip. "Looks like somebody got mad in the school cafeteria and threw mustard and stuff all over the place." I touched the different colors. "These are smooshed blueberries. And this looks like slimy eggs." I glimpsed her confused-looking face. "Can't you see the green beans right here?"

"Different people see different things." She scribbled notes without even looking up. Finally, she put the set of cards away.

The aqua-blue, sleeveless blouse Dr. Connel wore matched her eyes. Come to think of it, it also matched the grayish blue walls in the room. I slid my shoes on the floor, then stared at my white sneakers on the slate blue carpet. Was it me, or was everything perfectly color coordinated? *Creepy.*

"Now, I want to ask you a few more questions."

I pressed my feet into the carpet. "Thought we were done."

"Not much longer. I'm going to run through these questions quickly unless you need clarification or need me to slow down. Okay?"

I nodded. The faster the test, the faster I could go home.

"What kind of mood are you in?"

"You mean right now, or usually?"

"At this moment?"

"I'm good."

She frowned. "Are you happy, sad, depressed ..."

I said I was good. Didn't she know what that meant? Sheesh. I shifted in my seat, tired of sitting still. "Actually, I'm irritated at the moment."

She darkened a circle on the sheet with her lead pencil, then rattled off another question. "Do you ever see things that others might not see?"

Kinda like those blobs on the cards I just guessed at? "I'm not sure what you mean." I tilted my head toward the white rectangular box stacked on the table. "Were you able to see the things I saw in those cards?"

She smiled. "I was referring to visual hallucinations. Do you see people or images that aren't really there?"

Be careful. That's a question that'll get you thrown in a nut house quick. I shook my head, erasing the voice. "No."

"Do you hear voices that no one else hears?"

My heart stopped, then picked up speed. "Like right now?"

She glanced up from her bubbled sheet, the pencil hovering over the multiple responses. "Ever?"

I swallowed. Did the voices in my head count? I stared at the blue carpet, wondering how many people were carted off for talking to themselves.

"Cyndray, do you hear voices that are unheard by others?"

My thoughts battled. *Better not answer that one ... But I've got to answer ... What should I say?*

She tapped the paper with the pencil, seemingly anxious to mark my response. "Any *strange* voices?"

My own voice wasn't strange. I breathe a sigh of relief. "No."

"How many friends do you have?"

I shrugged. Couldn't count Danielle anymore. Janaclese for sure, but Miracle was just someone I hung out with because of Janaclese. And Kehl-li ... I couldn't stand that girl.

Dr. Connel waited for my response.

"I guess one, maybe two."

"Do your friends engage in any illegal activities?"

"No." Was this test about me or my friends?

"Do you have a boyfriend?"

"No."

"Do you practice safe sex?"

"No."

"Do you have more than one partner?"

"No! No, of course not!" I couldn't help screaming.

She stared at me and then looked at the answer sheet. "You said you didn't practice safe sex. You don't use protection?"

"I've never even had sex!" I banged my fists on the table. "You must be insane to assume I'd let anybody touch me like that!"

"Oh. Oh." The table shook as she erased a few marks, bubbled the answer sheet, then scribbled more words across her notepad. "Didn't mean to upset you. These are just standard questions."

Could she guess my mood now? I pulled at the collar of my blouse. If this was what A.J. went through, it's no wonder he was put in an institution.

I forced a deep inhale. *Calm down. Reel it in, girl, before they get you too. Don't let 'em get to you.*

A million thoughts circled my brain, and I felt lightheaded. The court system was already questioning my sanity. After that outburst, would I be committed too?

I forced a weak smile. "Look, there's been a mistake. I'm really not supposed to be here."

"Oh?" Dr. Connel's blue eyes widened as her lips froze into a tiny red circle against her pale skin.

Did she think I meant I wasn't supposed to be here on Earth like I was some alien or something? I had to straighten this whole thing out.

"See, Judge Chan thought I assaulted a cop, so she mandated anger management therapy. But I didn't go to therapy because I didn't need it." I lowered my voice. "Uh ...yeah, um ... sometimes I do get a little PO'd, but it's not a major problem or anything."

She seemed hesitant like she wanted to say something, but couldn't.

"Anyway, *everybody* knew I'd accidentally hit that officer. Since I didn't participate in therapy, the judge ordered a psych eval to see if there's something wrong with me." I chuckled. "That's how I landed in your office. I'm good, though, right?"

She opened and closed her mouth about ten times before speaking. "Cyndray, it's not a good idea for you to discuss your legal case with anybody except your lawyer. I'm simply conducting a mental assessment."

My mouth hung open. *If you can't help me, then what was the point of my being here?*

As if having read my thoughts, she continued. "You need to talk to someone, but that someone isn't me. Remember the informed consent I read to you?"

I nodded. Sheesh, I finally do the right thing, and it's the wrong person.

"Nothing you say to me is held in strict confidence. Unlike a regular psychologist, the results of this assessment will be shared with the court."

My shoulders slumped. "Everybody's gonna know about me and what happened?"

"Well, it's not going to be on the five o'clock news or anything, but your lawyer, your probation officer, and of course, the judge, has to see my report."

Sounded like they were in cahoots—everybody against me. "So what now?"

"Based on the findings, I'll recommend a treatment plan for a therapist if you don't already have one. Are you seeing anyone?"

I shook my head, focusing on the word treatment. Seemed no way to get around it. I could've avoided all of this if I'd painted a warning sign on my forehead at the mall. *Caution: Flammable When Touched!*

My shoulders vibrated when I chuckled. Me? Combustible?

The skin puckered above Dr. Connel's nose. "This is funny to you?"

"Yes, I mean, no." My smile met her frown. "Just this random thought about being a human torch." I bit my tongue, clamping down the giggles.

Dr. Connel's contorted face hardened. "Are you thinking about burning something down?"

I shook my head. Sheesh. If a person was sane before getting involved with the law, this court process could drive anybody mad.

Truth of the matter, I was starting to think that maybe I was a little cray-cray.

Chapter 23

JANACLESE

On the way to Aunt Alicia's, I sat in the backseat of what felt like a sauna and tugged at my seatbelt. I had one last chance to convince Mom and Dad to let me stay home alone while they handled their "personal business"—whatever that meant.

Tension stretched wide and deep in the car, circling me, Mom, and Dad.

"Why don't you trust me? I'm old enough to drive and responsible enough to have a job. Shouldn't that count?" I whined.

Mom gazed into her compact, powdering the beads of perspiration on her nose, while Dad sped across town. "Do you have plans, Janaclese?" She patted her face with a sponge.

"No, but it's the weekend and—"

"And our decision stands. Alicia's on bed rest. She'll need your help around the house."

"But can't I at least keep my car?"

"I thought you said you didn't have any plans." She twisted her neck toward the backseat and eyed me.

"I don't." I pouted my lips. "But still …"

Mom returned to powdering her nose. "You shouldn't need a car for the next two days. You can ride to church with Sam on Sunday."

Dad braked at a stoplight. "Your mom's right, sweetheart. Two days isn't that long."

Yeah, right. How was I supposed to look Aunt Alicia in the face? Pretend she wasn't a hypocrite?

But there was no need in arguing further.

Mom and Dad had finally united, two against one. Even worse, they decided to drive my Prius, claiming it had better gas mileage.

Dad accelerated when the light turned green. I stuck my head out the window, capturing a slight breeze, though sweltering heat still seeped into the car.

Mom fanned herself like she was about to burst into a flame. "Franklin, if you think for one second I'm riding two hundred miles without air conditioning, you're crazy."

Dad looked back in the rearview mirror at me. "It's not so bad. Is it, Janaclese?"

"Compared to an eternal burning hell? Maybe not," Mom barked at him.

We leaned into a curve as he steered to the right. "What do you want me to do? One minute, you're hot. The next, you're cold."

"It's called mid-life hormonal changes, Franklin. A sports car won't fix it," she said.

"Are we discussing that again? What does my Corvette have to do with your wanting air conditioning?"

That was my question too. But I didn't say a word. We'd entered a landmine, where only carefully crafted words could be uttered. The tactic of biting my tongue prevented any sounds from escaping my mouth and setting off more explosives. I'd let them fight their own little war.

Neither Mom nor Dad spoke.

Mom's neck and shoulder, stiff and rigid, and Dad's clenched jaw translated a looming verbal attack. But for now, the disturbing silence lingered.

Finally, our tires screeched into Aunt Alicia's driveway. When we stepped out of the car, music bounced from the house, inviting us inside.

A grin swept across Dad's face. "Is that a sax I hear playing?" He scooted onto the porch. "Sam must've dusted the old girl off."

A jazz tone flowing in unison with the piano swiftly transformed my parents' mood. Agitation crawled away from Mom, and she turned her spare key in the door's lock.

"They can't hear the doorbell over the music," she explained and entered the foyer with Dad following behind.

I grabbed my duffel bag from the car and trailed my parents into the music room. Uncle Sam waved his saxophone in the air. "Hey, family, come on in!"

Aunt Alicia glanced away from the piano. Banging one final note, she stood to greet us, her round pregnant belly slowly rising like the sun over the horizon. "We thought you'd be here hours ago."

Mom responded, but I stared at Aunt Alicia's belly, avoiding her face. Seeing her so full of the promise was the one thing that made me believe anything was possible—including my parents not divorcing.

But they were at odds.

Why couldn't Mom and Dad get along for more than five minutes? Seemed they only agreed when it came to punishing me—like not allowing me to stay home alone and taking my car for the weekend.

Dad's dimples, deep-set like mine, broadened as his smile stretched wider. "That music gave me flashbacks of how we used to really cut loose." He grabbed Mom by the waist and started swaying.

Mom swatted Dad's hand. "Stop fooling around. We need to get going. It's getting late."

Was Mom ever fancy-free like Dad? Maybe opposites did attract. Then obviously, repel. I would never let that happen to Hassan and me.

Dad placed one hand on my shoulder.

"Sam, Alicia. This is precious cargo we're trusting you with." He tilted his head and examined me for a few seconds, then frowned.

What was that all about?

Aunt Alicia waved my parents away. "Go on. We don't have kids yet, but we can handle a teenager." She rubbed her stomach.

Mom hustled toward the door. "Janaclese, don't forget to keep your cell phone on. I'll call you when we get there."

I nodded. Where in the world were they really off to? Could they finalize a divorce in one weekend?

"And I'll call again in the morning around 9:00. You should be awake by then. Not sure if we'll have another break until around lunchtime."

"Betima, will you give the girl a chance to miss us?" Dad patted my back. "I'll make sure she doesn't hound you." He waited until Mom had gone outside, then pulled me aside in the foyer. "Where's the diamond pendant I gave you?"

I slapped my palm to my neck. How could I have forgotten to put my necklace back on? Dad had given both me and Khara necklaces on our thirteenth birthdays to remind us he'd always be there.

Disappointment shone in Dad's eyes. "I know things are difficult right now. But, I'll always be your Dad, and I'll always be here for you like I promised."

I'd vowed to never take my necklace off, but when he broke his promise and left our family, I'd broken mine and only wore the necklace when he was around.

"I don't need a necklace to remind me of that." I tucked my hands in the back pocket of my jeans and rocked on my heels, forcing a smile.

Dad wrapped me in a bear hug, and I nestled against his broad chest, inhaling his wood-scented cologne. "It would mean a lot to me if you didn't take it off."

"Okay, Dad." I walked him to the car.

Mom sat in the passenger's seat with the door open, dusting the dashboard.

"See that?" She held up a white handkerchief speckled with yellow stains. "Pollen."

"Dad, you're gonna have to roll up the windows and turn on the air conditioning, even if you think it's less fuel efficient. Otherwise, Mom'll be so upset, she'll clean the entire car."

A twinkle sparkled in Dad's eyes. "At least your Prius will still get detailed this weekend. Besides, cleaning relaxes your mom."

I shook my head. Seriously? The stuff they fought about.

Dad winked at me and grinned. "Of course I'll turn on the air conditioner. What Betima wants, Betima eventually gets. Just thought I'd make her sweat for a minute."

"Dad!" I pretended to scold him. "Oh. I need my CDs."

I extracted my music, then we exchanged kisses and quick good-bye hugs.

"Love you," I called after them, waving until taillights disappeared down the street.

I trampled back into the house. The music had stopped, but apparently, it still played in Uncle Sam's and Aunt Alicia's heads. He held her from behind, her stomach facing outward, the back of her head leaning against his shoulder. Cheek to cheek they swayed back and forth, circling around the room. Was this real love?

Did Uncle Sam know Aunt Alicia's secret?

Maybe he was a part of it. My heart galloped. Why did I have to stay here?

I closed the door to give them privacy and then made my way to the guest room.

A bird chorus, chirping outside my window, awakened me. Their melodic sound urged me to get moving and gave hope that my day would be just as lovely as their singing.

Sunlight flickered into my barely opened eyelids. A stuffed giraffe, its long neck arched over a white wicker rocking chair, was mounted in a corner.

This wasn't my room.

Uneasiness gnawed in my stomach, interrupting the optimistic tune from the birds.

Evil foreboding, Mrs. Patterson had called it.

I rubbed sleep from my eyes and scanned the avocado-colored walls, the oatmeal carpet, the blue potted pansy flowering in another corner.

Shoot. Aunt Alicia's. Her guest room had been my bunker since arriving yesterday.

I lifted my sluggish body from the daybed and slipped into sweats and a tee shirt. My stomach complained. I needed to eat something. After splashing water onto my face, I ambled into the kitchen and opened the fridge—a bowl of mixed berries, veggies, and icky green liquid lined the half-empty shelves. Why hadn't they prepared for a guest?

Seemed they didn't want me here any more than I wanted to be here.

Good thing I'd stashed snacks in my bag. Could I survive off animal crackers and go unnoticed for two whole days? I closed the refrigerator and slogged back toward the guest room.

"Janaclese? You up?" The sound of Aunt Alicia's voice lassoed my feet.

I stumbled, then stood silent.

"Hold still, Allie. Gotta find a new spot," Uncle Sam said.

"Stick it right there." Exasperation traced Aunt Alicia's words. "Janaclese? Come here, sweetheart."

What could she possibly want? Would she know I was ignoring her if I pretended not to hear?

Better to not be rude.

I inched to their bedroom. The door, wide-open, exposed Aunt Alicia sitting on the edge of the bed and Uncle Sam kneeling beside her with a needle in his hand. They obviously weren't used to having anyone else in the house. I stood in the doorway with my hand on the doorknob.

Uncle Sam glanced at me. "The dead has arisen. You sleep okay?"

I nodded, then mustered my cheeriest voice. "Good morning."

An angry growl escaped from my stomach.

"Hungry?" Aunt Alicia puckered the skin on her thigh between her thumb and index finger. "Thought your belly would eventually force you out of your hole."

"Yeah. What time do we eat?" I looked away, not wanting to see her face or the whole needle episode.

"Allie's on a special diet. And I totally forgot to buy groceries." He waved the syringe toward the dresser. "Grab some money and my keys. IHOP has great waffles. I'd join you, but I've got to be at the radio station in forty-five minutes. You still tuning in?"

"Sometimes," I said, grabbing a bill and the keys to his Highlander. His weekly show 'The Bible Speaks' hardly aired anything relevant to me. I turned to leave the room. "My stomach thanks you. Do you want this door closed?"

Aunt Alicia shrugged. "Not really. You get to witness a human pin cushion. Prick here to test glucose levels. Prick there to control them."

My eyes locked onto the track marks lining her thigh. Why would God require so much of fragile human beings?

"It takes all of that to have a baby?" I bit my lip. Too late to retract such a personal question.

"Goodness, no." She shuddered, yet seemed less surprised by my question than I was. "My body's just stubborn and refuses to do what it needs to do without some direct intervention. If women had to go through this, the world's population wouldn't be anywhere close to seven billion. More like seven."

Uncle Sam drew medicine into the syringe, then repositioned the needle where Aunt Alicia pointed. "God doesn't put more on us than we can handle."

I'd heard that saying a million times. Our actions had consequences, didn't they? Maybe being impure had made Aunt Alicia's body stubborn. Like a punishment?

"I think I'll close this now." I shut the door and took a sharp inhale.

"Ow." Aunt Alicia's soft groan floated into the hallway.

"Did it hurt this time?" Uncle Sam asked, comforting her.

A pause followed, and I tried to tear myself away from the door.

"Just stings a little." She sighed. "I'm getting so tired of all of this. Sometimes it seems I'm forcing my own will to have this baby."

"We've already discussed that. When you have this baby, it'll be God's will."

"I just want to know for sure that this time is different."

Was this pillar of faith experiencing doubt? Paper rattled on the other side of the door.

"Honey, in three and a half months, you'll have your answer. Let's pray."

The rattling paper fell silent.

"Dear Lord—"

"Wait," Aunt Alicia interrupted Uncle Sam. "Did you notice anything different about Janaclese?"

My body tensed. *Me? Different?* Why would they talk about me behind my back?

"No. Like what?" Uncle Sam asked.

"She's quieter, less energetic. She practically slept from the time she stepped foot into this house yesterday until now."

"She's probably worried about her parents," he said.

"It's more than that, Israel."

My heart skipped. *Did she know I knew? Could she tell I was avoiding her?*

"You want me to talk to her?" Uncle Sam asked.

"No." Aunt Alicia's voice softened.

Good. I padded a few steps away from the door.

"I'll do it," she said.

I stopped. My legs wiggled like wet noodles.

She continued, "I have a feeling it's a girl-to-girl talk that's needed. Let's cover this in our prayer."

I listened to their heartfelt prayer. Realizing the intrusion, I grabbed my purse and walked out the door to Uncle Sam's Highlander.

Maybe I'd stay out all day. That'd leave one more day to figure out how to dodge Aunt Alicia.

And how to avoid our *girl-to-girl* talk.

Chapter 24

CYNDRAY

In your presence, my heart explodes. It goes … tick, tick boom,

'cause I'm your bride, and you're my groom …

The lyrics to the jazzy love song on Mrs. Samson's demo CD burned my ears as I tried to forget about my surroundings. For the umpteenth time, I was forced to listen to the same song because Janaclese couldn't seem to get enough of it. The song was supposedly about God, but I wasn't convinced. Sounded too romantic for me.

I tried not to let the music add to my anxiety at being in Janaclese's uncle's SUV. My muscles tensed. Janaclese had invited me to breakfast, and I'd agreed to go because I wanted to ask questions about Dr. Beverly from Redemption Temple in private. Mom and I had filled out the therapy papers for the court, and on first impression, Dr. Beverly seemed to be a cool therapist.

I breathed in the leather smell of the Highlander, but the familiar scent killed my appetite, nauseating me. The odor reminded me of the night I was trapped in a hotel with a few lowlifes. In Mrs. Samson's haste to find me, she'd grabbed Pastor Sam's keys and had driven his car—a secret rescue mission that rested between us.

"So let me get this straight." I eyed Janaclese. "You asked me to breakfast because Hassan said no?"

She gripped the steering wheel. "He didn't actually say no. He's busy today. That's all."

"Busy? Doing what this time?" Hassan had broken at least two dates with her already. Always some excuse concerning his family.

"The suit drive. Remember? His mom used to teach job skills to women and help them transition into the workplace?"

"Oh." I vaguely recalled her listing this as something they had in common. Both of their mothers did community service geared toward women. "Still doesn't make me feel better being second choice."

Janaclese side-eyed me. "Hassan is honoring his mom."

The leather seat squeaked when I wiggled, just as on that perilous morning I wanted to forget. I didn't like this SUV, the memories it held—even if it had carted me to safety. "Why're you driving Pastor Sam's car, anyway?"

"'Cause my parents took mine, and Uncle Sam is lending me his. He's going to drive Aunt Alicia's Volvo, I guess."

Thoughts of Tommy Dawg raced through my head. Ugly inside and out. I shuddered trying to shun him from my mind. My thoughts transitioned to Danielle. I shuddered again. I'd thought she was my best friend. Turned out, Janaclese, the Christian girl I could hardly stand had been the one there for me. And now, I had to return the favor. She got on my nerves, but I definitely had her back. I sighed and settled into my seat. That's what friends were for.

"Are you mad at me?" Apprehension filled Janaclese's eyes.

"No." I scrunched my face. Janaclese worried too much about nothing. "Why would I be mad at you?"

"You're lost in your thoughts, and you think I chose you last."

I smirked. "Girl, please. I don't care about that."

Janaclese nodded but didn't look convinced.

My mind bounced between the SUV smell and the in-take therapy session I'd finally had with Dr. Beverly the other day, but I wasn't totally absent-minded. "As long as you're treating me to free food, I'm good."

She glanced at me. "Actually, I was thinking we could grab something quick … like pastries. I want to go by Mom's to grab a few of her old suits to donate."

I sucked my teeth. "No breakfast buffet? We're gonna eat cinnamon buns for breakfast so you can roll through the 'hood chasing behind Hassan?"

She didn't answer.

I slammed my back against the seat, banging my head against the headrest. I hated this vehicle. Absolutely *hated* it.

Janaclese turned into a Starbucks and unbuckled her seatbelt. "You getting out with me?"

"No. I'll sit here, and people watch." I didn't want to hear her chipper chit-chat.

She hopped out of the Highlander.

I leaned my head against the window. A good laugh watching a sluggard slouch into a coffee shop, then bounce out like an addict might actually alter my mood.

But it didn't.

Flashbacks haunted me. Tommy Dawg pressing against me ... struggling to push his alcohol breath away ... sneaking out of the hotel ... crouching in the woods and waiting for sight of this very SUV ...

Why hadn't Danielle defended me? That's what *real* friends did.

"Which one—the blueberry scone or the zucchini walnut muffin?"

I startled. How'd she return so fast without my noticing? "They didn't have grits and eggs, or bacon?"

Janaclese smiled and tossed me the muffin. "This is better for you."

I resisted a growl and picked up the bag. I'd never admit how the tantalizing scent teased my taste buds.

We made our way across town. Before long, we parked the Highlander in her driveway. Pink and red azalea shrubs lined the walkway leading to her pale brick house.

"I'm just going to run in and grab a few suits Mom doesn't wear anymore. She won't mind since they're old." Her talking grew faster. "I'll just take the ones that are too small. You know, the ones she can't fit into? It's for a good cause, and she'll be happy—"

"Sounds like you're trying to convince yourself that it's okay."

"It is." Her wide eyes challenged me. "My mom says we need to do more to help those less fortunate."

I lifted her cell from the console. "Then call her. Tell Betima Mitchell about the good deed you plan to do on her behalf."

"Not now. But later." Smiling, she returned the cell to its pocket, hopped out of the car, and disappeared inside her house.

Ding.

I jerked my head toward her phone. Sheesh. Was that mommy-intuition? Just creepy the way nothing could be hidden from Mrs. Mitchell. Should I answer?

Ding.

Mrs. Mitchell wouldn't text. Was Hassan trying to reach Janaclese? Maybe he'd changed his mind about not hanging out with her today. Janaclese must be rolling in the deep to forgive him for kicking her to the curb two times in a row. I ignored her cell phone.

Ding.

Why didn't Janaclese ever keep her phone with her? I was surprised she'd charged the thing in the first place. I forced my eyes not to spy and tapped the armrest on the door instead.

Ding.

My stubby fingernails dug into the leather coating. Sheesh. Who'd keep blowing up somebody's phone when they obviously weren't available? Somebody desperate ... or stupid. I glimpsed the display.

Kehl-li? Definitely stupid. She couldn't want anything important. But in her self-centered world, everything was urgent.

I skimmed my phone apps, trying to decide which game to play while I waited for Janaclese. The sun's heat penetrated the glass and beat down on my neck.

"Aren't you going to help me?"

I looked up. Janaclese peeked above an armful of clothes. My eyebrows pinched tight.

"Touch your mom's stuff without asking? Nope. I'll pass." I looked down again and downloaded a game.

The trunk creaked as she struggled to open it. She tossed the suits inside, then thudded back up the steps into the house a second time.

I played solitaire on my cell as she made three trips back and forth from the house to the car. When she was done, I stared at her. "You look like a thief."

She frowned. "I'm not stealing. You know I'd never do that."

"I didn't say you *were* a thief. I said you *look* like one."

She quirked an eyebrow. "Tell me, Cyndray. What does a thief look like?"

I studied her face. Her braided extensions tucked back in a neat ponytail, the deep dimples in her cheeks now concealed by a serious expression.

But I knew better than to describe a thief.

She'd accuse me of stereotyping or something worse like being judgmental. "You wanna know what a thief looks like? In a one-word description—you."

"That's not funny." Janaclese turned on the CD player, blasting Mrs. Samson's love song. Again. "If it makes you feel any better, I packed some of my own clothes since I'm staying with Dad now."

"Whatever, Your Righteousness." I swatted a gnat flying near my face. Wonder why some people took things on purpose and got away with it, but people like me, who stole on accident, suffered the consequences. I smacked the audio control to switch from the CD player to the radio station, almost jamming the button. "And listening to the same musical voice has gone from phat to flat. In other words, from hot to not."

She backed out of the driveway, and we headed to Hassan's little stinky suit drive.

We rumbled down the street like clothes bouncing around in a dryer.

I clung to the handle on the ceiling. The road seemed less threatening after traveling it a million times like we'd done recently. Still, how could any driver get used to the narrow roads with faded lines separating the lanes?

"It's so rough over here." I exaggerated a pounce, nearly bumping my head on the car's roof.

Janaclese gave me a disapproving glance.

"I meant the road. Not the people." Though my statement could've referred to both. "Watch that pothole."

My head snapped forward.

"Oops." Janaclese's knuckles tightened around the steering wheel. She came to an abrupt stop. "Sorry about that. Your head okay?"

I rubbed my neck. "Let's just drop the suits off and head back to our side of town."

"We're here." Rays of sunshine burst from her.

I crumpled my face. "Uh, Janaclese. There's a strip mall on my left with a pawn shop, a tattoo parlor, and an exotic video store. And there's a Red Dot liquor store on my right. I don't see a church."

"Right there." She pointed to a tiny white building, positioned right next to the liquor store.

"The one with the banner that reads *Soul Food Served Here?*" I listened to the clicking of her turn signal. She couldn't be serious. "We're going in there?"

"The parking lot's full." She pulled into a space. "Lots of generous people coming to give."

"Or to eat soul food." A smile tickled my lips, "Think they'll have eggs and bacon? Maybe even barbecue sandwiches for lunch?" Maybe it would be worth it after all.

"I don't know. Hassan didn't say they'd have refreshments. Plus, it's not right, coming here just to eat."

"Girl, that's one of the duties of the church. Feed the hungry." I twisted my head to glimpse over my shoulder. "We're not exactly empty-handed. I think you have enough suits to justify two meals."

We hopped out of the car, and I scanned the perimeter. "Who's that ditzy chick waving at us like she knows us?"

"Where?" Janaclese's face brightened the moment she spotted the girl. "Oh, Samara. Samara Pitts from school."

"When'd she get blond hair?" I squinted. Was everybody changing this summer? "Looks like I'm the only one who likes being me."

"You're the only one who *can* be you."

I elbowed her. "You know what I meant."

Samara skipped over to the car. "Y'all must be here to see my daddy."

I cocked my head. Why on earth would we want to see him? "Who's your daddy?"

"The youth pastor." She rolled her eyes like I'd asked a ridiculous question—like he was this famous preacher.

"No, we're here to donate," Janaclese said.

"Suits?"

"No. Blood." *Who was the lamebrain now?* "Isn't this a suit drive?"

"Yep." She bounced like she had springs in her shoes. "That's totally awesome. Mostly adults donate."

"Well, Janaclese raided her mom's closet, and I'm seriously not touching those clothes." I watched Janaclese unloading the SUV. "You can help her take 'em inside if you want to."

Samara's pudgy face gleamed. "Sure. How'd you guys know about our suit drive, anyway?"

"Hassan Rayfield told me about it." Janaclese's head, poked inside the trunk, muffled her voice.

"You know Hassan?" Samara wrinkled her nose, and we just looked at each other. "Cool. His mom started this project. We continue it in her honor. I'll get a basket."

Samara raced off toward the church where a light-skinned girl with reddish-colored hair sat on the top step, her back against the porch. She was overdressed in long pants, Timberland boots, and a headscarf pulled close to her eyes. Strange. Why would she have on an oversized sweatshirt in sweltering heat? I walked to the trunk of the Highlander and stood next to Janaclese, who was no longer holding her mom's suits.

With squinted eyes, Janaclese gazed at the girl. She shook her head. "She's got to be burning up in all those layers of clothes."

The racket of metal being scraped across the asphalt snatched our attention to Samara. She pushed the cart to the back of the SUV. "Load your stuff in here."

Concern rested in Janaclese's eyes. She nodded toward the church steps. "Is that girl here for a suit?"

"Who?" Samara followed Janaclese's gaze. "Finale? No. She's in a different program."

"Finale? Like in the grand finale?" I scrunched my face.

"Yep. She's the last of eight kids. Guess her mom must've said this is the end, the last, no more children to come." She paused, then mumbled, "At least not from her mother, anyway."

I stared closer. The round lump of Finale's belly formed what looked like a baby bump. "How old is she?"

"Sixteen. I'm surprised y'all don't know her."

"Why would we know her?" Janaclese asked.

"Thought you were friends with Hassan. She and him used to be joined at the hip."

I lifted my eyebrows. "From the looks of things, she was joined somewhere else too."

Janaclese shot me a look.

"What? I'm just saying ..." I snapped my attention away from Janaclese's critical eyes.

"Yep. Sixteen and pregnant, just like on MTV." Samara dropped a jacket into the metal cart. "Except we get to witness a real-life episode."

"She's Hassan's friend?" Janaclese gulped. "Like girlfriend?"

"Used to be ... before he stopped coming to church here." Samara dumped more suits into the cart.

The look on Janaclese's face didn't help the thoughts racing through my head. I'd told her Hassan was no altar boy.

But a father-to-be?

I sighed. Anything out of my mouth would hurt Janaclese's sensitive feelings. I grabbed the cart of suits. "I'll just take these inside."

The wheels whistled across the asphalt and up the ramp as I pushed the cart inside the church. A sign pointed to the clothing drop-off area. I hustled to a large room, where a tall, middle-aged man wearing a baseball cap stood behind the counter.

"Dropping off?" His deep voice vibrated the room.

"Yes, sir." I emptied a few suits onto the countertop.

He examined the suits. A couple still had tags dangling from them, indicating they'd never been worn. "These yours?"

"No, sir. My friend's outside in the parking lot talking. I'm just bringing them in for her."

He read the inside label. "These are mighty expensive suits. Somebody's feeling pretty generous. We certainly appreciate the kindness."

I eyed the inside white stitching on a navy blue suit. It was monogrammed 'expressly for BM.' Figured Janaclese's mom wore tailor-made clothes.

The man grew quiet, fingering the label. He took off his cap and scratched his head.

His *bald* head.

I stumbled backward.

"My ... my friend's waiting for me." I turned and barreled out the door into the parking lot. "Janaclese! Janaclese! You'll never guess whose lookalike ..."

I didn't finish. Her gaze darted past me, and her lips formed an O. I swiveled around.

Sunlight danced on Mr. Clean's shiny head. "Young lady, you rushed off so fast, you forgot your receipt. For taxes."

I snatched the paper. "Thank you."

He squinted at Janaclese. "Aren't you Betima Mitchell's daughter?"

Janaclese squirmed. "Yes, sir."

"They're friends with Hassan," Samara said.

"Is that right?" His white teeth glistened. "Maybe you girls can keep him out of trouble." He turned to Samara. "When you're done out here, I need your help sorting sizes."

"On it," Samara said. "I can start now."

Mr. Clean and Samara walked away. He stopped, then spoke over his shoulder. "Tell your mother Curtis says hello."

I grabbed Janaclese's arm. "Uh-oh. Girl, you're in trouble now."

Ding. Janaclese checked her cell phone.

"For real, for real." I waved my hands. "No matter how you slice it, Mrs. Mitchell is gonna find out you were over here in Red Hill."

Janaclese's face transformed like she'd tasted something bitter and needed to spit it out.

"Okay, so here's the deal. Beat Mr. Clean to the punch and tell your mom you saw him before he mentions he saw you."

With shaky hands, Janaclese scanned her messages.

Suddenly, I remembered Kehl-li's obsessive texting. "If it's Kehl-li, then—"

She shoved me toward the Highlander. "Miracle's in trouble. Stranded at Zekiah Park. We've got to find her … and quick!"

Chapter 25

CYNDRAY

"There she is!" Before the words left my mouth, Janaclese dashed toward a park bench where Miracle was sleeping. I quickly caught up with Janaclese and peered down at Miracle. Didn't look like Miracle was in trouble to me, more like she was sunbathing.

"Miracle?" Janaclese knelt beside the bench as Miracle opened her groggy eyes and willed her body to sit up.

Upon closer inspection, her splotchy skin and dull eyes relayed that something was desperately wrong. I swallowed the lump forming in my throat. "Why were you sleeping on a park bench?"

"I must've dozed off." Her soft voice was barely audible. "Thanks for coming."

"No problem." Janaclese held Miracle's hand. "Are you okay? You look ... you look ..."

"Tore up from the floor up." I examined her from top to bottom. Her hair was decorated with yard debris, the ripped shoulder of her sundress disclosed a tiny bruise and the strap on her left sandal was broken. She was lying around on a park bench like a homeless person. "Looks like you've been in a catfight or something. Girl, what happened to you?"

Miracle looked at her feet, touched her tangled hair, then brushed her dirt-stained sundress. Blood oozed from her arm like cherry Kool-Aid. Her ragged and soiled clothing only told bits and pieces of her story.

She lowered her gaze. "I can't go home like this."

I put my hands on my hips. "You can't go anywhere looking like that. You—"

"It's okay, Miracle." Janaclese shot me a look as she patted Miracle's hand. "I have clothes in the trunk. I'll be right back."

Janaclese raced away, and within minutes she was back, carrying a small plastic grocery bag. She dipped her hands inside, then held up a pair of blue jean shorts and a multi-colored mid-drift, with a red tank top to wear beneath it. "Let's find a bathroom and get you cleaned up."

They latched arms. I strode a few steps ahead of them, navigating and following signs for a public restroom. The smell of a sewer alerted us when we'd arrived.

Janaclese stepped back, unlatching her arm from Miracle's. "I'll just wait out here."

I braved the stench and held the door open for Miracle, my nose hairs set afire. The rust around the faucets attacked my courage, and I refrained from going inside. "I'll wait out here too."

Janaclese twisted the toe of her shoe in the grass and waited a few seconds after the door closed before commenting. "Something's not right."

"Tell me something I haven't already figured out." I shifted my stance. "I'll bet she won't say a word about what really happened."

She shook her head. "I hope she talks because it seems like everybody's hiding something. I don't know if I can stand any more secrets."

"I don't mind talking."

I almost flipped backward when I looked up and saw Miracle standing next to me. I stood silent, gazing at her.

"So whaddya you wanna know?"

Why bite my tongue? "For starters, why do you look all busted and disgusted and—" Janaclese's slanted look became a flashing red light. Maybe I was going too far, but Miracle *did* ask. I extended my hand for Your Righteousness to proceed.

Janaclese locked arms with Miracle on one side of her and me on the other. I broke away and scrunched up my face.

"Tell us everything that's happened since your pool party." Janaclese's dimples slowly appeared. "I've missed you so much. And I just want to catch up."

They plopped onto the first bench along our path. Miracle sucked in a big gulp of breath, looked around as if uncertain, then, exhaling let it seep out. "Everything's so crazy right now. Judah, Kehl-li's ex-boyfriend, threatened to sue me for something I don't think I did."

Janaclese leaned forward to get the details, her eyes stretching wider as Miracle piled on layers to her story. "We pawned Mama's boulder necklace that Kehl-li stole, so I thought I'd take this modeling job to buy it back before Mama finds out." Tears streamed from her eyes. "But then, this model guy tried to, he tried to …"

Janaclese closed her eyes like she was mentally blocking out the scene Miracle was painting. My heart pounded like a jackhammer. How far had Miracle gone in this modeling job?

Tears had formed in Miracle's eyes before she swiped both cheeks. "I jumped from the bathroom window, and I still didn't get the money." Miracle's voice squeaked as she stitched together each strand of what had happened up to the moment we had arrived. "I bailed on the assignment and Kehl-li couldn't pick me up."

"Wait." I leaned into Miracle's view, unable to sit still any longer. "Kehl-li left you stranded? You were in a hotel room with a guy all by yourself, and Kehl-li didn't bother to stay with you or answer your text messages?"

"It wasn't a hotel, but a beautiful antebellum house … at least from the outside. Kehl-li responded to my text, but she couldn't drive back to get me. Apparently, she's ill."

"Sick is right." I stood up and stomped toward the parking lot. "I've heard enough. Let's go."

"Is Cyndray okay?" Miracle's question to Janaclese floated from behind me.

"Sometimes just mentioning Kehl-li's name tightens Cyndray's fists and places her in a boxing match."

I stopped beside the blue SUV, then spun around on my heels. "You know what? I really wanna say I told you so. But if I say I told you so, then you'll think I'm being mean. So even though I told you so is on the tip of my tongue, I'm just *not* gonna say 'I ... told ... you ... so!'"

I scampered into the backseat as Janaclese and Miracle hopped up front. I settled in my seat, but my insides remained jumbled. Anger wrapped my body in a straitjacket, and my nostrils flared as the wind whipped around the haunting odor of the Highlander. I never got the chance to tell Danielle off for abandoning me. But no way was I letting Kehl-li off the hook for what happened to Miracle.

Chapter 26

CYNDRAY

The Highlander came to a stop in Miracle's circular driveway. I could hardly wait to get out. I deserved an Oscar for putting on my sympathetic face for Miracle just to appease Janaclese. But now that we were parked in front of Miracle's mansion, I would pretend no longer.

"One word—stupid. Maybe two words—stupid morons," I said.

"What are you talking about?" Janaclese's eyebrows met to form a straight line.

"I'm talking about you and Miracle if you ever trust Kehl-li again."

"Kehl-li wouldn't have left Miracle without a good reason." Janaclese narrowed her eyes as she placed a supporting hand on Miracle's arm. "Let's go inside to hear her side of the story."

I rolled my eyes. Janaclese's logic seemed stuck like a bottle full of ketchup that wouldn't flow. Sometimes I wanted to shake her good sense to the front of her brain.

"Fine." I jammed my face in hers. "But fair warning, I'm going in swinging." I stood back, crossing my arms, challenging her to argue. And quite frankly, I didn't care who came out limping. I'd be good with one strong punch in Kehl-li's 'oh-so-beautiful' face.

"Remember," Janaclese's voice held warning, "we agreed that kind words soften Kehl-li."

Flattery had worked the last time, but I was in no mood for sweet talk.

"Don't tell me I don't have a right to speak my mind," I said.

"Take it easy, okay?" Janaclese sidestepped around me. "We'll get to the bottom of this."

Miracle shifted, seemingly uncertain, her wide eyes roaming between Janaclese and me.

The hexagon pattern of the brick driveway stretched before us. We walked inside the mansion. Though the walls were massive, they closed in around me, and I felt like I was crawling through a winding maze. We'd invaded the enemy's territory. And Kehl-li was gonna get what she had coming.

I grabbed the banister and hoisted my leg up each step, following Miracle to Kehl-li's room.

A small lump lay under a down comforter, with arms propped beneath a pillow. Raspy breathing escaped from the bed.

I took two large steps and towered over Kehli-li's stiff body.

"Get up." A deep roar blasted from me.

Kehl-li lifted her head slightly, then crumpled back onto the pillow. Her face held crease lines from the imprint of her palm.

I leaned over, snatched the comforter, and tossed it onto the floor. "Get up."

"Cyndray, calm down." Janaclese grabbed my arm, as Miracle stooped to recover the comforter.

"What kind of person leaves their best friend stranded?" I pulled away from Janaclese. "Anything could've happened to Miracle."

Kehl-li turned her back to me. Just like a snake, she slithered into a coiled position, hugging her knees to her chest.

A wave of anger tackled my insides. My breath shortened. Suddenly, I was in a dingy hotel room screaming at Danielle for letting Tommy Dawg put his hands all over me. "Don't you care? How can you watch someone being violated and do nothing?"

Tears jammed my eyes. Why wouldn't she say something? Make me understand her rationale. With clenched fists, I kicked the bed. "Say something."

"She lost her voice." Miracle, also in tears, shook her head at me. "Please ... just let it go."

"Oh, she's about to lose a lot more than her voice," I yelled.

"Everything's fine now. Look at me," Miracle pleaded. "I'm okay."

"Well, I'm not." I hovered over the bed, then marched over to the dresser. "Kehl-li, you're a poser." Sweeping my hand across the bureau, I sent items flying across the room. A soft bristle brush landed on the bed next to her.

"That's enough, Cyndray," Janaclese ordered. "We don't solve problems by having temper tantrums."

"Or name calling." Miracle sniffled.

"What! You're taking her side?" I huffed. "*I'm* not the villain here."

I clenched my fists. How could Miracle not see I was defending her? And why would Janaclese turn on me when I'd stuck by her the whole summer?

They glared at me.

"I see how it is." I jerked my head. "Always my fault. The more things change, the more they stay the same." I dashed from the room, reversing my entrance into the mansion. Outside, the air didn't seem so thick. But I couldn't loosen the chokehold of anger squeezing me. I needed to run ... hit something ... slam something into pieces.

I grabbed a stone from the flower garden. Kehl-li's name was written all over it. I strutted to her candy apple red mustang parked in the driveway, its color now deepening to blood red. I flung my arm back. "This is from all of us."

As my arm clutched the stone in mid-air, Janaclese suddenly stood between me and the car.

"*Vengeance is mine says the Lord.*" She didn't blink.

I squeezed the rock tighter. "Don't quote Scriptures to me."

"I'll stop when you stop. 'Be *angry, yet sin not.*' Never give the enemy an opportunity. You smash Kehl-li's car, no telling what she'll do."

"Mmooove!" I spoke slowly through clenched teeth. "Get outta my way."

Janaclese blinked rapidly, tearing forming in her eyes, but she stood her ground. "I'm not gonna let you do something stupid. Especially, something you'll regret five minutes from now. Let me help you."

Help me? I pushed down my own urge to cry. She had tears surging down her face. What comfort could I receive from a wet blanket? My short breaths came too rapidly. Dizzying darkness surrounded me. I fell to my knees to keep from passing out.

"Good choice." Janaclese muffled in the background of my loud thoughts.

What was wrong with me? Sheesh, I wanted to scream. Why did I let Kehl-li get to me like that?

"Breathe, just breathe." Janaclese moved closer to me.

I pressed my throbbing temples. *God, help me. I can't have a meltdown. Especially not here in public.*

"Back there, in the park." I stopped to control my quivering voice, then began again. "In the park, you said everybody was hiding something."

"Yeah. All of these secrets. It's too much." Janaclese knelt beside me.

"Were you talking about me?" I turned to face her.

She squinted like I was an alien. "Are you crying?"

I sucked in my tears. "Do you know something about me? 'Cause if you already know, I don't wanna keep torturing myself, trying to keep you innocent."

She placed a hand on my shoulder but frowned. "I'm not innocent. Why does everyone keep saying that?"

"I was almost raped." The word choked me.

"*What?*" Janaclese's face softened as she started to open her arms. But an automatic gesture to hug me was quickly withdrawn. She looked into my eyes as if suddenly realizing why I hated being touched. And seemingly knowing I wouldn't repeat myself, her words spilled out quickly. "I'm so, so sorry. Tell me when, who, where?"

The story came out in short bursts, like my breaths. "Last spring … a friend of my 'used-to-be' best friend … in a hotel."

"What were you …" Her words slowed. "… doing in a hotel?"

"I shouldn't have been there." The bitter taste in my mouth turned my stomach, constricted my throat. I shouldn't have done a lot of things that night. I shouldn't have lied to my parents or trusted Danielle or agreed to party in a hotel room. It was all my fault.

"Just talk to me."

A small weight lifted from me. Still, I massaged the rock. Without resisting, I let Janaclese put her arms around me. "I ... I don't know where to begin."

"The knees are the perfect praying position. Since we're both on our knees, why don't we start here?"

I inhaled and blew out a huge breath. Talking about what had happened wouldn't make me look cool. But I wanted that feeling of freedom I'd had when I'd shared long-held secrets with Mrs. Samson.

The rock slipped from my hand. "Okay, God ...You win. I already gave you my life. But now, I surrender all. Everything—my thoughts, my will, and my emotions."

Chapter 27

JANACLESE

I swayed back and forth on the porch swing at Aunt Alicia's, not wanting to go inside. Not wanting to deal with her or anything else this evening.

A full moon hung high in the sky. Its brightness illuminated the night, yet my world seemed dim, dark ... ugly. After we left Miracle's front yard, Cyndray took hours un-stuffing the secrets she'd held clogged inside for so long. Seemed I was now holding her distress.

Aunt Alicia rescuing Cyndray from a gunman? I tightened my grip around the rough metal of the swing's chain. I didn't know much about my own family.

When I eased into Aunt Alicia's house, Beethoven's symphony crashed into my ears. I headed to the guest room, the tune of 'Moonlight Sonata' trailing me.

"Hey, stranger." Aunt Alicia stood in the kitchen mixing berries in a blender. "You're just in time for a blueberry smoothie."

I waved, determined not to be deterred or distracted.

"How's it going?" The whirring of the blender competed with the sounds of classical music.

"Bad day," I answered just as the blender stopped.

Aunt Alicia chuckled.

"Sweetheart, you've never seen a bad day in your life." Still smiling, she poured herself a drink. When her eyes met mine, her smile vanished.

"Janaclese?" She put her glass on the counter and moved toward me, "What happened? You wanna talk about it?"

I raced to the guest room. The clicking of the door closing was my only response.

An hour after I'd holed up in Aunt Alicia's guest room, a soft knock landed on the door.

When I didn't answer, Aunt Alicia poked her head inside. "May I please come in?" She held up a watering pot. "I don't mean to disturb you, but it's time to feed my pansies."

I lay still, pretending I was half-asleep.

She dallied in the room, sweet-talking her flowers like they were her children. After about five minutes, she sounded like she turned in my direction. "Janaclese, I bet you're wondering why I love pansies so much."

I held my sigh. If I acted interested, would she leave sooner? I opened my eyes and propped my elbow on the cotton sheet, my face against my hand.

"Blue pansies were the first flowers your uncle ever gave me. Israel said they look delicate, but they're the strongest plants he knows. They can bloom in winter and even survive ice storms."

I looked at my aunt's tall, slender frame. From the back, there was no sign of "the promise" she held in her womb.

"God's creation is marvelous." She fingered a heart-shaped petal. "I noticed He did the same with people." She turned and looked at me, her belly extended, "the promise" in full view. "We seem so delicate, but we're strong enough to survive the cold, harsh months."

I averted my attention, surveyed the room, then rested my eyes back on her stomach. Wasn't that the pep talk Uncle Sam had given her this morning? Was she also still trying to conjure enough faith to continue believing?

"How do *you* believe without a shadow of a doubt?" My eyes challenged her, dared her to be honest and admit she wasn't a pillar of faith like everyone thought.

She sniffed her flowers. "These blue pansies only emit a fragrance at night. Come smell."

I didn't budge. Just waited for her response to my question.

Aunt Alicia put the watering pot next to her pansies. "Everyone doubts sometimes. The key is to choose to believe in the midst of it."

Her poised and confident reaction quieted me. Uncle Sam's soft snores, creeping from the other room, dominated the house sounds.

She placed one hand on her back, seemingly arching it further. "Israel goes to bed especially early on Saturday nights because he wants to be fresh when he preaches on Sunday mornings. He had a difficult time relaxing until I assured him you were okay." She rubbed her stomach and smiled with tenderness. "Hope he doesn't worry so much when our baby arrives."

I repositioned my weight on the mattress.

She scanned my face. Raising her eyebrows, she asked, "*Is* everything okay?"

I considered Hassan, Finale, Cyndray, Kehl-li, and Miracle, feeling like there were layers of weight. I swallowed. Not to mention there'd been no contact with my family the entire day. I hadn't checked in with anybody, and Mom hadn't bothered to call me either.

Twisting my body, I gave a humorless laugh. *Was I okay?* When was the last time I felt okay? "Why doesn't Mom fight for our family?"

Aunt Alicia sighed. "Who says she isn't fighting?"

"If she is, then she has a fine way of showing it. Giving Dad divorce papers, making him go away with her to speed up the process."

"Hmmm … interesting you'd think that's what's happening."

"What am I supposed to assume?" My voice rose. "Nobody tells me anything. You all keep secrets from me like I'm a baby." I waited for her reaction, but she toyed with her plants. "But that's okay. The truth's finally leaking out."

She stopped. "The truth? We all have varying perceptions of reality, but there's only one Truth."

Now I was alert—fully awake, ready to talk. "The truth is, things aren't always what they seem. People aren't always who you think they are."

"I agree. You want to expound on that?"

I folded my arms. Did she think I was too much of a "goody" to expose her? "How could you be so deceitful? Organizing a lock-in to tell girls not to have sex before marriage when you didn't wait?"

"And you're angry?" With narrowed eyes, she shook her head. "Why?"

Did she really not understand? "That's being a hypocrite!" My voice sailed higher than I expected, contesting the loud snoring down the hall.

Aunt Alicia, seemingly unnerved by the intensity in my voice, grabbed pillows from the white wicker rocking chair, then sat on the edge of the daybed. She carefully scooted back, placing the pillows behind her before leaning against the wall. "It hurts to know you think I'm a hypocrite."

"Well, I ..." My voice fell silent.

She pursed her lips. "But I understand. You think I'm telling you one thing, yet I've done another, right?"

I nodded.

"I wasn't raised in the church. My past isn't pretty, but it is my past. I'm not ashamed of what led me to God. As ugly as it may be, I'd like to use my testimony to help others."

Quietness settled between us.

"Janaclese, there are many ways to learn. Wise people learn from other people's experiences. I say *wise* because personal experiences can sometimes be cruel and bitter."

"Was yours?" I hoped my question didn't ring as mouthy or too judgmental.

She frowned. "The consequences were. That's why I advocate abstinence."

"You want to expound on that?" I asked, mimicking her.

Her slight shuffle rocked the bed. She hesitated, and then began speaking. "Emotional and mental bondage can make you believe you're unworthy of God's promises, so you physically cause the manifestation of that promise to terminate. Follow me?"

Sounded like babble. "Not really."

"Whatever you believe, you make it a reality. For example, when you don't think you can succeed at something, you're likely to fail without giving succeeding much effort. In my case, I didn't think I could, *or should*, ever mother a child."

"Because you were a night club singer?"

"Not just that. Also, the lifestyle that came with it."

We sat in silence, engrossed in our personal thoughts.

I eyed her. "You think I should believe my parents will stay together?"

A big grin plastered across her face. "I don't care what it looks like, I believe they'll reconcile." She chuckled, staring off into space. "Old Salt and Pepper are gonna be just fine." She glanced at me. "That's what we called them when they were dating."

I frowned. "Like Salt-n-Pepa—the rap artists?"

"Oh, no. As in seasoning and spice. Let me get my old scrapbook." She scooted off the daybed and waddled out of the room.

I held back tears, remembering how easy faith seemed a year ago. *God, why's it so hard to believe? Make me believe again.*

"Here it is." Aunt Alicia passed me the album.

I held it against my chest. As angry as I'd been, Aunt Alicia was still one of my favorite people. Always there to help me, comfort me. "Can I give you a hug?"

Her eyes danced. "Absolutely. I love hugs."

I crouched on my knees and reached up toward her neck, giving her a big embrace. "I'm sorry, Aunt Alicia."

She smiled. "For what?"

"You know ... avoiding you and thinking the worst."

"Next time, just ask. Okay? Now slide over and make room for your pregnant auntie."

She nestled next to me, and we flipped through the pictures of her and Uncle Sam, Mom and Dad—playful, carefree, loving teens, then more serious young adults. One picture showed Aunt Alicia's face smeared in blueberries.

I pointed to the photograph. "You've always loved blueberries, huh?"

"Yes, indeed. My favorite." She smacked her lips. "Believe it or not, I crave them even more now."

"Yeah, I smelled your blueberry smoothie earlier."

"Check this photo out." Aunt Alicia reared back and laughed. "Betima doesn't know I still have that one. Franklin convinced everyone in the club she was this major superstar. People interrupted us the entire night asking for her autograph." She snorted. "Might not have been so bad, if he hadn't passed her the mic to sing. Everybody stared in anticipation. She turned to me, heat steaming from her ears, 'Allie, I'm gonna choke that man.' I snapped her picture, just as she took off running after him."

I laughed. "Dad still teases her like that."

"A few grinds of pepper, a pinch of salt. So different, but flavorful together."

My eyes darted across the page. A knife stabbed my stomach. "Who's that guy standing there next to Mom? Do I know him?"

"One of Betima's classmates." She flipped the page and pointed to another photo, refocusing my attention elsewhere. "This is before your mom started wearing dungarees to work."

I glanced at Mom in a business suit, holding a briefcase and kissing Dad, but my thoughts were still on the previous photograph. Why did Aunt Alicia move away from the last picture so quickly? Was that man a younger Mr. Clean when he wasn't bald?

Then I remembered something Mom had said, and Aunt Alicia's voice faded …

She flipped the page again. "I gotta show you this one. Look."

I looked, without seeing. My thoughts were deep. Was Aunt Alicia hiding something about my mom and Mr. Clean?

Aunt Alicia's voice repeated in my ears. *Next time, just ask. Okay?* But somehow I couldn't.

Chapter 28

CYNDRAY

My eyes felt irritated as I texted Janaclese to '*hurry up.*' Leaning against the kitchen drawer, I ignored the knob digging into my hip. Something crackled in the background, like a cat playing in a paper bag. *Come on!* How long could it possibly take for her to answer?

"Cyndray!" Mom yelled from upstairs. "Check the stove!"

Glancing over, I saw smoke pouring out from the rattling lid on the front burner.

"Yikes!" I dashed around the island, switched off the burner, grabbed a potholder and removed the pot. So that's why I heard crackling? I'd totally forgotten to watch the rice for Mom.

"Everything all right down there?"

"Yeah!" I screamed back, hoping I hadn't completely destroyed dinner.

I stirred the overcooked mush with a wooden spoon, scraping the sticky substance from the bottom of the pot. I turned my face away. Did yellow rice always smell like burned popcorn when it was overdone?

"Then why does it smell scorched?" Mom's voice descended into my ears before the telephone rang. "Did you burn the food?" When I didn't answer, her voice boomed with another command. "And get the phone!"

Sheesh! When did I become the maid? I hustled toward the desk that held the phone, wondering what was Mom so busy doing upstairs anyway? I stopped mid-step and stared at the caller ID on the display. *Robert Scott.* My probation officer calling me at 6:30 p.m.? It was still three hours till curfew.

The telephone rang again.

I snatched the receiver from its cradle. "Hello?"

"This is Mr. Robert Scott. I'm calling for Cyndray Johnson, please."

"It's me. And I'm where I'm supposed to be," I said, already getting an attitude.

"I'm not calling about your curfew." He spoke between chews on something. "Were you notified your request has been approved by the court?"

My heart pounded. I'd made a lot of requests. Obviously, the one to leave me alone was being denied. "What request?"

"Counseling at Redemption Temple." Mr. Scott smacked in my ear. "But it's not that Youth Encounter class you keep mentioning."

I knew that. "Yeah, we got the letter last week."

"You'll be meeting with a Dr. Beverly every Tuesday evening ... starting tonight."

I knew that too, which is why I needed Janaclese to hurry up. "I'm on it. We've already met with her and filled out the paperwork."

"Oh." He sounded disappointed not to be telling me something I didn't already know. "Just remember your curfew hasn't changed. Says here, your sessions only last an hour. You're still expected home every night by 9:30 p.m."

"Yeah, Mr. Scott, I know. I got it." I rolled my eyes. *Can we hang up already?*

A lull settled in our conversation, and his smacking grew louder.

"Mr. Scott, the letter didn't mention the number of sessions. Is it still six weeks like the SOS program was supposed to be?"

"Judge says it'll take as long as you need."

"So maybe even less sessions?"

"That'll probably be based on how well Dr. Beverly thinks you're progressing, but you don't have to rush through the process." He swallowed with a big gulp. "Your probation is six months."

"Yeah, don't I know it."

"Good luck tonight. I'll call back at 9:30 for a quick check-in."

Don't bother. "Yeah, okay."

We disconnected as Mom clumped down the stairs carrying a wicker basket. "Who was that?"

"Mr. Scott."

She checked her watch. "What did he want?"

"Making sure I knew about tonight's therapy, so I don't miss it." I pulled out my cell phone, searching for a message from Janaclese. Where was she?

"I came down to tell you that Janaclese just pulled up." Mom scrunched her nose and bolted toward the stove. "Did the rice burn?"

"Might be salvageable. I gotta run." I darted outside, letting the door slam behind me. The heat of the sun warmed my face.

Janaclese sat in her Prius waiting to drive me to Youth Encounter, the front windows down, her eyes covered in dark shades.

I hopped into the passenger's seat. "Sorry to keep you waiting."

She gave a lazy shrug like she was too exhausted to care. She started the car, blasting the sound system.

"Ow." I pressed my hands against my ears and then fumbled with the volume. "What's the matter with you? Are you deaf? Sheesh."

"Sorry. Didn't seem so loud when I turned the car off."

"And what's up with you listening to that same old stupid song again?"

"It relaxes me. I dance to it … well sorta. I choreographed a routine in my head."

"You're starting to bug me, you know?" I wrung my hands together. *Wish I could relax.* "Why would you dance in your head?"

"My dance shoes are at my mom's. Forgot to pack them when I left."

I twisted my WWJD bracelet. "Well, you should've grabbed them when you were stealing her suits."

Janaclese rolled her eyes. "Plus, there's no space to spread out in Dad's shack."

"As much as you love dancing, you should try whooping it up outside bare feet, like a real African princess."

I watched as she clutched the steering wheel tighter like I'd plucked a nerve. "You got something against dancing outside bare feet?"

"Not that." She swirled a braid around her finger. "You think that Finale girl's having Hassan's baby?"

I sighed. "I don't know. Maybe."

She glanced at me. "That wasn't supposed to be your answer. You're supposed to assure me Hassan's not the father, encourage me a little."

"I've been *encouraging* you the entire time to stay away from Hassan. You play with fire, you get burned. And to think you wanted to be more than friends."

One hand on the steering wheel, she removed her sunglasses and placed them in the center console. "You make me sound stupid."

"Not stupid. Just unbelievably naïve. If I were you, I'd straight out ask him."

The worry in her eyes echoed in her voice. "Seems like every time I trust people, I get stabbed."

"Humph. You and me both." I slanted my eyes in her direction. "I'm meeting with Dr. Beverly tonight during Youth Encounter."

She presented a tiny smile. "Good. You'll like her."

I rubbed my forearms. "You ever talked to her?"

"Once or twice … when Mom and Dad first separated."

Meeting with Dr. Beverly two times to get better? I can do that. "Well, how're things going with your parents?"

She shrugged. "Don't know. They got back late last night. Dad dropped Mom off at home and didn't mention anything when he picked me up. Aunt Alicia thinks they'll reconcile, and I should keep believing. But truthfully, I'm struggling with trusting her too."

Janaclese didn't seem to know the half about how sweet her Aunt Alicia really was. "Mrs. Samson's on the up and up. Nothing down low about her."

Janaclese flinched as she turned into Redemption's parking lot. "My aunt's hiding something. I'm so tired of all the lies."

Tiny dark patches lay beneath her eyes. I'd detected her unusual lack of zeal, but I hadn't noticed how beat up she looked till now.

I checked my watch. "Time to go inside. Don't wanna be late for my meeting."

She looked up at the church. "I don't even wanna walk through those doors. Can't we just sit here for a minute?"

The knots in my own stomach gave me an idea of what she was feeling. "Maybe you should take my slot and talk to Dr. Beverly."

She leaned back in her seat. "I'll be fine. Just need to collect my thoughts. Figure out what to say to Mom and Hassan when I see them."

"You haven't spoken to your mom, yet?"

"We talked this morning, but the whole suit donation thing didn't come up. She wants me to work at the Wellness Center on Saturday." She waved her hands. "They're sponsoring this Paint the Park Pink event."

I opened the door, then swung both feet onto the parking lot, my back facing Janaclese. I spun around. "Um ... I hope you've collected enough thoughts 'cause that looks like your mom cutting the rosebush beside the church."

Janaclese adjusted the rearview mirror. Horror spread across her face. "Oh, no, no, no! Is she wearing pajamas?"

Mrs. Mitchell's blue satin outfit flowed with her every moment.

"Looks like a nice leisure pantsuit," I said.

"Oh, brother. She must've discovered her suits are missing." Janaclese held her stomach and sucked in a deep breath. "You don't know Betima Mitchell like I do. She's not wearing her usual gardening dungarees. Mom's making a point of not having decent clothes to wear."

"Then come clean and just tell her." Janaclese's drama made my heart pound faster than I wanted it to. I had my own stuff to resolve. "I'm sorry, but I've gotta go to my meeting."

"Wait."

I pivoted to face her.

"Be honest with Dr. Beverly. She can help you."

"You worry about being honest with your mom. She's probably the *only one* who can help you." I laughed. "Aren't you coming inside?"

She swallowed. "No. Not yet."

I trampled across the parking lot, heading toward the front entrance of the church. I didn't want her mom to see me either. She'd probably ask why Janaclese wasn't with me, and I'd have to make up an excuse then corroborate with Janaclese so we didn't contradict each other. Sheesh. That girl was making my life too complicated.

The snipping stopped when Mrs. Mitchell spotted me. She waved a gloved hand. "Hello, Cyndray!"

No way could I sneak past her now. Might as well act normal. "Hi, Miss Mitchell."

"*Mrs.* Mitchell." She twisted and pulled at the foliage. "*Mrs.*"

What was that deliberate correction about? *And why're you walking around in pajamas?*

"What're you doing?" I asked.

"See these thorny leaves?" She pointed to the bush. "They're called suckers, and they're keeping the roses from budding."

I crumpled my face. "I thought all rosebushes had thorns."

"The leaves on this bush should be glossy and dark green with five leaflets." She broke off a stem. "This sucker is light green with seven leaflets. Tricky, but see the difference?"

Counting the leaflets, I nodded. "Sheesh, how'd you notice something small like that?"

Mrs. Mitchell leaned in and pressed her lips together before speaking. "It can be deceptive, but only the top half of the rosebush has blooms. Something had to be zapping its energy, stealing the nutrients." Her eyes bore into me. "When you have a problem like this, you can't just cut back and prune. If you want something to flourish, you've gotta dig a life-sucking sucker up by the root."

Her words almost knocked me over. Did she know about my issues?

I stuttered. "We … we're still talking about the rosebush, right?"

She narrowed her eyes. "Isn't that what you asked about?"

"Yes, ma'am."

"Then keep up."

I breathed, relieved she wasn't talking about my life. It didn't matter what Janaclese said about her mom or Mrs. Samson. They were all right with me.

"One more thing," I said, smiling.

Mrs. Mitchell tilted her head. "Yes?"

"Does this getting rid of suckers thingy only work when you're wearing pajamas?"

With a twisted face, she looked down at her nightclothes. "That's another issue I have to get to the root of."

Grinning, I headed up the steps and into the church for my counseling session. Hope Dr. Beverly could dig up the suckers in my life.

Chapter 29

CYNDRAY

I scooted through the church doors and walked down the winding hallway that led to Dr. Beverly's office. The sound of high-pitched voices grew louder as I edged closer.

"I can't believe enrollment is so low for the lock-in. You'd think the teens would be interested in the topic of sex." The voice belonged to Brianna Nicole, my Youth Encounter instructor.

"There's still time." A second voice, presumably Dr. Beverly's, responded. "Every year we get an influx of registrants at the last minute. Just keep reminding them. You're doing an outstanding job. Just keep that in mind, regardless of the results."

"Thanks. I should get to class. Expecting a lively discussion tonight."

I read the announcement for the lock-in posted outside of Dr. Beverly's office as Brianma Nicole shot past me. Not sure what she'd think if she knew I needed counseling. I lingered close to the wall, practically hugging it until she passed and escaped down the hall.

"Cyndray?"

I jerked my head around and stared at the sisterlocks neatly pulled away from Dr. Beverly's angular face.

"Are you going to pretend you're reading that poster or are you going to come in for your session?"

A smile crept across my face, greeting the grin on hers. Maybe I liked her already.

She glanced at her wrist. "Follow me. We need to get started right away."

I trailed her into the room, where it sounded like a stream trickling in the background.

"Sit wherever you're comfortable." She extended her hands out.

Eyeing my choices, I decided to sit on the orange L-shaped couch. I pushed against the back of the seat, and just as I expected, the front raised upward, allowing me to recline.

Dr. Beverly sat behind her desk, propping her elbows on its wooden surface and clasping her hands together. "So, what brings you here today?"

Whoa. This lady got straight to point. Guess I'd better do the same. "I just wanna know if you can help me."

She unclasped her hands. "That depends."

Here we go again. I sat upright, kicked against the foot rest to lower the recliner, then inched to the edge of my seat. "Depends on what?"

"You." She gestured at me. "If you're honest, I can help you get to the source of whatever is bothering you."

"How're you gonna do that?" When I'd started to spill my guts to Dr. Connel, she informed me that she was the wrong type of therapist. Before either of us got too comfortable, I needed to know Dr. Beverly was the real deal. "What kind of psychologist are you?"

"I'm a counselor, not a psychologist."

I tugged at my WWJD bracelet and squinted, trying to hide my disappointment. "Oh. I thought you were a psychologist."

"I'm trained as a Cognitive Behavioral Therapist, but my approach is eclectic. Not that that means anything to you."

It didn't. I just needed some fast help. I looked at her bookshelf. One section filled with puppets, action figures, and dollhouse furniture; the other held hardcover books. I recognized the thick dark blue one with the title DSM. I'd googled so many psychological symptoms, and that book had some pretty scary diagnoses in it. Next to it was a small book, *What to Do When You Don't Know What to Do.* I felt my eyebrows hitch. Sounded appropriate for me.

"Now that you know a little about me, why don't you tell me about you. Why are you here?"

"I have to get court-ordered therapy; might as well be here." When she didn't respond, I continued. "It's mandated, remember?"

"That much I know. How did you come to be involved with the law?"

I explained the mall incident as if she hadn't already read my report. "If the cop hadn't touched me, then I wouldn't have jerked away and accidentally hit him."

"But you were already angry before he touched you. From what I understand, anger is what made you march out of the store, forgetting to pay for your swimsuit. Why were you so upset?"

"Kehl-li." Just saying her name rattled my nerves.

"Did Kehl-li touch you?"

"Not physically, but she touched my nerves. All her stupid talk about boys and kissing like she's some kind of expert."

"Those things make you uncomfortable?"

I stared into space. Dr. Beverly's questions were coming too fast. What was she really asking me?

"Those things make you uncomfortable." Her voice lowered, and now, rather than asking a question, she was telling me.

My body itched. "Maybe."

I wrapped my arms around my stomach and scratched my elbows. Wasn't a secret I hated being touched, but maybe all the talk about romance and boyfriends didn't sit well either.

"I'm curious as to why. Why do those things make you uncomfortable?"

I shrugged my shoulders.

"If you're not ready to open that door, I understand."

Be honest with her. Janaclese's words sailed across my mind.

"There're too many doors—slam one shut, another opens." I sighed. "I can't keep them all closed."

She got up from behind her desk, sat beside me on the orange couch, then pointed toward the space where I stared. "What if we slowly opened just one door together?"

I slanted my eyes in her direction. "What are you doing, Dr. Beverly?"

"You don't mind if I join you, do you? Thought we could slowly open just one door together."

For some reason, my heart started pounding. "You're missing my point. I don't want to open any of the doors. I want them *all* closed." I brushed my palms against my jeans. "Teach me how to permanently seal the doors, please."

"Let's reflect on that." Her calm voice opposed the hurricane brewing inside me.

"You asked me why I was here." I fought to keep my voice steady. "I didn't come to reflect or think about the past or recall any old memories. We don't need to open no doors. I'm here to move forward."

"Tell me, what are you feeling right now?"

That I really don't like you after all. "I feel like you're trying to trick me."

"I'm not trying to trick you. Why do you feel that way?"

"Yes, you are. Because if I open a door, I'll just get mad. And you'll just tell Judge Chan how I reacted and everything will spiral out of control again."

"So, you're telling me all of the doors you want sealed lead to anger and that frightens you? Feeling like you have no control must be pretty scary, huh?"

Heat flushed through my body. "Who said anything about being scared?"

"Then give me the right words. Tell me what you're feeling."

I bit my lip, uncertain if I could explain the sudden frustration, the anger of not trusting that I should explain it.

Tiny beads of sweat formed on my hands. I made a fist, then spread my fingers to flex them.

"If you don't have the words, can you point to where you feel sensations in your body?"

I flattened my palm against my chest.

She leaned forward. "Tightening?"

I nodded, noticing my chest rising and falling in rhythm with my noisy breathing.

"Try breathing from your diaphragm like this." Dr. Beverly demonstrated a technique, and I tried to follow her. "Breathe in and out from your gut, not your chest. Tell yourself to relax."

Relax. Relax. I mentally uttered. *Relax!*

"Anger has purpose, but we have to understand how to use it appropriately."

Dr. Beverly educated me on why God had created anger as a warning for fight or flight, and how uncontrolled anger led to headache and heart disease. I listened until I realized I was calm again.

"I don't know exactly what's behind those doors." A sisterlock escaped her tidy bun and covered her eye. "But, I want you to know those events are like movies, and your mind is a wide-screen television." She brushed the twisted hair from her face and stared directly into my eyes. "Who controls the channel on the TV?"

I squinted. "I guess whoever's watching … they can use a remote control."

She smiled. "You are the remote control for your thoughts. When we control our thoughts, we control our behavior."

I sat quietly, letting her words sink in.

"That's some pretty strong girl power. Don't you agree?"

I liked the idea of having control and power; yet, I'd never thought of it the way she described.

She leaned back in her seat. "This week can we agree to work on the breathing exercise and switching the channel?"

I nodded, wondering about my control and power. Maybe I did like Dr. Beverly … but could I trust her to open the doors with me?

Chapter 30

JANACLESE

I watched as Cyndray's long legs sauntered up the steps and into the church. I bounced my knee below the steering wheel. What had she and Mom talked about? Did they mention anything about me?

Mom continued lopping off stems and dropping them into a plastic yard bag. Using the back of her hand, she wiped sweat from her brow, then stooped down to look at something below the rosebush. Odd. She hadn't looked in my direction, not even once.

Maybe Cyndray hadn't ratted on me.

Putting my hand on the side of my seat, I pushed the lever up, reclining the seat back. Youth Encounter only lasted an hour and a half. I could camp out by myself that long—even longer if I had to, especially if it meant avoiding people.

I cracked the window open and closed my eyes. Thoughts of Hassan flooded my mind.

What if he'd gotten Finale pregnant? No way—it didn't make an ounce of sense. Not once had he tried to kiss me, even after my silent hints of wanting him to.

My heart flipped. But what if Finale was the reason Hassan always pulled back? What if she was really why he'd canceled our last two dates?

My insides quaked. If he was cheating on me, then I'd tell him—

Tap, tap, tap…

The rattle on my window startled me. I jerked my eyes open and twisted my head around.

"S'up, Shawty?"

I knotted my face. "Hassan?"

He grinned. "It's me in the flesh, baby. Whatcha doin' chillin' out here all by yourself? You taking a nap?"

I raised the seat lever back until I was upright. Hassan's warm smile, his dancing, light brown eyes—the color of sun glinting through a glass of clear apple juice—instantly dissolved my angst. My face relaxed. "Just thinking."

"Thinking? About what?"

"Um … stuff."

"What kind of stuff?" He gazed into my eyes, his bright smile dimming into a frown. "Are you alright?"

I swallowed, then looked at the steering wheel. *God help me be strong. I've gotta get to the bottom of this Finale thing.* I lifted my eyes. "We need to talk."

"O-kay. Am I in trouble?"

"You can decide that for yourself."

Hassan raised his eyebrows, then threw both hands in the air. "I'm all yours. Shoot."

I glanced around the parking lot. Mom was gone. Still wouldn't look good for anybody to see me sitting in my car, talking to a boy when I should be inside the church at Bible study. "Not here."

He jingled his keys. "My truck or your Prius?"

Better to leave my car in case Cyndray came looking for me, or if Mom, by chance, had noticed where I'd parked.

I opened my door and popped out. "Can we make it back before Youth Encounter lets out?"

"Of course. I mean … depending on where you wanna go and if my girl ain't acting moody today." He patted the hood of his truck.

"Just drive around the block. I'll walk back if I have to."

We skidded away from Redemption and circled the block.

Hassan parked on the far side of a convenience store. "Is this good enough?"

"Yeah," I said, wondering where to begin with my questions.

He lifted a mint from his pocket. "You get my message?"

"What message?" I asked, shaking my head when he offered the candy to me.

He unwrapped the peppermint and popped it into his mouth. "I texted you today."

"Sorry. I'm pretty bad about checking my phone."

"I see. Just wanted to know if we can hang out this Saturday."

My heart thumped with the boom of a million firecrackers, then fizzled flat like a burned-out sparkler. "You've already broken two dates."

He did a double-take, then settled his gaze on me. "Is that what's eating you? I told you I had to babysit my sisters."

"I know what you said, but—"

"But you obviously didn't believe me." He shook his head. "I'm not *that* guy."

I bit my bottom lip, warring fear of asking about Finale and worry of upsetting him even more.

His jaws clenched. "Not like I left you hanging or stood you up."

Tears welled up behind my eyelids, but I refused to let them fall. *Be strong, stand your ground.*

He tilted his chin down and furrowed his brows. "I don't have a lot of flexibility with going on dates. I thought you'd be different. Thought you'd understand my unique situation with my sisters. I gotta help Pops raise Khadijah and Nneka."

I swallowed the uneasiness. "You could've brought them along. I wouldn't have minded."

"Can't you see *I* would've minded?" The intensity in his voice strengthened. "I want a normal relationship like every other guy. When I'm with you, I don't want any distractions. I want to give you *all* of my attention."

Oh, God. How could I be so selfish?

I closed my eyes, forcing the tears back.

"Are you crying?" His voice settled against my silence. "Please don't do that."

"Okay," I whispered, trying to breathe a normal pace.

"If I were a swearing man, I'd swear on Moms's grave, I'm telling you the truth. I canceled our last two dates to babysit."

The sincerity of his words broke me. "I know. I believe you. It's just that I'm so mixed up inside."

He cupped my hands into his larger ones. "Look at me."

Please, no more letdown. I turned to face him, confirming the truth in his deep-set eyes.

"I know your tender heart is fragile. And I promise I will never, *ever*, do anything on purpose to hurt you."

My stomach did something funny. Something unnatural.

How could I possibly bring up Finale when Hassan was so kind, so sweet to me?

"It's not just you." I sighed. "It's my family too."

"Your parents' separation?"

"That ... and some other stuff."

"Rainy day stealing your sunshine?"

"Right now, feels like I'm in the midst of a storm."

Hassan scooted toward me. "Come closer."

I slid across the bench seat, where he tucked me into his arms. I rested my head against his shoulder, inhaling the fresh scent of his cologne mixed with his peppermint breath.

"Before Moms died, she said I had to be like an eagle."

"What did she mean by that?"

"Don't know." He gestured, and my head bounced against his hard chest. "But one day when I was missing her, I googled the eagle. Guess what happens to eagles in storms?"

I hunched my shoulders. "What?"

"If eagles get caught in the sky while it's thundering and lightning, they aren't even tossed about or taken off course."

"Really?" I tilted my head and searched Hassan's face. "Maybe they can predict the weather, so they just don't even fly if it's bad out. Wish humans could do that ... predict the bad storms and avoid them."

"The weather doesn't matter to an eagle. They fly above the storm. In fact, they use the winds of the storm to soar even higher. I think Moms meant when things get rough, use your circumstances to rise up."

How'd this boy from the 'hood, as Cyndray called him, get so smart? I basked in his embrace and looked up at the sky. Daylight had disappeared, and now black shimmering satin arced overhead, decorated by tiny rhinestone patterns.

"Janaclese?"

"Yes?"

"Are you ready to trust me?"

I nodded against Hassan's chest.

"Then give me another chance. Let's spend some quality time together on Saturday. Maybe the picnic we planned a long time ago?"

Store light spilled into his truck, illuminating the nightfall, casting a silhouette of his muscular frame on the dashboard and me lodged next to him. The peaceful cadence of his breathing swaddled me in comfort, absorbing all of my doubts about our relationship.

Hassan nuzzled closer, wrapping his warm arms around me even tighter. A single tear rolled from my eyes and landed on his arm.

"What's wrong?" He stared down at me.

"Nothing." I sniffled. "Nothing's wrong. Everything is so right."

I tilted my head upwards, taking in every inch of his handsome face. Even the flaw above his right eye added character. I reached up and traced the scar's outline, wanting to ask how he'd earned this badge of honor, yet not wanting to spoil the moment with unnecessary words.

Hassan smiled and leaned in, narrowing the gap between our faces.

My heart thudded, and a tingling sensation spread through my entire body like a flame of fire.

Eyes opened or closed? What was the perfect posture for a first kiss?

We nestled so close, I could almost taste the peppermint on Hassan's breath. I closed my eyes, puckered my lips ...

Ding.

"Is that your phone?" Hassan shifted his shoulder. "You better get that."

I didn't want to leave his cuddly cradle, but I bolted up and checked the clock. Bible study wasn't over 'til another ten minutes. Who was cutting in on my action?

Sliding my finger across the cell phone screen, I opened the message from Cyndray. *Miracle and Kehl-li aren't here. Where the heck are you?*

I pressed my palms against my eyes absorbing the wetness. "It's Cyndray. If she's late getting home, she'll be in hot water." I powered off my phone. "We have to go back now."

"Figures." Hassan chuckled. "You know your girl's a blocker, right?"

I laughed. "I was thinking the same thing."

Chapter 31

JANACLESE

I backed away from Cyndray's driveway, trying to recover the safe feeling I'd had in Hassan's arms.

When I told her I'd planned to go out with him on Saturday, she'd initially lost all patience, railing me about being too trusting. But then took deep breaths and calmed down. She apologized, then admitted she could learn a thing or two from me to overcome her own trust issues, something Dr. Beverly apparently uncovered during her counseling session.

Cyndray wanting to learn how to trust from me? I didn't know about that—not with how suspicious I'd been of Hassan. But after our talk, I'd decided to give him the benefit of the doubt. Maybe I'd feel better if I did the same with Aunt Alicia and Mom.

As I drove up the path to Dad's shack, a deer romped across the driveway, joining an entire herd camouflaged among the trees. Fireflies, dancing in the darkness, flitted their lights off and on like mating signals. Love was everywhere. I breathed in the fresh air, remembering the magic spark between Hassan and me.

Headlights shone in my rearview mirror only seconds after I turned my car off.

Kharee must've forgotten something important. When he slept at Dad's, he still let me have his bedroom. But he never came home this early even on weeknights.

I stepped from my car triggering the motion sensitive light to flash on. "What'd you forget?" I said over my shoulders.

"Nothing."

I whirled around, squinting. "Mom? I thought you were Kharee. Why're you here?"

She jerked her neck back and barked a surprised chuckle as if I had some nerve to be questioning her whereabouts.

"I meant to say ... is everything okay?" She still looked ridiculous in her pajamas.

"I'm fine. How are you?" She raised her hand to her forehead.

"Good," I said.

Where was this conversation going—did she want to know about her suits? Why I'd missed Youth Encounter? *What?*

"Tried to catch you before you left church tonight," she said, her right hand massaging her temple.

"Oh. Cyndray's mom wanted her home right after Bible study." I spoke as fast as I could, answering the next question before she asked. "Rushed off, drove her straight home so she wouldn't get into trouble."

She nodded, then passed me a small sheet of paper folded in half. "Give this to your Dad."

Feeling wary, I accepted it. What was it? Were they fighting again?

I headed up the steps, onto the porch, then turned back. "Dad's home. You can come in."

Mom massaged both of her temples, her tired eyes glistened in the light. "I need to get home. My head's about to explode."

The front door creaked open, and Dad barreled onto the porch.

"Thought I heard voices." He looked past me, a confused expression taking over his face. "Betima?"

"Here, Dad." I passed him the note. "It's from Mom."

"You drove all the way out here, in your pajamas, for this?" He shook his head, unfolded the note, and scanned the content. "The Paint the Park Pink event isn't until Saturday. I think I can remember what we discussed."

"I wrote it down because we always argue about what I've asked you to do."

"We don't *always* argue."

Pinching the bridge of her nose, Mom sighed. "Yes, we do, Franklin. I had to write it down."

"No, we don't."

"Yes, we do."

My gaze bounced back and forth like a needle in a time bomb, looking at Mom, then Dad, then again at Mom. "Are y'all gonna stand here disagreeing about not disagreeing?"

Dad pulled a pen from his pants pocket, jotted words on the paper, then shoved the note back to me. "Here, give this to your mother."

I scrunched my face. "Are you serious?"

Worn-out from the drama, I took the paper from Dad then reached out to brace my weight against the porch column. The column shifted, and I stumbled.

"Jana!" Dad raced into action, swooping me up like before. "I told you to be careful. That column's not safe."

"Then fix it." Mom's frustration sparked my memory of how she'd very often nagged Dad to repair broken appliances around the house.

"In time," he responded as he lowered my feet onto the porch.

Steadying my balance, I glanced at Dad's scribble—'I still LOVE you'. He'd used exclamation marks, capitalized every letter in the word 'love,' apparently trying to drive a point home to Mom.

I hastened to give her the note, practically tossing it because of my excitement.

She stared at the paper, her already moist eyes tearing even more. "A four-letter word?"

The way she sounded, you'd think he'd written a cuss word.

I zoomed in on their strange language—spoken and unspoken.

Mom stared at Dad. "What did I tell you about using big words you barely know the meaning of?"

My heart dipped. For the first time since they'd split up, I noticed something I hadn't seen before. The pain in her eyes wasn't just from the stress of a headache. Her facial expression reflected what I'd felt with Hassan—a wrestling match of loving someone who'd disappointed you. All this time, I'd blamed Mom for their separation. But now I wondered.

What had Dad done?

"I'll call you later." Mom turned to leave, mumbling something about her head.

"Betima, wait." Dad hustled down the steps after her, desperation ringing in his voice.

With a quick wave good night, I strolled into the house, slamming the screen door on my heels.

Would Mom choose to trust Dad like I'd done with Hassan, or was my parents' relationship too complicated for second chances?

Strangely, I didn't have the energy to worry about it.

Chapter 32

JANACLESE

No matter how much I'd cleaned my room at Dad's, the cheesy smell of my brother's feet refused to abandon the premises. I pulled the covers over my head, trying to escape the world of nachos, trying to soak in the eucalyptus calming fragrance I'd sprayed on the sheets.

But it wasn't working.

I tossed and turned in the rickety bed, creaking the springs and going in and out of sleep. Faces, familiar and unfamiliar, darted in and out of my dreams. I pressed my eyes together, determined not to open them till daylight. Finally, sleep overtook me.

"S'up, Shawty?"

"Nothing." I almost melted from the sight of Hassan's dreamy eyes.

He stared through me as if I hadn't said a word to him, yet he kept talking. "You ready?"

"Of course! I've been waiting for you all day," I said, excitement zooming inside.

Smiling, Hassan opened his arms and extended his hands. "Let's go."

I leaped toward him, smiling. Instead of extending his hand to me, he turned and embraced another girl. He dipped her like they were dancing, then kissed her.

I tripped and clattered to the floor. Was that Finale? Why were his lips plastered against hers?

"Hassan, what are you doing?" I asked.

He didn't answer me.

I scrambled from the floor, my fists opening and closing like a gulping fish out of water. "I trusted you. I trusted you!"

But he didn't look at me.

Hand in hand, he and Finale walked away, acting like they didn't see or hear me.

"Hassan!" I bolted straight up, my heart splitting my chest and sweat trickling down my face.

The room slowly came into focus. Only a dream. *Thank God!*

Calming my nerves, I settled back into a deep sleep.

Hassan and I held hands as we walked along a sandy beach. Out of nowhere, a giant wave toppled me, collapsing me into the water. Panic set in as I flailed my arms, battling to come up for air.

"Calm down. I got you." Hassan held onto me. "You're safe. Just stand up."

Wobbling, I clutched his hands and stood to face him a little embarrassed that the water only broke against my knees while I'd thought I was drowning.

Staring into his eyes, I saw nothing but tenderness. And I couldn't hold back what I was feeling. "Do you know how long I've—"

"Sshh …" He placed his index finger next to my lips, then removed his hand. His soft whisper landed in my ear. "Me too."

Cheek to cheek, I turned my face toward his.

"What the heck are you doing?" Cyndray's voice filtered between us. She yanked me away. "We've got to go."

My eyes flashed open.

Ugh. Why did Cyndray have to ruin my dream?

The bed felt like a steam bath. I folded the covers back. No wonder I was so hot, I'd fallen asleep in sweat pants.

Readjusting my position, I checked the time. The digital clock flashed 2:08 a.m.

I hated waking up in the middle of the night having to go. Eyes half closed, I ambled down the hallway, trying not to fully awaken. Maybe I could recapture that special moment with Hassan.

Low voices and a dim light streamed from beneath Dad's bedroom door, enough to light my path. He must've fallen asleep with the TV on again.

I quickly relieved my bladder, using the last of the toilet paper. Now I'd have to cut on the light to replace the roll. After a quick survey, I discovered no rolls under the sink or in the cabinet.

Sauntering down the hall, I tapped lightly on Dad's bedroom door before attempting to enter. No need to awaken him for a non-emergency.

I turned the knob.

The door was stuck. *Weird.*

I braced my weight against the door, but it didn't budge.

Why would Dad lock the door when we respected closed doors? Was he okay?

"Dad?" I whispered, then banged the door when there was no response.

He must've turned the TV off because the room was dead quiet, other than the shuffling of feet.

Dad appeared in the doorway. "What is it, Pumpkin?"

"Out of toilet paper. Sorry to wake you."

"Uh, no problem. I'll get it."

"I got it," I said, attempting to push past him.

He sidestepped and blocked my entry.

I twisted my face at him. Why didn't he want me in his bedroom?

An awkward silence hovered between us. What was that odd look in his eyes?

I swallowed. *No, God. No.* I swung around and sped toward my room.

Dad's voice chased after me. "Jana, I—"

"I got it!" I yelled, and I wasn't referring to toilet tissue.

I stalked to my room, grabbed my purse, and ran out the back door.

Chapter 33

JANACLESE

Parked at the 24-hour Zippy Mart, about five miles from Dad's shack, I replayed the night's event in my mind, unable to make sense of what I'd seen and heard.

Where could I run to? Who could I call at this late hour?

With trembling hands, I pushed the power button on my cell phone. Three missed calls from Dad displayed. No way I'd talk to him right now.

Kharee was probably awake, but I didn't want to talk to a guy. Maybe Khara would listen and understand my rage.

I punched in the numbers to call my big sister.

The phone rang several times before she finally answered. "Janaclese? What's up?"

Music played in the background, along with several high energy voices. Was she in summer school partying?

"What's the matter?" She repeated her question with urgency. "Everything okay at home?"

She had to know something wasn't right if I called her in the first place, let alone ringing her phone at this hour.

"No," I managed to croak, my raw voice hoarse from all the crying.

"You're scaring me. Is Dad sick?"

"Worse," I said, sniffling.

Khara yelled for the people in the background to be quiet, and the music volume abruptly shut down.

"Put Dad on the phone, Janaclese." Her shrill voice trembled.

"I can't. I left." My insides crunched together.

"You left?" Her patience seemed thin. "Where are you at 2:30 in the morning?"

I fumbled through the story, telling Khara where I was and why I ran from the scene.

Silence settled on the line before she finally spoke. "There's gotta be some misunderstanding. Dad would never do something like that."

My stomach screamed in pain, but I was quiet. How could I confirm what she said after what I'd seen with my own eyes?

"Yeah, he wouldn't do that to Mom, especially not with any of us right there in the house." She sounded unsure like she really needed to convince herself that I was wrong.

My phone beeped. I glanced at the caller ID—Dad was calling again.

"Is that your phone?" Nervousness rang in her voice.

"It's him." I didn't even want to call him 'Dad.'

"He's probably worried. You shouldn't be out this late, anyway." Khara sighed. "Just go back, okay?"

"No. Not by myself." Like a child afraid of the dark, I didn't want to face this alone. I needed someone to hold my hand. "Can you come with me?"

"*Now?* Kharee's closer. Call him."

"No." My voice was firm.

Silence lingered a few seconds before she conceded. "Oh, all right. I'm coming, but I'm calling Kharee too."

Khara and Kharee always relied on the buddy system in tough times. I used to wish I was a twin like them. They'd battle like unrelated adversarial species, but if anything major ever happened, they stuck closer than bark on a tree.

"What about Mom?" Khara cut into my thoughts.

"What about her?" I asked. "She wasn't feeling well earlier when she came by the shack. You think I should wake her up?"

"No, not until we have the facts. Things aren't always what they seem."

How many times had I heard that in the last few months, even uttered those very words myself? But with all the lies and betrayal, trust wasn't coming easy.

"Janaclese, stop worrying. You don't wanna make yourself sick over this. Remember your stomach migraines."

Too late for that. My intestines gnawed themselves.

"Trust me. You don't have to protect Mom. If Dad is having an affair, Betima Mitchell already knows. She knows everything."

I'd been half-asleep when I went to Dad's room, but I was pretty sure of what I saw. Then again, maybe my thoughts were exaggerated. *God, I hoped so.*

But what if Khara was right? For sure, nothing slipped past Mom. Could this explain the disappointment in her eyes I'd finally noticed? How could our family be so screwed up?

I'd timed Khara's expected arrival to the shack just right. She pulled into the driveway only seconds behind me.

As soon as I opened my car door, Khara glided over to my Prius, her diamond necklace emitting sparkles into the night. "You okay?"

I touched my bare neck, realizing I'd forgotten to wear my pendant again. I peeped at her through swollen eyes. "Thanks for coming."

She hugged me. "No problem. We're gonna get to the bottom of this once and for all."

I wrapped my arms around my waist, following Khara into the yard, my head down.

When she came to a sudden halt, I almost collided with her.

She squinted. "Did you call Mom?"

"No. Why?" I asked.

She pointed to the side of the house. "Isn't that her car sticking out over there?"

My heart pounded faster when I saw the back of the Volvo, its red taillights reflected by the motion sensitive porch light.

"Maybe Dad called Mom because he was worried about you," Khara said.

"Or maybe Kharee told her what was happening. You called him, right?" I stared at her.

"Yeah, but he agreed we shouldn't say anything just yet." She rolled her eyes, then narrowed them at me. "You said Mom was here earlier, and she didn't feel well. Was she driving her Volvo?"

My foggy mind raced. Had Mom driven her car or the minivan? I shrugged. "I don't remember."

"Well try to remember, because I'm gonna be more than hot for coming all the way over here because of your vivid imagination."

Khara's temper flared. She was no-nonsense like Mom, though she'd never admit it. In fact, she worked overtime to prove how different they were.

"If Mom was in Dad's bedroom, then why didn't he just say that? And … and why didn't I see her car when I left?" I argued to justify my actions, but deep down I knew the answers.

Probably because I'd left out the backdoor on the opposite side of the house in a blind rage. But why mention that now?

We eased into the shack.

Dad snatched his head up, anxiety coloring his face. "Young lady, don't ever run out of this house like that again!" He held the cordless phone in his hand and gestured it toward me. "And from now on, you're gonna keep your cell phone on and start answering the phone whenever your mom or I call you."

Was he seriously scolding me at a moment like this? Lowering my eyes, I stared at the swirly pattern on the carpet.

"Janaclese, do you hear me talking to you?" His voice was low, yet stern.

For sixteen years, I'd heard how my chipper spirit had come from Dad. People said we both had an easy, automatic smile that revealed the dimples he'd stamped on me like his very own fingerprint. But in this chaotic moment, all of those common threads that knitted us together were threatening to break.

Kharee bolted through the front door. "What's going on?"

"That's what we're here to find out." Khara plopped onto the loveseat, and her eyes seemed to challenge Dad. "Where's Mom?"

"She's sleeping—"

"No, I'm not … at least not anymore." Mom straggled from the bedroom in her blue satin pajamas, curled onto the couch, then eyed everyone in the room. "Somebody called a family meeting?"

"Not me." A three-person chorus, minus me, responded to her question.

I stood silent.

"Then somebody mind telling me why we're all up at 3:00 in the morning?"

All eyes stared in my direction.

Mom shifted against the arm of the couch. "Janaclese?"

"Well, I … I thought." The right words stuck in my mouth.

"I'm listening," Mom said.

I pointed to the bedroom door. "It was locked. I heard voices, and I assumed it was the TV, but Dad wouldn't turn on the light … or let me come in." Why was I rambling like a senseless idiot? "I needed toilet paper for the other bathroom."

"I see." Mom was too calm. She nodded toward the twins. "And why're you two here at this late hour?"

"Tsk!" Khara clicked her tongue the way she did when she was either disgusted or annoyed. She crossed her arms and rolled her neck. "Your favorite daughter accused her father of having an affair, said Dad was cheating on you big time."

Kharee burst into out-of-control laughter. He galloped toward Dad and extended his fist. "You got game, player."

Dad's eyes bulged from his face. I expected smoke to seep from his ears.

Kharee whipped his fist back. "Whoa, big fellow. Sounds so ridiculous, it's uber-humorous."

But Dad didn't laugh. And he hadn't said much since Mom first entered the room.

At dizzying speed, I spun around and headed toward the back bedroom.

"Janaclese. Come back in here. We need to talk." Dad's slow, deliberate words buckled me. My legs froze.

They expected me to be a part of an 'adult' conversation? I swiveled around.

"Sit." He pointed to the ottoman.

I plopped down on the squeaky, leather footstool beneath Khara, who sat cross-legged on the loveseat. Kharee hovered above her, leaning an elbow against her chair.

Dad shook his head. "What kind of man do you think I am?"

Before any of us could answer, Mom jumped to his defense. "Your father's a good man. He was taking care of me. My migraine was setting in fast, and I almost blacked out. Franklin took my keys so I couldn't drive home."

My mouth slackened as I bent forward. Why would that have been such a big secret?

I swallowed before speaking. "But he wouldn't let me come into the bedroom or switch on the light."

"Honey, my migraine headaches are different from the ones you have in your stomach. It's been years since I've had an episode, but when they occur, I have extreme sensitivity to lights and sound."

The hurt in Dad's eyes was evident. "Cheating on your Mom? Why would any of you rush to that conclusion? Haven't I set a good example of being a man of integrity?"

"I told her she was being silly, snatching me out of bed in the wee hours. I've got class first thing in the morning."

I glared sideways at Khara. Don't know why she was acting all innocent and studious like she wasn't partying when I called—probably the only reason she agreed to go to summer school.

Mom sighed. "You shouldn't feel too bad, Franklin. I believe Janaclese suspected me of the same thing last month."

The swirls in the carpet meshed together into one ugly pattern.

"But why an affair?" Dad's disappointed voice shook me. "We have more respect for each other than that. Just because we're separated doesn't mean we're not still married."

I spoke up. "You guys seem to get one step closer to getting back together, then you take two steps backward like you're headed toward divorce. You're always fighting."

"Not *always*," Dad emphasized the word like he'd done with Mom. "If we were considering a divorce, we'd tell you."

"Yeah? Well, you never told us you were considering separating." Spontaneous tears flowed down my cheeks. "Why'd you split up in the first place?"

Mom hoisted to her knees and raised the window behind the couch.

Did she feel the heat too? After sweating in the hot seat, I appreciated the cool nighttime breeze.

Zapping noises from mosquitos being fried by the Bug Zapper filtered through the screen, erasing the silence among us.

Kharee finally spoke. "Dad forgot to cut the grass and trim the hedges. Mom hates that kinda stuff—that's what happened. That's why they separated."

"No, from what I remember, it was the dishwasher." Khara's faced looked stressed, and she clutched her diamond necklace.

Had she ever taken off her pendant like me, or did she keep her promise to wear it despite Dad's broken promise to always be there for us?

"Dad never replaced the broken part on the dishwasher." Khara pulled at her gold chain, threatening to snap it loose.

I didn't want to hear any more speculations. I wanted the truth from the horse's mouth. "Why'd y'all split up?"

"Your dad left me." Mom spoke through clenched teeth. Batting her eyelashes, she looked away.

"Betima, you asked me to leave, so I left," Dad corrected her.

"I was frustrated." Mom's voice was low. "You weren't supposed to actually *leave*."

Dad furrowed his brows. "How was I supposed to know that?"

Tears streamed down Khara's face. "Are you kidding me? Our entire family has been traumatized because of *your* miscommunication? I was miserable being home from college ... trying to decide where to spend my holidays!"

I knew Khara avoided coming home from school every chance she got, but I didn't know she'd taken their breakup as hard as I had.

After all, she was still wearing the necklace Dad gave her, holding on to his promise.

Kharee reached down and squeezed Khara's shoulder, then addressed our parents. "Dad, how many times have you told me not to listen to a woman's words, but pay attention to her heart? And Mom, you always told us to 'say whatever we mean and to mean whatever we say.'"

More awkward silence saturated the living room. Quiet, yet not peaceful.

Mom's contorted face mirrored the unspoken pain we all shared. "I'm so sorry. I never meant to rip our family apart."

Dad scooted onto the couch next to Mom, lacing his left fingers through hers, their matching wedding bands meshing together. "I'm sorry too. We were both wrong."

My heart thumped. Hadn't she stopped wearing her ring because of Mr. Clean? Isn't that what she'd told me in the garden?

"I ... I ..." The blunt remark lay trapped in my mouth. Maybe now wasn't a good time to remind her of what she'd said.

Sounds from a croaking frog interrupted my thoughts. A mournful howl outside the window sent creepy chills down my spine. Hard to believe that earlier this same night, I'd experienced the sappy sweetness of love, where everything in nature mimicked romance.

Apparently, romance wasn't all there was to love. How could love be so complicated, so hard?

Now that the door was opened, my family walked through it. I gazed at Dad and Mom, Kharee and Khara—questioning, explaining, clarifying, and even yelling and crying. The brokenness we'd suffered left us all crippled, limping along the best we could.

But this seemed a moment for healing, yet I couldn't concentrate.

My mind floated in and out of the room to Hassan, the safety net who padded my heart, eased my tension and allowed me to rest despite my family tension. I needed him to whisk me away, and day-dreaming was the next best thing to escape.

Awkward laughter pulled me back into the room.

"I followed the money," Kharee was saying, in response to why he'd moved away from home and made Dad's place his crash pad.

My heart staggered. Maybe they wouldn't ask me the same question.

"Mom's purse strings are too tight. The honeys expect a brother to have more in his pockets than lint balls." Kharee grinned. "Besides, Dad lets me roll in his Corvette. You won't even let me see the inside of your Volvo."

Mom shooed his words with a waving hand. "If you'd get a real job ..."

"I work." He pointed to a small crack in the wall that started at the ceiling and ended at the window's top edge. "That'll disappear during the shack-attack."

"Is that what y'all call this construction project?" She laughed, looking up at the ceiling. "While you're up there, fix the roof and make the rain spots go away, and then I'll be sold."

"Can I hold you to that?" A gleam lit Dad's eyes.

Mom's eyes stretched wider than the full moon. She'd only spent the night because of her emergency. She wasn't a snob, but Dad lived liked the people she helped. Her expression was priceless, and it turned the tide to gut-wrenching laughter.

I sat arms crossed. I didn't know why forgiveness wasn't coming so easily for me. I'd been ready to hang Hassan out to dry, but one conversation had brought us closer. Could I trust that this was happening with my family?

What had Hassan said about rainstorms making you better? Did you ride the waves to overcome? I wracked my brain trying to remember his exact words.

"You and Dad do that?" Khara's high pitch directed my attention back into the room.

Mom cleared her throat. "Uh ... yeah. How do you think y'all got here?"

"That's disgusting." Khara screwed up her nose.

Kharee hid his face behind a throw pillow as his shoulders shook.

And my mind scrambled to catch up on what I'd missed.

"What's so funny?" Dad asked.

"It's like we know it, but now that we *know* it." Khara shook her head. "It's just disgusting."

La la la … la la la. I wanted to plug my ears and drown their voices like a three-year-old. But somehow, I'd obviously managed to cross that invisible line of being mature enough to handle such topics.

Mom raised her eyebrows at the three us. "What's disgusting is the thought of my unmarried children engaging in premarital sex. And I pray that isn't the case."

Did she really pray about stuff like that?

Mom glanced at Dad, prompting him to speak up. "I agree with your mom. She and I are the only married people in this room. Sex should only happen in the context of marriage."

What triggered this conversation? Was it the assumptions about their presumed love affairs?

No questions about where my parents stood on sex, but they hadn't mentioned a word about saving your kisses for marriage. If it was an individual choice, I'd already decided mine.

My thoughts skipped to Hassan. Four more days 'til Saturday, our special date.

Warmth layered my stomach, but the heat from four pairs of gazing eyes burned my face.

What'd I miss this time? Were they talking about me?

"Humph," Mom said. "She's always been creative, but lately her vivid imagination has soared to greater heights."

Khara yawned and stretched her limbs. "Yeah, but if Janaclese hadn't let her fantasies run wild, then we wouldn't have spent the last three hours in an impromptu family meeting, solving this issue. When was the last time we talked like this?"

Suddenly, I noticed hints of daylight snaking through the window. We'd talked, cried, and laughed through the night. Suppose it was about time for sincere apologies and forgiveness. I mustered the words. "Sorry, guys. I didn't mean to interrupt your sleep, or cause any confusion."

"Actually, pumpkin." Dad winked at me. "You've helped bring clarity to a whole lot of muddle."

He stared at Mom for a few seconds. She stared back at him. And I gawked at them both, trying to figure out their non-verbal language. Finally, Mom squinted, then nodded her head, smiling.

A wide grin mapped across Dad's face before he turned to his three children. "I know you think we don't share decisions that affect us as a family. We've made some mistakes, and we've apologized—to each other and now to you. We hope you can forgive us for our poor model of what we believe is a God-ordained marriage." He sucked in a deep breath. "We've been talking … dating, really …"

My heart pumped like a rapid, African drumbeat.

"… trying to sort out how we got off track and map out the rest of our lives together."

Faster and faster, the drum rolled in my chest.

"How do you guys feel about us reconciling?"

Clash.

There it was. Cymbals clanged together, crushing my jittery heart.

When your prayers are finally answered, it was supposed to be a good thing. Perhaps even the happiest moment in life.

Then, why wasn't that the case for me?

Chapter 34

CYNDRAY

I stood at the Hen Pen register taking an order for my pimply-faced customer.

"I'll have a number four, with a Diet Coke. Oh, and make it large."

The last thing she needed was a large soda to wash down an equally large pod of greasy fries and chicken. But I wasn't supposed to say that. Probably not think it either. I filled the order just in time for my fifteen-minute break.

"Be right back." I pushed my timecard into the metal slot to clock out of work. "Going on break."

Strolling past the cash registers and onto the opposite side of the customer's ordering counter, I entered the mall, happy for a few moments of freedom. Not much mid-week traffic in the eatery compared to the weekend, but still, on days like this, I'd rather not be working.

I dialed Janaclese's number, expecting to leave a short message to convince her to attend Redemption Temple's lock-in with me. Ever since my counseling meeting with Dr. Beverly, I'd toyed with the idea of going, but I wasn't keen on going alone.

Her cell's ringing sang in my ear.

"Hello?" Janaclese's chipper voice sailed through the line.

My knees buckled, and I steadied myself. She'd actually answered her phone?

"Cyndray? Are you there?"

Any slight movement could knock me over. I became a statue.

"Why are you calling and not texting? Cyndray, is everything okay?"

"Gimme a minute. I'm still processing the shock of not getting a recorded greeting. Is this really Janaclese Mitchell?"

"It's me. Surprised you didn't text. Dad told me under no circumstances am I to turn off my cell phone. And what's worse is that I have to answer every time he or Mom calls. Can you believe that? I'm so bummed that he's decided to be so strict."

"About time you listen to somebody," I interjected.

"Well, I don't like wasting my battery. If I really needed to call someone, then my phone might be dead …"

Didn't she have a charger? We'd discussed that before. I checked my watch. Ten more minutes before my break ended and I hadn't had a chance to tell her why I'd called in the first place.

Janaclese rambled on. "And I don't like my parents having access to me every second of the day. You know what I mean?"

"Um-hm." I understood that but wished she'd finish yapping.

"You're never gonna believe the bomb they dropped on me last night. Well, actually this morning. My entire family—I mean me, my parents, and my twin siblings, that is—talked all night long. Totally unbelievable what they said. I'm still trying to grasp it."

"Come up for air, will you?" Janaclese was on a roll. Was she nervous about something?

I checked my watch. Five more minutes, and I hadn't even mentioned why I'd called her in the first place.

"Mom and Dad are getting back together."

Though her tone was flat, excitement shot through me. "What? That's great news!"

"The timing is all off. Why'd they decide to get their act together now?"

Scowling, I tapped my foot. Hadn't we all prayed for her parent's reconciliation? Why'd she seem so panicked? I pressed the phone to my ear.

"With Mom around all the time, no way I'll be able to talk to Hassan late at night—let alone hang out with him. Dad doesn't watch me like a hawk. *But Mom?* I'll have to dress in black and slip in and out of my window like a cat burglar."

"She's not that bad," I said.

"You've never lived with her. Multiply the little control you've witnessed by one thousand. Then you'll have a remote clue of the freedom I've just lost. A year and a half ago, one decision ruined my life. With Hassan, I finally found a way to be happy. Now here they go again. One decision and my life's on the brink of disaster again."

Janaclese's drama struck a nerve. "Are you *that* pressed to get with Hassan, you'd prefer your parents not getting back together?"

"Of course not!" Shock registered in her voice. "I'm not saying that. I'm just saying I don't see how I can date Hassan *and* live with both of my parents."

"Date Hassan? Is that what y'all are doing?"

"I told you we're planning to hang out this Saturday."

"Oh. He hasn't called to cancel, yet?" Sarcasm was too tempting.

"Don't hate." Janaclese's weak chuckle sounded doubtful.

She'd been around me too long. Was even starting to talk like me. "I ain't hating. Just hoping you face the facts. Did you ask him about Finale?"

"She never came up."

"Uh, weren't you supposed to purposefully bring up her name?"

"Things aren't always what they seem."

"Yeah! All the *more* reason to ask Hassan about his ex."

She was quiet on the other end. Hard to understand why all of sudden she wanted to believe in Hassan without a shadow of doubt. Anyway, she'd mentioned something about painting the park with her mom on Saturday. How did she intend to wiggle out of that for a date with Hassan?

I checked my watch. Sheesh, only one minute left.

"I gotta go." I could barely disguise the irritation in my voice.

"Are you mad at me?"

Yes, for being borderline stupid. "My break's almost over."

"I didn't realize you were at work. Why'd you let me hog the conversation? I'm sure you called for something. What's up?"

"Never mind."

"Cyndray?" She hesitated. "I didn't mean to fall in love. It just happened, you know?"

"Yeah, whatever," I said.

"I know you're worried I might get hurt. But Hassan promised he'd *never* do that to me."

"And you believe that?" Like Hassan was God, claiming to never leave or forsake her.

"I believe in him."

Why couldn't Janaclese see she was changing? Maybe it wasn't Hassan's fault that she was sneaking around donating suits, missing Bible study, doing anything to get a glimpse of her man. But the old Janaclese would *never* deceive her parents. And she wouldn't have mixed feelings about them getting back together either.

"I'd feel a lot better if you told your mom the truth. It's the right thing to do."

"Oh. Speaking of the right thing to do, I've been meaning to talk to you about apologizing to Kehl-li."

I grimaced. Why did Your Righteousness have to act like she was the only one who knew what was appropriate? "I get it. It's easier to see the telephone pole in somebody else's eyes, right?"

"Huh?"

"I've already decided to set things straight with Kehl-li."

"Oh." She sounded surprised. "Well, I'm happy to hear you plan to resolve it because I don't want the beef between you and Kehl-li to affect me and Miracle again. I'm wondering what's going on with her. You think her mama found out what happened last weekend?"

I sighed. "How am I s'posed to know what's going on at the Rand mansion? Sheesh. You better worry about yourself." I hoped my sharp tone would hit a nerve. *Whatever you do in the dark, will come to the light.*

"Miss Cyndray, when'd you start quoting Scriptures?"

"When you prayed I'd be more like Jesus."

"I never prayed that."

"Well, somebody must've." I checked my watch—ten seconds. "Gotta go!"

I powered off and hustled back to the Hen Pen. Next break, I'd apology to Kehl-li. *Sheesh.*

Chapter 35

CYNDRAY

"So, Cyndray ... how did the last assignment go?" Dr. Beverly raised her eyebrows.

I sat on the orange couch that was becoming my usual spot in her office. "You wouldn't believe I had to use that breathing technique as soon as I left here last time. But I've been switching the channel."

"Good. Is it helping your decision-making?"

"I don't know. I broke down and apologized to Kehl-li the other day. Figured if I kept thinking of her as an enemy, then I'd continue behaving like she was one."

"I'm proud of the progress you're making so quickly. Readiness to change makes a big difference in therapy."

I settled deeper into my seat. "Well, I don't think I *feel* any differently about Kehl-li yet."

"I see."

The gleam in Dr. Beverly's eyes made me wonder if my feelings about Kehl-li would eventually change too. But she didn't say more on the matter.

"Today, I want to get a picture of any disturbing experiences you may have had. I need for you to take a few minutes to recall any events that may have been upsetting ... that have caused you to be angry."

"That should be easy since people claim I'm mad all the time."

"No one knows you better than you know yourself, Cyndray. People's perceptions aren't always accurate. And sometimes what we respond to isn't really the culprit." She hesitated, then pulled out a white sheet of paper. "In terms of this exercise, the event could be something that happened recently or something that happened years ago. What stands out to you?"

The windy night in the hotel swept through my mind. I shivered.

"Are you cold?"

I stared straight ahead.

"I know some things are difficult to talk about, but I need you to be as honest and open as you can. As a reminder, everything you discuss with me is confidential."

It was great knowing that Dr. Beverly wasn't like Dr. Connel who had to share her assessment of me with Judge Chan. I bit my lip. "*Everything?*"

"Everything. Unless you report child abuse, hurting yourself … or someone else for that matter," she quickly added. "In that case, I'm bound by law to get you to safety."

I nodded.

"When you're ready, tell me the event you're thinking of."

I swallowed. "He was so drunk. Tommy Dawg is what my friend called him. I can still smell the stench of alcohol and cigarettes on his breath."

"Was Tommy Dawg a friend you trusted?"

"I didn't even know him. I was sneaking off to a hotel party with Danielle. She's the friend who betrayed me." The shivering had stopped, and now I pulled at my collar for air. "I told her I'd changed my mind about wanting to hang out, but she wouldn't listen, and Tommy Dawg wouldn't let me leave."

"That sounds frustrating. Did Tommy hurt you … or make you do something you didn't want to do?"

"His hands were all *over* me. He thrust his body against mine, jamming my back into the wall." I closed my eyes and arched forward, feeling the hardness of the door, seeing the gun in his hand. "I don't think I'd ever seen a real-life gun before."

"A gun was involved?"

"Yeah. Tommy tried to force me to have sex. Don't know why he wouldn't believe I was a virgin." Tears threatened to fall. I searched Dr. Beverly's face, "I don't go around hooking up with strangers."

She nodded. "I know."

My breathing slowed. I don't know how she could possibly know that, but it felt good hearing her say it.

"Did he force himself on you?"

"He tried, but I got away. I tricked him into thinking I needed time to get ready. When I came out of the bathroom, he'd fallen asleep." I sucked in a gulp of air. "I must've crouched in the woods for hours waiting on Mrs. Samson to come get me."

"Alicia Samson? Pastor's wife?"

"Yeah. She used to be my mentor."

"I see." She paused. "Well, tell me, how does your story end?"

"I'm here. I survived. Just wish I could kick him. HARD!" I lowered my head. "Should probably kick myself."

"The lingering anger is only one chapter in your story. Do you feel responsible for what happened?"

"Who else can I blame? I shouldn't have lied to my parents or disobeyed them." I pulled at my WWJD bracelet. "Just gotta be careful next time."

"Careful?" She squinted. "When lying to your folks?"

"Careful not to trust anybody. Careful not to let anybody touch me."

"Hmmm ... how's that working for you?"

I twisted my lips. Getting mad when the officer touched me is what landed me in anger management therapy.

"Did you know guilt makes people feel angry?"

I slouched in my seat. "People touching me makes me angry."

"And people, like Kehl-li, always talking about boys and kissing and sex makes you angry too, right?"

I could feel my heart thumping in my stomach. *What is she getting at?*

Dr. Beverly left her desk and sat next to me. "Look at this." She shared a grid she'd drawn with lines connecting several circles. She pointed her pencil to a box. "Here's where you are." She lifted her pencil and pointed to another area on the page. "Here's where you want to be."

Based on her chart, I wasn't just dealing with anger. Underneath that circle, she'd placed guilt, shame, self-doubt, and a feeling of no control over my situation—which was spot on. Otherwise, I wouldn't be in mandated therapy.

"I think your anger is motivated by guilt. It seems that when someone touches you, it triggers negative memories of a situation where you felt little control. Does that sound right?"

"I don't know, maybe." I touched one of the lines. I wanted to hear more.

"Lying to your parents wasn't a good idea, but had you known how that party would turn out, would you have gone anyway?"

"No! Never!"

"Then you have nothing to be ashamed of. What Tommy did wasn't your fault. You trusted Danielle and she failed you. The entire world is not like Danielle and Tommy."

"In my mind, I know that."

"Every day, you have an opportunity to write more to your story." She traced a line with her finger. "And make decisions that get you from here to here."

"How?" I really wanted that future box of no anger.

"Your assignment this week is forgiveness."

I jumped up from the couch. "No, I won't do it." She couldn't expect me to call Danielle. *And Tommy Dawg?* That was out of the question!

"I can't call Danielle or Tommy to forgive them. I won't do it."

"Not other people. I'm talking about forgiving yourself."

"Oh." I breathed a sigh of relief.

"That may be harder than you think, but you'll get there." She motioned for me to return to my seat. "The other issue is trust. Can we work on trusting one person you're unsure about this week?"

I plopped down on the couch and quirked an eyebrow. "Like boy-crazy Kehl-li?"

"Maybe. Seems pretty normal to talk about boys at your age."

So being uncomfortable talking about kissing and sex at my age is abnormal? Maybe I was right about being the strange and crazy one.

Dr. Beverly rambled on about trusting people, but my mind was so full, I only caught snatches.

It made me wonder how had Janaclese been able to trust Hassan so quickly? At the beginning of the summer, he was a stranger. Now she was in love. *God, what's wrong with me?* I couldn't even get close enough to anybody to trust them.

Dr. Beverly seemed to notice I'd grown quiet. "Maybe not Ke-hl-li. Just whoever you think is deserving of trust, but you've withheld it. Doesn't have to be a big thing like divulging a hidden secret, but something small."

"Okay." I had no idea how this assignment was going to work.

Chapter 36

JANACLESE

"Eck!" I wrinkled my nose. "This is disgusting."

I stared at the fuzzy green substance on the circular metal blade in the juicer. Mold along with remnants of fruit and vegetable pulp stared back at me.

"Who forgot to clean the juicer?" I screamed for everybody within earshot to hear.

Nobody answered.

The steady thump of a basketball bounced in the yard as Dad and Kharee engaged in a little father-son challenge.

I peeked out the window, lured away from my anger by their laughter. Why couldn't our entire family remain as close as Dad and Kharee?

"Booyah!" Dad slam dunked the ball into the goal, then gave an exaggerated swagger. "What you know 'bout old school, young blood?"

Kharee waved Dad away. "That was smooth, but let me teach you some new skills."

Turning away from the window, I scooted to the fridge and pulled out the pint of fresh strawberries, keeping my eye on the clock. My plan was to make chicken salad and freshly squeezed fruit juice for my picnic with Hassan. But if I had to keep cleaning everything first, there might not be time.

Twenty minutes to go. *God, I hope he doesn't have a last minute cancellation.*

As I added water to the blender and swished it around, the mold floated upwards, showing the gunked blades. I held my breath at the smell. This was gonna take forever.

Behind me, the screen door slammed. Khara came sailing through the front door.

"Where's Dad?" She stared at me like I kept Dad hidden in my pocket. "I need to talk to him."

"Out back balling with Kharee," I said, practicing my hip vernacular.

She grabbed a spoon and scooped out some chicken salad from the container on the table.

I poked her. "Hey! That's for not for you."

"Chill-lax. I'm just taste testing so you don't poison anybody with your lack of cooking know-how."

"Well?" I waited for her approval.

"Not bad." She gave a slow nod. "Actually pretty good for an amateur cook. You taking it over to Mom's Paint the Park Pink event?"

My heart dipped. I turned and started to rinse the strawberries, not wanting to see Khara's judgment. "I'm not going."

The spoon clacked on the counter.

"Mom said she needed *all* of our help."

"I know, but I work for the Center all week. And today, I just wanna hang loose."

"Probably smart not to go. Me-maw says it's gonna rain—might even storm."

Khara's conversation was casual, but my heart pumped like we were speaking about something intense.

"Only a slight chance according to the News Channel forecast," I said, dropping lemon slices and a few strawberries into the juicer. "Besides, rain has been forecasted for three days, and we haven't had anything but a drizzle."

"Tell that to Me-maw's arthritis."

I spun around, dripping water from my hands to the floor. "Late afternoon or evening showers?"

Khara scoffed. "She's not *that* accurate, but it's coming." She lowered her head and studied me. "Why're you so jumpy and wishy-washy?"

"I'm not!" I grabbed a dish towel, dried my hands, then placed the remaining strawberries into a reusable Tupperware container.

She pointed at my chest. "Exhibit one, you're wearing your necklace again."

I clutched the diamond pendant dangling from my neck. "So? I promised Dad."

She chuckled. "That didn't stop you from taking it off before. You think he didn't notice?"

"He only said something last week," I said, wondering why she was so concerned.

Was it a crime I needed proof to trust Mom and Dad would really get back together?

Ding.

I raced across the room and grabbed my cell phone. Message from Hassan. He'd better not stand me up.

What's ur address? I'll pick u up.

Good—we were still on. Bad—he wanted to pick me up.

I texted back. *Thought I'd come to ur place.*

He responded in a flash. *Goin' deep in the woods. Truck's better.*

My fingers couldn't type fast enough. *Will park my Prius and hop in with you.*

You sure? OK.

Safer to risk leaving my car unattended in Red Hill than have Hassan meet my folks for the first time today. I was about to set my phone down when I noticed a text from Cyndray.

Paintballing w/guys in one hour. Coming?

I responded. *Can't. Date's still on—YAY!*

"Must be something mighty important the way you jumped to that phone."

I turned and found Khara smirking. I blinked, astonished. Just that quickly, I'd forgotten she was in the room and that we were in the middle of a conversation.

"Group of kids from Unity going paintballing." Hopefully, that unrelated tidbit would throw her off.

"So you want me to tell Mom you decided to go paintballing?" She stretched her eyes and pointed at me. "Neat freak you and messy paintball?"

Best to ignore her direct question and not even bother arguing that she was more obsessed with cleanliness, like Mom, than me.

"Whatever happened between you and Kohl?" I asked.

She expelled a nervous chuckle. "We broke up. Why'd you ask that?"

"Just wondering if you stopped being friends because Mom didn't like him."

"Mom didn't like him? Hmm ... I never knew that." Her scrunched face relaxed. "Found out Kohl wasn't a Christian. We were unequally yoked."

"But he went to church with us all the time."

"You can swim in the ocean every day, but that doesn't make you a fish. Kohl was *only* interested in a relationship with *me*, not God."

"Oh. I see." At least Hassan was a Christian ... I think. We attended the same church, but did I really know him? "How do you *really* get to know somebody ... um, like a boy you think you like?"

"What do you mean by *really* getting to know a boy?" Khara narrowed her eyes. "You haven't been—"

"No!" I hadn't meant to be so adamant.

She gave me a doubtful look. "Then how'd you know what I was about to ask?"

"I don't. But if you're talking about being physical, I've never even kissed a boy." Though the guilt of having thought about kissing stabbed me.

"Then calm down."

Why'd I even ask her anything? Bringing up the subject of boys only roused her suspicion. I focused on packing my basket.

"Communicating and spending time together are ways to get to know somebody. But I usually check a guy's wallet. And my girl-friends think the best way to study anybody's habits is to ramble through their garbage."

I folded napkins and placed them inside. "Gross."

"Well, you asked." She bit into a strawberry and closed her eyes, savoring its taste before flicking its hull into the garbage. "Dad still out back?"

I peeked out the window again. "Yeah, he's cleaning the grill. Guess Mom put that on his 'to do' list for today."

Khara pushed through the screen door, then circled back. "By the way. Just so you don't mistake me as your air-headed big sister, I know you're not going paintballing with that picnic basket."

I gulped, feeling my eyes widened with fear. Oh, no!

"The chicken salad's good, but I'd take a couple of PB&J sandwiches for back-up." She turned to leave again, then swiveled back like she'd forgotten something else. "Oh, almost forgot. When I saw Mom yesterday at the Wellness Center, she had on pajamas."

Another gulp. *Oh, no, no!*

Khara held the screen door half opened, "When I asked, she said one of her children swiped her business suits when she and Dad went away last weekend. She's hoping whoever did it will confess. I assured Mom I was on campus. For the life of me, I can't fathom why Kharee would be interested in a bunch of women's suits. So that leaves you as a prime suspect."

Two gigantic gulps. *Oh, nooo …*

Chapter 37

JANACLESE

Twenty minutes after texting Hassan "on my way" I knocked on his door, leaving behind all thoughts about Mom's plan of flaunting around in pajamas until I admitted I'd donated her suits.

Today, Hassan and I would spend time alone together, communicating and doing what Khara said would help me get to know him better.

Loud hip-hop music spat from an old sage green Cadillac that drove past the Rayfield's house. I watched as it paraded in one direction, then circled back twice before someone finally answered the front door.

"Hey, Khadijah." I smiled big and wide, hoping she hadn't forgotten my face, but not sure she'd recognize me with braids. "I'm Janaclese."

"I know who you are." As usual, she sounded irritated with me. "You know the drill."

"Yep. Wait out here, right?"

She didn't bother responding. Just rolled her eyes and yelled for her big brother. "Taaa—lent! That boo-gee girl's here."

Boo-gee? How'd she figure I was bourgeois? I sat on the steps examining my shorts and tennis shoes. What made Khadijah think that I thought I was high society and better than her?

"Hi-ya!" Nneka's beautiful smile met mine when I popped my head up. She pounced into my lap, hugging me with the comfort of embracing an old favorite stuffed animal. "Where ya been?"

"Thinking about you!" I pinched her cheeks.

She giggled. "You gon' marry my big brother?"

I chuckled. "We're just good friends."

"Ooooh. Sparkly." She fingered the diamond pendant around my neck. "Can I have it?"

"My dad gave this to me, and I promised him I'd wear it. You know how important promises are, don't you?"

The door snatched open, and Khadijah stuck her head out. "Nneka, git outta that girl's lap. You're too big to act like a baby."

"It's okay, Khadijah. We all need a hug sometimes." Nneka's plastic hair beads mashed against my chest.

Khadijah put her hands on her hips and glared at me. "We 'on know you like that."

Nneka's beaded cornrows clickety-clacked in my face as she fidgeted, looking sideways at me, then glancing up at Khadijah.

I relaxed my grip, allowing her to slip from my lap. But what I really wanted to do was hug Khadijah. What was it like not having a mom at her age? If she'd soften just a little toward me, I could at least be her surrogate big sister.

"Come on, girl." Khadijah grabbed her little sister's hand and led her away from me. "Don't beg for anybody's fake jewelry. It'll make your neck itchy and crusty. Someday, I'll buy you a real diamond necklace."

I was about to comment when Hassan strolled from around the corner of the house. His infectious grin triggered a wider smile from me.

"Yo, Shawty. Sorry to keep you waiting. Had to help Pops out back."

"No problem. Your sisters were very good company."

Hip-hop music blasted from the street, and Hassan's smiled faded. He eyed the car as it slowed down in front of the house. He looked at his sisters. "Get inside and lock the door. I don't want y'all outside today."

Khadijah frowned. "Pops said Nneka could play in the yard if it's not too hot."

"Well, it's sticky and muggy." He peered down the street. An uneasiness seemed to sweep over him and his jawbone set tight. "Just stay inside. Pops'll be in soon. He's in the shed fixing the lawn mower."

"What about you and her?" Khadijah nodded at me. "You going off with her?"

Hassan's shoulders stiffened. "Yeah, right after I check the mailbox."

He headed up the driveway, and I sprang from the steps, hustling next to him. "Everything okay? You seem tense."

"I'm good." He zeroed in on the mailbox, stopping a few feet in front of it, then turning his attention toward the sky.

I felt my brows furrow. What was he gawking at? Was he checking for rain clouds? I looked up, following his line of vision.

A pair of old rugged boots dangled from the powerline. But why did that seem to upset him?

With clenched fists, he banged the top of the mailbox.

I jumped between Hassan and the mailbox just as he was about to smash it or rip it open—I didn't know which. "Something's wrong. What is it?"

The familiar thumpity-thump of the hip-hop beat grew louder as the same Cadillac inched closer.

"Don't move," Hassan said to me.

He pressed my body against the mailbox and fiddled with the front of my ripped-neck tee shirt.

"What are you doing?" I asked. Was my shirt too low? I'd cut away the crewneck, making it more stylish.

"Trying to hide your necklace, and it's not working. Wrap your arms around my neck."

"Why?" I twisted my nose at him.

"Trust me." He moved his hand from the front of my shirt, then fumbled with the clasp on my necklace. "I can't unhook it. Pretend we're making out."

"In broad daylight? Are you crazy?"

"Just do it." His voice was stern.

I didn't move. But I wasn't being stubborn—at least not on purpose.

In warped speed, he thrust my hands around his neck like he suspected I was clueless. "Lay your head on my shoulder, Janaclese ... like a slow dance."

Without questioning, I did as instructed, feeling his rapid pulse beating.

The car stopped in front of us, rattling my nerves even more.

Suddenly, Hassan popped my chain, landing the diamond necklace into my bra.

"Hassan!" I gasped.

He pivoted, facing the driver of the car.

"Already got the lady screaming your name?" The driver's grin revealed a gold front tooth. An assortment of chains layered around his neck glinted in the sunlight. "Must be your new girl. She gotta name?"

Hassan stared at him. A different look, I'd never seen in his eyes, bore into the guy.

Knots formed in my stomach, but I waited. Was Hassan going to admit that I was his girl, introduce me or something?

Obviously, Hassan knew this guy. At least one of us needed to be friendly. Bouncing to the car, I extended my hand to the driver. "Hi, I'm Janaclese."

The guy held my hand, running his thumb over the back of it. "Soft and smooth as cocoa butter."

I glanced back at Hassan, and his eyes flinched.

The driver brushed his lips against my hand, tickling my skin with a wet kiss. "And sugary sweet."

I pulled my hand away, wanting to wipe it against my shorts, but not wanting to be rude.

"My boy seemed to have lost his manners." The driver smirked. "I'm Rev."

"Nice to me you, Rev. You and Hassan friends?"

"No!" Hassan yanked me away from the car, the way I'd seen Khadijah handle Nneka. "And he said *Reb*—as in Rebel!"

That creepy look was in Hassan's eyes. What happened to the glow I'd grown accustomed to?

"What do you want?" Hassan shouted at Rebel.

"Had to make a run in your 'hood. Saw you out here, just wanted to holler at my boy."

"I'm not your boy."

Reb lifted his eyebrows. "Oh. So it's like that now?"

"Always was, always will be."

I watched as they engaged in a staring contest.

Rebel finally grinned. "Well, I guess I better make my drop ... special delivery for my incapacitated customers."

No way was I going to judge this guy—even if it was the so-call "'hood," as Cyndray kept reminding me. "Cool. You work with the handicapped or sick?"

Reb looked me up and down. "I guess you can say that."

"Me, too—sorta. I assist the elderly. What exactly do you do?"

"I'm a street pharmacist."

My heart staggered. *Did he mean a drug dealer?* I pushed the thought away. *Things aren't always what they seem. Like, I wasn't "boogie" like Khadijah's accusation.* "If CVS or Walgreens delivered, that'd be one less thing for my clients to worry about."

"Good to know somebody appreciates and respects my work." He sneered at Hassan. "I like your girl."

Hassan pulled me closer, but still didn't speak or take his eyes off of Reb.

The car rolled forward. "Hey, Janaclese. Wouldn't mind seeing you around here more often. Your presence adds a little class to the ghetto."

"Thanks." *I think.*

Not until Reb's Cadillac was out of sight did Hassan turn his attention from the street. He jetted toward the house—focused on another mission.

I opened the mailbox, grabbed a handful of letters that Hassan had initially intended to get, then raced to catch him. "Hassan. The mail."

He spun around, seized the mail, kept moving ... mumbling, "You shouldn't have come here. I told you I'd pick you up."

He walked so fast, I skipped to keep up. Why was he turning on me now?

"Reb knew your car didn't belong in this neighborhood. He wanted to check you out."

"What?" I was getting a workout just from running up the driveway. "Will you slow down and tell me what you're talking about?"

We reached the porch, and Hassan plunked onto the steps. He hadn't communicated what was wrong, and now he pushed me away, outright saying I shouldn't have come. How could I get us back on the right track of getting to know each other?

"You were being too nice, too *friendly* with him. You have to be hardcore with guys like that. Not all smiley, showing your cute dimples."

He said 'cute' real ugly-like. As if he thought I was flirting with Reb.

But it wasn't fair. First of all, I wasn't taught how to be hardcore. Never had to be tough. And second, hadn't Hassan mentioned my friendliness was what attracted him to me? How he adored my smile and cute dimples?

Was this jealousy?

I sat on the porch, right above the step Hassan occupied. It had to be stress creating this unnecessary conflict. There was no need for him to think Reb was interested in me one bit.

Placing my hands on his shoulders, I pressed my fingers into his flesh, rotating them in a circular motion, pushing in and out like kneading bread at Me-maw's. It was exactly how I'd seen Mom and Dad help each other relax over the years.

His shoulders slumped, and tension seemed to gush from them.

I leaned closer to his ear and whispered, "Reb called you his boy. I just wanted to be nice to your friend."

Hassan twitched, and more knots formed beneath my hands when his neck stiffened. "He's a drug dealer, Janaclese. A gang-leader … not even close to being an associate of mine."

"What?" My hands pressed into his shoulders. "But he knew you. He called you—"

He covered my hands with his, stopping the massage. "And now he knows you too and the car you drive. Once Reb runs your tag, he'll know your address. You shouldn't have come here."

"Seriously?" I didn't need everybody always trying to protect me from everything. I pulled my hands away from his, stood up and marched to my Prius. Obviously, he didn't want me around. Maybe he needed another excuse to break our date. But trying to scare me away? Ugh!

"Janaclese!" The sound of Hassan's voice chased me.

I didn't bother turning around. My eyes burned, and he hated seeing me cry.

If I acted fast and just left, I could outrun the tears before they raced down my cheeks. I opened the trunk and picked up the picnic basket. Maybe Nneka could have a tea party if Khadijah trusted my food.

I didn't hear Hassan's footsteps, but I felt his energy drawing closer to me. It was a strong magnetic force, a gravitational pull I couldn't deny. So when he wrapped his arms around me from the back, I wasn't startled. Just needed to keep the tears in check.

"What're you doing?" he asked.

I squiggled free, then turned to face him, straining to push down frustration. "Give this to Nneka."

"Nneka?" Lines decorated his forehead. "I thought you and I had a date."

I swallowed. Why wouldn't he snag the easy out I'd given him?

"Listen, Shawty." He glanced around. "Living in Red Hill makes me crazy protective sometimes."

I sniffed back a tear and considered him. Behind him, his sisters watched us from inside their window. I gave a slight nod. Being locked in the house, all holed up like his sisters, could drive anybody nuts. Why didn't his family move? I knew the answer wasn't always so simple. And I also knew better than to ask Hassan that question.

"When Reb's Cadillac sputtered back and forth, I knew he'd spotted your car. I wanted to keep you safe. A girl like you can't walk around Red Hill sporting diamonds and pearls."

"Oh!" I drew my hand to my chest, then breathed a sigh of relief. The necklace was safely tucked away. I stiffened my shoulders and lifted my chin. "I'm not afraid of Reb or people like him. I'm also not scared of your neighborhood, so you don't need to baby me or feel pressured to take care of me, even if you think I'm too soft."

"I don't want you to be hardcore." He extended an apologetic hug.

I skirted his embrace. "That's not what you insinuated."

"Sorry if I hurt your feelings."

"You didn't."

I don't know why I pretended to be tough when all I wanted to do was fall into Hassan's arms. I shoved the basket into his hands. "Give this to Nneka."

I walked around to the driver's seat, then hopped behind the wheel.

"Please, Janaclese. I really want to spend time with you today. I-I ... I can't seem to stop thinking about you. When we talked the other night, something fascinating happened, like a connection." Hassan kicked at my tire. "Aw, man, you don't know what I mean."

"Yes, I do." Sometimes there were no sufficient words to describe being in love. But the light that had returned to Hassan's eyes spoke volumes. "Let's go."

Chapter 38

JANACLESE

Just us two—Hassan and me—alone, together, at last!

No stressful thoughts of my family and no weight from him needing to protect me. For the next few hours, I'd shelter Hassan from the outside pressures—*not* the other way around.

"We'll picnic on the other side of this stream." Hassan nodded at the distance, then presented his dreamy smile like he had fond memories. "Me and Pops fished here a few times."

We'd walked deep into the woods. I had no idea where we were. "Is this still part of Red Hill?"

He laughed. "No, this is the country. What Pops calls being in the cut. I told you I'd take you where your Mom's eyes couldn't see you."

I smiled, remembering our bike outing. Today wasn't as hot, but the sun was shining. So glad I hadn't brought an umbrella like some flake. I stared into the shallow water, seeing nothing but flat rocks and large boulders. The heat made me crave the cool wetness, but I hadn't worn a bathing suit. "I could jump right in and swim."

He winked with a playful grin. "And hang your wet clothes on a branch to dry? I promise not to look."

"Yeah, right." I chuckled, then slipped off my sneakers and rolled up my pants legs.

"Careful. The rocks are slippery."

Holding my shoes, I leaped across the narrow stream like a ballerina in a stage performance.

He seemed impressed, and my insides warmed higher than the outside temperature.

"Right here is where we picnic." He set the basket down and spread the blanket. "You're obviously a dancer."

"Good guess." I couldn't contain my smile, remembering how he'd lifted me on the day we met. My plan of us getting to know each other was working perfectly. I pulled my iPod from the basket and turned up the volume. "Listen and watch."

I performed a solo variation with bare feet in the grass to ease his mind ... and mine. Gracefully, I leaped and landed in preparation for a triple pirouette. Three clean spins, only a slight wobble, and I ended my combination by lifting my leg high as the sky in arabesque.

"Wow!" With an earphone dangling from his right ear, Hassan's eyes were planted on me. "Do that leap thingy again."

"Maybe later." Panting, I smiled, exercising my only willing muscle after my intense 'call of the wild' dance. Cyndray's suggestion of dancing outside in bare feet, instead of a dance floor, was more physically straining. I reached for the fresh fruit juice I'd made. "Did you like it?"

"Like it? Loved it dot com! The food's good, your performance was wonderful, the—"

"I'm talking about the song."

I'd also downloaded Aunt Alicia's love song to my iPod. It reminded me so much of Hassan, I wanted him to hear it. Perhaps it would make him think of me too.

"Oh, yeah. This track is hot. Kind of a neo-soul flavor. Sounds a lot like Alicia Keys." He turned to look at me. "She doesn't sing contemporary gospel, does she?"

I shrugged and wrinkled my nose. "It's not Alicia Keys, and how'd you know it was a gospel song?"

"The lyrics." He didn't skip a beat, just started singing the words. "You're the lover of my soul. You complete me. Yes, you make me whole."

Hmm ... how come *he* got that so easily when I had to argue with Cyndray every time she heard it? Was he really that different from other boys?

My heart fluttered. "Do you think it's possible to love like that?"

"I guess. I mean, the songwriter is obviously in love with God. It's probably a good example of what to expect in a relationship with Him." He shrugged. "Don't know."

I sprawled across the blanket, rolled over on my back and looked up at the treetops. With a response like that would he ever try to kiss me?

Hassan nudged me in the side, taunting me. "Can't believe you made a brother beg to spend time with you today."

"Was it worth it?" I teased back in a sleepy voice that sounded shamefully seductive.

"Um-hum. Sure was." He seemed even less energetic than I was. Having hiked so long in the sweltering heat and so deep in the woods for total isolation had already drained us.

Mostly evergreens towered high above our heads, allowing just a few rays of sunlight to peek through. I inhaled the fresh forest scent of cedar and soaked in the peaceful quietness. The natural haven, with no other signs of human life, gave the impression that we were literally alone in our own little universe.

"You feel lost without your cell phone?" I asked, yawning.

"Glad you made me leave it in the truck. Probably can't get a signal anyway."

I'd parked my car in Red Hill and ridden to our secret hide-out in Hassan's truck. Sure hoped his truck was ready and willing to leave when we were. The rust bucket—Cyndray called it.

"Does it bother you when Cyndray picks on your truck?"

"My truck beats her BMW any day."

Hassan's response didn't make sense and confirmed he was half-asleep.

"Cyndray doesn't have a car." I closed my eyes.

"Exactly. My truck is better than taking the bus, metro, or walking."

An electric current surged through me, and I giggled. "BMW—I get it."

When I finally settled down, I realized the chuckling had zapped more of my energy.

Alone together, without any distractions. Still, Hassan hadn't tried to kiss me. My tired mind couldn't conjure a list of 'why-nots.' Besides, whatever time it was, the evening had to be young.

Snuggling into the crook of his arm, I let my body completely relax. The stream we'd crossed trickled a lullaby and soon, I drifted off to sleep.

A wailing siren shook me awake. What was that noise?

I bolted upright, taking in nothing but darkness and the lump that lay beside me—Hassan. This wasn't a dream. How long had we slept?

"Hassan, wake up." The wind sounded like a runaway train rumbling off track. I shoved Hassan. "Wake up!"

"I'm up, I'm up!" His eyes roamed the perimeter like a searchlight.

The trees danced faster in the shadows, and without another warning, the sky split open, spewing a cascade of heavy rain.

"Run," he screamed, grabbing the picnic items.

I dashed in search of shelter as torrential sheets of rain blinded my path. Swaying branches whipped at me, and I jumped, sidestepped, refusing to break my stride until I found safety.

But something was chasing me.

Deeper and deeper I fled into the woods, with no sense of direction, no inkling of my whereabouts.

"Janaclese!" The thunderous voice repeated my name while I fought against the angry elements and its threats.

A cedar tree fired a broken limb from its crown. I angled my arm, shielding my face from the falling debris crashing all around me. My sore feet scurried in the darkness while the echo of my name grew farther and fainter in the distance. Not until I was sure I'd outrun whatever was chasing me did I stop. Breathless and stumbling about, I slowly turned to look in all directions. It was daylight again. But where was I?

And where were Hassan and his truck?

"Hassan!" I yelled. "Hassan!"

Barreling through the brush, Hassan rushed to my side.

"What's happening?" My voice shook. "Where's your truck?"

"It's back there. You ran in the opposite direction, so I followed you."

"We have to go back." I lunged toward where he'd pointed.

He grabbed my arm. "We can't. It's too dangerous."

"I gotta get home, I gotta get home." I shook my braids, now heavy from the drenching rain.

"I promise I'll get you home, but we have to wait the storm out, and then—"

"No time to wait. I gotta get home, I gotta ..."

Whatever comforting words Hassan offered, my mind couldn't hold them. There was room for one thought.

I had to get home.

Chapter 39

CYNDRAY

I army-crawled flat on my belly to stake out the enemy's territory. Pine needles, rocks, and other earthy debris pressed against my stomach as I snaked along the hard ground preparing to blast my opponents.

Paintball was supposed to be fun. At least that's what I thought until the guys went all Rambo and started employing military strategies like the US Special Forces. Now here I was crouched behind a makeshift bunker like GI Jane, trying to avoid getting splattered.

All I could do was wait to shoot. Or be shot. I sat still.

My mind drifted. What was Janaclese doing on her private date with Hassan? Surely not playing hide and seek like me and Trevor at the moment. Most of my teammates were already in the dead box, so winning this little war game was totally up to me.

The smell of dirt tickled my nostrils, and I wiggled my nose to squelch a sneeze. Leaning to the left, I spotted movement behind a tarp about ten feet away—yes! I readied my paintball gun and pointed straight at the target.

"Surrender," a voice from my right side commanded.

I turned my focus away from my target and toward the voice. Trevor? Where'd he come from?

A devilish grin trekked across his sweaty face. "Give it up, Cyndray. My range is too close to shoot you."

Splat!

"Ow." I dropped the gun and grabbed my thigh. "That hurt, you idiot!"

Micah darted from behind the tarp. "You don't get pity 'cause you're a girl. If you're gonna play with the big boys, then man-up and stop whining."

I jerked my head up at Trevor. "Did he just call me a sissy punk?"

"I didn't hear anything like that." He doubled over in laughter, reaching to help me up. "I'll walk you to the dead box."

When I took off my head gear, I noticed Trevor staring at me. "What?"

"You're pretty spunky. Ever think about coming to sparring class again?"

"Are you kidding me? I almost got creamed on my first match," I said, rubbing my hands against my thigh.

He chuckled. "That was a fun night."

"Yeah. A funny sight." I got lost in the pitch of his laugh.

Fine with a PH—the only word to describe Trevor's chiseled face that spilled drops of sweat down the side. Even the dirt caked to his shirt emphasized the rock-hard muscles underneath. It wasn't just his physique. He was down to earth and nicer than any boy I'd ever met.

But why didn't I have feelings for him like Janaclese had for Hassan? Was I really that messed up?

"Where're your girls today?"

Girls ... plural ... as in more than one? Was he discreetly asking about Kehl-li?

"Janaclese is hanging out with another friend."

He raised his eyebrows. "Miracle and uh ... what's her name?"

I shoved him. "Boy, you know Kehl-li's name. You were practically drooling at her feet at the pool party."

"Not me. She's not my type."

"Yeah, right. Kehl-li's *every* guy's type."

"Don't get me wrong. She's hot and all. Her walk, her style, totally sweet!"

Did I look like I wanted a blow-by-blow on what made Kehl-li so desirable? I did my best to tune Trevor out.

He insisted, "But even with all of that, she's not my type. Girls are like cars."

"Humph." I cocked my head. "I was told cars defined boys."

He shrugged as if blowing off the conversation, but I wanted to know more. "Just out of curiosity, what kind of car is a girl like Kehl-li?"

"An expensive one." He spoke without hesitating. "A dude would have to shell out money constantly for the upkeep. My dad says if you can't afford the maintenance, why bother?" He paused. "But to ride in a Lamborghini? Man, I'd do almost anything—"

"Excuse me." I put my hands on my hips—thought he'd said Kehl-li wasn't his type. "Then why didn't you kiss her?"

"Kiss who?"

"Kehl-li."

"I thought we were talking about cars." He scrunched up his face. "Kehl-li wanted to kiss me?"

Didn't he remember her totally draping herself around him at Miracle's pool party?

Narrowing my eyes, I asked, "You can't tell when a girl wants to be kissed?"

"Uh, no." A sheepish grin crept across his face. "Can't say that I can."

Would it totally creep him out to tell him I wanted to kiss him? I meant ... not *wanted* to kiss him, but *needed* to kiss him, to see if I was normal like other girls.

No doubt Janaclese and Hassan had finally kissed on their date. I wasn't there to interfere. When those two were together, a total bonfire blazed.

All I wanted was to feel a tiny spark.

I moved closer to Trevor and looped my arm around his, the way Janaclese would do. Nothing. Absolutely nothing different came over me.

The surprised look on Trevor's face began with a tiny smile and ended with a big grin. "What's up?"

"Did you feel a magnetic force pulling us together?" I asked.

"Um ... was I supposed to?"

My experiment wasn't working. Elevating onto my tiptoes, I kissed Trevor's cheek. "What about now? Any sparks?"

"Not really … but, if you want a *real* kiss, I'd be okay with that."

I took a deep breath. It was either now or never. A golden opportunity to get two for the price of one—a chance to prove I was okay *and* gain evidence that kissing wasn't such a big deal.

Closing my eyes, I leaned in.

"Ouch." I rubbed my noggin.

"Sorry. I didn't mean to bump your head."

I touched my forehead. "Maybe we should keep our eyes open."

We eased our heads toward each other. Closer, closer … without any thought, I automatically shut my eyes. My lips trembled, barely brushed his. Then …

Snap, Crackle, POP!

My eyes flashed wide-open. "Did you hear that?"

Trevor scratched the peach fuzz on his chin. "Yep. Saw it too."

"Like fireworks?"

He raised his gaze to the sky. "More like thunder and lightning."

As if God Himself was denying me my first real kiss, out of nowhere, rain poured from above.

"Unbelievable." Giggling and arms outstretched, I focused upwards and turned in circles like a three-year-old in awe of something they'd never seen. "Totally unbelievable."

"Cyndray. We need to take cover."

Lightning flashed overhead like a psychedelic disco ball.

I stopped spinning. "If you give me a head start, I'll race you to the building."

Trevor laughed. "The track champion needs a head start?"

"Go!" I sprinted ahead before Trevor had a chance to figure out what was happening.

Still giggling, I let the thunder, lightning, pelting rain, and his insane laughter chase me to shelter.

Chapter 40

JANACLESE

I don't know how long Hassan and I squatted beneath the grassy mantel that jutted out from the slope above us. Could've been minutes or even hours, but it seemed like days.

The steady rain poured with a vengeance. And regardless of what Hassan said to make things better, thoughts of home never left me.

What would Mom and Dad say if I didn't make it home before too late?

Pain shot down my cramped legs and traveled to my aching feet. I looked down. "My shoes. I left my shoes."

"I grabbed them. They're in the basket." Hassan opened the lid and reached inside. "Here, I'll help you put them on."

He loosened the strings, and I slipped my feet into my damp sneakers.

"You see that cabin?" He pointed toward a steep hill that looked more like a mountain from my position.

I squinted and craned my neck, unable to fully see what he was referring to in the hazy, gray distance. "You think somebody's camping there?"

"Not if they paid attention to the forecast." He gave me a side glance. "Wanna make a run for it?"

"I can barely see two inches in front of me." I hesitated. "How far away is it?"

"Much closer than the truck, and it'll be too dark to see anything soon. If someone's there, maybe they can help us."

Hope prickled my insides. "Okay."

Holding hands, we trudged up the slick hill, layered with hard slippery rocks. Seemed the more we climbed, the farther we got from the cabin, which was now hidden behind a boulder.

"Are you sure you saw a cabin?" I hoped it wasn't wishful thinking, a mirage solicited from desperation.

"It's up there." When he released my hand to gesture, I stumbled and slipped on the rocks.

"Hassan!" I grabbed hold of packed earth, extending my left leg and tucking my right knee into a narrow crevice. "I can't do this."

"Grab my hand." He pulled at my arms.

My heart thudded. The slippery mud could cause me to fall and break my leg. I closed my eyes and bit my lips. "If I let go, I'll … I'll fall."

"I got you. Just don't look down."

With eyes fully shut, I couldn't look anywhere. How did I get myself into this? Why hadn't I gone with Khara to Paint the Park Pink?

"Open your eyes, Janaclese. I won't let you fall—I promise."

"Promise?" *How can he promise you something like that?* Cyndray's words floated across my mind. "Cross your heart?"

"If I cross my heart, I'll have to let go."

"Don't let go!" I flashed my eyes opened as I spoke.

The sky rumbled overhead, and suddenly, torrential rain poured down again. I grabbed Hassan's hand, and he helped me scramble up the rocky slope. The wind whipped at us, forcing us to move even slower. Yet, we trudged forward.

When the blinding rain tapered off, an old wooden cabin came into view. My heart skipped. He hadn't imagined it.

We pounced onto the porch, and Hassan knocked softly.

When there was no response, he pounded harder.

Still no answer.

"May—" Shivering wet, I sneezed. "Maybe they can't hear above the roaring wind."

He frowned. "Maybe nobody's home."

My heart sank, dragging down hope with it.

"Wait here." Hassan stepped down from the porch.

"Where're you going?" My voice shook just as hard as my quaking insides.

"Wait here, Janaclese." Hassan rounded the corner of the cabin.

Moments passed, and I didn't see or hear anything. Finally, I could wait no longer.

"Hassan?" I tottered onto the ground, landing in the middle of a mud puddle. Dirt splattered onto my legs, and I resisted squatting right there and crying. "Hassan?"

The front door swung open, and Hassan scurried to my aid. "You okay?" He grabbed my hands and led me onto the porch.

"What took you so long?" I clutched him with a vice-like grip.

"Went looking for a key."

"Did you find one?"

"Not exactly."

My stomach churned. "Then how'd you ... you broke into someone's house? We're breaking and entering?"

He caressed my arm. "It's okay. We're seeking emergency shelter."

I looked up at the sky. A rolling dark cloud slowly sipped the daylight, warning night would arrive sooner rather than later.

"I can't do this. It's not right. It's ... it's illegal."

Lightning sped across the sky, pursued by a clap of thunder.

My heart thumped, and I stepped inside the one room cabin, the smell of damp pine convincing me it was safer in than out. Dead eyes, plugged into deer heads mounted on the walls, gazed back at me. Goosebumps crawled along my flesh. This had to be a hunter's haven.

"Sit right there while I take a look around."

I knew he didn't expect me to plop down all comfy in the gray and tan plaid chair overdue for a shampoo. My muddy legs reminded me I had no room to be scornful. "Gotta clean up. Don't wanna ruin the furniture."

"Bathroom's over there."

I skirted in the direction he nodded, then flipped the switch. *Great.* "No lights."

The sound of a million whistling tea kettles echoed through the cabin. I glanced at the empty stove, then eyed Hassan.

His face twisted. "What the—"

Chapter 41

CYNDRAY

What was that? I jumped when the rumbling thunder echoed in the building. Why did I always have to be the last one picked up?

I waited inside the paintball office for my mom to come get me. Knowing her, she was waiting for the storm to pass since she knew I was already safe inside.

"Wanna try calling again?" The old man's gentle concern was probably driven by his desire to close shop and head home.

"No, someone's coming." *When?* I couldn't say, but my parents wouldn't abandon me.

The man moved in slow motion, rearranging the head gear for the umpteenth time. Although he looked as old as Methuselah, his straight charcoal hair sat on his head, thick like a forest. Had to be a wig.

"You like working here?" I patted my feet against the tile floor and made small talk to pass the time.

"Keeps me going." He dusted the cans of paint, turning them to make sure the labels faced forward. Then he walked over to the gun display on the side wall, behind the counter.

Methuselah's back hunched over so close to the ground, he could've crawled and moved quicker. What was he doing working in a high energy place like this anyway? Watching him do the same thing over and over again was like rewinding a horrible flick.

He stepped from behind the counter and crept to the doorway. "Looks like headlights coming this way."

"Might be my mom." I jumped up from my seat, squeezed past him and snatched the door open.

A blustery wind blasted inside, tackling me to the floor. As I held the door's handle, it slammed shut again.

"Whoa." Methuselah tried to help me up, but I practically pulled him to floor next to me.

"I'm okay!" I scrambled to my feet and noticed his shoulders shaking.

Was he having a seizure?

"Sir?" I bent downward to see his face.

He waved his arms in the air. "You're like a kite."

I straightened my back. Was Methuselah laughing at me?

"Flowing through the air, light as a feather." He snickered.

"Well, yeah. Didn't know I needed to arm wrestle the wind."

My phone chirped, and I slid it from my pants pocket.

"Wait for your mom to pull up to the door." He passed me an umbrella. "Looks like you're gonna need this too."

"Thanks." My phone chirped again. Mom was calling me. I took the umbrella while trying to answer my phone. "I'm coming, I'm coming."

Methuselah stood next to my shoulder, attempting to hold the door ajar as I multitasked.

Pressing *talk* with one hand, I snapped the umbrella opened with the other. "Hello … hello?" The wind battled the umbrella, and I yanked it back through the door, lifting Methuselah's toupee from his head.

"Oh!" With both hands, he covered his bald spot, causing the door to squeeze the umbrella into its frame.

My jaws dropped. I tried to restrain my laugh but failed miserably. "I'm sor—" The chuckles wouldn't stop even with my mouth closed. "Sorry. So sorry."

Mom's Audi honked outside, and my cell phone chirped again.

I grabbed his wig from a spoke on the damaged umbrella and passed it to him. "Um, see ya around." What else could I say?

He placed the wet toupee on his head, looking crooked and crazy.

I sailed out the door laughing, then hopped into the front seat. "Hello."

"Hi." Mom glanced at me and squinted. "Oh. You're on the phone?"

Still giggling, I nodded and held up my index finger. "Hello?"

"Is this Cyndray?" The caller's voice wasn't familiar to me.

"Who wants to know?"

Mom checked the rearview mirror, then skidded onto the wet pavement. Rain pinged against the windows.

"This is Betima Mitchell."

Janaclese's mom? "Hey, Mrs. Mitchell, what's up?"

The windshield wipers swished a steady beat, almost drowning the low voice on the other end of my cell phone.

"Did you go paintballing today?" She sounded distant and unusually formal.

"Yes, I'm just leaving. Sorta shut the place down." I chuckled.

Mom slowed the car to a near stop and clicked on her signal. The solid yellow lines in the road, barely visible through the rain, made staying in the right lane a challenge.

"The weather's bad, and we haven't heard from Janaclese."

I gulped. "Um … well …"

"I know she didn't go paintballing. Khara seems to think she's out with a boy."

My heart dropped like an unexpected dip on a rollercoaster.

"Sweetheart, please. If you know anything about where she could possibly be, just tell me."

I stared at the fading lane. *How much should I tell? Where was the line?*

"Cyndray, it's important. My little girl could be in danger."

"Hassan. She and Hassan went on a picnic this afternoon. I have no idea where."

"Hassan? Do I know this young man?"

"He goes to Redemption Temple." *But he lives in Red Hill. Should I mention Red Hill?*

"She met him at church?" Her quizzical voice rang high.

"Um … Kinda."

"Well, either she met him at church, or she didn't."

I didn't clarify, and she didn't pursue the issue.

"What's his last name? Do you know it?"

"Hassan ... uh ... Hassan Raymond ... Richards." I closed my eyes to block distractions. "I'm sorry. I can't remember, but I'm pretty sure it's an R."

She sighed. "I guess that's more than anybody else knows. Thanks."

"Mrs. Mitchell?"

"Yes?"

"You don't have to worry about Janaclese's safety. Hassan's not the type who would hurt her."

"Thanks, I was referring to the bad storm. But thanks."

Mom's tires splashed water onto our driveway just as I clicked off the phone. She turned off the ignition. "Everything okay with the Mitchell girl? Her mom seemed worried."

I sat motionless in the passenger seat, a tingling spread across my chest.

"Cyndray?" She waited for my response.

I nodded slowly. "Yeah, I hope so."

Through the windows, I saw the house lights flick off and on. *Whatever you do in the dark, will come to the light.* Bits of my last conversation with Janaclese raced through my mind.

Aw, Janaclese, I told you ... Sheesh!

Chapter 42

JANACLESE

"It's gonna be stupid dark soon," Hassan said, slamming one drawer shut and opening another.

As the daylight dimmed and shadows formed on the walls, we rifled through drawers searching for candles, matches, flashlights—anything that illuminated.

"Found it!" I shined a flashlight in his direction.

"Great. Now let's see what else is in here." Hassan rummaged through the cabinets below the kitchen sink, pulling out a small grill and lighter fluid. He opened the practically bare cupboards, finding a knife and a pack of saltine crackers. "Not much."

I quirked an eyebrow. How long did he think we were going to stay here?

He turned the flashlight on me. "Look at you. You're soaking wet, and I don't want you to get sick."

As if on cue, I sneezed so many times in a row it sounded like a secret code.

Walking into the living room, he lifted a hunter's camo jacket from a nail on the back of the door. "Here put this on. Lay your wet clothes across the chair, so they can dry."

I tilted my head. "What about you?"

He held up matching oversized pants, then pointed to a small closet. "Found these hanging in there."

I walked into the bathroom, leaving Hassan to change into the pants. "How long do you think it'll be before we can head out again?"

"Depends on the weather," he yelled from the other room.

Heaviness pulled my chest. What was happening at home? What were my folks thinking?

I slipped off my ripped-neck tee shirt, then eased out of my jeans. Fastening each button on the camo, I stared at my divided image in the cracked mirror, then felt my knees buckle. Wasn't there a saying about a house divided not being able to stand?

The oversized army jacket swallowed me, its massive tail came below my knees. But who cared about how I looked? My world was crumbling. If I'd only been honest with my parents, told them about my date. Now my only goal was getting home.

Heaping my clothes into a bunch, I stepped from the bathroom. My diamond, loosed from its broken chain, fell to the floor. *Dad!* Oh God, I needed to get home to hug Dad, kiss Mom … to come clean.

Swooping up my jewelry, I raced into the big room "We can't stay—"

I grimaced, cutting off my own words.

"Huh?" His bare chest exposed, Hassan busied himself in the kitchen combing through the picnic basket, making himself at home.

Why didn't he cover up—keep on his wet shirt just on principle?

"You look warmer," he said, spreading strawberries on a napkin.

"I look a hot mess, but it's better than shivering in these damp clothes." I spread my articles across the back of the musty couch, avoiding looking at his chest. "Listen, we need a plan to get home."

He passed me a napkin. "These strawberries won't make it past tonight. Here, you might as well eat 'em."

Eyes on the napkin, I took one plump strawberry and bit into the sweetness. "Why don't we share?"

"I'm good. We have two peanut butter and jelly sandwiches left. If we get hungry, let's share one tonight and save the other one for breakfast."

PB&J … it was Khara's brilliant idea to pack them. But why was Hassan rationing the food and planning for breakfast? I focused on his face. "I was thinking we could rest for a while then head out tonight."

He nodded. "We should probably get some sleep. Tomorrow might be rough, and we need to save the flashlight battery."

He walked toward the bed. "The picnic blanket got a little wet. Only saw these two extra blankets. Better to just lie on top of the covers."

Heat crawled up my neck. Was he serious? I couldn't make eye contact long enough to tell. Instead, I scanned the room, focusing on the dusty brown curtains sagging at the windows. An overnight date was out of the question.

Finally, I looked at the bed, then at Hassan. His expression said he didn't see a problem.

Hassan tested the bed while I stood motionless. I tried to swallow, but my mouth was dry as if coated with the thick dust layering the curtains.

"Oh." His eyes widened as if remembering something. He stood and crossed the room to where a big accent chair waited in the corner. He pushed the chair next to the bed, then plopped in it. "Better?"

My breath evened. "Yes." I scooched onto the edge of the bed and turned out the flashlight.

He was right. It was stupid dark. The creepy eyes from the stuffed deer glowed. Murmuring noises, intensified by the blackness, moaned and rumbled outside the wooded cabin. None of it was as loud as the silence that lay between Hassan and me.

"Hassan, are you there?"

"I'm right beside you, Shawty."

A scratching noise raised the hair on my arms. "Do you hear that?"

"Probably just a tree branch against the window."

"Oh." Knowing what it might be didn't ease my nerves. My leg muscles tensed. "Are you afraid?"

"Get some sleep. Everything is gonna be fine." He reached over and touched my arm. "I'm right here beside you."

Without hesitating, I laced my fingers through his, desperate to know he was there as I closed my eyes really tight.

A weird feeling rested in my belly. I lay with my eyes shut, feeling the daylight against my eyelids. What was I supposed to remember? There was something important I needed to do.

I inhaled an unpleasant damp odor. But then I felt him move closer to me. I smiled recognizing the sensation I felt when Hassan was within ten feet of me. I slowly opened my eyes and took in brown curtains hanging over a tattered rug.

Suddenly, I remembered everything.

My heart pounding, I turned over in the bed.

"Hey, you. Shawty, you awake?"

The sour taste in my mouth stopped me from verbally responding. Under different circumstances, having Hassan stand next to my bed, seeing the scar above Hassan's right eye would've been a welcomed greeting. Hassan was dressed in the shirt he'd worn yesterday. I squinted. How long had he been awake?

"I'm going to see how bad it is out there and if there's a clear path to the car."

I bolted from the bed, aiming for my dry pants. "I'm coming with you."

"No." An immediate answer flew from his mouth. "You'll be safer here."

Not expecting his response, I lowered my head, afraid to say what I was really thinking. What if he got lost and didn't make it back? What if he got hurt and *couldn't* make it back?

"It'll be easier and faster for me to go alone." His voice softened.

My insides twisted, and I gave him my mom's worst glare. Was he ditching me because he thought I'd slow him down?

"Am I too much to worry about?" I searched his face, but his eyes hinted nothing to confirm my accusation. "I promise I won't be a bother." I fought tears. "Hassan, don't leave me … please."

"I promise I'll be back." He walked over and put his hand on my arm. "I promise I won't leave you."

Or forsake you. Guilt nibbled at my insides. I'd forgotten to pray. *The Lord is my Shepherd*, I began.

I shall not want, Hassan added.

He makes me lie down in green pastures, I mouthed the familiar prayer. *He leads me beside the still waters.*

We finished the 23rd Psalm together, and he hugged me.

I pulled away before I couldn't let go. "Be careful and hurry back."

After studying my face, he kissed my forehead. "I will."

Chapter 43

JANACLESE

Pacing the floor, I checked my watch. *God, it's been two long hours. What could possibly hold him up for two hours?*

Once again, I peered through the window. Branches and litter decorated the yard. One uprooted cedar I hadn't noticed the night before lay on its side. Where were the singing birds?

A sharp twinge pricked my stomach, alerting me I hadn't taken my migraine medicine. If I wanted to avoid being sick, I had to stay calm.

I sat for a moment, wringing my hands ... *Hassan, please be careful.*

I stood and looked out the window again. Maybe I should search for him. What if I leave and he returns, and we miss each other? My restless legs made the decision. I wiggled into my half-dry jeans, then hopped around on one foot trying to slip into my still damp tennis shoes while skittering for my basket. He wouldn't have gone too far without me.

One hand on the door ... and I sensed his presence. I paused, listening to his footsteps sliding through fallen leaves before landing onto the porch. I swung the door open, breathing a sigh of relief. "Hassan!"

With straight shoulders and a high chin, his confident smile instantly calmed me. Surely, we could head home now.

"Are the roads clear? Did you find the truck?"

"We can leave." His confident smile faltered for a second, appearing hesitant.

I gave him a questioning look, noticing he didn't answer my questions.

"The roads are clear, and you spotted the truck?"

"We've just survived a major storm. Trees are down everywhere, power lines are low, foreign debris—"

"So you didn't see the truck?"

"I didn't make it that far. It's pretty slow going, and I knew you'd worry, so I turned back."

I'd worry? This wasn't just about us. We both had loved ones who were probably sick with worry. I sighed, the smell of mud permeated my nostrils. "It's just ... um, our families."

"I know you're concerned, but—"

"And you're not?" My trembling lips snapped at him.

He tilted his head. "You're treating me like I caused the storm—like I planned to trap you here."

"Well, you did suggest hiking all the way out here to a special, secluded place." I planted my hands on my hips.

"Only because you kept saying your mom's eyes are everywhere." He brushed his hand through the air like he was painting the sky. "You're trying so hard to get away from your family, you even convinced me to leave my cell phone in the truck. Trust me, Janaclese, some of us like being connected to our families and *wish* we had a mom who cares."

"You know what?" I wagged my finger, feeling sparks of anger. "Do you know what?"

"What!"

I stalked down the steps. "I can find the truck by myself."

Before he dared speak to me again, I dashed toward the woods. I didn't care that I didn't know where I was going. I didn't care that I didn't have the key. Pride, anger, fear—I don't know exactly what—propelled me down the hill with much less effort than struggling upward the previous day.

Before long, I groped my way into the woods, pushing back briars snapping at my legs. New smells and sounds combined with my unfamiliarity of the surroundings, heightening my senses. I lost track of time and direction as I deepened among the trees. But I wasn't worried.

Hassan was dead on my trail.

I knew it because I felt him. That indescribable magnetic force hadn't left me. It moved when I proceeded, stopped when I rested and turned in every direction I took.

The faint sound of lapping water filled my ears. The stream! We'd crossed it right before our picnic. I hustled into a steady trot, the bulky basket hitting my side, Hassan's energy tracking me. As I got closer, the pitch of the water grew louder, resonating like roaring thunder.

I ran until I reached it, suddenly skidding to a fast stop. My heart followed.

The shallow stream was swollen.

Wider, deeper, and accelerated water rushed through it. How could something so tranquil quickly turn to turbulence? I couldn't hold back the tears this time. "No, no, no ..."

I turned to face Hassan, and he placed a hand on my shoulder but offered no words.

"Are we still fighting?" I drew in a sharp breath, not wanting what we shared to suddenly change like the stream had done. "'Cause if we are ... then, then ..."

"Then we start over." He held my hands. "I'm sorry."

His apology was accepted. But I wanted him to fix it, rewind time and make the nightmare go away.

A quick scan of the area uncovered paper and debris floating all around us—high in the battered trees, along the moist grass and even in the rust-colored stream. Water had settled in practically every hole or low spot it could find.

"How did you know we needed to move to higher ground?" My low voice shook.

Hassan shrugged. "I didn't ... I just wanted to keep you safe."

"I'm sorry for blaming you," I said.

"I'm not God," he responded with a straight face.

Exhaustion precluded me from asking what he meant. It also blocked any rational thoughts of getting to safety. I didn't want to argue. I wanted to keep moving, get home, but I was clueless. "Should we try to cross it?"

"Not here. The current looks powerful, but it's still early enough not to be at its worst. Maybe if we keep walking, we can find a shallower area to cross. We have to wait and see."

We needed a real plan. "What if that doesn't work? Then what? What if the water's still raging?"

"Then we turn back." He picked up a stick and started walking in a take-charge fashion. Glancing over his shoulder, he spoke as I stood still watching him. "You don't have to trust me."

What choice did I have? I skipped to catch up. "I trust you, Hassan."

"No, really." He stopped, picked up another stick, studied it, then tossed it aside. His pace quickened. "Gotta practice what you preach."

I sidestepped a low-hanging branch. "What are you talking about?"

"Faith." He directed me around a pothole. "It comes easy when everything's going well." He stooped to examine a branch cast to the ground. "But as soon as tragedy strikes … something unexpected happens … warriors become wimps. That won't be my story."

I paused considering his words against the past few months of my life. Hadn't planned on it being my story, either. I frowned, brushing my dirty hands against my shirt. Is that what he thought of me now that he'd seen the real deal?

"How can a soldier win a war if he never fights any battles?" He thrust the stick in my hand. "Use this one."

Soldiers, wars … I just wanted to find the truck and go home. I had no idea why I needed a stick, but I took it. It didn't take long to discover it helped me balance along our muddy trail. We must've walked miles before the stream narrowed. Two hours later, we'd scarcely covered three miles, but we found a bank where the stream narrowed a bit.

Hassan dipped his stick into the water, then measured it against his legs. "Must be about three feet deep. Can you see the rocks?"

"Yes." But staring into the flowing water made me dizzy. I blinked. "I don't know if I can wade through."

"Follow me and stay on the rocks." He skipped to the first one. "It's like dancing. Just like before ... leap and balance."

A warrior, not a wimp. I focused on my landing before my feet left the ground.

"Good," he said, before hopping to another rock. "Do it again."

Jumping from rock to rock, I became intense, blocking out Hassan's applause and his encouraging cheers. Half-way across, something wiggled past the rocks, and I squelched a scream.

"Hassan," I whispered. "Wh ... what's that?"

Worry lines marked his forehead. "Where?"

Unable to move my lips or my feet, I pointed.

Moments of focused gazing led to his face relaxing into a grin, then an outright laugh. "Seaweed. It's just seaweed."

"Are you sure?" My heart pumped.

"Positive." He stirred his stick around in the water, then held up algae. "See?"

How was I supposed to know that?

I leaped and skidded across a slippery rock. Losing my focus and balance, I fell to my knees and splashed face downward into the water. Bobbing up, I spewed gritty water from my mouth, leaving a sour taste on my tongue. Panic swept over me as my stick moved further away.

Oh God, I'm gonna drown, die right here in the wilderness.

"Stand up," Hassan yelled.

"My ..." A chill from the cold wetness made me shudder. Coughing and sputtering, I scraped my knee against a rock as I tried to spread my body. "... stick."

Why couldn't I stand up? My muscles tensed, and my body folded into itself. Like all the other debris, my body started to be tugged downstream.

Hassan launched from a rock to grab hold of my shoulders. "Janaclese, I've got you. Stand up."

I pulled at him, and he twisted my hands away. "Look at me. Don't fight. Look at me."

My gaze flitted from his calm face closing in on me to my floating stick getting farther away. I needed to focus.

"You're okay, Shawty." He repeated soothing words in an even voice. "Everything's all right."

When I finally stood, we waded to the other side of the stream, the water barely reaching my waist.

I swallowed. "I'm sorry. I don't know what happened. I can swim."

"I know. I remember from your friend's pool party." He didn't sound angry or judgmental, but did he think I was a flake?

"You probably won't believe this, but I used to be on the swim team. Was actually thinking about being a lifeguard next year ... um, maybe ... um, I'm so sorry." Why was I rambling? This is *not* how I wanted us to get to know each other. "My friends say I talk too fast sometimes."

"I like it when you do that." He laughed. "Not panic and try to drown yourself, of course. But when you talk so freely about everything and nothing in particular, it relaxes me."

I wanted to bear hug him for saving my life and not making me feel stupid. Instead, I clasped my hand in his. Both wet, we walked and talked until the landscape looked somewhat familiar again, letting the midday sun dry us off.

"The truck's just around the bend." Hassan raced ahead of me.

I looked up at the sky, clear and blue like there had been no angry storm clouds yesterday. My thoughts swerved to how quickly things had changed from the little tiff Hassan and I had earlier in the morning. I'd vowed our relationship wouldn't be like my parents, yet there we were fighting anyway. What if we hadn't fought? Maybe disagreements were somehow important. *Especially if there was reconciliation.*

A smile tugged at my lips, and I grinned—*Make up like we'd done.*

Skedaddling around the corner, I hustled along to reach Hassan.

Shoulders slumped, he looked straight ahead, frowning. I searched his face. The confidence had vanished.

Heaviness pressed on my chest. I followed his gaze. A large limb from a pine tree lay across the busted windshield. Glass glistened in the boggy road and on the grass.

The heaviness sank to my stomach.

I wanted to encourage him like he'd assured me, but my faith was waning. "What now?"

"We pray," came the solemn response.

Chapter 44

JANACLESE

"Phoenix! Here, boy!"

Barking dogs and a man's voice, followed by a series of whistles, interrupted our prayer.

Hassan's eyes narrowed into tiny slits as he looked into the sunlit sky. "You thinking what I'm thinking?"

Releasing his hand, I straightened. Thoughts of getting home had ruled my mind for the last twenty-four hours, but of course, he must've already known that. I gazed into his face. "What're you thinking?"

"Might be an answer to our prayer." He pointed toward the barking. "Let's head in that direction."

The barking grew louder as we trampled along the muddy, grassy path. When we reached the source of the sound, an elderly white man was loading hound dogs into a wire cage on the bed of his pickup.

"Hello," Hassan called out.

The elderly man stopped tussling with the dog leashes and jerked his head around. "Yeah?"

"Any chance you headed into the city?" Hassan squeezed my hand as he spoke to the gentleman whose leathery face appeared worn from too much sun.

"Hadn't planned on it. Roads pretty tore up after that microburst." More wrinkles outlined the man's eyes, making him appear older than he probably was. He studied us for a second, then proceeded to unhook the leashes from the dogs. "What're y'all doing way out here anyway?"

Hassan gestured toward me before speaking. "My friend and I got stranded in yesterday's storm."

"Yeah. That microburst came suddenly, did its damage and left just as quickly." The latch rattled as he closed the dog pen. "I lost my hound out here yesterday training for rabbit season. Thought I had all seven of my dogs, but one didn't come back."

I counted six restless canines in the metal cage. "We didn't see any stray dogs out there, sir."

He scratched his head. "Couldn't have gone too far. They usually stay pretty close. I've been out here all morning. Guess I'll be back again tomorrow." He looked up at the sky, then darted his eyes past us. "That your truck busted up back there?"

"The Chevrolet?" Hassan nodded. "Yes, sir."

"Well, I'm Mr. Archer. Y'all climb on in. I can get you as close as the roads'll let me."

Hassan grabbed my hand again, took two steps toward the truck, then yanked me back as if suddenly startled. His eyes narrowed.

I knew that look. It was the same expression he'd worn when he'd stood between Reb and me.

Following his line of vision, I noticed a gun standing upright inside the truck.

"Excuse me, sir." Hassan pulled me aside and whispered, "Janaclese, I'm not sure about this."

"Why not?" I tried to control the desperation in my voice. "We have to get home."

Hassan arched his brows. "He's got a .22 rifle in his truck."

"So? He said he lost his dog while training for rabbit season yesterday."

"You don't need a gun to find a lost dog. I don't trust him."

"We need help."

He folded his lips inward.

I shook my head, then Hassan's reluctance hit me. White man with a gun, the two of us cast away where no one would think to search for us. I glanced around. The thick brush and low vines seemed to stretch for miles. We had to take a chance. "Just because he's different, doesn't mean he's bad."

"He looks like maybe he shouldn't be trusted."

"And he's probably thinking we're ghetto hood-rats up to no good. But he's willing to help us. Besides it's Sunday."

His eyebrows lifted two inches. "What? People don't commit crimes on Sunday in the suburbs where you live?"

"I meant the church is probably praying for us today. Aunt Alicia is probably about to lead praise and worship just before Uncle Sam preaches." A wave of nostalgia swept my inside. "With all the prayers covering us, we're gonna be fine."

"How can we be sure he—"

"We can't. Try the faith thing you reminded me of earlier." I braved my way toward the truck, ignoring Hassan's doubt.

He stayed on my heels, not once allowing space between us.

As we clambered onto the long bench seat, the relief of going home sank in. Yet, dread trailed the thought of my parents being upset and worried all the time I was away. "Mr. Archer, I need to call my parents. May I use your cell phone?"

"Technology ... now that right there is the main cause of the generation gap. My grandchildren can't even hold a decent conversation. Don't even know if my great-grands can talk. They keep their faces plastered to a screen while their fingers flick up and down like nervous robots."

My stomach soured. Did that mean he didn't have a cell phone?

Hassan and I glanced at each other, seemingly thinking the same thing—just because you were born in the early twentieth century, didn't mean you had to stay trapped in a time capsule.

"Ain't got no cell phone, and I don't want one." He started the engine. "Who your folks?"

The messy roads wouldn't permit Mr. Archer to take us further than the Zippy Mart convenience store, which was five miles from Dad's. Exhausted, we trudged our way to the shack.

"We're here," I said, hesitating before going up the steps.

"Your dad's gonna be relieved I got you home safely." Hassan's face didn't match his calm words.

When I climbed onto the porch and peeked through the window, my heart tumbled. "Oh, no."

"What is it?" Hassan asked, standing next to me.

"My ... my mom's here."

Through the opened curtain, I saw the dimly lit living room where my parents had announced their planned reconciliation two weeks ago. Mom sat in the corner of the couch, turned away from Dad, her head buried in its arm. Dad's hand rested on her back, comforting her.

"We'd better go get this over with." Hassan raised his fist to knock on the door.

"Wait." I pulled his arm away. I hadn't imagined us facing both of my parents together, at the same time—the tag team was a double threat.

"Janaclese, what are you afraid of?" Concerned colored his voice. "We haven't done anything wrong."

I lowered my head. How could I tell him?

"What is it, Shawty?"

Hearing my pet name melted my insides. "My parents don't know about you."

Hassan's eyes bulged. "What?" He took a step backward. "Whadda you mean 'they don't know about me'? We've been talking on the phone and seeing each other for weeks."

I was quiet. That always seemed the best approach to keep people calm, especially when they were threatening to explode.

"Sure, Pops never met you, but trust me, he knows all about you." Hassan spoke as if he were struggling to control his disappointment.

I opened my mouth to explain, but no words came out.

He shook his head. "So you've been lying to hang out with me?"

"Not exactly." The low, soft words seeped from my mouth.

"Sneaking around is like lying." He turned around in a circle, rubbing his head. "Are you ashamed of me or something?"

"Of course not!" The shock in my voice seemed to jolt both of us.

"Then what? What is it?"

"I just haven't gotten around to telling them yet."

He rubbed his forehead. "This is hard enough for me. Having to explain to your parents where I've been overnight with their daughter. Now you're telling me they didn't even know I exist?"

My stomach clenched. I'd never considered this scenario—bringing home an unkempt, Tarzan-like boyfriend to meet my parents for the first time. They'd be glad to see me. But what about seeing him?

Hassan sighed and lifted his fist toward the porch column.

"No, don't touch ..."

Crash!

The column landed straight through the window, shattering the glass.

Within seconds the front door swung open. Dad stood front and center with Mom pulling up the rear. One look at me and they leaped over the fallen column.

"Janaclese! Are you okay?" My parents just about squeezed the life out of me—hugging and asking questions all at once. "We were worried sick. Where were you?"

I pulled away from the huddle and glanced over at Hassan. "I ..."

Dad's gaze flitted back and forth like he'd just noticed I wasn't alone. His shoulders stiffened. "What happened ... and who's this?"

Hassan extended his hand. "Sir, my name is—"

"Hassan," Mom said as a matter of fact.

As if by habit, Dad properly obliged a handshake, then quickly withdrew his hand. The confusing frown on his face grew deeper when he turned to Mom. "You know this fellow?"

The same question had raced through my mind.

"I know *of* him." Still holding my hand, Mom sidestepped a piece of glass.

"I know this looks bad, but I can fix it," Hassan said.

Was he referring to the column or this awkward situation? Truthfully, I didn't know how he'd repair either.

"Let's step inside." Dad's usual light nature was buried beneath seriousness.

Broken glass, splintered wood, and a few shingles cluttered our narrow pathway into the house. The humid, musty odor that settles after a good rain created stuffiness inside the shack.

"I'm sorry about the column, sir." In a jerky motion, Hassan scraped one hand across his head, then rubbed both hands down the legs of his jeans. "My pops and I—"

"No discussion of the column just yet, son." Dad's bloodshot eyes didn't blink. "How'd you end up finding my daughter and bringing her home?"

Did Dad mean to be so gruff?

"Uh, Franklin." Mom eyed the debris scattered beneath the broken window on one side of the living room, then gestured toward the kitchen. "Maybe we can talk in there."

She led us into the jumbled space, which now doubled as Dad's workstation. Several flat sheets of white paper covered the glass kitchen table, along with sketch pencils, pens, a ruler, and a compass.

I fidgeted with the tail of my shirt. "I really have to use the bathroom."

"Franklin?" Mom squeezed my hand and seemed to want Dad's permission for me to be excused.

Dad nodded without removing his gaze from Hassan.

Mom tightened her grip on my hand and escorted me to Dad's room. "Use this bathroom in case your friend needs the one in the hallway."

"Okay," I said, twisting my hand free from hers.

As soon as the door clicked shut, I heard frantic dialing. She must've hit speed dial then clicked on speaker phone.

"Hello, hello? Any news?" Khara's panicky voice rang clear.

"Your little sister is home safe and sound." Air spilled from Mom like it had been cramped in her lungs.

"Thank God! Is she alright?"

"Seems to be." The shakiness in Mom's response accompanied sniffling. "After all the worrying, I'm just so relieved."

"Me too." Khara paused, then shot the next question off like an afterthought launched from a cannon. "You're gonna get her, right? I mean, Janaclese disobeyed Dad by not keeping her cell phone on. And this is the second time in two weeks she's kept us up all night. Was she with that Hassan boy?"

I jerked the faucet on. They'd suspected all along? How did they know Hassan's name?

"We haven't talked yet," Mom said to Khara.

I splashed water on my face, trying to cool the heat creeping up my neck. Like my own swaying emotions, I sensed Mom's relief and disappointment.

Khara spoke again. "Regardless of what you find out, you should make Janaclese wear a leash."

I frowned.

"A leash?" Mom asked.

"Yeah, the child safety harness for kids who wander off from their parents."

Would she do that? I adjusted the water to just a trickle to overhear their conversation.

"That would be embarrassing." Mom's chuckle sounded strained, but at least she'd laughed.

"I'm not kidding." Khara sounded hurt. "When have you *ever* cared about embarrassing us just to teach a lesson? For crying out loud, you're still walking around in pajamas."

"Leisurewear," Mom corrected her. "And I get your point."

I dried my hands and opened the door before she actually agreed with Khara's insanity.

Mom glanced at me, then spoke more hurriedly into the phone. "Call Kharee and Me-maw, then ask your Aunt Alicia to please initiate the church's phone tree. Our prayers have been answered."

"Sure thing, Mom. Tell Janaclese welcome home. And by the way, Target sells the leash—"

Mom hit the speaker button, muting Khara's voice. "Thank you, Khara. She just stepped back in. I'll call you later."

After disconnecting, Mom stared at me for a brief moment. "Are you okay?"

I nodded, pushing down the lump in my throat. "I'm sorry. I didn't mean to get stranded and worry everybody."

She rose from sitting on the bed. "Let's join your father. That way, you don't have to repeat your story."

We walked back into the kitchen where Dad stood above Hassan as he sat at the round glass table talking on the phone. Dad hadn't bothered clearing his blueprints and drawings to make the room more presentable.

Hassan pressed the phone to his ear. "Pops, you know me better than that ... yes, sir ... I left my cell in the car." He glanced at me, then quickly broke eye contact. "Yeah, Pops. We went back for it, but the truck was crashed."

I couldn't read Hassan's expression, so I eyed Dad. How much of our story had Hassan already told him through his phone call?

As soon as Hassan clicked off the phone, Dad picked up the ruler from the table and started lecturing. "Is it me or has the world gone crazy?"

Nobody answered.

He smacked the ruler against his palm. "Some dating rules may sound archaic to you young folks, but we're a family of traditional values."

I tucked my hands by my side. I knew my family's values. Maybe that was why I hadn't wanted my parents knowing about Hassan. Who else in the twenty-first century assumed dating was the same as courtship, and courtship was *only* for marriage?

Dad placed the ruler down—a slow, deliberate, controlled motion yet, his jawline flinched. He stared at Hassan. "Do you normally date girls without getting their parents' permission?"

Under the table, Hassan bounced his knee. "Uh ... actually, sir ... uh, I don't date."

My heart slammed into the pit of my stomach. That sounded so wrong.

Dad closed his eyes and took a deep breath.

The moment would've been a good time for me to jump in and explain, but my little courage was no match for Dad's anger nor Mom's disappointment.

Mom sat quietly like she was biting back words of her own. And Dad's broad hands covered his entire face as he raked them up and down his cheekbones.

He glared at Hassan, then squinted. "Son, I'm just a tad bit confused—and concerned—about your last statement. So, you just randomly take girls out on picnics, but it's not considered a date?"

"No, sir. I didn't mean it like that." Hassan's leg kicked forward beneath the table. "Janaclese and I are good friends, and I'd very much like to date her. I thought … I just thought …"

Dad's patience waned. "Well, before you get to thinking too much. Let me clear something up. Janaclese isn't allowed to date anyone we haven't met and given the okay. I don't know the rules of other girls' homes, but you should *always* show respect by asking first."

Hassan lowered his head, then gave eye contact. "Mr. and Mrs. Mitchell, I'm sorry for offending you. I should've asked to see your daughter. The next time—"

"Next time? Slow your row, son. You're mighty confident to assume there will be a next time. When it comes to Janaclese, even if you want to sit next to her in the church pew, ask."

Did Dad really have to swim that far out? My eyes pleaded with Mom.

"Franklin." Mom tried to reel Dad in. "The kids have been through a lot. Can we table the interrogation for now? I'm sure they're tired and hungry."

Dad fidgeted. "I'd drive you home, but your dad says the road to your street is closed. Might be open tomorrow."

My thoughts sped to my Prius. Had Hassan's neighborhood been hit bad enough to wreck my car? *Lord, please don't let this nightmare get any worse.*

Mom scooted her chair from the table and headed toward the refrigerator. She unloaded lunch meat and condiments, then circled over to the breadbox. "Janaclese, go get cleaned up in your dad's bathroom. You and I will sleep in his room tonight." She untwisted the bread tie and took out a few slices. "Franklin, you and Hassan can have Janaclese's room."

"He's staying the night?" My wide eyes and high, shrill voice wasn't meant to convey excitement. My parents had shocked me.

But their hard stare piercing my core told me I'd shocked them even more.

Chapter 45

JANACLESE

"Sorry I made you worry," I said to Mom while pulling back the top sheet on Dad's bed.

"As a mother, that's what I'm genetically wired to do." She lifted a throw pillow from her side of the bed and sat holding it.

"Were you worried something really awful had happened to me?"

"Deep down, I knew you were okay. At least I'd prayed and believed God had you covered." She patted the pillow. "I found myself worrying about whether you were hungry or if you'd dressed warmly enough. And then, I wondered if you'd remember to pray."

"I did. We prayed together."

"Hassan prayed?" She sounded surprised and pleased.

"Um-hum." I climbed into bed, then slanted my eyes without turning to look at her. "Were you concerned that I was with a boy?"

"Yes … well, no … okay, maybe just a little." Mom's indecision made me look at her. She sat on the edge of the bed, hugging the throw pillow, twisting its tassels around her fingers. "I didn't tell your dad I suspected you were with Hassan because I didn't want to deal with his questions or struggle with the 'what-ifs' in my own mind."

So that explained why Dad seemed shocked to see Hassan, but she didn't.

"How'd you know? Who told you?"

"When you didn't come to Paint the Park, Khara tried to cover for you. She said a group of kids went paintballing. At first, it was no big deal—just wished you'd told me you had other plans." She glanced at me with misty eyes. "Don't know how, or *when*, we stopped talking."

I could feel the guilt on my face as my heart dropped, and I remembered what Hassan had said when we were at odds. "Now's a good time to start again."

Mom nodded. "After the event, your dad was loading the grill when the storm came out of nowhere. I called the local paintball store, and the owner put Trevor on the phone. He said he hadn't seen you all day." Her words slowed. "That was bizarre. You've never lied to us."

I chewed my lip, considering defending myself. Maybe I misled Khara, but I hadn't outright lied.

"So I called your sister back, and she mentioned you had a picnic basket like you were possibly meeting a boy."

I bit my lower lip a little too hard. The salty taste of blood brushed my tongue.

"I found that even more strange." She sighed. "Long story short, Miracle gave me Cyndray's number."

"Cyndray?" My mouth dropped. *My best friend ratted me out? Seriously!* "Cyndray mentioned Hassan?"

Mom eyed me. "Yes, but she implied he was a good boy, a member of our church who wouldn't hurt you." She repositioned her hunched posture on the bed. An unusual throat noise escaped as she tilted her head toward me. "Why didn't you tell me you were interested in this young man?"

I gulped. "I tried that day at the Center when you were working in the garden—right before you and dad left town together."

"I thought that was hypothetical."

"Maybe at the time, but it escalated."

"Escalated?" She frowned. "How far have you gone with him?"

"I don't know," I muttered, feeling as if somehow I'd messed up.

She tossed the pillow aside. "Haven't we discussed this?"

"Yes." My slow nod contrasted her jerky movements. "How far is too far?"

"Oh, Janaclese!" She covered her mouth with her hand and then stood and paced the floor. "Did you … you didn't … I'm afraid to ask."

"I slept—"

"Heavenly Father, most High God! Carry me, Jesus ..."

Mom's theatrics pushed me to my limits. "See! This is why we don't talk. I didn't do anything wrong. So what? I slept in the room with someone of the opposite sex." I waved my hands for emphasis. "That's it. That's what happened!"

She cocked her head to the side. "You didn't sleep in the bed with him?"

"No." I pressed my lips together. "But honestly, that wasn't because of me. It was Hassan's decision to let me sleep in the bed while he slept on a grungy chair. Sex was the last thing on my mind. I wanted him next to me because I was scared, Mom." Tears automatically flowed as I spoke. "I was so scared."

She pulled me into her and cradled me against her shoulder as she rocked me. "I know, baby. And I understand."

I pulled away so I could breathe. "You know what's worse?"

She waited.

"All I could think about was getting home. Getting home because of what you've preached to me about boys and the appearance of evil. Hassan helped me see it wasn't rational to dash through the woods in the middle of the storm or to cross a swollen stream just to get home. But I was so desperate to please you—to be your good girl—I couldn't even think right."

Tears tracked down Mom's cheeks. She sniffled. "Must've been traumatic, and that's why cell phones are important."

Was she still trying to teach me a lesson like it was my fault I ended up stranded?

"Even if I'd had my cell phone, there was no reception out there."

"And that's why we communicate truthfully with our loved ones beforehand." She wiped tears from her face. "We don't get angry and move out in the middle of the night when we're questioned about our whereabouts. We don't sneak around to date when we think it might be forbidden. We discuss issues and come to an agreement."

Why was she bringing up old stuff? "So you're mad now?"

"No, honey, I'm relieved." She squeezed me in a tight grip. "And I'm happy to have you home and so glad we're talking."

"Yeah, but you still didn't answer my question."

"What is it, baby?"

"I know you waited for marriage, and you want the same for me. But how far is too far?"

"Oh." She made that funny noise with her throat again. "Well … I guess it varies from person to person."

Was she being serious? "Mom, *how* did *you* and *Dad* abstain?"

She pulled at her pajama shirt collar, then fiddled with the sleeves. "Your father and I practiced group dating. When we went out alone, it was usually to public places like concerts, skating, and bowling. You know? Places where other people were *around*, even if they weren't *with* us."

"You didn't trust being alone with Dad?"

Mom's muscles tensed. "I don't think that was it."

"Then what? Because I trust Hassan."

Her eyes stretched wide when I mentioned Hassan's name.

Mom took a deep breath. "Sometimes when two people fall in love, they don't think clearly about premarital sex. You can never undo what's already done. As much as I loved Franklin, I still didn't want to gamble. And I didn't want any regrets."

"Not everyone has regrets, you know."

"But there's no guarantee." Her comeback was quick. "Besides, I used to be a worrywart."

I chuckled under my breath. As far as worrying, that apple hadn't fallen far from the tree. Evil foreboding is what Mrs. Patterson had called it. Probably why Mom and I suffered from migraines. Tension spilled from my body, and I relaxed. Seemed we had something in common. I cocked my head. "Used to be a worrywart?"

Mom face relaxed into a smile. "Okay, so I'm working on not being overprotective." She waved her hands as if shooing me. "I had so much going on back then, I didn't need to add an unwanted pregnancy or sexually transmitted diseases to the list."

"They didn't have condoms back then?"

Mom's arm jerked, releasing the pillow onto the floor. She placed it back onto the bed, then tugged at the top sheet until it was tight. She seemed to search the room for something to straighten.

I felt a slow smile creeping up. "You and Dad do a good job protecting me, but contrary to belief, I don't live under a rock."

She tucked a loose strand of hair behind her ear. "I know. Your dad had this talk with Kharee, and Alicia was naturally Khara's first choice. I hadn't expected you to have these questions so soon."

"Mom, I'm sixteen. I'm not ready to have sex, but I am ready to talk about it."

"That's why we planned the lock-in. I thought it would be easier without parents around."

Easier for who? The parents? "I'd prefer a one-on-one with you."

She slowly nodded. "Okay ... well, alright. I don't think abstinence is just about being safe. Lots of people practice safe sex, and still end up hurting emotionally."

I nodded. That sounded about right.

"There's a difference between love and sex. And there are many ways to show someone you love them, *without* engaging in sex. When I waited, I never felt used or exploited or that Franklin was with me for any other reason than he cared about me."

"But when you're so careful and always afraid of getting hurt, doesn't it take away the fun?"

"For me, it was the opposite. Actually, the option to *not* have sex made me less afraid, and I ended up relaxing and having more fun. Especially considering the negative consequences of some who chose the alternative." Mom smiled. "Your virginity is a special gift. You don't just give it away to the first interesting guy who comes along. There'll likely be more suitors. Wait for your husband."

"Yeah, I hear you. But kissing isn't wrong, is it?"

"It can be. If purity is your choice, then it's dangerous to place yourself in the way of temptation. And, quite honestly, I'd rather you didn't open certain doors that can lead to sex." She grunted. "Not everyone understands or respects their partner's desire to wait. Peer pressure, bullying in a relationship ... it's real. Some people have raging hormones. Cuddling, holding hands, even being unsupervised in the same room is too risky for them."

"Hassan and I aren't like that."

"That's good. But here's a little motherly wit to put under your belt. Some relationships start off slow and innocent, then blossom into something more. Others just need a small spark to explode into a wild, out-of-control flame. I don't want you going through that."

I yawned, seeing her point, but the conversation was about to get too personal.

"I know you have strong feelings for Hassan, or you wouldn't have been misleading in your actions. But when purity is the goal, you reach it through abstinence. You have to make the decision to remain sexually pure for yourself, without pressure from me or anybody else."

"Yeah, okay." I didn't want to talk about sex anymore. Not when it specifically boiled down to Hassan and me. I stretched my limbs like LeMew, Mrs. Patterson's overweight feline, then turned onto my side.

"Sleepy?"

"A little." I rubbed my eyes as my mind raced over the day's events. "Mom, you should've seen Hassan's truck when we finally found it."

"I heard him on the phone with his dad." She tilted her head. "Did he say Pops?"

I yawned again. "Yeah. That's what he calls him."

"You're beat." She clicked off the lamp on the nightstand. "Lights out, Janaclese."

Being without light reminded me of Hassan again. "Man, it's stupid dark in here."

She bent down and kissed my cheek. "I can still see you." She raked her hand through my hair, snagging her ring on my three-strand twists. "I've gotten used to these braids, but this new funky, hip talk ... I don't know."

I laughed. "Good night, Mom."

"Janaclese ..." She didn't move from my bedside. "Naturally, I worry about you. But, I want you to know I really do trust you. You're a good girl. But I don't love you just because you're good. I wouldn't withdraw my love or think any less of you for your mistakes. I don't expect you to be perfect. But I do expect you to be honest with me, to strongly consider your choices, then choose wisely."

I rolled over on my other side. "I can feel you next to me, but I can't see you."

She sighed. "But you can hear me in the *stupid* dark, right?"

I giggled. "Yeah, that's when it's so dark, it's crazy ridiculous—like you can't see your hand when it's right in front of your face. And you open your eyes wide, but you think they're still closed, and ..."

In the midst of my rambling, Mom reached down and gently stroked my face. Her touch, warm and soft like velvet, released more tension from my body.

And within minutes, I was out.

Chapter 46

JANACLESE

I lay in bed breathing in the calm. The feeling of being cloaked in somebody's arms gave me an unexplainable peace. I didn't want to move.

A tiny shift onto the pillow next to mine awakened a citrus fragrance—Mom's perfume. I flashed my eyes open and remembered … I was home. I'd slept with Mom.

I squinted against the sun and check the room. Where was she?

With a sigh, I realized it wasn't Mom creating this sensation anyway. I bolted upright. Hassan had to be near. How else could I explain the safety net concealing me? Excitement and adrenaline stirred inside. I threw back the covers and dashed into the bathroom to make myself presentable. After working in haste with my limited resources, I stepped into the hallway, meeting Dad.

"C'mon slowpoke. We've gotta get the boy home to his folks." Dad handed me a raspberry toaster strudel and practically pushed me out the door.

"But I thought the roads were closed?" I asked, wiping my eyes in case I'd missed some crusty gunk.

"Morning news says the main streets are now open. Probably just a few potholes on the boy's street like his dad mentioned last night, but it's not dark like last night. We can get close enough to walk him home if we have to."

I sighed. Not because it was still early, and not because my body was still too tired and achy to think about anything like walking. I sighed because Dad had regressed to calling Hassan "the boy."

We trailed into the yard where Mom stood talking to Hassan.

My heart sank as I took in the purse in Mom's hand. How come they didn't wake me up? Were they about to force Hassan to leave before saying goodbye to me, and then meet his pops without me?

With a creased face, Hassan nodded at Mom and Dad. "Thanks for everything, sir … ma'am."

He hadn't even bothered to look at me long enough to part his lips for a good morning. Dad must've scared the dickens out of him last night. At his next glance in my direction, I smiled. "Morning, Hassan. Did you sleep well?"

A brief return smile ripped across his face before he muttered, "Yeah, considering I had a pit bull sleeping on the floor at the foot of the bed as my guard dog."

I jerked my head around to my parents. Did they hear that?

Dad was doubling back inside the shack for some reason. Mom had walked ahead and now held open the front door of the car. "Sorry about the hospitality. Space is tight in this cozy cottage, and I didn't want anybody on the living room couch. Don't know how well we got up the glass and all last night."

I rolled my eyes. When had Dad's shack become a cozy cottage to Mom? They'd verbally reconciled, but neither had made an attempt to move in with the other. And I could bet my entire savings—a whopping $500—that Mom would never, in a million years, move into the shack, now called "cozy cottage." Why had I been so worried about that?

"No problem," Hassan said. "I talked to Mr. Mitchell, and I'll help him repair the column and the window right away."

I squinted. "But that column was already…" My fluttering heart prompted me to hesitate. "Never mind."

If Dad was trying to punish Hassan by getting free labor from him, then I'd use it to my advantage and make it worth the while for Hassan. Being confined to the house, yet forced to see my man every day? Priceless.

I scooted to the car and slid into the backseat next to Hassan.

"Janaclese, up here with your dad." Mom stood next to the front passenger's seat. "I'll ride back there."

What did they think we were going to do in the backseat in their presence?

I scuffed to the front seat, slapped on my seat belt, then recalled my conversation with Mom the night before. Everything was in the open. I had nothing else to hide.

Dad hopped behind the steering wheel already conversing. "The county's going to need a backup cleaning crew to keep the storm water drains from clogging. Otherwise, we might get some street flooding."

I settled into deep thoughts. I wanted to spend every waking moment with Hassan. Isn't that what people did when they were in love? My heart sank. *If that were true, then why are my parents still living apart?* Now that Mom knew about Hassan, I didn't have to sneak around her anymore. She could live with Dad…or he could live with her. *God, whatever it takes, please bring my parents back together like a family again.*

Dad maneuvered the car around a plastic recycling receptacle lying in the street.

"I know your father well," Mom was saying to Hassan in the backseat.

I glanced behind me. No surprises there—she knew everybody. Just another reason why I'd kept my crush a secret. Thought they'd scare Hassan off with the whole "meet the parents" ordeal. There was no turning back now. I was about to meet Hassan's pops for the first time.

"How do you like living in Red Hill?" she asked Hassan.

The bleep of an ambulance behind us faded Hassan's response. On instinct, Mom ushered a short prayer as the screeching siren grew louder, then passed us.

I held my breath with relief that she'd been interrupted during her turn to grill my boyfriend.

"Franklin, do you mind stopping by the house to check on it since we're out this way?"

Dad sat stiffly, his eyes nailed to the road. "Honey, we've got to get the boy home. Then pick up Janaclese's car."

I bit my bottom lip, feeling the tension rising. Did Dad really have to keep calling Hassan "the boy"?

"It'll only take a minute." Mom's voice sounded anxious. She'd been stranded at Dad's, waiting to bawl me out for not showing up at her event. "I just want to be sure everything's okay. Hassan, do you mind?"

"That's cool. Janaclese mentioned Mr. Mitchell designed it." A wide grin stretched across Hassan's face. "I'll bet that joint's tight."

I tensed. Funny how Hassan's slang seemed over-emphasized and weird now that my parents were around. I wanted him to talk normal, impress my folks.

Dad eyed me, but I couldn't pick up his expression. He adjusted the rearview mirror. "The house isn't huge, but a bit more spacious than my place."

"That's not what he meant," I said, blushing and feeling like a translator. "The joint's tight. He thinks it must be nice."

As we approached Mom's neighborhood, more sirens filled the air. Dad clicked on his signal and pulled to the shoulder of the narrow street. Blue and white swirling lights of a police car shot past us. Up the road, in the opposite direction, the clanging of a fire engine sounded. We watched as it made a right turn several streets ahead into Mom's subdivision.

"Heavenly Father." Mom seemed to not have any other words.

Dad checked his mirrors, twisted the steering wheel, and looped back onto the paved road. Soon, he turned down the path the emergency vehicles had taken.

We rode in silence, taking in the sight of uprooted trees and fallen power lines. The red, white, and blue stripes of a tattered flag, detached from its pole, waved from the branches of an oak.

"Franklin." High emotion rang in Mom's voice.

"It's probably not as bad as it looks." Dad's monotone voice spoke more than the comforting words he attempted. *It was probably worse than we could see.*

Suburbia reflected the aftermath of a passing storm that had shown no favoritism based on social status. Neighbors stooped over debris, looking as if they'd toiled for hours, searching for goods and cleaning trash and broken tree limbs from their usually manicured lawns.

I swallowed hard, gulping down guilt from having complained about waking up so early. Glancing over my shoulder, I saw Mom's misty eyes. She was so used to helping other people across town, but now her own neighborhood was in need.

Dad turned the corner onto Mom's street and stopped the car.

A throng of people blocked the roadway watching a raging inferno. We couldn't see what was burning, but we could hear the crackle of wood above the murmuring crowd.

"Is everything alright, Mr. Mitchell?" Hassan's curiosity sparked mine.

"Dad?" One look at Dad, and I knew something wasn't right.

"Betima, the street's crowded. I can't go any further. We should—"

But Mom was already out of the car, making her way to the swarm ahead.

"Betima!" Dad raced behind Mom without even shutting off the engine.

I couldn't move. What was happening?

Hassan hustled up front and switched off the engine, then tucked Dad's keys in his pocket. "C'mon, Janaclese. Maybe we can help with whatever they need."

His words spurred me to action, and I jetted after my parents. "Mom ... Dad ..."

"Keep her back, Hassan!" Dad's command made no sense. Didn't they need me?

But then I saw it for myself—our two-story house engulfed in hot flames.

"Let me go." I wrestled against Hassan's grip. "I have to help."

"Stay with me, Janaclese." Hassan cupped me in his arms.

Mom's frantic scream pounded my ears. Heated words—fast, furious —rotated around me. The smell of charcoal burned my lungs, my throat, my eyes. Too much, too sudden to grasp. I couldn't take it all in. Didn't want to.

Cramps zigzagged across my stomach—marching, stomping, angry, hard. My knees weakened, barely able to hold my body. Billowing black smoke dimmed my vision. The voices became inaudible, and my teary eyesight blurred until darkness was complete.

Chapter 47

CYNDRAY

Even though the storm had caused several closures, the church was open, and counseling had not been canceled. Fist in air, I was poised to knock when Dr. Beverly's office door swung open.

Her dark brown eyes sparkled with surprise when they met mine. "Oh, um … come in, Cyndray." My counselor checked her watch, then held up a slip of paper. "I'll be right back. Gotta run this note over to Pastor Sam before he starts Bible study."

"No problem. Take your time." I watched her sisterlocks bounce as she darted down the hallway.

After stepping into her cozy office, I made my way to the L-shaped couch in the center of the room where I'd sat for my last three sessions. Therapy with her seemed to be working. With the lights turned low and the relaxing sound of a waterfall, I was tempted to sneak in a nap on the bright orange sofa.

Kicking my legs up on the couch, I extended them and reclined on my back, looking up at the swirly white designs on the ceiling. An intricate pattern mapped into what looked like a humungous spider web overhead. But when I concentrated on small sections, I visualized different pictures—a flower, a cheerleader with pom-poms … or was that a Congo dancer with maracas?

I squinted, then shook my head. Why was I concentrating on something that didn't matter?   Maybe if I put the same effort into solving my problems, I wouldn't need therapy at all.

The door creaked open, and Dr. Beverly boogied back into her office. "Everything's been kinda crazy since the storm."

Crazy? I smothered any sign of surprise that a therapist would use that word.

"Cyndray, sit up, please." She swept my feet from her couch. "How are you today?"

"Good. Really good, I think." I sat upright, thinking how much I'd grown to really like my no-nonsense counselor. Today, her sisterlocks hung beneath her shoulders, not pulled back or pinned up like usual.

"So tell me about your last assignment. How did it go?"

"Found out I'm normal." I searched her face for a reaction. "I'm just a regular, ordinary girl."

"Mmm-hmm." Her light chuckle didn't expose whether she thought otherwise. "And you derived that conclusion, *how?*"

Last session, she'd asked me to find one person to trust. I'd done that.

"I wasn't afraid to kiss Trevor," I spouted out.

Except for the trickling waterfall, the room was quiet. I tried to read Dr. Beverly's expressionless face.

"Tell me more about the kiss," she said.

My heart dropped. Was she asking for details of what was supposed to be my first kiss?

Dr. Beverly tucked a section of locks behind her ear. "Any thoughts or feelings about what made you kiss Trevor?"

Somehow saying I wanted to fit in or be accepted didn't sound right. I settled for the next best answer. "You did."

She blinked, slowly at first, then more rapidly. "When did I tell you to kiss Trevor ... or any boy for that matter?"

"I thought you wanted me to risk trusting someone."

"Well, yes, I did say that. But I meant confront your fear of trust so we can address the underlying issue. I never saw being touched, or in your case, kissing a boy as the real concern for you."

"You didn't?" I leaned forward. "Then what's my problem?"

She tilted her bottom, settling deeper into her seat. "That's what I'd like to help you uncover."

The room was quiet again, and Dr. Beverly didn't fill the silence. I knew she wouldn't. She'd sit and watch me until I was ready to say more.

"I didn't feel weird in my belly when Trevor and I agreed to kiss. Maybe a little awkward, but slightly more comfortable than worrying about when and if it was ever going to happen. Or *how far* ..." I mumbled the rest under my breath, remembering the details about Tommy Dawg I'd already shared with Dr. Beverly.

"I see." She pursed her lips. "Let's talk about what you're really afraid of."

"*Afraid?* Who said anything about being scared?" My heart galloped like a race horse breaking out of starting gate. Images of Dawg pressing against me flashed through my head. "I just don't want anybody forcing me onto a road I don't want to travel down."

"Mmm-hmm ... I see." She paused, then locked her fingers together.

Studying her facial expression, I got nothing. Absolutely no insight. I scrunched my brows. "What're you thinking?"

"Well ... sounds like an emotional conflict to me. I imagine you must've felt some confusion because you obviously traveled down a road you didn't want to be on. You despise being touched, yet you—"

"That's not the same!" Why was she making me sound so crazy? Like my words and actions didn't line up? "Kissing Trevor was on my terms."

"Mmm-hmm ... I see."

"No, you don't see." My voice cracked. *Ugh!*

She sucked in a gust of air, then slowly released it. "Deep breaths, remember? Deep breaths will ease the anger."

Air couldn't flow through my flared nostrils fast enough, and I noticed beads of sweat forming on my arms. I didn't understand myself, so how could Dr. Beverly possibly understand me? I waited until I could soften my tone before speaking. "Sorry. It's just that you say 'I see' like you understand."

"Never apologize for how you feel. Not in here." She unlocked her fingers and opened her hands in yoga style. "This is a safe place for expressing yourself, no matter what emotion you feel, but I do need you to help me understand."

"I see." Mimicking her, I rolled my eyes. Today, Dr. Beverly with her perfectly crafted words sounded more like a therapist than a friend, and I hated it. "I wish you wouldn't treat me like a patient."

"How do you wish to be treated?"

"Like the normal human being I am." I couldn't control the rise in my voice. "I don't even know why I'm here."

"I remember why you said you wanted to see me when we first met, and I'm thinking of the progress you've made. How have things changed?"

Good question. Things were the same—if not worse. Counseling wasn't fixing me. Thought I'd confronted my trust issues and concerns about being touched by kissing Trevor, only to discover kissing wasn't my fear? All I wanted was to feel normal, but somehow I felt more like a hypocrite. Like a wimp, who'd gone against what she really believed.

"I thought you were gonna fix me, tell me how I could be normal." The last thing I wanted was to end up depressed like my mom. Or worse, shipped off to an institution like my brother, A.J. Dr. Beverly knew about my dysfunctional family. She'd recorded my family history. Why couldn't I have been born in a stable family like Janaclese's?

"If you think you're broken, your job is to discover ways to repair yourself. My role is to guide you through that process. I thought we were clear on that."

I shook my head. "I need answers."

"You have the answers within yourself. Just dig deeper."

When she pointed at me, I tucked my hands beneath my bottom to lessen the probability of acting on my thoughts. The batteries in my metal remote control were apparently dead. It was a shame how badly I wanted to break her artificial French-manicured nails for quoting some jacked-up lyrics she probably heard in an old song. *The answers are within yourself… humph.*

"I thought you could help me not mind being touched like a normal girl."

"Mmm-hmm ... I ss ..." Sounding like a hissing snake, Dr. Beverly caught herself just as the word 'see' almost escaped her lips. "Tell me more about not being a normal. When did you decide this was an issue?"

I responded with silence. What was I supposed to say? Insanity was in my blood?

"Correct me if I'm missing something, but earlier I thought I heard you say you didn't like worrying about *how far* a kiss would go and that kissing Trevor was on *your* terms. I didn't know your actions were about being normal."

Sweat moistened my palms, and my armpits started itching.

Dr. Beverly gazed into my eyes like she was staring into a crystal ball. "I'm interested in knowing about the last time you felt abnormal. Can you tell me about that experience and what it was like for you?"

Dr. Beverly waited for an answer. The silence lingered until it turned hostile.

I squirmed, rubbing my arms against my sides.

"I'm hearing not feeling normal is a concern for you."

Did silence have a voice? I hadn't uttered a word. How did she hear anything from me except my rapid breathing?

"Perhaps you're wondering if you're like other teens your age."

Her soft, gentle statement was spot on. Truth be told, I suspected something very bad had to be wrong with me. I was way more mature than Janaclese, Miracle, and Kehl-li combined. Why wasn't I ready for a real relationship with a boy? Dawg couldn't have had that kind of effect on me. After all, I survived.

"I've been exposed to more stuff than my friends. I've seen more, done more ..." My voice tone split, and I whipped my hands out from beneath my tailbone and waved them. "Except, you know ... *that.*"

A blank expression preceded her next question. "*That* meaning ... uh, what exactly?"

Was she having a slow moment? Sheesh! The only thing worse than a dummy was pretending to be one. "Sex. I told you last time I was a virgin. I've never had sex before."

"I'm assuming you think you should be at that stage because your friends are." She paused but continued when I nodded. "Maturity in one area doesn't guarantee maturity in all areas. Actually, being more worldly—so to speak—could be why you're hesitant and prefer *not* being touched by the opposite sex. Maybe you've seen what intercourse can lead to."

Yeah. I'd seen plenty, but I wasn't sure that's what bothered me. "Am I off a little bit?"

"By *off*, are you asking if I think you're normal?"

I nodded again. I had to worry about things like that since my mother and brother had mental issues. I had to pay attention to all the signs. We weren't like the Mitchells. Even through the separation, the Mitchells were more together than any family I knew.

"What everybody else in the world is doing shouldn't be the measuring stick for what's right for you." She smiled, then lifted her eyebrows. "It's perfectly normal not be ready for sex at your age."

"Were you ready at sixteen?"

"We're focusing on you, not me." She tilted her head as if shocked by my question, then pursed her lips before speaking more gently. "But if it helps, I don't think most people are emotionally ready at that age."

"I guess if I had all those giddy feelings about doing it, then made a conscious choice not to do it, then perhaps I'd feel better." But those feelings hadn't surfaced for me, and my words seemed too inadequate to explain. I used my hands to gesture as I tried again. "I want to be the kind of person who can push her emotions aside and make a decision to abstain on purpose—not someone who abstains because she has no feelings and doesn't care about whether she kisses a boy or not."

"But you are abstaining on purpose. Lots of people—girls and boys—engage in sex just to follow the crowd. They don't necessarily *feel* anything either. I'd much rather be in your shoes."

"Really?" My heart fluttered. *I wasn't a hopeless case?*

"Sure. Think about having to control raging hormones. Do you see how blessed you are not to have those challenges?" She glanced at the clock which indicated our time was almost up. "One day, I suspect you'll get there—the giddiness and all. You'll remember this conversation and wish for a day when you could simply hang with guys without thoughts of crossing the friendship line."

I sat processing her words. Was I really the lucky one? Everybody else was anxious about having a boyfriend. Frankly, I could care less. And that was normal? Didn't it make me just a little crazy worrying about not being worried?

Dr. Beverly cleared her throat. "Any final thoughts before we end our session for today?"

Too bad our time was up just when I was starting to feel better about not being normal. "So feeling weird about kissing and sex is okay for me right now?"

"You've been through a rough patch that may have caused you to feel the way you do. Your feelings are perfectly normal for now. Embrace them. Let them serve in helping you make wiser choices. Might also keep you out of trouble."

"So it's okay to not be okay?"

She smiled. "As long as you're on the way to being okay."

"Oh. I almost forgot to mention it; I registered for the lock-in like you suggested. Guess I'll learn more about purity and waiting from God's perspective."

"I'm sorry, but the church had to postpone this year's lock-in. The note I gave Pastor Sam was to announce our community out-reach on that date. In light of all that's happened with the storm, we needed to reprioritize." Worry lines surfaced between her eyes. "I hope the teens understand. I know how much they were looking forward to the lock-in."

Not the ones I know. Janaclese had outright refused. "I'm sure it'll be fine."

She smiled and walked me to the door. "If you have urgent questions ... you know, about what we talked about ... feel free to call me."

Strange how all of sudden she didn't come straight out and say sex. I didn't have any more questions about kissing. Seemed kissing didn't make me more— or less— normal. And sex definitely didn't. And for me, it was normal not to be normal. At least for now.

I scratched my head. What did "normal" really mean anyway?

Chapter 48

CYNDRAY

I stepped out of Dr. Beverly's office. Random hallway noises overlapped with chatter. With practically everything in the community closed, Bible study seemed unusually crowded tonight. I strained my neck, searching for signs of Janaclese among the pockets of people settled along the corridor.

"Boo!" A bear-like tackle from behind was followed by a low whisper, "Is your head on straight?"

Recognizing Janaclese's spirited voice, I turned and saw my friend's big dimples. I playfully pushed her away. "My head's on straight. Dr. Beverly just talked me out of killing you. Where have you been?"

"You haven't heard?" Her bewildered eyes widened, but she was anything but speechless. Words tumbled and jumbled from her mouth in the usual Janaclese way. "Mom and Dad finally met Hassan. Talk about embarrassing. And guess what else? After all that sneaking around, I heard Mom tell Hassan she knew his pops very well. And we were on our way to actually meet his pops when Mom suddenly wanted to check on her house after the storm, but we were too late because it was on fire. And then, today—"

"What?" My brainwaves swirled like a spinning top. "Slow down. You said house fire? I thought you were on punishment for being caught with Hassan."

"Hassan and I are old news." Her face grew serious. "My mom's house caught on fire. We managed to save some stuff, but she can't live there right now."

"You're kidding right?" I found no humor reflected in her eyes. "What happened?"

"The police are still investigating. They think the storm damaged Mom's propane tank. The inspector and adjuster are coming this week too, so we'll find out what's what."

Her expression changed as her attention split between me and the other activity around us.

I felt empty. All I could think about was loss. Janaclese's loss. And I had nothing to give her. "Your mom must be devastated."

"You'd think." She looked past me and stared down the hallway. The light in her eyes dimmed.

Laughter floated through the crowd, and I traced the sound to Janaclese's mother, reeling back on her heels while conversing with Mr. Clean. Her chortling became silent for a few seconds as she gasped for more air, then spilled into the hallway like a rain shower. For someone suddenly displaced from her home, she was seemingly in good spirits.

Mrs. Mitchell had on a hideous, deep purple sweat suit—looking like the Barney character from educational TV, but at least she didn't have on pajamas like the last time I saw her. Must be the only clothing she had left from the fire.

"So you decided to work out and get in shape?" Mr. Clean asked Mrs. Mitchell.

Mrs. Mitchell patted her pear-shaped figure, her hands landing on her purple stomach. "Round's a shape, isn't it?"

Maybe it was a blessing in disguise Janaclese had gone back home to get more of her clothes to take to her dad's shack. At least she wasn't dressed like an eggplant. I turned to look at Janaclese's outfit but met her protruding eyes and flaring nostrils. Deep down, I felt awful. "I'm so sorry, Janaclese."

But she acted like she didn't hear me. Her gaze remained fixed on her mother.

I scanned the hallway and noticed Miracle giving Mrs. Samson a side hug. Kehl-li stood with her arms folded, seemingly annoyed. That wasn't surprising. But something was strange about the way Miracle and Mrs. Samson held on to each other. Like a child who'd found a favorite lost doll, Mrs. Samson smiled and wiped her eyes, clinging to Miracle.

"Wonder what's going on with them?" I asked Janaclese, referring to Mrs. Samson and Miracle.

Janaclese held a hard, cold stare in her mom's direction. "I'm wondering the same thing. After all my family has been through, why is he here?"

Mr. Clean pointed his index finger in our direction, and Janaclese and I glanced at each other, certain their conversation had moved to us.

"See how she's all giggly?"

"She's just being friendly." Though I had to admit, every time I'd seen Mr. Clean and Mrs. Mitchell together, she'd acted like a school girl.

"My parents said they'd reconcile." Her eyes narrowed. "Mom didn't even come back to the shack after our house burned. We've been through a flood and a fire. Not even hail or high water can make them reunite, but—"

"But nothing," I said and elbowed her. "That's your problem, you keep letting your 'but' get in the way."

She was supposed to be teaching me about trust. Lately, I had to remind her that things weren't always what they seemed.

Mrs. Mitchell made her way across the hall over toward us. "Hello, Cyndray. You girls ready?"

Upon closer inspection, I could see worry hiding behind Mrs. Mitchell's smile and also lingering in the shadows of her eyes. Too bad Janaclese couldn't see it.

"I guess so. Are you driving me home?" I asked.

"Yes, Janaclese still doesn't have her car or her cell phone. You've heard about the fire? We've had a lot going on lately."

"We could've taken care of my car today." Janaclese's chest stuck out farther than I'd noticed before. The girl was puffed up.

Mrs. Mitchell cocked her head but bit back words. No longer concealed, a troubled smile surfaced across her face.

"*You* must've had other plans," Janaclese said to her mom.

The difference between Janaclese and me is that I'd had to walk on eggshells around my sensitive mother most of my life. I'd developed the skill of knowing when life had hit too hard, and Mom didn't have the strength to hit back. Janaclese had never needed to learn to recognize when her mom was falling apart. Perhaps it had never happened. Maybe that's why she couldn't see what I saw beneath Mrs. Mitchell's pseudo-cheery smile.

"Is Mr. Clean why you didn't come to Dad's last night?" The accusation laced in Janaclese's words plunged over me like dangerous waters.

And watching Mrs. Mitchell reminded me of why I've never liked swimming in the ocean. I've always been afraid of getting caught in an undertow beneath the calm surface water.

Mrs. Mitchell jiggled her keys, then turned to leave. "Let's go."

I double-stepped to follow Mrs. Mitchell. Janaclese stood planted by Dr. Beverly's office.

"I wouldn't want you to drive out of your way to the shack." She spoke to Mrs. Mitchell's back. "I can call Dad to get us."

I instantly regretted being lumped into the collective 'us' she referred to.

The forceful wind from Mrs. Mitchell's about-face unsteadied Janaclese's stance. She rocked back on her heels, her face switching to an uneasy expression.

"Is there something you want to ask me about Curtis, little misses?"

"I already did," Janaclese responded in a shaky voice, then glanced in my direction. Whether it was to impress me or to garner support, I still remained silent. She returned her attention to her mother. "Is that man why you didn't come to Dad's last night?"

"Excuse me." With a concerned face, Dr. Beverly stood at the entrance of her office with her hand on the door knob. "Maybe you should step inside, out of the hallway. I can leave you alone for privacy."

"You don't need to abandon your office, Vivian. This will only take a minute." Mrs. Mitchell skirted past Dr. Beverly. "Janaclese, Cyndray. Come on in."

Before I could refuse, Janaclese had pulled me inside. I wanted to flee the scene. No way—no how—was I a part of whatever was about to go down. But Mrs. Mitchell had addressed me too, and intimidation made me submissive.

"The man you keep questioning me about is respectfully named Mr. Curtis, not Mr. Clean," Mrs. Mitchell said.

My fault for the name calling. Squirming, I flicked my toes against the insides of my shoes. Why did I have such a bad habit of labeling people based on looks?

"Curtis heard about the fire and wanted to let me know someone donated suits to his church that might've belonged to me." She looked at me. "He recognized Cyndray as the generous donor, yet I'm wondering how she had access to my closet."

My guilty heart plummeted. Should I confess? I knew I should've kept my hands off those monogrammed business suits. But Janaclese was upset when she learned about Hassan's pregnant ex-girlfriend, Finale, so I took the suits inside for her.

"They were donated for a good cause," Janaclese piped in defense. "Besides, you never wear them."

"That was stealing," Mrs. Mitchell snipped.

Janaclese turned toward Dr. Beverly. "Dr. Beverly, is stealing any worse than cheating?"

"I'm not here." My counselor waved her hands. "I'm not hearing this conversation because I'm not here."

I frowned. If Dr. Beverly thought she was invisible, then she needed therapy too.

Mrs. Mitchell's face twisted. "This is ridiculous. Why do you keep implying I'm cheating on your father?"

Janaclese swiveled back toward her mom. "In the garden, I asked if you'd taken off your ring for Mr. Clean. You said 'yes.'"

Narrowing her eyes in deep thought, Mrs. Mitchell slumped down onto the orange L-shaped couch. She sat still like an invisible weight held her in place, rendering her motionless. Suddenly, the shroud of wrinkles on her forehead made way to even lines when she burst into hearty laughter. Her shoulders shook, and she snorted between the words she spoke. "I was distracted, and I thought you said 'to keep it clean.' Sweetheart, when I'm working in the dirt, I take off my ring to keep it clean—not for Mr. Clean."

Mrs. Mitchell's ringtone changed the focus in the room. She struggled for composure. "Excuse me, ladies." She pulled out her cell phone, slid her fingers across the screen, and pressed the phone to her ear as she spoke, "Betima Mitchell ... you have them with you? ... Great ... Sure, hold on." She lifted the phone from her ear. "Vivian, what room is this?"

"Huh?" Dr. Beverly shifted her gaze from her computer screen. "Oh. Room one thirty-six."

"Thanks." Mrs. Mitchell repeated the information to the caller, then disconnected. She refocused her attention back on the earlier conversation. "Janaclese, I hate kicking this issue around like a soccer ball. I just wanna score a goal and move on. For the record, I have never been unfaithful to your father. And definitely not with Hassan's pops."

I jerked, then gasped. Sometimes my hearing was a little staticky. But I was certain she'd said Mr. Clean ... uh, Curtis ... was Hassan's pops. Had I heard right?

Trying to close my gaping mouth, I threw a glance at Janaclese who skipped over whatever Mrs. Mitchell had just said and kept arguing.

"We all lost something in the fire," Janaclese insisted. "I needed you. Dad needed you."

"You know how sometimes only a mommy can fix it?" Mrs. Mitchell relaxed on the couch. "That's the kind of day I had yesterday after the fire. I needed Me-maw."

My attention was divided. My ears listened to the exchange in the room, while my mind scrambled through its archives, trying to place whether I'd ever seen Hassan with Mr. Clean.

When Hassan showed up at Miracle's pool party, Mr. Clean was there too. But they weren't together. I shook my head. *Was the night Mr. Clean had shown up at Youth Encounter the same night Hassan's raggedy truck wouldn't start?* I thumped my head, but couldn't remember.

"Where were you last night," Janaclese insisted, stronger.

"Your Dad suggested I stay at Me-maw's because I was exhausted." Mrs. Mitchell sighed. "He was concerned my fatigue would trigger a migraine, so I stayed and rested."

I banged my fist against my head. *When and where else had we seen Mr. Clean?*

The answer was in the front of my brain when a knock at the door threatened to interrupt my thoughts even more.

"Must be my suits." Mrs. Mitchell stood up, but Dr. Beverly scooted from her desk to answer the door.

The suits. Mr. Clean had accepted the suits. I wracked my brain. Sheesh! Hassan wasn't there either.

Dr. Beverly flung the door open. "Yes?"

"Sorry to interrupt."

My gaze flitted toward the familiar voice at the door. Dr. Beverly angled her body, blocking the entrance—I guess to protect privacy—and I couldn't see anyone.

"My pops asked me to bring these suits to room one thirty-six."

My heart dropped. I snatched my gaze toward Janaclese whose opened mouth was speechless, confirming my exact thought.

I'd heard right—Mr. Clean was Hassan's dad!

Chapter 49

JANACLESE

The best way to get your mind off of your own problems is to help someone else in need. At least that's what Mom and Dad tried to convince me of as they shoved me out of the door and sent me on my way to Mrs. Patterson's house.

Mom said there was lots of paperwork she needed to fill out. She was probably using that as a lame excuse to avoid answering more of my questions. But that was okay. Focusing on my relationship with Hassan made me feel better anyway.

I shook my head, thinking about the past week. Hassan's pops and Mr. Clean one and the same? How'd I miss that?

The buzzing thought was a permanent distraction, making me less than productive at Mrs. Patterson's house. I placed a box of Raisin Bran in her cupboard.

"I've unloaded all of the groceries, Mrs. Patterson. Do you need anything else today?"

"No, that just about does it." She lifted her attention from studying the store receipt I'd given her and winked. "I ain't keeping you from a hot summer date, am I?"

I lowered my eyes, embarrassed. The whole church knew I was stranded on a date during the storm. "No, ma'am. I told you before, my parents don't really allow me to date."

"Nothing wrong with dating at your age. These young parents don't mean no harm trying to prevent the bad, but I think they're the ones causing it. Oughta just let things take their natural course. Seem more normal that way to me. Especially nowadays. Kids suppressing so much, it's hard to know what to feel and who to feel it for." She tilted her head toward Heaven like she was giving God the

411 or perhaps pleading with Him. "Boys and girls confused about their sexuality, you know?"

When she turned and looked at me, I nodded my head so she'd know I was listening, although Hassan and I weren't confused one single bit. We loved each other, which is why I had to rush home before he left the shack for the day.

"Well, if you don't need me for anything else, I'm gonna head on out."

"Shoo." She pushed me through her forest-like living room, and I giggled when LeMew's fur brushed against my legs. "Tell your mother hello for me and that I'll see her in church on Sunday."

I was so happy to have my Prius back in good shape. I strapped on my seatbelt and drove down the street, my thoughts racing faster than the speedometer.

Mr. Clean and Hassan, father and son? Hard to believe Mom withheld such vital information. And I hadn't even had a chance to talk to Hassan about it—but today I would.

Several miles down the road, my new cell phone vibrated. My parents had put me on a different calling plan and upgraded my phone. Sounded like a reward, but it wasn't. I had a different number, and none of my friends knew it. I hadn't backed up my contact list before Dad dropped my old service plan, so I didn't know their numbers either. And worst of all, my parents could track my whereabouts from the GPS in the phone.

The phone jiggled on the passenger's seat.

I seriously thought about not answering, but the vibrating wouldn't stop. I eyed the caller ID knowing full well it was Mom, and knowing full well I'd answer her call if I didn't want to add more limitations to my long list of restraints.

"You could've told me," I answered the phone with my new normal greeting.

"What took you so long to answer the phone?" She responded with her usual way of ignoring my comment and with an edge of 'get over it' in her tone.

Mom had known Mr. Clean was Hassan's pops ever since she and Hassan talked in the backseat of Dad's car on the way to her house. Didn't seem fair for her not to mention it, but she stood by her lame excuses.

"I'm driving. Just leaving Mrs. Patterson's house," I said.

"You're ten miles from Mrs. Patterson's house. You left early?"

Without responding to her, I eyed the clock on the dashboard. I supposed her question was more of a statement she expected me to validate. But I didn't.

"Are you talking hands-free?"

"I'm using the Bluetooth." I rolled my eyes. What did she want? To check my schedule? Add another prohibition to my 'do not' list?

She and Dad had made sure that I wasn't at the shack for the last two weeks when Hassan was there working on the column. But today would be different.

If things went as planned, I'd have fifteen extra minutes to question Hassan about Mr. Clean. I hadn't seen or spoken to him since the fire. He didn't have my new number, and I couldn't remember his no matter how hard I'd studied the dial pad.

"I'm gonna be a little late getting home this evening." Mom's hesitant voice echoed through the phone. So that's why she'd called. "Your Aunt Alicia had a doctor's appointment today, and I need to visit with her."

My focus snapped to the unborn baby, my stomach gearing to rumble. "The baby ... Aunt Alicia hasn't—"

"No." Mom didn't dare let me finish the sentence. The entire family knew not to speak the words "loss" or "miscarriage" concerning Aunt Alicia's pregnancy. "She's okay. Everything is fine. I'll call again later if there's more news."

Everything didn't sound fine, but I disconnected the call, leaving unanswered questions sloshing around in my head.

After parking in the driveway, I trudged up the walkway, entered the shack, and headed to my room. That bad feeling, evil forebodings—or whatever Mrs. Patterson had called it—settled over me. Aunt Alicia's pregnancy represented belief in miracles, faith for the unseen, the hope of long-held dreams. What was she going through? I placed both my hands on my belly. If there was no baby, then ...

"Why're you looking all droopy, Snoopy?"

I pivoted, turning away from my bedroom and now facing the kitchen.

Khara held a large wooden spoon under the sink's spigot. Water splashed off the spoon onto the sink's edge. She glanced down at my hands and frowned. "What's wrong? Is it your stomach again?"

I brushed my hands from my belly and shook my head. "Mom called. It's Aunt Alicia."

"Oh. Don't worry. It's just a few routine tests." She dipped the spoon into a glass pitcher, stirring slowly. "Simple precautions. That's all they are. Precautions."

"Are you sure?" I eased further into the kitchen, the scent of fresh strawberries and lemons teasing my senses and offering relief from anxiety. "Because Mom said she's gonna be late getting here."

"I know. Mom's late. And you're early." The wooden spoon clinked against the glass as she stirred and stared out the back window. "Surprise you didn't run straight to the backyard."

"Huh?"

"Dad's got Hassan working harder than an Old Testament Hebrew slave. Even the Egyptians occasionally let the Israelites slop around in the mud pit for a break. Look at him."

I skedaddled to the window. "Hassan!"

How had I forgotten so quickly why I'd rushed home? And why didn't I feel him near me? Maybe I was too distracted with the news about Aunt Alicia. I checked my watch—ten minutes before Hassan's quitting time. We needed to talk. I scooted toward the door.

"Janaclese Mitchell!" Khara spat my name out of her mouth like sour pickle juice. "Get back here right now."

I turned on my heels, restraining irritation. "What?"

"Boys don't like all that excitement. Too much attention scares them. You have to play it cool. Let him pursue you."

What was her problem? Did I need advice from someone who couldn't keep a boyfriend? Maybe I should tell her Hassan didn't like pretense. That he liked girls who kept it real. That I didn't have to calm down because Hassan loved everything about me—especially my enthusiasm.

"Here." Ice cubes clinked when she thrust an eight-ounce glass into my hands. "Don't be all willy-nilly. Take him a glass of strawberry lemonade. And for goodness sakes, will you calm down?"

I took a deep breath, but I couldn't settle the bubbles inside my tummy making me all giddy and flighty at the same time. I stepped onto the back porch, allowing the screen door to slam shut.

Hassan didn't even look up. He braced one hand on a worktable, positioning a nail on a board, and raised the other hand with a hammer above his head, then slapped the tool repeatedly against the slab of wood.

Gliding over clumps of crabgrass, I ambled toward Hassan. The cubes jangled beneath the hammering, but Hassan was undisturbed. Didn't he feel me getting closer?

"Thirsty?" The banging must've drowned my words. I spoke louder. "THIR … STY?"

The hammering stopped, and Hassan looked up.

"Hey, you." The smile that had melted my heart from day one spread across his face but escaped his eyes. He glanced toward the shack. "What're you doing out here? I thought your parents had shipped you off to get you away from me?"

"Not a chance." My heart sank, and I broke eye contact for a second. Why hadn't he called me 'Shawty' like usual? I extended the glass toward him. "Have some strawberry lemonade."

"Rescuing me from the heat?" He wiped his forearm across his forehead, raking away the sweat before taking the drink.

Small droplets of water had formed on the sides of the glass. When we touched, the wetness of my hands moistened his. He didn't seem to mind.

Hassan leaned his head back and guzzled the drink. "Mmmm … that was good."

"Are you done for today?" I raised my eyebrows and flashed an enticing grin.

He placed the empty glass on the table and pointed. "Gotta put these materials in the shed first, then lock-up back here. What's up?"

I picked up a few nails from the table. "I haven't seen you in a while and thought we could talk for a few minutes."

He eyed the shack again. "Your folks might not like us out here unsupervised."

"Mom and Dad aren't here at the moment." I dropped the nails into the box.

He twitched his shoulders. "Janaclese, I don't like sneaking around with you. If we can't be on the up and up, then … then, maybe we can't be."

"It's not like that." I figured he was still frustrated that my parents hadn't known about him before the storm. That was another reason I'd wanted to talk. I quickly added, "Khara's inside."

"Still doesn't make it right." He waved his hands between his chest and mine.

My heart dropped. I knew "it" referred to "us," that he'd meant something still didn't make *us* right.

"Why did you lie about seeing me?" His face looked tense.

"I didn't lie. I just kept quiet about having a boyfriend. That's not the same thing as lying."

"And you considered me your boyfriend?" His chuckle was fused with sarcasm. "Where I'm from, we call it a part-time lover, since you and I could only hang out on my side of town. Seems to me, I wasn't allowed to enter your world because you were ashamed of me."

"I was never ashamed of you."

"Yeah, okay. That explains why you wouldn't let me pick you up from your house. You always visited me or met me somewhere else, but never out in the suburbs where you live."

"Not because I was ashamed of you." He had it all wrong. I moved my head from side to side. "That's not true."

"Look, I watched you from the backseat of your Dad's car. You hated your mom talking to me and the way I answered your Dad's questions."

I lowered my gaze. Maybe his slang sounded weird around my parents, but I wasn't ashamed of him. I couldn't speak. This wasn't the conversation I'd intended to have with him. Looking up, I searched his face for understanding.

"Don't get me wrong. Your folks are mad cool, but I'm not their kind of peeps."

The thing is … my parents wouldn't have approved of me dating anybody. If only I could make Hassan know that.

"They don't want a guy like me for their beautiful princess." He picked up the board he'd hammered and latched it under one arm, then reached for the saw. "Guess I can't blame them."

"I can understand if you're mad at me, but don't insinuate my parents are stuck up, because they're not." How could he possibly think we were different? "As a matter of fact, my mom dated your pops in high school. Did you even know that?"

He froze. Yet, he didn't turn to look at me.

"Did you know my mom and your pops were in love a long time ago?"

He still didn't answer. He stacked the saw, nails, and hammer into a box.

I stood watching. My emotions bounced like a ball in a fierce tennis match. Part of me wanted to beg his forgiveness, hold him, and make him understand how much I loved him. But his frustration also fueled mine. Why was he being so difficult, ready to give up on us and simply walk away? I wanted to smack him for not seeing my heart and feeling what I felt.

He carried the timber and materials into the shed.

I scurried behind him and shut the door.

"What're you doing?" Hassan bunched his eyebrows together.

"Look in my face and tell me you don't love me, and I'll believe you."

"I never said I didn't love you."

"Then tell me you don't want to be with me anymore and I'll let you walk away from me."

"It's not that I don't want us to be together. We can't." He shook his head. "We just can't."

The tightness in my stomach rose to my chest and threatened to choke me. I'd forgiven Hassan for standing me up on several dates. I understood when he needed to babysit Nneka and Khadijah. I'd overlooked him not telling me about his pregnant ex-girlfriend, even when my gut said I should ask. I loved him enough to trust him.

Now I had to prove it. "Why can't we be together?"

"Because it can't work. It never works. Girls like you go off to college and forget about guys like me. My pops said we've got to be even and on the same wavelength."

Maybe his pops was referring to whatever happened between him and Mom. I didn't care about that stuff anymore. I simply wanted the two of us to be happy again.

I eased closer and soft words fell from my lips. "I believe we both have to be Christians. That's all." *Didn't Khara say that?*

He turned, lifting the wood saw from the box and placing it on a shelf.

I inched behind him, blocking any room for escape.

Hassan jerked around, his jittery motion spilling the box over, clanking nails against the hard floor. He stooped to gather the nails.

I knelt beside him and stared into his face, searching …

"What?" He seemed annoyed. Maybe he was too hot to act cool. Perspiration trickled down his hairline.

Cupping his sweaty hands into mine, I wrapped them around my waist. "Kiss me."

His narrowed eyes seem to question my sincerity.

"I mean it." I leaned forward.

"No." He pushed me away. "Not here. Not like this."

Tears welled in my eyes. I couldn't let them fall, especially knowing how much it bothered Hassan. "But … but …" I gulped. It was too late. No amount of resistance could stop the flood.

"Sshh …" Hassan pulled me into his chest. "I don't want to do anything to make you cry."

How could I tell him it wasn't what he'd done, it was what he *hadn't done*—and the guilt of what I wanted him to do that was about to overtake me.

"Why won't you kiss me?" I asked.

"Your first kiss should be special."

"I happen to think this … what we have … is, is pretty special." I bit my trembling lips, locking the floodgate. "You're special to me."

"Look Janaclese, you're special to me too. I love you, but I can't open certain doors."

I could feel my lips quivering, not understanding at all why Hassan was rejecting me, especially if what he was saying—that he loved me—was true.

"One kiss from you is too tempting for me. I will want more."

Was he talking about sex? I looked into his eyes, questioning him without words.

He lowered his head. "Most guys would kill to be alone with a girl as wonderful and innocent as you, who *thinks* she only wants to kiss."

"You couldn't stop at a kiss?" I asked.

"Yeah, I could stop. But I wouldn't want to. And I know you aren't ready for that."

I wasn't ready? That must've meant he was ready, which must've also meant he had crossed the line before.

"It's her, isn't it? You did it with her and got her pregnant, didn't you?"

The skin buckled on his forehead. "What are you talking about?"

"Your ex-girlfriend, Finale."

"How do you know about her?"

He wasn't denying it? My heart raced. He wasn't gonna tell me how wrong I was?

I jumped up from the floor. I wouldn't waste another minute sharing how I knew about Finale.

"Where're you running off to? I'm not—"

The end of Hassan's sentence drowned in the ocean of emotions gushing from me. He loved me, but he couldn't be with me. He had another responsibility, another relationship to fix.

He had to be with her.

Chapter 50

JANACLESE

My chest felt empty like someone had ripped my heart from its chamber.

I walked slowly at first, but with each step, the hole grew bigger, so I quickened my pace, trying to outrun the widening chasm before it swallowed me.

I didn't feel Hassan running after me like usual. How could I feel anything with no heart? Only his words chased me … "I'm not …"

Tears cascaded down my face, gushing like water from an uncapped fire hydrant. The back door was locked. I ran around the house, sprinted up the front steps and bumped into Mom, too blind to initially see her standing in the doorway.

"Janaclese, what's wrong?"

I shook my head and bolted in the opposite direction. When I reached my Prius and grabbed the door handle, Mom's hands stopped me.

"Baby, what is it?" A panicky concern rang in her voice.

No words left my mouth, and I moved my head from side to side as if to clear my mind of what had just happened. If I could wipe my mental slate clean, then maybe my heart would jump back inside.

"I'm not letting you drive anywhere like this. What's going on?"

"He … he …" The words were trapped.

"Who?" Mom's panic seemed to heighten.

"Ha …"

"What?"

My "he-ha" must've sounded like a dying donkey. I couldn't say Hassan's name, or even talk about him. I looked to see his father's Nissan rolling out of the driveway.

Mom's investigative lawyer instinct seemed to kick in. She turned in the direction of my gaze, then whipped out her cell phone before pressing a few buttons.

"Hello … Mrs. Mitchell?" The voice on the other end inquired.

I'd covered my face but jerked my head back around when I recognized Hassan's voice. The taillights on the Nissan turned red, and the truck stopped. Words somehow tumbled from my mouth. "He—Hassan—he broke up with me."

A myriad of expressions raced across Mom's face in a split second, creating a mosaic. She clicked off her cell, then waved "go on" to the Nissan.

I don't know how I ended up in bed. But I lay in what looked like a quarantined sick room. Propped beside the bed, a tiny square-shaped trashcan wadded with tissues, overflowed onto the floor. A remnant of unused Kleenex lined a half-empty box next to my pillow. The cracked window permitted some ventilation, but the room's stale odor begged to be fully aired out. My closed bedroom door completed my voluntary confinement.

Except for an occasional head poking through the door to check on me, I'd been pretty much left alone—dazed, in and out of sleep, wrestling with new emotions and old memories, trying to recall if I'd ever felt like this and survived.

I was six years old when Grandpa died. The one thing I understood even back then was that death was final on earth. And as hard as I tried to hold Grandpa in my heart like Me-maw had said, it still hurt knowing he wasn't coming back. That's how I felt about Hassan and me—a grievous death.

Hassan wasn't coming back, and trying to hold him crushed my insides like an elephant stampede.

After a couple of days, Mom still hadn't spoken about Hassan the entire time. No words of comfort, not even admonishment for not heeding her warnings concerning falling in love. She let me stay in bed, and as long as I was asleep, I could breathe. But as soon as I opened my eyes and remembered, I struggled for air.

Two rapid knocks on the door didn't wait for an invitation to "come in." Mom stuck her head into my room. "I'm almost done with breakfast. You want to try a bite?"

I hadn't eaten in two days. Didn't think I could keep anything down. It wasn't hunger, but irritation that welled up in my belly. At least that was something other than numbness.

Mom eased into the room. "I'm worried about you. How do you feel?"

"Like I died and went straight to He—"

"Janaclese! Pull yourself together."

Giving her my back, I faced the wall. I could've said Heaven, but she didn't let me finish. Besides, why was she so appalled? Was it the intensity of my language or my true feelings?

My emotional gauge spun toward frustration. "Why don't you say I told you so?"

"Sweetie, I didn't see this coming any more than you did."

Mom saw everything, and sometimes she acted like she knew more than God. But she had no idea Hassan would break up with me, tear my heart to shreds like paper?

I curled into a ball, desperately wanting to revert to being a baby and letting mommy fix it, make it all better. This wasn't a boo-boo she could rub healing balm on, but I needed an ointment to soothe my broken heart.

I sighed. "Just tell me how to stop the hurt."

She lowered herself onto the bed, the springs in the mattress creaking. "You keep moving."

"It aches to move." Didn't she understand that?

"It's the only way to push the hurt away—one step at a time, one day at a time."

My puffy eyes felt wrinkly like dried raisins; still, tears managed to squeeze from them, saturating my pillow. Did she know how bad the pain was? She'd barely blinked twice when she and Dad separated. Just like Hassan walked away without looking back. Why was I born so super sensitive? Why was I even born?

"Janaclese, I can't protect you from this type of disappointment. If I could, I would. I'd do anything to lift this from you."

How about tracking Hassan down and recovering my stolen heart? The aching cavity was too hollow and painful to bear. "Feels like something's missing."

"I know, baby." She caressed my arm. "Ask God to fill the gap."

I didn't want to ask God for anything. It seemed lately He only wanted to trade one thing for another. I sniffled. "Every time I ask God to give me something, He makes a trade and takes something else away."

She looked through me like I hadn't spoken like I wasn't really visible. I felt tiny as if at any moment I'd completely fade away. Maybe my disappearance had already begun.

"That's how it's supposed to work," she finally said. "You ask God for peace, He takes away the worry."

"I asked God to let you and Dad live together under one roof, and He burned your house down. I'm sorry you're forced to live in the shack."

"Oh, baby. I'm here because I *want* to be here. What happened with our house is not your fault. I prayed the same thing ... that we'd all be together. This shack is our home because we live in it together."

I propped on one elbow and blew my clogged nose. "Our clothes and furniture ... we lost practically everything."

"We have what's important. We have each other."

I lowered my head. Why were thoughts of losing my first love bombarding the surface?

"What is it?" Mom asked.

"You and Dad have each other. I lost a good friend." I tasted the salty tears flowing into my mouth. "I guess if I wasn't so sensitive, it wouldn't feel so bad."

She sat in silence for a few seconds before speaking.

"I'd do anything to keep you from hurting unnecessarily, but some pain is good for you. It gives you an opportunity to see your own strength. You don't know your own strength, Janaclese. Don't ever stop being compassionate and *sensitive*. Those character traits have never made you weak. It's where your strength lies."

My core sputtered a faint lub-dub. Was that my heart clamoring back to life? Did being sensitive really make a person strong?

Mom's lips did that funny upside down U-shape. She pointed to the antique floor-length mirror Dad had stored in the corner of the room. "Why don't you look in the mirror and tell me what you see?"

The lub-dub stopped, and the tiny spark of hope died with the rest of me. I flipped over, placing a decorative pillow over my head.

"You can't ever expect a boy to be the center of your joy, and you can't lie in bed forever on the sidelines of life." Mom's muffled voice traveled through the pillow, and her voice tone switched as suddenly as my emotions had. "Many people would die for you, but nobody … I mean *nobody*, can live for you."

I flinched. Why wouldn't she take the hint and just leave? I squeezed the pillow tighter against my face.

"You've got to crawl out from under and be an active participant in your own happiness."

When she lifted her weight from the bed, the mattress elevated. I listened as her quiet footsteps padded back and forth across the floor. The door opened, then clicked shut.

Finally!

Drenched in an emotional tug-of-war, I wrestled and hugged my pillow like a lifeline until sleep waves drifted me away.

Hours passed before I awakened to the giggling sounds of children playing outside. It wasn't dark, but it had to be evening time. The lawn sprinkler was set to go off at any moment. I forced my body to turn in the bed.

EEK! I double blinked into focus. Mom had positioned the mirror so I couldn't help but see myself.

I looked hideous. The hair extensions had creased my face making me look more like Rip Van Wrinkle than Sleeping Beauty. My scalp itched, and I knew it was probably just as flaky as the dry skin on my face and the rest of my body.

"Yooou caaan't catch me!" The kids' sing-song voices and squealing laughter sounded like happiness I'd never know again.

I studied my reflection, then turned away. *How long was I going to be this pitiful?*

What if Mom was right about pushing the hurt away, about me being strong? Could I create my own happiness by participating in life? I gently touched my braided extensions. They reminded me of Hassan and his little sister, Nneka.

Oh God, I feel like dying. The ache tugged my insides, and I tugged my braids. The hair extensions, a constant reminder, had to go. If only I could muster the energy to climb out of bed.

"I did it! I did it! Told you!"

The thrill of having achieved something reverberated from the voice outside and hit me in my gut. The faith of a small child led to success.

My heart quickened when a familiar Scripture scrolled through my head. I spoke it aloud, allowing the words to penetrate. "*I* can do all things through Jesus Christ who strengthens *me.*"

"Strengthens" resonated in my core, awakening a thumping lub-dub in my chest. It wasn't long before the word flowed through my veins and soothed me like medicine. God's strength could get me through this.

Fill the gap, Lord.

Willing my body from the mattress, I allowed my feet to touch the floor.

Chapter 51

CYNDRAY

When Janaclese came to my house, I knew something was terribly wrong. She'd awkwardly stood in my foyer squinting, like her head hurt or the sun was in her eyes. Her braided extensions stuck up every which way, like live tentacles.

"Giirrll." That's all I could say when I touched her hair.

"Can you help me take them out?" She wrapped a braid around her index finger.

My eyes widened. "That'll take FOR. EV. ER. We need back-up if you don't want your hair to break off." Seeing her eyes water, I softened my tone. "Like special hair conditioner."

Janaclese's face brightened. "Miracle's mom! I need you to come with me."

The ride to Miracle's house was quick, but the entire time I tried hard not to picture Janaclese as the Greek monster, Medusa, who had venomous snakes dangling from her scalp. I failed miserably.

We ran the doorbell, and Miracle opened the door. The overhanging chandelier glinted in the sunlight, casting a shadow on Janaclese's withdrawn face. She twirled a braid around her fingers and held one out for Miracle to observe. "I asked Cyndray to help me take these out, but I needed to see if your mom had any special hair conditioner. Cyndray says it's tangled and will break my hair off if I don't use a good conditioner first."

I sucked my teeth. "If your mom can't help us, then we need to call 911. Janaclese's hair is jacked up."

Miracle gave a warm smile. "I have some of Mama's products in my bathroom." She touched Janaclese's matted hair and scrunched her face. "You're going to undo the braids all by yourself? Why not go back to the salon across town or to your mom's Wellness Center?"

"I can't." Janaclese hesitated, tears crowding her eyes. "I can't go to Red Hill, and I don't want to be around a lot of people I know right now."

I put one hand on my hip and scoffed at Janaclese. "Friend or no friend, I ain't going back to that salon in the 'hood with you. No way!"

"Kehl-li and I can help." Miracle shifted her weight. "I mean if you want us to. I'm not trying to be pushy or anything."

A smile tugged at Janaclese's lips, and she glanced at me. "I could use a few good friends right about now."

The three of us— Miracle, Kehl-li, and I—crowded around Janaclese, each with a pair of scissors snipping her braids.

Every time the synthetic hair dropped to the floor, Janaclese tensed. "Y'all aren't cutting my real hair are you?"

I sighed. "Girl, will you relax and let us do this? Don't know why you went to the 'hood and got these extensions in the first place."

"I just wanted—"

"To impress Hassan. We know. And look where that got you. He called it quits. Now hold still."

"What ... breakup ... happened ... Hassan?" Kehl-li's words and Miracle's jumbled together, annihilating any form of a coherent sentence.

Janaclese looked a little wounded, so I shut up and let Kehl-li have the floor.

"Did Hassan dump you?" Kehl-li batted her sparkly eyelids. Before Janaclese answered she added, "I knew you couldn't handle a boy like Hassan. He needs someone more mature."

"Someone mature like you? Ha!" I snickered. Didn't take much for Kehl-li to make my blood boil. "Do you think wearing glittery eye shadow and finger painting your lips makes you more mature? You look like an art project."

"Let's not go there, talking about looks." Kehl-li tossed her hair. "Hassan is the kind of guy who needs a girl who treats him like a man. He's practically eighteen." She directed her question at Jana-clese. "Did you even kiss him?"

Janaclese squirmed in her seat.

"Let's not go *there*." I returned Kehl-li's hard stare, and she backed down.

"Hassan and I had a mega fight." A somber response sailed from Janaclese. "I just don't think I'll ever laugh or be happy again. They say love's a battlefield."

"More like a game. Play at your own risk." I rolled my eyes.

"Not a battlefield or a game, but definitely a gamble," Kehl-li said.

"Yep." To loosen the strands, I dripped more papaya-scented, orange liquid onto a braid, thinking more about love and romance. "How can something so simple be so complicated?"

We interrupted each other, finishing sentences, agreeing, dis-agreeing. Everybody had a different idea about relationships and what love should be like.

"It's been such a bummer summer." Janaclese sighed, then filled Miracle and Kehl-li in on the latest details of her life, pausing for an occasional sarcastic "mm-hmm" from me. "And now Aunt Alicia's baby might be challenged."

Kehl-li's fingers curled as she unraveled an extension. "Is she go-ing to keep it?"

Sounds of scissors snipping filled the momentary quietness as black strands of hair puddled onto the floor. No one dared speak ini-tially. Apparently, we were all shocked by Kehl-li's absurd question.

"Girl, don't make me accidentally cut you." Blades clicked as I held my scissors in the air. I still couldn't stand too much of Kehl-li. "Why would you ask something so senseless and inconsiderate?"

As if she hadn't heard a word I'd said, Kehl-li stared at Jana-clese and inquired again. "Is your Aunt Alicia going to give her baby away?"

"Of course not!" Janaclese recoiled, springing a braid from my grasp. "Giving up her baby isn't an option."

"People do stupid, thoughtless stuff like giving their babies away all the time. Don't they MiCha?"

The scissors fell from Miracle's shaky hands, landing with a clink beside the stool.

"Tell 'em," Kehl-li insisted.

Miracle gulped. "Kehl-li doesn't think Mama is my biological mother. I'm not so sure anymore either."

"Are you serious?" Janaclese's stool tipped over as she turned to look at Miracle. "You're kidding, right?"

Confirming yes or no didn't flow from Miracle's mouth.

"Sheesh, I thought my family was dysfunctional, but y'all ..." I shook my head and pointed the scissors at the three of them. "Janaclese, you're included too. Y'all gotta lotta mama drama. And I'm the one in therapy?"

Kehl-li and Miracle gawked at me.

"I'm just saying ... I'm working out my little issues by talking to someone and y'all need to do the same thing."

"Humph." Kehl-li turned up her nose. "I don't have any issues, though I did notice you had a few problems."

"Girl, please. My biggest problem is you. And as soon as I find a flyswatter or some bug spray that problem will be resolved."

"Stop it, stop it, stop it!" Janaclese banged her fists on her thighs. "Please, I want all the secrets, the lies, and the fighting to stop."

I cocked my head. "And I want to click my heels three times and get the old, chipper Janaclese back. I don't like the one who thinks she'll never laugh again. I want to wave a magic wand so the weeping willow that replaced my friend will just go *POOF*. What do you want, Miracle, um, MiCha ... whoever you are at the moment? Do you have any requests? One personality, perhaps?"

"I'd like very much to get Mama's boulder necklace back," Miracle said.

I rolled my eyes. "If the necklace has special powers to make you bolder, you definitely need to get it back and wear it like a choker."

"She said boulder not bolder," Kehl-li smirked at me, then looked at Miracle. "Saturday's our last chance to try."

Janaclese twisted on the stool, her legs dangling. "What did you tell me happened to your mama's necklace?"

I slathered mint conditioner onto Janaclese's head, softening her hair. My eyes watered from the strong concentration.

"We pawned it at the beginning of summer for $500.00. We thought we'd make the money to buy it back, but the man at the pawn shop doubled the price," Miracle said.

"Oh." A worried expression settled on Janaclese's face. "That's not right."

"Tell that to the owner," Kehl-li snapped, then walked over to the intercom and switched on the radio. She rejoined our circle, pointed to the audio system and whispered, "In case Imo is listening."

"I don't know what to do." Miracle lowered her eyes.

"Just go get it back." I bobbed my neck.

"That's what I've been telling her for weeks," Kehl-li said. "Saturday's our last chance."

Janaclese swallowed. "We can't go on Saturday. It's Community Day at church. Everybody's going to be there."

"Might be the best time." I put my scissors down and ran my fingers through Janaclese loose hair, feeling for more braids underneath. "Actually, if everybody's there, then they won't notice right away if you aren't."

"See?" Excitement coursed through Kehl-li's voice. She poked Miracle's shoulder. "Isn't that what I told you?"

Hard to believe she'd agreed with me two times in a row.

Miracle shrugged. "We can try. Janaclese, can you and Cyndray come too?"

"You know Betima Mitchell expects me to be at Community Day." Janaclese looked at Miracle. Her lopsided smile parted before she spoke. "I guess maybe if we went early enough, I could sneak away." She gazed up at me. "Do you have to work on Saturday?"

"No. I'm good. I'd already made arrangements to be off for the lock-in. I'm in if you're in."

Kehl-li grinned. "Then it's a date!"

Looking at Janaclese, I was unable to contain myself. I bellowed into full blast laughter. "Hakuna Matata!"

They stared at me, probably wondering what was suddenly so funny.

"Um … should one of us call your therapist?" Kehl-li's face was serious.

"I'm sorry, Janaclese." Words surfaced between my breaths. "Simba."

Kehl-li giggled. "Janaclese does look like Simba from the Lion King."

We'd taken out the braids. Janaclese's coarse hair framed her face like a big, desert tumbleweed. She'd come here looking like Medusa, but now her hair was a fierce lion's mane, loose and fanning out in wild directions.

I wrestled to restrain myself, but the laughing and singing were contagious.

Janaclese dashed from the stool and looked in the vanity's mirror. She stared blankly at herself for a few seconds, then a gut-wrenching laugh shook her body like an earthquake. A loud guttural roar launched from her.

Janaclese was laughing again, and that was a relief.

"Hakuna Matata," I sang, wishing the meaning of the words were true for all of us.

Chapter 52

JANACLESE

Laughing with my friends seemed to have been the remedy for my blues; and as promised, when Saturday rolled around, I found myself helping Miracle.

"C'mon. Let's go inside." Kehl-li twisted around in the front seat and glared at Miracle, who sat next to Cyndray in the back of my Prius. She narrowed her eyes. "MiCha, I thought you had on your big girl panties today."

We'd been parked in front of the pawn shop for ten whole minutes, while Miracle tried to conjure up the nerve to buy back her mama's boulder necklace at the same price they'd traded it for. The angry man had said "no deal," and he'd meant it.

Even Cyndray acted irritated by Miracle's sudden change of mind to confront the manager. She bobbled her head. "The only way you're gonna get what you came here for is to get unstuck from your mouse trap, Miracle."

With all that I had going on with Hassan and my own family, I didn't have much motivation myself. *But, really?* Was that Cyndray's insane way of encouraging Miracle?

Miracle pulled the seatbelt away from her chest and slid her hand up and down the smooth polyester fabric. "I was just thinking maybe we could tell Mama the truth and let her and Daddy figure all of this out."

"Oh, yeah, like that'll go over well. Imo needs another reason to not trust me. Let's add thief to the list." Kehl-li huffed so hard I could almost see black smoke streaming from her nostrils. "Never mind. I'll handle this by myself."

"But, Kehl-li—"

"Let Miss Big Stuff work this out." Cyndray interrupted Miracle's pleading and frowned at Kehl-li. "She was probably the one who talked you into pawning the necklace in the first place."

"For your information, Cyndray, I can handle my business. The question is can you *mind* yours?" Kehl-li opened the passenger's door, then glanced over at me. "Keep the car running."

When I nodded, Kehl-li jerked her head toward Miracle and chided. "Infant!"

Miracle tugged her seatbelt.

"Don't mind her, Miracle. If you're not comfortable, then …" I hunched my shoulders upward. "Then I guess you're just not comfortable. Period."

The sucking sound of Cyndray's *tsk* emphasized her frustration. "If you had a backbone, then I would've gladly backed you up. But I ain't fighting nobody else's battle."

"I didn't ask you to," Miracle said. "Why does my decision make you think I'm spineless?"

"'Cause it's your mama's necklace, and you're *sitting* next to me." She pointed toward the pawnshop. "Not in there *standing* up for your rights."

"Isn't it my right to do whatever I think is best?"

"Yeah." Janaclese let out a light giggle. "And not succumbing to your bullying makes her pretty strong if you ask me."

"I didn't ask you." Cyndray sat staring out the window, pensive. Her hand tightened around the door handle, immovable and fixed like her focus. Finally, she spoke without turning to look at me. "Sorry, Miracle … wasn't trying to bully nobody. You have the right to feel whatever you feel."

Wonder where that was coming from?

"Thanks, Cyndray," Miracle said.

I smiled and looked in the rearview mirror at Cyndray in the backseat. "Awww … that's so nice. I'm tearing up. I think I'm gonna—"

The driver's door whipped open.

"Slide over. Hurry up!" Kehl-li forced herself into the car. "Scoot over!"

Her urgency left no time for questioning. I unbuckled my seatbelt and leaped across the middle console, landing into the passenger's seat just as my Prius spun away from the curb.

"What's going on?" I couldn't control the panic in my voice. "What happened back there, Kehl-li?"

"Nothing." Kehl-li glanced at the side view mirror.

"Doesn't seem like nothing to me." Cyndray leaned forward in her seat, eyeing the speedometer. "You're going 60, and the speed limit's 45."

Kehl-li glanced over her shoulder. "Will y'all chill out? The speed limit is a suggestion for learners, not experts who know how to drive."

"Huh?" I contorted my face. *What was she talking about?* "Slow down, Kehl-li."

"We just need to cross the tracks, get to our side of town." Kehl-li scanned the rear view mirror. "Then I'll slow down."

Was somebody following us? I twisted my neck to look behind our car, but nothing suspicious caught my attention. We zoomed down the narrow, bumpy road. The Prius, a racecar, soared toward the railroad tracks like it was the finish line in the Indy 500.

"Lights-flashing-train's-coming." My quick words merged without pausing. "Stop!"

Kehl-li slammed on the breaks, and the seatbelt tightened across my ribcage.

"I don't see a train," Kehl-li protested.

Cyndray cocked her head. "I know you're half blind, but are you deaf too?"

Red and yellow lights flicked off and on across the metal bar above the railroad tracks. The constant ding of the crossing bell and a low whistle warned of the train's arrival as a zebra-striped barricade slowly descended to block traffic.

"We can make it." Kehl-li drummed her fingers against the steering wheel while jerking her head in one direction of the tracks, then the other. "I know we can make it."

"Don't even think about—"

Kehl-li floored the gas pedal and accelerated toward the tracks.

Cyndray's words melted into a disbelieving shriek.

"Jesus!" I braced my hands against the dashboard.

The train's whistle screamed.

The tires scraped against metal, then bounced off the first set of tracks.

My breath caught in my throat, and I squeezed my eyes shut, trapping inevitable visions of our death.

Another bump against metal sent us bouncing as if the car was on a trampoline.

Eyes still screwed together, I counted the last seconds of my life.

Kehl-li careened into a sharp left off the tracks, and the car came to an abrupt stop. Nervous laughter sailed from her.

The train's whistle bellowed, quaking my insides like I'd somehow swallowed it. But slowly the sound faded, and that's when I noticed the quietness in the car.

I opened my eyes and waited for my heart to beat. "Did we make it?"

My words broke the silence and thawed Cyndray's statue-like pose. She banged both fists on the headrest in front of her. "Kehl-li, do you have a death wish or are you on a suicide mission? Let me know, 'cause I value my life, and I wanna live. Do you hear me? I WANT TO LIVE!"

Kehl-li's rolling eyes said 'shut up' before she actually responded decently. "I choose life too."

"Could've fooled me. I know stuff is pretty jacked up for you right now, but for me, things are just peachy. Maybe Dr. Beverly can help you too."

From the side view mirror, I could see the flashing blue light on the patrol car behind us. My heart slowly found its rhythm and picked up pace as an officer slid from the vehicle and quickly walked toward the Prius. I swallowed. The last thing I needed was more trouble.

"Let the window down." I pointed to the driver's side. My eyes zoomed straight to the black leather duty belt wrapped around the uniformed officer's thick waist. Shiny metal handcuffs hung from a loop between a bottle of spray and a small white nylon rope. A handgun was snuggled against the officer's hip.

Kehl-li pressed the button to lower the window. "Yes?"

The officer bent forward and looked inside the car. "Young lady, do you know why I approached your vehicle?"

"No, sir. Is there a problem with the car?" Kehl-li glanced toward the passenger's seat and pointed at me. "This car belongs to her. I have a convertible."

My heart skipped time. Mom and Dad would have zero tolerance for a traffic violation.

With a straight face, the officer spoke again. "I need to see your license, registration, and proof of insurance, please."

Kehl-li tossed her hair and dug through her purse, pulling out a small case. She unfolded the visor above her head, and looking at herself in the mirror, slathered on apple-flavored lip gloss.

The officer cleared his throat and patiently repeated his request.

Kehl-li sighed. "Janaclese?"

"You're the driver," I snapped.

"*Your* license." The officer nodded at Kehl-li, his patience seeming to thin. "And *the car's* registration and proof of insurance."

I opened the glove compartment and produced two documents.

Between clenched teeth, Cyndray whispered to Kehl-li. "You choose life? Well, maybe you're about to get it. Now hurry up and show the police your fake license before you wake up with taser burns."

"Here, officer." Kehl-li handed over her license and a fake ID landed on the console. "This photo makes me look like a hobo. I look so much better in person."

"Wait here."

When the officer walked back to his police car, Kehl-li tucked the fake ID back in her purse and tossed the boulder necklace to Miracle. "Hide this under the seat."

Miracle scrunched her face. "Why do I need to hide it?"

"'Cause she stole it," Cyndray barked. "I ain't going back to court ... not for aiding and abetting a fugitive."

I tried to blink back my astonishment. What else was I going to find out today? From the rearview mirror, I stared at this stranger sitting in the backseat—first admitting to therapy, now court. Maybe Cyndray was hiding more stuff, like being in a witness protection program or something. I narrowed my eyes at her. *Do I even know you? Or Miracle? Or Kehl-li?*

"Stop looking at me like that!" Cyndray snapped. "Kehl-li's the thief."

Kehl-li stroked a bristled brush through her hair. "How can somebody steal what's rightfully theirs?"

"Guys, come on." I took a deep breath and my chest heaved in, then pushed out. "I think we're in enough trouble as it is."

Kehl-li powered her nose.

"Why do you always irk me?" Cyndray exclaimed, studying the back of Kehl-li's head. "And I don't know why you're getting all pretty for your mug shot. I'd be too afraid of being Hammer's girl."

"Who's Hammer?" I asked, wondering how I was going to explain yet another incident to my parents.

"Hammer in the slammer ... some random serial killer she'll probably have to bunk with." Cyndray's panicky voice concerned me more than the police officer.

"We're not going to jail," I insisted. At least, I hoped not. I was forcing myself to stay calm, though my mind frantically searched for a believable story as I pictured myself calling my parents from the police station.

"Easy for you to say. Who's gonna get us out of this jam?" Cyndray wrung her hands. "Certainly not my parents."

The officer walked back to the Prius. "This car is registered to Franklin Mitchell. Is anybody related to him?"

"He's my dad," I offered.

"Lawyer Mitchell is your mom, then?"

"Not anymore." I swallowed.

The officer's eyes stretched. "Come again."

I couldn't think or talk straight. "My mom *used* to be a lawyer. She's licensed, but she doesn't practice anymore."

The officer's stern face turned toward each of us and paused a few seconds as though he was mentally running our profiles through the America's Most Wanted list. "Look. I could write you up for speeding, but I'm just going to give you a warning this time."

My heart thumped, still too afraid to be fully relieved. Was he going to search the vehicle for stolen merchandise?

"Where're you headed in such a hurry?"

"Community Day," we said in unison. At least that was the truth. We had to get there before anybody found out we weren't.

He smiled. "Me too. How about a police escort?"

Chapter 53

JANACLESE

The officer didn't pull up to the church with loud sirens and flashing lights to attract everybody's attention. But he managed to alert Mom we were on the way. Why else would she be standing with Dad at the church's entrance?

Kehl-li pulled the Prius right beside where the green and white police car stopped, and all of us girls hopped out, awkward to see my parents.

"They're good girls," Dad was saying to the officer. "Thank you so much for escorting them here. Teens aren't always the wise decision-makers we'd like them to be."

We stood quietly, embarrassed to hear their conversation as if we were invisible. Apparently, the officer had seen Kehl-li jumping the tracks in front of the train. He'd decided to write a warning because he recognized my parents' names and knew their sentencing would be harsher. Lucky me!

"Sorry, Mom." I lowered my head, not wanting to meet the disappointment in her eyes.

"All is well." She hugged each of us. "And the good thing is that all of you get to spend the next week helping out at the Women's Center—all day. It's such a joy to serve!"

"Not me." Kehl-li's smile matched the excitement in her voice. "Maybe I could take a raincheck. I'll be totally swamped with packing my clothes because I'm headed back home next Saturday."

"MiShelle mentioned that. But we've worked out a nice little schedule so you don't feel left out. It'll be a fabulous send-off, I promise." Mom looked over at me. "Talk about clothes ... Janaclese, there's a tent set up for those in need of a few garments. Your friends can help you replace some of what you lost in the fire."

"Yes, ma'am." Anything to get away from the police scene.

"Is she seriously going to make you wear used clothing?" Kehl-li frowned when we were a few feet away.

"You wear my stuff." Miracle jumped to my defense. "And most of it isn't new."

"But it's like new since you only get one wear out of them." Kehl-li delivered trial-size hand soap from her purse and pumped the foam onto her hands like a germaphobe.

We walked toward the tent. Maybe they'd have gently used items that fit my size and taste. With school starting, most days I'd be in a uniform, but I needed more jeans for the weekend.

"MiCha, can we just find Imo and give her the necklace? She won't be ballistic with so many people around, and she'll understand about the police when she realizes we risked our lives to get her necklace back."

"You think that'll work?" Miracle cocked her head to the side.

"Yeah. Even if she gets mad, she'll calm down by the time we get home."

Kehl-li had always been manipulative. I'd noticed the fake ids that had fallen from her purse in the car. Her leaving to go back home was probably a good thing. I smiled at Miracle to let her know I'd be fine shopping without her.

When they left, Cyndray started talking again. "Kehl-li didn't want her prissy hands touching other people's donated clothes."

I shrugged. That was a possibility, but I hadn't given it any thought. I picked up a pair of Levis and measured them against my legs. "What do you think? Long enough?"

"I don't know. I guess so." Cyndray shook her head. "Why does it feel like no matter how hard I try, trouble is just standing in line to attack me? If it wasn't for your upstanding parents always doing service for other people, we'd be in jail right now."

"What Kehl-li did, speeding and all, wasn't exactly our fault."

Wiggly lines tracked Cyndray's forehead. "I know; but in the eyes of the law, we would've been guilty by association. Do you think she stole the necklace back?"

Some people were capable of doing just about anything. But I'd also learned not to jump to conclusions. I looked at Cyndray. "Kehl-li said she didn't steal the necklace. I guess we have to take her word until she proves otherwise." I tugged at a random pair of jeans folded under a stack, remembering how I'd been wrong lately from assuming the worst. "Things aren't always what they seem."

"I have to work so hard to stay out of trouble. Other people seem to get away with murder. Just doesn't seem right."

"If we keep modeling the right behavior, I think Kehl-li will get it." I eyed a decorative pair of jeans with designs on the back pockets. "What about these?"

"You just gon' sit in the same spot all day?" A whiny voice distracted Cyndray from answering me. "Ain't fair we gotta stay under this tent with you the whole time!"

I turned toward the salty voice.

The little girl's bony elbows protruded when she put her hands on her hips. "What's wrong with you anyway? This is ridiculousness."

When she snatched her tiny body around and flopped down in a wooden folding chair, I recognized Khadijah. And sitting next to her … Hassan!

My heart dropped.

Cyndray elbowed me. "Isn't that Hassan and his feisty little sister?"

I nodded.

Before I could usher her in the opposite direction, Cyndray had bounced over to Khadijah. "What's up? You remember me?"

I tried to swallow the cotton balls in my mouth. Should've occurred to me Hassan would be at Community Day, manning the clothing donations.

Khadijah looked Cyndray up and down, then turned her head away like she didn't want to be bothered. "I might."

"Aw, c'mon. Don't you remember me visiting your house? I'm Cyndray."

Khadijah twisted her neck back around. "I know who you are. You're friends with that 'boo-gee' girl that made my brother act stupid and get lost in the storm." She shoved Hassan. "Tell her to split, Talent."

My heart started into overtime. The community, local churches, plus anybody affiliated with Redemption Temple was probably here. I made a beeline for the exit.

"Janaclese?" Cyndray spoke my name in full volume. "You talking about that girl right over there?"

I stopped in my tracks, feeling the sting of eyeballs spearing me. I turned to see Cyndray pointing at me, making it impossible for me to go unnoticed.

"She's not bourgeois," Cyndray said. "We just have to teach her how to loosen up and be a little more street savvy."

A pair of eyes peeped out from behind Khadijah's chair. "Janaclese!"

I smiled when Nneka raced over and tumbled into my arms, knocking the jeans onto the ground.

"Where you been *this* time?" Her beaded hair clanked when she looked into my eyes.

"Still thinking about you," I said, swinging her into the air, then gently landing her onto her feet.

Nneka scrunched her face. "How come you don't visit us no more? Talent don't wanna do nothing fun since you stopped coming around. He works all day."

"Is that right?" I held her hand as she pulled me over to Cyndray and her family.

"Yeah. Khadijah says he's making us boring like him. Khadijah's real mad."

"That's ridiculousness." Cyndray folded her arms and mimicked Khadijah who had her lips poked out. "We could be double-dutching or getting our faces painted. Why don't we just leave boring Hassan right here with 'boo-gee' Janaclese while we go have some fun?"

Khadijah's eyes lit up, and Nneka's tiny hands slipped from mine as she latched on to Cyndray's.

"Hey!" I tickled Nneka's sides. "You're willing to abandon me for face-painting?"

She giggled, then looked at her big brother with pleading eyes. "Pleaasse … can we go with Miss Cyndray? We promise to be good."

Hassan shrugged his shoulders like his energy was drained. "Stay together and listen to her."

"YAY!" Nneka bounced up and down as the three left the shield of the tent and trooped into the sultry heat of the sunshine.

When they'd tramped a few yards away, Cyndray turned around and gestured for me to talk to Hassan.

Trying to ignore the butterflies in my stomach, I finger-combed my hair and plopped down where Khadijah had been sitting. Not like I had any control over him talking to me. Hassan sat leaning forward, elbows propped on his knees, with his fists balled next to his cheeks.

"So, how have you been?" I asked. From the looks of it, worn-out, maybe sleepy.

He offered a side glance. "I'm making it."

"Whatcha been up to?"

A long sigh sounded. "You heard Nneka. Working day and night."

"Why's that?"

"Keeping busy. That's all."

He unfolded his body, stretched out his legs, and flashed a half-smile. "You changed your hair back. You look great."

"Thanks." Too bad I couldn't say the same about him. He looked broken down. Like his raggedy truck, Cyndray always teased about.

We both sat in silence, staring at yellow patches of grass. Guess our conversation was stalled like his raggedy truck too.

Awkwardness rested between us like a partition, daring us to cross the line and simply talk. Why wouldn't he say something else first?

I watched the second-hand circle the face of my watch three times. Hassan's engine wasn't cranking, and I didn't have the keys to start it. Finally, I stood up to leave. "See you around, Hassan."

"We were *never* boyfriend and girlfriend."

I paused. When a wound is trying to heal, you shouldn't rip the scab off. It hurts just as bad as a fresh cut. Words squeezed from my constricted throat. "I got the memo the first time."

"We were just friends."

Why did he have to twist the knife in my chest? "Hassan, I get it. I wanted more. You didn't. It's all good."

I walked away, and he jumped up and grabbed my arm.

"Not us ... me and Finale." His eyes bore into mine. "I'm not the father of her baby."

My heart skipped. "Why didn't you tell me when I asked you?"

"I tried, but you ran away."

My expression must've seemed doubtful because Hassan eased closer to me and started talking.

"The three of us—me, Finale, and Reb— you remember him, don't you?"

I nodded, recalling Reb's Cadillac creeping up and down Hassan's street.

"Well, we hung tight back in the day. But Reb and I never saw eye to eye on certain things." He shook his head. "It's too complicated for a girl like you."

A girl like me? I chewed my lip. "Then make it plain and simple for me to understand."

He ran his hands down his thighs, then raked them across his head—a nervous gesture I'd noticed before. "Where we're from, things are different. People hustle. Some sell drugs to survive, and others take them just to escape what they've survived." He scratched his head. "Love is a funny thing in my world. The tenderness of it ..." He hesitated, wrangling with his words, forcing them to flow. "People confuse kindness with love. I mean love *is* kind, but all acts of kindness ain't about love. You follow?"

I wanted to comfort whatever was troubling him, but I couldn't give him an easy out. Not after he'd hurt me. "Maybe. Keep talking."

"Reb could afford to do kind things for Finale that she mistook for love. Now she feels trapped with a baby on the way." He lowered his voice. "Finale and I have never, um … I've never."

My heart softened at his struggle for words. "Never?"

He looked around nervously and shook his head as if he was about to reveal a dangerous secret.

"Never. I plan to wait for marriage—and that's unusual where I'm from, especially for guys. Don't get me wrong. I'm no punk. I just …" He sighed. "You mind sitting with me for a moment?"

Hugging myself, I wondered if I should sit for a while. Suddenly, a neo-soul voice, accompanied by string instruments, burst into the air. The concert was starting.

I looked around and spotted Khadijah staring at a group of kids double-dutching. Two girls jumped rope in symmetry, their high knees lifting up and down in quick jog-like motion.

Hassan tugged my arm. "I—I need to talk to you. Will you sit with me?"

I diverted my attention away from the jump ropes and singing, then sat back down in the folding chair, prompting him to sit next to me.

"I'm sorry about everything," he began.

"You apologized when you broke up with me. You don't have to apologize again."

"Nah, that was my bad." He studied me for a second. "I mean, breaking up with you was the worst thing I could've done."

"I'm okay with it now." A blender whirred in my stomach. "No worries. I'm good."

"But I'm not." He lowered his head. "I can't sleep. I can't eat. Sometimes, I can hardly breathe."

My insides felt squishy. *Was he telling the truth?*

"My world is dark and cold without you, Janaclese. There's no light, no warmth …"

"Where'd you get those tired lines—Hallmark greeting card or Mahogany?"

"What?" He glanced up, his brows knotting together.

"I've already forgiven you," I said.

"You have?" I couldn't tell if Hassan was shocked or relieved. "You're always nice and so sweet."

"You're pouring it on pretty heavy." I worked to hold back a smirk.

"And honest." He chuckled. "This is what I can't get enough of. I've missed you so much. I was afraid I wouldn't see those dimples ever again."

Seemed like I couldn't get enough of him either. His irresistible smile sent an electric shock through me, liquefying my insides. I tried not to cave because I needed to make him understand something important. We weren't *that* different from one another.

I straightened my face. "I've also chosen to wait for marriage. We live in the same world, Hassan. When yours is dark, mine is too."

He stared at me.

"The only thing that's different about you and me is our viewpoint on *whether* we're different from each other. Nature couldn't distinguish us. Apparently, the storm didn't know to rain only on your side of the tracks. The entire community has suffered together. Just look around, look at me." I patted the jeans on my lap. "Our worlds aren't colliding. They're interacting, pulling through the aftermath together. That's how life should be, how relationships *are* *supposed* to be. I'm sorry you didn't see that."

The squishiness in my stomach sloshed around.

Hassan sat silent and numb-like, with a strange look on his face. If he couldn't tell me what he was thinking, then fine. I didn't have the time or the energy to try to decipher the male psyche.

I stood up to leave. "Despite everything that's happened, I have enough courage to still love you. The thing is, you've got to be brave enough to let me."

Letting go of a first love wasn't easy. But this time, I didn't run. I walked away.

Chapter 54

JANACLESE

The fast beat of stomping feet kept time between the two ropes. Whipping against the paved parking lot, the rope's sound mixed with musical instruments in the background. Sing-song voices counted a rhythmic pattern of numbers.

Khadijah, glued to the same spot, looked on longingly. Probably like her brother, letting imaginary differences hold back what her heart desired.

I pulled up beside her. "Bet it's not as hard as it looks."

She looked up at me and rolled her eyes. "I know it's not hard."

"Well, I can't double-dutch either," I said, letting her know it was alright, and that even though she thought I was "boo-gee," we had something in common.

"That figures." Her attitude flared. "And for your information, I *know* how to jump double-dutch."

"You do?" *Then why aren't you jumping?* I choked down a smart remark. "Then maybe you can show me how to do it."

She focused on the ropes and the girl's Adidas tennis shoes, her eyes moving up and down in tandem with both. "'Cause that girl right there is double-handed. That's why the ropes keep collapsing, making everybody get out."

"Then why don't you turn for them?"

She twisted her lips. Right away, I could see the problem— Khadijah wasn't a people person like her little sister, Nneka. She didn't know how to make friends.

The rope snapped together, and the next girl was out after two steps.

"Hey. My friend says she can turn for you."

A wide grin mapped across the freckled face of one of the girls turning. "Here, take my rope. My double-handedness gets worse when I'm tired."

I watched Khadijah turn a few rounds, then jump, her side ponytails snapping against her brown face.

"Go, girl!" I cheered her on until the ropes collapsed.

"Told ya!" Her chested heaved up and down, practically breathless.

"Wait. What's that on your face?" I gestured to touch her cheeks.

She reeled back, squirming and batting my hands away. "What?"

I placed my hand on my heart and sighed. "Oh. Don't worry, it's gone now."

Khadijah brushed her cheeks. "What'd you see? What was it?"

"I don't know." I scrunched my nose. "It sorta looked like a smile."

A grin tugged at her lips. "You got jokes. But you ain't got no jumping skills."

"You got me there."

She stopped and looked at me. "I can teach you if you come over again."

"You're inviting me over?" I smiled. "I'd like that."

"Hassan would like that too. And especially Nneka."

"Speaking of Nneka …" I pointed to where Cyndray and Nneka stood in line waiting for food, their faces painted identically as sparkly purple and pink butterflies. "You hungry?"

"After all that jumping? Yes!" She darted away, then circled back. "What about you?"

"Go on with Cyndray." I looked at the change in the stage setup. "I think my aunt and uncle are about to sing."

I found a center spot in front of the stage, noticing the bread in Aunt Alicia's oven had fully risen. In the past, she'd suffered the disappointment of miscarriages, but faith had kept her going, not allowing her to wallow in sorrow.

Uncle Sam blew his saxophone, then Aunt Alicia's contralto voice harmonized a soothing tune. The song lyrics from the CD I'd listened to a million times swarmed around and enveloped me.

"Hold me in your arms, keep me safe from harm ..."

How many times had I wondered if she was singing about God or romantic love?

"Don't know what I'd do, if I didn't belong to You ..."

Warmth coated me like a second layer of skin, and for the first time, I really got it—God had held me because I was His. He loved me first. And I loved Him back.

Despite my doubts and insecurities, fear and rejection, God was there to bring me through. He'd shown me His love and how it worked through a supportive family, good friends by my side, and an entire community pulling together to help each other.

I drank in the moment. Right here and now, I loved this place, this feeling of love and safety.

A familiar wave of energy enveloped me, further cocooning me from the outside.

Hassan had to be near.

I stared straight ahead at the platform where Aunt Alicia sang, and Uncle Sam blew his saxophone.

"Isn't that our song?" Hassan's soft whisper fell into my ear.

Even though I wanted to look at him, acknowledge I'd heard him speaking, I couldn't. I was captured by the truth of the lyrics, the realization that God was my first love.

Hassan laced his fingers through mine and squeezed.

My heart fluttered, and I didn't oppose clasping his hand. Yet, my feet refused to stand still, moving gently with my swaying body.

"Go for it," Hassan encouraged.

I'd danced for him, but now I only wanted to dance for God.

Releasing my hand from his, I glided ahead, abandoning all thoughts of who was watching me. I transitioned my body by rising high on the balls of my feet. My spontaneous, unrehearsed choreography didn't matter. He'd accepted me for me, and I loved Him with all my heart. I *had* to express it.

With a clear mind, I was free to dance, free to worship. I ended my routine with a grand allegro, traveling across the lawn, soaring into the air, and landing perfectly with my head and hands held high, pointing toward Heaven.

"And let's give a hand to our dancer, Janaclese Mitchell!" Aunt Alicia announced over the mic.

Applause spilled forward, and out of courtesy, I smiled and extended my usual pas marché.

But it wasn't for them. *Thank you, Lord, for loving me.*

Smiling and waving at me, Mom and Dad embraced each other from the corner of the stage as Aunt Alicia began her next set.

I weaved through the crowd, finding Cyndray standing with Hassan and his little sisters.

"Girl, you were fabulous!" Cyndray slapped me a high five. "Gonna start calling you J-Fab! What do you think, Khadijah? Was that dance legit?"

"She did alright. But not as good as that ice cream gon' taste." She docked her hands in their usual position, then looking up at Hassan, swung her hips to one side. "You promised."

Nneka latched onto my leg, and I scooped her up.

"You coming with us to get ice cream?"

I rubbed my head against hers, clanking her beads. "Maybe next time."

"Nneka, get down." Khadijah tugged at her little sister's dangling legs. "You're way too big to be held, always clinging on to people."

I placed Nneka on her feet. "Come here, Khadijah."

Tentatively, she scooted next to me and wrinkled her nose. "What?"

I did what I should've done a long time ago. I wrapped my arms around her, squeezing gently.

"Get off of me." Khadijah squirmed.

But I could tell she liked being hugged.

Laughing, Cyndray joined in and sandwiched Khadijah. "I used to hate it too. But if you stick with Janaclese, you'll get used to these rib-crushing hugs."

"Let me out of here!" Khadijah demanded, without much resistance.

"Let me in." Nneka slithered into the circle, tightly packing herself inside.

"Why are y'all leaving a brother hanging? Break me off a piece of love too." Hassan dove in laughing until we all tumbled to the ground.

Khadijah sat up and wiped the wide grin from her face. "Now can we get ice cream?"

"Yep. I'm with you, Khadijah. That's enough Janaclese-love for one day. Kinda overwhelming." Cyndray brushed off her pants and passed me my cell phone. "You dropped this."

Hassan's eyes widened. "Is that a new phone?"

I nodded.

His eyes switched to tiny slits. "Did you get a new number too?"

I nodded again. "My parents."

"Then that explains why I couldn't reach you. What's your number?"

Trying to contain my giddiness, I gave Hassan my new number.

Grinning, he grabbed my phone, pressed in a few numbers, and handed it back. "Call me, Shawty."

Shawty. I chuckled. The words kissed me like fresh summer rain.

Holding hands, the family trooped toward the ice cream booth. I stared after them. *He called me Shawty.*

Cyndray checked her watch. "We'd better skedaddle. Your parents were serving hotdogs, and they need us over there in thirty seconds. And they wanted me to tell you—"

Her voice faded from the loud machinery as we passed a tall Shred-It truck. I noticed a stack of magazines, and sitting on top was Kehl-li's favorite—*TotalDiva.*

I elbowed Cyndray. "Did you ever read that article about '28 First Kisses?'"

She stopped walking. "Yep. I sure did. What about it?"

I pointed to the stack of magazines, as a uniformed guy lifted the stack into a bin. "Looks like somebody thought it was trash."

"It is. You can't have twenty-eight *first* kisses." She giggled.

I laughed too. "It's an oxymoron."

Cyndray slanted her eyes. "Wait. Did you call me an ox or a moron?"

"Neither." I laughed even harder. "Never mind."

My phone dinged. I scrolled to the text message. *Just checking on you, Shawty.*

The tingling started around my ears and worked its way down my arms. *I like when he calls me Shawty.*

"Hassan called me Shawty," I said to Cyndray.

"He always calls you that. What's the big deal?"

I wobbled, trying to keep my feet steady. "I can't imagine a kiss being any better."

"What? Are you lightheaded from too much sun?"

And I couldn't imagine her understanding. I laughed. *Twenty-eight first kisses?*

Guess I didn't need that, after all.

THE END

About the Author

Wife, mother, sister, friend, teacher, student, research psychologist, writer, daughter of His grace.

A graduate of Clemson and Columbia Universities, Sandra's love for multiculturalism has taken her around the world to collect stories. She's a non-fiction author, published in Encounter magazine, and a member of ACFW.

Available in bookstores and Amazon in e-book and print.

Made in the USA
San Bernardino, CA
17 October 2018